Alan Sillitoe

was born in 1928, and left s… factories until becoming an … Ministry of Aircraft Production in 19…

He began writing after four years in the RAF, and lived for six years in France and Spain. In 1958 *Saturday Night and Sunday Morning* was published, and *The Loneliness of the Long Distance Runner*, which won the Hawthornden Prize for literature, came out the following year. Both these books were made into films.

Further works include *Key to the Door*, *The Ragman's Daughter* and *The General* (both also filmed), The William Posters Trilogy, *A Start in Life*, *Raw Material*, *The Widower's Son*, *Her Victory*, *The Lost Flying Boat*, *Down From the Hill*, *Life Goes On*, *The Open Door*, *Last Loves*, *Leonard's War*, *Snowstop*, *Collected Stories*, and *Alligator Playground* – as well as eight volumes of poetry, and *Nottinghamshire*, for which David Sillitoe took the photographs. He has also published his autobiography, *Life Without Armour*. His latest novel, *The German Numbers Woman*, is due to be published soon.

BY THE SAME AUTHOR

Fiction

*Saturday Night and
    Sunday Morning*
*The Loneliness of the
    Long Distance Runner*
The General
Key to the Door
The Ragman's Daughter
The Death of William Posters
A Tree on Fire
Guzman, Go Home
A Start in Life
Travels in Nihilon
Raw Material
Men, Women and Children
The Flame of Life
The Widower's Son
The Storyteller
*The Second Chance and
    Other Stories*
Her Victory
The Lost Flying Boat
Down From the Hill
Life Goes On
Out of the Whirlpool
The Open Door
Last Loves
Leonard's War
Snowstop
Collected Stories
Alligator Playground
The German Numbers Woman

Non-fiction

Life Without Armour
    (autobiography)

Poetry

The Rats and Other Poems
*A Falling Out of Love and
    Other Poems*
*Love in the Environs of
    Voronezh and Other Poems*
Storm and Other Poems
*Snow on the North Side
    of Lucifer*
Sun Before Departure
Tides and Stone Walls
Collected Poems

Plays

All Citizens are Soldiers
    (with Ruth Fainlight)
Three Plays

Essays

Mountains and Caverns

For Children

*The City Adventures of
    Marmalade Jim*
Big John and the Stars
The Incredible Fencing Fleas
Marmalade Jim on the Farm
Marmalade Jim and the Fox

ALAN SILLITOE

The Broken Chariot

Flamingo
An Imprint of HarperCollins*Publishers*

Flamingo
An Imprint of HarperCollins*Publishers*
77–85 Fulham Palace Road,
Hammersmith, London W6 8JB
www.**fire**and**water**.com

Published by Flamingo 1999
9 8 7 6 5 4 3 2 1

First published in Great Britain by
Flamingo, an Imprint of HarperCollins*Publishers* 1998

Alan Sillitoe asserts the moral right to be
identified as the author of this work

Author photograph by David Sillitoe

This novel is entirely a work of fiction. The names,
characters and incidents portrayed in it are the work of the
author's imagination. Any resemblance to actual persons,
living or dead, events or localities, is entirely coincidental.

ISBN 0 00 649305 X

Set in Galliard

Printed in Great Britain by Clays Ltd, St Ives

Part One

Part One

One

Housemartins swooped to neat mud nests under eaves because the young were always hungry. It was unlucky if they didn't trail back every spring. Last year none came, and her mother had died, though in their innocence they were not to be blamed.

Maud looked on with pleasure, fascinated by such graceful devotion, pale and vibrant bellies in curving flight again and again above the window. She could almost hear the sound they made in their passage through the air. It was industry of a Darwinian sort, and the fact that they would still search out the house when all who lived in it were dead was merely a reflection on countryside life.

The gilt-bordered mirror above the fireplace reflected her straight nose and blue eyes, and she did not know whether she liked what was there, though wasn't disturbed that no alternative could be expected. The lines of her mouth showed a determined spirit that had so far found little to brace itself against.

At twenty-one she was tall and robust, with a fine sweep of brown hair descending along both sides of marble-smooth skin. Such a pre-Raphaelite profile had the usual masculine aspect that put off most men except the weakest and those – given her congenital sense of self-preservation – could never be interesting.

The eldest of four daughters from an East Anglian clerical family, her father had wanted a first born son and, rather than not forgive her for having wilfully refused to be one while in the womb, treated her as soon as she left the arms of her mother as if she was. For reasons which would have been laughable if known, she secretly enjoyed trying to be a boy, which pleased her father who, however, expected that she would resume her female identity in time to find a husband.

3

A year after his wife died the vicar gave up his rattling velocipede and bought a Daimler touring car. How the wish for one came to him when there were so few in the district was hard to say. Perhaps an advertisement in *The Graphic* or *Bystander* had changed from the sketchy drawing and become in his eyes a monument of colourful utility. Or maybe the death had been a liberation, and the motor a consolation in his grief.

The vehicle was brought over from Coventry by two men in long pale dust coats one Thursday morning, and they sat in the study with a satchel of papers, a bottle of Sandeman sherry, and a packet of cigars on the table. The pony was sold, its cart hauled through the orchard by the gardener and left to decay in the paddock.

Maud turned from the mirror and saw her father's surprising acquisition on the gravelled space before the front door of the rectory. The book fell closed, her place in *The Old Wives' Tale* lost at the sight of what couldn't come to life without human hands to move it, the strange agglomeration between four wheels calling to her as if every metal part was magnetized.

After several slow pacings around the pristine machine she knelt to peer at its inner mechanisms, stroked the tasteful leather seats, opened the tool box, dipped her fingers in the petrol container, tried its perfectly fitting doors, ran a hand along the sturdy mudguards, and felt an insane wish to put her lips to the steering wheel. The whiff of oil and fuel excited her, the whole lovely beast in tune with her heart and her future perceptions of the world. A friendly hand at the shoulder signified her father's gratitude for such approval. 'I've always wanted one,' he said, 'and we can certainly afford it.'

She had regarded him as a cheerful bigot, but should have known he was prone to accept more items related to the changing world since having a telephone installed. She asked if he would call the garage in Yarmouth, for someone to come and show her how to drive about the grounds. She sensed he was half afraid of what might become a Trojan horse brought into his household, and was surprised when he agreed.

In a few weeks she was taking him on excursions to his favourite Norfolk places, becoming more and more competent with each meandering circuit. He took great pains, with a tinge of malice, she thought, in fussing with the map to choose parallel routes and keep her from the better roads on which he said she drove too fast. Yet she noted the faint pleasure in his fear when, along the occasional straight stretch, she wondered at her reckless dishonesty on topping the twenty mile an hour limit.

The sandy highway south of Yarmouth, scattered with loose stones, laid traps for cartwheels and the vulnerable tyres of automobiles. Inclement rain increased the peril and the motor, of which she felt herself the captain, stalled by a hedge. At steam clouding out of the radiator her father went into a spinsterish panic – though she wouldn't dare tell him so – not knowing whether to go for help and leave her at the mercy of straying wayfarers, or send her on alone to face the danger of ambush by uncouth holiday-makers from London while he guarded the machine. He need not have worried, for Maud in her leather driving coat, hat and goggles, could stare down any potential molester.

They sat in the high seats, taut and silent with indecision, she unwilling to speak, and wondering if her father ever would. A light rain drove against them, and with it over the sandbank came a line of men in khaki, advancing towards the road in skirmishing order. 'We've been for a swim in the sea,' the young officer with his platoon of Territorials explained.

'Must have been cold,' Maud said.

'Freezing, actually,' he laughed. Seeing their plight he and his men piled arms and thought it unusually good fun to manoeuvre the motor towards the town. Maud suppressed her chagrin so as to enjoy the encounter, and honour was appeased when after half a mile the handsome young officer suggested that his men empty their regulation water bottles into the radiator, so that she was able to drive the car at little beyond walking pace to the garage, where a mechanic was soon labouring over the trouble.

'Hugh Thurgarton-Strang.' The dark-haired lieutenant gave his card to the vicar. Maud noted how he had studiously taken in the situation, as well as his easy confidence and humour, unlike the waffling young men she sometimes met with. She also saw that he was taller, which few men were, and how impressed he was with her presence and the proud way she had looked at the landscape, pretending not to notice any of his qualities, hat in hand and hair blowing about her face.

The vicar, who thought it his best adventure for years, asked Thurgarton-Strang to tea at the Queen's Hotel. 'It's just along the road,' and promised a pint of beer for each of his men at the neighbouring public house.

'Sorry, sir.' Thurgarton-Strang refolded his map into a neat calico case. 'I'd jolly well like to, but we can't stop now. We have to surround Blue Force by morning.'

Maud's invariable response to her sisters from then on, when she was asked to do something, was a shake of the head, and laughter as she replied: 'Can't do it. So sorry. Got to surround Blue Force by morning!' a new catch phrase in the family which recalled the young man's intelligent and amusing features.

She became adept at learning from such breakdowns. Fitting the spare wheel with jack and spanner after a puncture passed an enjoyable half hour. Every part of the frame and engine fascinated her by the obvious way each could be put together if she looked long enough at the manual. After a while she was allowed to drive her sisters to the beach at Cromer.

She waited every Tuesday for the *Financial Times* because Mr W. G. Aston, the well-known motor expert, wrote an article and responded to queries on the problems of the road. Maud wrote him a letter comparing the difficulties of fitting the bolt valve to ordinary valves, and telling what was likely to happen if certain precautions were not taken. She explained the problem cogently and with some wit, under the signature of M. Holt, so that Mr Aston in his printed reply assumed her to be a man, which both irritated and amused her.

A greater adventure for the vicar came about on Maud suggesting that all five should go on a tour to the Continent. They would drive around Flanders and Northern France, and visit cathedrals. His bald pate turned pallid as she spread a map over the library table. 'We're in the Association, and they'll take any trouble off our shoulders. We'll get the magic triptych fixed up, so there'll be nothing to pay on the motor at the customs.'

The French drive on the wrong side of the road. What about petrol? How would they find their way? Foreign maps weren't the same as

English. Then there was the problem of different money, apart from the fact, he concluded, knocking the ash from his pipe on the dogs in the fireplace, 'that my French isn't proficient.'

'Well,' Maud said, 'my French is all right, if I shout it loud enough,' and she convinced him on all issues, though without mentioning the attraction for her of there being no speed limit: gendarmes with stop-watches didn't hide like sneaks at bends in the roads.

Extra tyres were strapped on the footboard, the locker topped up with spare parts and sparking plugs. A leather satchel bulged with maps and documents, a phrase book with Baedekers and Michelins in the glove box.

Maud and her sisters stood on the top deck, and sang most of the way across the Channel, while their father was silent with anxiety and scepticism. When the car was swung off the steamer in Boulogne he suggested putting up at the Hôtel du Pavillon Imperial et Bains de Mer for a couple of days so as to recover from the crossing, but Maud was adamant for driving out of town. 'We must do at least a few miles today,' and they passed the first night in the Hôtel de France at St Omer.

'Got to surround Blue Force by morning!' her sisters let out in their shrill voices, while Maud paid off the porters for taking in the luggage.

After a minute examination of the church of Notre Dame they struck south for Amiens, so that the vicar could read his Ruskin in the cathedral. 'You're the captain of the ship,' her happy father said a few days later, 'so we'll go to Beauvais and then to Reims,' at which place she stood on the pavement to take off her dust coat and said to herself: 'Not another blasted cathedral!'

After a round of the ecclesiastical gems of Belgium they were rewarded at the end of their three-week tour by a few days at Ostend. The girls drank coffee and ate ices in the cafés, and made fun of common tourists coming off the boat from Dover, while the vicar, between walks up and down the beach, sat in the hotel lounge collating his notes.

When war began in 1914 Maud put on coat and goggles, and drove to Norwich, giving a lift to half a dozen volunteer soldiers on the way. Her experience and mechanical skill left no alternative, she said, but to enrol in an ambulance unit, but she fumed and brooded when no one wanted her, or she was sent from place to place, and felt herself sinking into an impossibly complicated maze of offices and organizations.

In six months she was driving an ambulance in France. From dressing stations near the front line to base hospitals she transported her cargoes of pain and misery, and sometimes death, and wept inwardly at the awful tribulations of the wounded, and swore with the sulphurous colour of any trooper at whoever mishandled them in or out and made their plight worse. A staff officer wanted to marry her, but she believed in love at first sight, deciding it was better to live an old maid than fall prey to whoever had the same idea.

She refused work in the administration of the ambulance service because it would take her away from motors, in spite of the hardship and the miserable squalor of stoppages on broken rainswept roads. In October 1918, resting one morning between goes at the starting handle, she recognized Colonel Thurgarton-Strang. His horse drank at a village trough, and when he mounted, his dressage was perfect. 'I've seen you before,' she called, above the boom and crack of distant gunfire. 'Yarmouth, when my father's car broke down. Long time ago, now. Don't suppose you recollect.'

He saluted and smiled. 'Of course I remember. Always hoped I'd see you again.'

'Well, now you have.'

'I'm astounded and delighted.'

'Got to surround Blue Force by morning!'

'We most certainly will!'

They laughed together, then he led his battalion of mainly eighteen-year-olds towards the German rearguards, whose machine gunners could not prevail against his enthusiastic young, who knew nothing of muddy stalemates in the Salient or on the Somme.

They met on the Rhine six months later, and Maud realized his place in her heart since their first encounter. 'You've hardly been out of my mind,' she said. They strolled the balcony of the hotel at Bad Godesburg while the orchestra played the old familiar tunes in the dining room. Maud smoked a cigarette, and Hugh took her statement as flattery, thinking that you ought not to believe a woman when she said something good about you. 'There's nothing I'd like better than to believe you.'

She put a hand on his. 'I never say anything I don't mean. I wouldn't know how.'

All he wanted was to be the husband of this delightful woman. 'I'm quite sure', he told her, 'that I shall love you forever – if you'll have me.'

They were married at St Mary's-All-Alone by an ex-chaplain uncle of Maud's, the ceremony as much a regimental as a Christian affair, with an arbour of glistening swords to walk under, and so many dress uniforms that to Maud the gathering seemed like a scene of peace after a rabid and pyrrhic war.

In India the Thurgarton-Strangs avoided the oven heat of the plains by renting a house in Simla, living in a style helped by Maud's thousand a year on the death of her father. Hugh expected their first child to be a girl, given the family from which Maud had come. This would not have disappointed him, but the dark-haired ten-pound baby, sound in wind and limb, was a gift for both, and they were pleased that he was stoical enough to make no sound at the font when he was christened. Their happiness was so intense – undeserved and precarious, they sometimes felt – that they could not resist doting on Herbert who, being new to the world, and having nothing to compare it with, thought such treatment normal.

His earliest memory was of being pushed in a large coach-like perambulator by a uniformed *ayah* along a track flanked by poplars. The continual trot of horses going to the polo ground was counterpointed by monkeys and birds performing an opera in the Annandale gardens. Above his cot he heard the clatter of raindrops on rhododendrons, violent splashes suppressing the voices of birds, and even his own when he gurgled for his nurse. Thunder gods growled among the deodars, then played to such a climax as seemed to burst the biggest granite globe asunder, sliced clean in two above the earth by a blade of lightning, which set him screaming.

The nurse was familiar with infants who were frightened, so he rarely wailed for long before she carried him – like a precious melon, Maud once said – to the covered terrace of the bungalow.

On calmer days, teething fractious hours, when he grizzled at the

9

miasma of inherited dreams, his *ayah* laid him by the edge of a stream and, snapping off a hollow reed, directed the water from a few inches above, so that drops coming out of her home-made conduit on to his forehead with such gentle regularity soon put him to sleep. 'You must have been too young to remember,' Maud said in later years. 'Or we told you about such incidents.'

He may also have imagined them, or they were culled from his dreams, the worst of which was of the nightmare meteor cleaved in half by an enormous blade of white fire. 'The splintering of monsoon artillery,' his father laughed.

Self-sacrifice was at its most poignant when Maud and Hugh took him to England, and left him in a boarding school which had everything to recommend it for a boy of seven except pity.

Two

The prospectus which moved Hugh and Maud to banish Herbert read: 'Clumpstead, Sussex. Preparatory for the Public Schools and the Army, situated in a most healthy position on the summit of Clumpstead Downs. Climate most suitable for Anglo-Indians. Exceptional premises and grounds of 25 acres. Teaching staff of University Graduates. Latin a speciality. Rifle range, swimming, ponies for riding. Every attention given to physical development.'

No sooner was Herbert left – abandoned, was the word he used – than the description seemed to be of some other establishment altogether. As for the healthy position, the climate was one to kill or cure, autumnal mist preceding rain that swept icily in from the sea, and snow whitening the school grounds before any other place in the area. The rifle range was in the dead end of a sunken lane and mostly unusable due to mud, and the ponies for riding must have been retired from some coal mine in the north after being worked almost to death. The swimming pool was a hole in the dell, and physical development meant little more than running and jumping whenever no time could be given to mediocre lessons due to the masters being either blind drunk or in bed with a cold.

Most of the teachers behaved when sober as if children had been put on earth to be beaten and terrified, while the boys had only each other to abuse for entertainment. Herbert, controlling his misery, learned to hold the first at bay by guile, and the latter by more violence than any among them could equal.

Apart from cricket, the only sport the boys were encouraged in was boxing, and Herbert's instinct told him that subtlety of manoeuvre was unnecessary if you forced a speed out of yourself which no defence

11

could hold back. They said he had a black speed, a devil's drive, a killer's fist, but the skill Herbert even so developed made his attacks deadly. A not quite matching adversary blooded Herbert's nose but he bore on in, scorning all cheers at his courage, learning that whoever drew blood first was three-quarters the way to winning.

He loathed boxing, but endured it by making his opponent pay for the inconvenience, fighting ruthlessly only so as to get more quickly out of the ring. He discovered the joy of being someone previously unknown to himself, vacillating between imagining he would either murder such a stranger if or when they became properly acquainted, or accept him as a friend for making him feel better able to survive. Who he really was, or wanted to be, he couldn't say, though he secretly liked the sportsmaster's remark that: 'You must have been born with the soldier in you,' a quality Herbert showed only when necessary.

Putting on weight and height, in spite of the thrifty diet, made him less likely to be bullied. He began to feel invulnerable though without turning into a bully, which at first made others suspect him of holding demonic punishment in store for some harmless remark, which an unfortunate boy would not realize until too late was a painful insult.

Hugh and Maud, when home on leave, were unable to understand why he showed no happiness. He was heartless and faraway, even for a boy of eleven. Hugh put an arm on his shoulder to point out Firle Beacon from the garden of their furnished cottage, and Herbert moved as abruptly as if he had been touched by fire.

'He was just being a manly chap,' Maud told him, after Herbert had gone to bed. 'Anyway, it's his age.'

Hugh paused between the measuring out of his whisky. 'I remember being like that as a boy myself,' he said with regret, 'and would have given anything not to have been.'

She held his hand, that strong pragmatic hand perfectly in harmony with the eye of his sharp intelligence. 'He'll learn to love us when he grows up. In the meantime, my dear, we'll make do with each other.'

'That'll always be so.' He put down the glass to fill his pipe, 'but it's a shame children can't realize that parents aren't much beyond children themselves, in certain ways.'

'I often wonder if I shouldn't have had another child or two. Then we wouldn't need to dote so much on Herbert.' She recalled her feelings after his birth: No more of that. He tore me to blazes.

Hugh stood up before going out to close the shutters. 'No regrets. One child's enough with which to surround Blue Force by morning!'

The new blazer needed some name tapes, and Maud picked up the needle. 'I'll tell you what we'll do. We'll take him to the cinema tomorrow. They're showing *Fire Over England* again.'

'Good,' he said. 'I haven't seen it myself.'

Herbert was sustained by the hope of one day getting revenge on his parents who callously condemned him to a school which, without experience of any other, he thought was the worst in the world. They deserved to pay even for sending him home to any school at all. Having waited for him to be born, he imagined them gloating over the ease of his first years, then springing this deadly trap. What other explanation could there be? Everyone knew what they did, and if they didn't the crime was all the greater. He evolved a potent fantasy of luring them to a valley in mountains as remote as those of Baluchistan seen from the top deck after leaving Karachi. The boulder behind the tree on the left bank of the stream was so vivid he could almost touch the moss. Taking an axe from his rucksack, he chopped them bloodily down, no pity at the look of horror as they died.

He wrote the daydream as a story, every stark detail sketched in words of fiery resentment, and the English master said it was an excellent piece of composition, though moving his head from side to side, as if in his experience he had read much similar work. Then with his tone laced by a threat he told Herbert to put it in the dining hall stove and never to pen such a whining screed again. 'In any case, don't you know, boy, that you may never see your parents more? There's a war coming on. In the meantime, write five hundred lines for your lack of filial love. Exodus chapter twenty verse twelve first line.'

Thereafter the scene of carnage came to him less frequently, for which he was glad, because living the murder through in his mind had left him weak and ashamed, though the sense of injustice against grown-ups took a long time to go away.

When the Second World War began there was a change of teachers, and his school was evacuated to Gloucestershire. The buildings were an even gloomier pile, all the boys listing gleefully its apparent illnesses of dry rot, rising damp, and deathwatch beetle, wondering how long it would be before the whole lot collapsed and buried them in a mound of dust.

It was as if the war had been sent especially to enthral them. Sitting in the library every day to hear the six o'clock news was like being in a cinema, and Herbert craved to take part in the glorious actions being fought. He performed well enough in class to keep ahead of many, but his greatest interest from the age of thirteen was devoted to the Army Cadet Force. The khaki uniforms were made out of last war misfits, but with cloth gaiters fastened, belt pulled tight, and cap angled on, he found it a glamorous transformation from school uniform. Maybe soon he would get into proper kit, because the war was bound to be on when he was old enough.

At times of despair he imagined a gaggle of Heinkels skimming like the blackest of black crows low over woods and fields on a deadly track to the sheds and towers of the school. His childhood nightmare of a world exploding in two and falling to crush life and soul out of him was overpainted by a smoking ruin in which everyone was dead or half-buried except himself and a few cadets coming from cover at the end of a tactical scheme. They would work tirelessly to rescue the living, especially those he saw reason to hate, so that he could go on hating them; or they would nobly clear up the mess and scorn all praise for their cool bravery among the as yet unexploded bombs. But the only sound of war in this backwater of England was the occasional wailing alert due to German bombers straying from the main path further south, or the dream-like ripple of ack-ack in the Gloucester direction.

He and Dominic Jones were enthused by yarns of conflict and exploration in *King Solomon's Mines*, *Treasure Island* and *Sanders of the River* but, above all, by *Kim*. Herbert saw himself as a district commissioner in some remote province of Africa, the ruler of an area as big as any country in Europe, sitting by the tent door at dusk while his native bearer set out supper on a camp table. Puffing at his pipe, he would see a range of purple-coloured mountains to be trekked through the following week, into an equally extensive territory administered by

Dominic, a social and courtesy visit before coming back to his own zone for another six months, no doubt fighting through an ambush of rebellious tribesmen on the way.

They talked of enlisting into the army, as an easy escape route into a wider world. The war would be on for years, and give them time to take part in an almost abortive and bloody but finally glorious attack on the mainland of Europe as members of a do-or-dare commando unit. On their return as heroes they would be cheered. Dominic pictured them with caps at a jaunty angle, toting walking sticks, and each with an arm in a sling. 'Let's chuck in a black eye-patch for good measure,' Herbert laughed, at comforting fantasies which, by their nobility of unreality, fed his spirit and made life easier to endure.

The first sentence of Ovid's *Metamorphoses* – his favourite reading – stayed in his mind for a long time: 'My task is to tell of bodies which have been changed into forms of a different kind.'

And into different minds, he supposed, because if you altered one the other must change as well. But what body, and what mind? Who gave them to us? And who the hell was it fixed me up with mine, I would like to know? Whoever it was had made a different job of him compared to the others. For example, he didn't know, for much of the time anyway, what mind and what body had been given him, because the relationship they had to each other didn't always correspond to how he felt. Even so, he could handle them all right because his outer casing of memory and experience was strong enough to let him control them, and would protect him until such time as he didn't need either any more. Nevertheless, it was difficult, one might almost say a fight, but since everything to do with the world was fighting, and since he enjoyed fighting, he kept bleak misery away.

Such uncertainties were no bother when, loaded like a hiker and clutching his single-shot Boer War rifle, he set out on the five-mile obstacle course, eager for cold air after the rigid stuffiness of class room or dormitory. He changed in a few minutes from a more or less clean schoolboy into the roughest of filthy-dirty ragamuffins as he went over a wall with rifle and kit, hands quick at the nets for speed, a metamorphosis not described in Ovid. He crawled through irrigation pipes, then waded a ditch, avoiding the splash of boots into cress and frogspawn. On his belly under pegged nets he relished the soil whose odours recalled Simla so keenly. He crossed the broader stream by a Tarzan rope, ballet-danced along a tree trunk and panted up a hill steep enough to be called an escarpment so that he could only get to the top by cunning zigzags. A hundred yards more or less on the level between scrub and sheep holes, he wended through a zone of bushes, and finally up fifty steps before dropping a dozen feet into home base, laughing at the poor sap who broke his ankle last year, while Herbert with his big stride made the course quicker than anyone else.

He absorbed the mixture of art and precision in map reading, able with no problem to transform in his mind the diagrammatic scheme on paper to the reality of fields and woods on the ground. He seemed made for the rough-house of minor tactics, manoeuvres and field days, and even drill with its fuss of polished boots and drying blanco. Most of all he looked forward to annual camp when, whatever the weather, he and Dominic set up a tent and cooked their mess in tins over the smallest of fires – careful because of the blackout – by a stream inside the wood.

Whether cold rain dropped on to khaki serge from the tent lining, or moisture fell from breath and sweat after a day in dry heat being stuka'd by flies and midges, Herbert was relaxed enough to be himself and not who anyone expected him to be. At which times he wasn't bothered by that first sentence from Ovid at all.

Nor was he when he manipulated the Bren, the Short Lee Enfield and the Sten, learning how to fire and pick to pieces and put them together again, hearing the satisfying click of symmetry from metal parts that fitted so perfectly into place. He got high scores on the range, and didn't care that each bull's eye at the butts winked at a despised face to be obliterated. By sixteen he had grown into a marker on which others formed their ranks. To pass his certificate 'A' (Part One) was easy, and made him the obvious candidate for promotion, so that he went up stripe by stripe to the rank of sergeant.

Problems subordinated to routine and discipline became no problem at all, and he couldn't dislike such a life when there was none other he felt he could deserve, an attitude which gave him less problems to contend with. Tall and lean, he had the same dark hair and Roman nose as his father (broken after a harder match than usual) with Maud's well-shaped lips and blue eyes.

Hugh's missives from active service were short and curt: 'I'm happy to hear about your attachment to the Cadet Force. Don't forget that one day the army will be your home, so always let me know of any progress. I'm sure you'll make a good soldier.'

In more frequent letters Maud, this time driving an ambulance on the Burmese frontier, told him to do well in academic subjects, and not spend more of his time playing soldiers than was necessary to make him a credit to the school. In the meantime she was sorry not to be seeing anything of him, but she was sure he understood it was all due to this blasted war.

Herbert also enjoyed days when the whole school set out in a mob on a cross-country run through brackeny woods, and by fields along muddy hedgerows where it was hard to maintain a sense of direction if you were leading. Keeping landmarks in view was good practice in going ruler-straight from A to B and not getting lost.

He wondered whether Uncle Richard, a retired clergyman who lived in Malvern, had learned the same as a boy. If so he hadn't remembered much. The sleepy aspect below his domed bald head, and his black rather shoddy clothes gave Herbert no confidence in his ability with the motor car when he drove to the school one Saturday and took him to tea at the Abbey Hotel.

He smiled at the clumsy old buffer not being able to see much beyond the length of his car, during the sick-making twenty-five miles an hour along leafy and unsignposted lanes though it pleased Herbert in that at any moment a five-ton army lorry (or tank for preference) might speed around the bend in front and give a touch of real life to their journey as they clambered bruised and maybe even amused out of a ditch after being overturned.

Knowing how much his uncle enjoyed such outings Herbert felt no need to talk, and in any case it wasn't done with a grown-up who might be shepherding only by way of duty. After every excursion the old man slipped him a quid, drooling and winking at how vital the odd sovereign had been in his own schooldays; which must have been before the Flood, Herbert smiled, relishing the added padding to his stomach which the copious tea provided. 'Thank you', he said, folding the lovely green note into quarters and putting it in his pocket.

For an otherwise blank hour of the week Barney the English master, who had served as a pilot on the Western Front, read to them from a Penguin Book called *Caged Birds*, about RFC officers imprisoned by the Germans during the Great War. Barney may have been one of them, since he related their adventures with such feeling, but nobody bothered to ask. Herbert borrowed the book, to go through it by himself, as if to memorize the cunning mechanics of escape. Dominic scorned such interest in boring anecdotes of compasses hidden in jam stones, and maps concealed between the linings of overcoats, or secreted inside cucumbers which were sent to the prisoners in Red Cross relief parcels.

Herbert was enthralled by the deception played by the grounded fliers on their captors during months of patient labour. Their plans incorporated the tiniest details, as little as possible left to chance or luck. Those who tried were the elite, and the ones who got clean away were the heroes. He finished the book in his favourite refuge of the library, then took down the large twenty-year-old *Times Atlas* and turned its pages to various countries of the world, but came back to the double sheet of southern England to mull over the place names and decide on what dot he would most like to be.

Parents who could spare themselves from work of national importance came for a quick look at their sons, bringing what food or comforts they could. To Herbert they appeared gaunt and miniature, out of place among the paths and high-up crenellations, people from the outside, another world.

Dominic's people drove up the lane in a Vauxhall Kingston Coupé, an elegant vehicle admired and wondered at by all the boys. When his sister Rachel also stepped down from the running board the car seemed even more the right motor to call at their gloomy school. Herbert wondered where they had found so much black market petrol, as he pressed against a bush to view them across the V for Victory Garden.

Rachel seemed angelic compared to her squat, pimply, ginger-haired brother. Staring was not done but, unable to resist, and though his jacket was wet with dew, Herbert fixed on her peachy cheeks, crane-like neck, and tied-back blonde hair swaying between slender shoulders as she strolled along the path.

A year younger than Dominic, she looked down on him by height, and also no doubt in spirit. Then she spotted Herbert and, quicker than any lizard, pushed the point of her tongue out and back, forcing him to wash away the tide of crimson at being caught like a dismal snooper.

Schoolwork clocked the weeks along, time he thought could be better spent though he did not know how or in what place. Rachel's face glowed in front of his eyes, a phantom to induce restlessness and longing, which detached him further from a system more oppressive than any German prison camp. He became less boisterous, even taciturn, which he supposed was due to something called growing up.

The precision of Latin, maths and history enticed him into high marks at every test, though he scored the minimum in French. Barney the English master occasionally praised his essays, especially a sparse yet colourful few pages on his reaction to the D-Day Landings called 'The Taking of Treasure Island'. Herbert described a skilful campaign fought by the crew of the *Hispaniola*, gave them Allied names and armed them for mutual slaughter with modern weapons. The *Hispaniola* was a tank-landing craft, and Ben Gunn commanded the French Resistance on shore.

Barney smoothed his bald head, and tapped his artificial leg with a ruler. 'Such comparisons shiver the timbers of credibility, but the imaginative exercise, plus the writing, keeps it afloat. However, in places there's a little too much striving for Johnsonian orotundity – but, nearly top marks.'

A convoy of cumulonimbus clouds blackened a wide track from the hill in the west, and an autumn storm played over the school as they were leaving the sports field for tea. A cloudburst at the same time as the lightning sent hailstones like shrapnel to pepper the science sheds and make the lawns dance. Herbert paused, sheltering in the colonnade, and the sudden all-illuminating flash seemed meant for him alone. His eyes didn't flicker, his firm gaze ready for another which, in his exhausted state after the game, lit his interior sufficiently for an idea to be planted and begin to grow.

A sulphurous explosion, synchronized with a bolt of lightning, shivered the windows, recalling the storms of Simla and his infant nightmare of a world divided, when the tree-covered sphere hovered as if to fall on his cradle and crush out all life. He could smile at such fear because the split had merely parted the bedrock of his existence and enabled him to see himself as two people instead of one.

The effect was to lighten the weight he seemed always to be carrying, though too many pictures went through his mind for him to pull out any that were connected, or even made sense, and he didn't at first respond to the call of Simpson the games master: 'Come on Thurgarton-Strang! Get a move on!' Realizing that the name was his, Herbert sprinted after the others, wondering the strange thought as to how much longer he would either run when commanded, or recognize the name thrown over him like the disabling net of a gladiator in the arena. He laughed so loud in his strides that Dominic, trying to keep up, wanted to know what it was all about, and got a sharp elbow for his unanswerable question.

The Cadet Force did no campaigning because there was too much snow, followed by floods. An uninviting frontier of lapidary green lay between Herbert and the outside world. Even the birds looked as if they needed a tonic. Waterlogged fields beyond the trees made him shiver to look at them. His only diversions were trips with Uncle Richard to the Abbey Hotel in Malvern, and he afterwards treasured the pound note, which he kept in reserve with others for better weather.

The deepest gloom of the season was to be illuminated by a theatrical performance in the games hall, organized by the ingenious Latin master. Herbert joined the group to avoid the embarrassment of being co-opted, and fancied there might be some interest in acting a person he most certainly was not, on being given the part of Phaeton, from Ovid's *Metamorphoses*. 'I have to give a lecture by Phaeton on Fate,' he quipped to Dominic.

His sky-blue coat was fitted together by the matron from old curtains, and the golden horned helmet made out of papier-mâché painted by Barney. A cluster of bulbs backed by a suspended mirror lit up the Sun God's palace. Dominic, wrapped in an unused skirt of the secretary's, was to play Clymene the mother, which part made his life a misery for weeks.

Herbert's recitative, 'as befitted a mythological character' – said the dramaturge, designating his pompous self – was to be spoken with panache, a style which came easily once Herbert had been through the tedious work of memorizing, and learning how to fit in with the speech and action of others.

Transforming himself into the pampered and irresponsible Phaeton, he assumes a privileged strut when his mother informs him, now that he is grown-up, that Phoebus Apollo the Sun God is his father. After much boasting to Epiphus of his descent from a deity – no less – he swaggers off to the Sun God's Palace of Light to be acknowledged.

Phoebus Apollo tells him it's true that he is of divine origin, and Phaeton is so in love with the golden words, even more perhaps than he is with himself, that he wants to hear them again and again. His father, to convince him that he is indeed of a godly line, decides to prove it by telling him he has the power to grant any wish he cares to make.

Phaeton expatiates on the golden precision of time, and declaims on the Sun God's control of the calendar, without which the earth would exist in eternal gloom. The only wish he could possibly make is to have a go at driving his father's chariot of the sun across the heavens, from dawn in the east to darkness in the west.

Half-wild horses are already snorting and whinnying behind the stable doors and Phaeton in his eagerness moves forward to open them, but Phoebus pulls him back, while all the spectators of this mighty drama yell for him to do so. Phoebus regrets his promise. 'Only I can control them in their anger at having to go, and stifle their hurry to get there once they begin.'

Phoebus argues eloquently that the fiery chargers, once harnessed to the chariot, obey no one but him, and even he needs all his power to keep them on course. He knows for a certainty that Phaeton, his very own and handsome son whom he has just met, will be killed if he tries to drive a vehicle for which he has not the strength, skill or experience. 'Ask me anything but that, my own resplendent lad!' Phaeton ignores such piffling appeals to reason. 'You are a god, and promised to grant me a wish, any wish, and a god cannot go back on a promise.' Phoebus is forced to relent. 'As my sun chariot each day is driven across the sky, so Fate must also take its course. Oh Fate, be kind!'

Phaeton exults as the steeds are led prancing and snorting out. He gets into the chariot – bodged together from a barrow out of the garden but decorated with blue paper and silver stars. Putting forth all his strength, with a heart not constant enough for any possibility of fulfilling his task, Phaeton sets off in hope of triumph.

The first stage is easy, as the animals smell the heavens and the distance they have to go, but everything happens as his father had predicted. In despair he watches his son struggle with the reins. Phaeton cannot believe that horses won't obey the laws of his dashing confidence.

Refusing to listen, they miss the signals, play wilfully and maliciously, zig this way and zag that, though Phaeton hopes they will sooner or later come to heel and take him calmly on. The struggle is noble and prolonged. Such half-tamed horses don't like to obey. Phaeton fights valiantly until, disastrously losing control, the end is certain. Yet there is something in Phaeton which enjoys this part of his travail (played to the full by Herbert) even when the chariot is breaking up.

Pieces slew all over the universal stage, a small piece, a bigger one, then one wheel, and the other. The four horses of Phaeton's apocalypse spiral across the sky to leave a wake of appalling destruction among the planets and on earth. Only when Jupiter hurls a sizzling thunderbolt and sends Phaeton to his doom is the universe saved from further havoc.

Herbert's speeches turned Phaeton into himself and himself into Phaeton, as he willed the horses to avoid his fate. At one moment he regrets that Phaeton did not take the advice of Phoebus Apollo and ask for a different wish – and he thinks of so many now that this had gone wrong – yet he exults in the glory of what he had become, and in the catastrophe he had provoked, accepting the change from nonentity to immortal charioteer, though it had cost him his life.

Three

Summer went on tramlines, winter on bumpy tracks. Every day after Christmas was endless and onerous, classrooms pungent with the stink of mildewed wood and damp wallpaper. Herbert knew something was wrong, that the life he was living was no life at all, so that when daffodils along the pathways opened into cups of brilliant yellow he told himself in the cold showers one morning after a run that he'd had enough.

Dominic responded in the one sure way to encourage him. 'You'll end up in awful trouble. You're bound to get caught.'

Days were dragging by so ponderously he knew that when looking back on them it would seem as if they had gone quickly. A spot of table tennis in the games room didn't help. 'I won't be. I'd rather die than stay in this prison camp. In fact I have to go before I do die.'

'I'll miss you, then.'

'Same here.' His compass for the escape came out of a Christmas cracker, and though the north point took minutes to settle it would have to do. He stole keys to certain doors, and knew how to open windows which were supposed to be locked; in any case there were so many that not all of them could be. His bag of essentials was concealed under an evergreen bush in the wood, wrapped against the wet in an anti-gas cape purloined from the cadet stores. Eight pound notes folded in half thickened his wallet.

'Can I come with you?'

'Keep your damned voice down, and serve.'

'I'll be no trouble. Curse it, I missed!'

'A person only has a chance to get clean away if he's by himself.' Herbert was sorry he'd told him. 'Do it later, if you like.'

'I'll be no good without you.'

'Oh, stop whining, or I'll give you a bloody nose. Just remember me to Rachel.'

'She doesn't care about you. She thinks you're stuck up. She wrote it in a letter.'

'So much the worse for her.' He put an arm on Dominic's shoulder, then took it away in case anyone else came in. 'Let's pack up this stupid game.'

'What about your parents?' Dominic believed he was trying to live out one of his fantasies. 'Have you thought of them?'

'You must be crackers.' He couldn't find the right tone, so shaped his most effective sneer. 'Haven't seen them in years. I even forget what they look like.'

'They'll be very cut up.'

He certainly hoped so. 'Serve 'em right. I'll bump into you one day, I expect.'

Seeing him unassailable, Dominic promised to turn Nelson's blind eye on his escapade, wished him good luck, and, fatuously, hoped they wouldn't recapture him before reaching neutral territory.

Wearing plimsolls, and boots around his neck, he went after midnight into the headmaster's study and found his Identity Card in the alphabetical file, heartbeats calm, steady fingers following his flashlight's beam.

The main door, daunting and heavily studded, was unbolted, but even so he slid up the library window without it squeaking and went over the sill. Good field craft enabled him to reach the outer fence, where he used a rope hidden behind a greenhouse cloche to scale the wall in the best *Caged Birds* tradition.

Darkness made him feel more than usually cold, though his battle-dress was buttoned and scarf well folded inside. Under cover of the wood he pulled on his boots, laced them well, and put the plimsolls under his arm. He had counted the paces in from a certain post so as to find the bush which covered his few possessions wrapped in the cape. Picking up a dead stick to poke the cabbage-smelling soil he wondered why it wasn't where it was supposed to be. Such mishaps always occurred when you set out on the great escape, but cold sweat pricked his face as he prodded the soft earth in different places, and looked under all shrubs within reasonable radius.

Fury at his incompetence would betray him. There was no saying how wide of the mark he was. If you made one mistake you made another. And then another. To bolt without a change of civvy clothes, toilet articles, penknife, and Barney's copy of *Caged Birds* would turn him into a cadet-scarecrow never daring to show his face. Luckily the school ordnance map was folded into his tunic pocket, as well as a few other odds and ends.

He stood a full minute without moving, telling himself that his exploit was now in the realm of real life. He was over the wall, but could go back if he liked, and be warm again in bed, where he had a dummy of himself made of pillows and discarded kit. Barney's flashlight was dim, and he had chosen a night before he might think to install a new battery. Who, in any case, would dream of someone doing a bunk? He wanted to go back but couldn't, because it was safer to push on. I'd look a right fool getting caught on my way back because I'd turned yellow.

Hang around much longer and I'll be seen and recaptured. He returned to the edge of the wood, took out his luminously dialled compass, and once more measured the paces in. The moonless night was no help, since all the bushes looked and felt the same in his beam of light, already less brilliant than when he had set out.

Another navigational run in, with more methodical poking, and the stick tapped what he was looking for. A sneeze shot out that must have been heard for half a mile. Of course, it always did at this stage. He stood awhile, still and silent, holding his nose to stop another. Using his handkerchief to mop the mucus, he thought it exceptionally bad luck to be stricken with the full house of a cold on getaway night.

Trees and hedges were indistinguishable in the dark and, well behind his timetable, he used his compass to cross fields, his previous daylight reconnaissance only a vague help. The outline of a great elm took out the mixture of stars and cloud, made the night a deeper pitch of black. He paused to get a bearing, and the fluting bars of an owl's beat startled and prodded him on till he broke through the hedge at the exact point where the lane forked. Exulting in his skill – and jolly good luck – all he had to do now was march half a mile by the cover of the right-hand hedge and find the main road.

To move without noise meant putting the plimsolls back on, but he didn't have them. Another mistake. They must have dropped while poking for his bundle among the trees. Now his pursuers would have a clue as to the direction. Listening for the noise of bloodhounds, he heard only the wind which hid the sound of him knocking claggy soil from his boots against the bole of a tree.

Anyway, I'm not a caged bird bloke in bloody Germany, he smiled. I'm on the run from a rotten school, and they'll never catch me. At the junction both ways seemed feasible. Either could lead to disaster, so he shrugged and headed to the right because the sky seemed faintly lighter that way.

After half an hour's carefree stroll a lorry came grinding up behind. Daylight showed in grey patches above the trees, and the birds were waking up, so he would have to be more careful. Walking along the inside of hedges and going from field to field would mean making only a few miles before nightfall, so he thought it best to get into a couldn't care less mood and nonchalantly put his thumb up for a lift.

An RAF corporal with a bushy moustache and big tobacco-stained hands helped him into the back. 'Going far, lanky?'

'Bristol, eventually,' Herbert said.

'So are we, right to the station.' The man winked while lighting a cigarette. He offered one, which was declined. 'You aren't a deserter, are you? Bit early to be about. What's in that bundle? Swag?'

Herbert pressed his tunic to make sure of the wallet in his inside pocket. 'Good Lord, no. I'm off to Bristol to meet a friend.'

The corporal laughed. 'A bint, eh? We're to pick up some erks back from France. War'll be over soon, anyway.'

'I sincerely hope not.'

'I suppose a lot of you young 'uns do. I've done four years, and can't wait to get out. The Russians are near Berlin, that's one good thing. It was on the wireless last night.'

Herbert had heard the same, and felt they had no right to be, because he still wanted the fray of battle, dazed by smoke and noise and not thinking of death or wounds. Draped with ammunition and a heavy machine gun, he zigzagged along the street of a German city.

But the corporal was right: it was getting towards the end, which for a while made him wonder why exactly he had broken out.

Sombre fields and hills beckoned him to the comfort and security of captivity, as he had supposed it would at this stage of the escape, but he smiled the unhelpful notion away, and only knew that he was hungry. The squalid bomb-damaged streets of Bristol put him in two minds about the war in Europe ending. The fact could only be good, though while standing in line for a wad and char on Temple Meads station he assumed that the Japanese would go on fighting for at least another three years. He might – and it brought a smile – meet up with his father in the jungles of Arakan. 'Hello, Herbert! Good to see you. All right?'

'Yes, sir.'

'Splendid. Now, we've just put a bridgehead across the river down there. Take your platoon over, and see that we keep it, there's a good chap.'

He got on the London train before any policeman could loom up with a pair of handcuffs. Everyone standing in the corridor could be his enemy, but freedom belonged to him alone, as long as he looked as if he owned the train and had every right to be on it. Gloating at having outfoxed his pursuers so far let him put on his most superior and supercilious expression.

His only plan, if plan there was, had been to get to the nearest big town and then clear of it. With luck and intuition he had succeeded. Acting on impulse might make him harder to track down. He locked himself in the toilet, as his carriage wheeled at speed through the Wiltshire Downs, changed into jacket and trousers, and dropped his khaki rig out of the window just before Hungerford. Back to a different seat, where no one could possibly know him, he read a few pages of *Caged Birds*, which firmly bolted reality out of his mind. Time went as fast as the train, a dotted stream of pale smoke when he glanced out, as if denoting the uncertainty of his expedition.

At Paddington he went through the ticket barrier and into the welcoming noise of London with a group of soldiers. Motors and cartwheels brushed his heels as he ran across Praed Street into a luggage store. The grubby yet strong-looking case had belonged to a sailor, an RN service number crested along the side. He latched and unlatched it, felt the material and gripped its handle. The man in a khaki overall behind the counter wanted four pounds, but called out he could have it for three when Herbert turned to leave. His belongings fitted easily, which made him feel a traveller at last.

A ten-mile radius of built-up area was protection from the world so far unknown. A needle in a haystack had nothing on this, and on Edgware Road a sign drew him into the Underground. After a while he felt so much like being buried among the mummies of an Egyptian tomb that he got out and walked by Cambridge Circus to Trafalgar Square.

His packet of day-old bread unwrapped from a clean handkerchief surprised him by its quality, when in school they had complained of it tasting like baked mud. He sat on a step to eat, and couldn't decide whether the lion on its plinth was sternly telling him to call his freedom a day's outing in London, and to get back to school by dark, or encouraging him to look sharp and stir himself to move further away than he was already.

Flights of pigeons swooped for his crumbs, though few enough were left. A pall of exhaustion came over him. He hadn't eaten enough, but it would have to do. When you had escaped from a prison camp it was dangerous to go into a café, and if he had to sooner or later that would be soon enough. He stood up, determined to go his way, a glance at the stone man with one eye and one arm high on his pillar who, he felt, would approve of his escape and watch over him.

Traffic was turmoil, people disturbing. He turned about and went into the post office to buy an air-letter form and zip off a paragraph telling his mother what he had done. She wasn't to worry, but if she did, so what? such concern being her affair and not his. It was a matter of protocol more than filial tenderness. You always let your parents know where you were.

He carried his case up Charing Cross Road, wondering whether he had done right in sending the news. It was vital not to betray his whereabouts, but they were so far away that the letter would take weeks to reach what outstation such folks were holed up in. By then he would be somewhere else altogether. Anxiety was lessened by looking in bookshop windows, at the gaudy covers of bigamy and murder. He wanted to buy one, for a real adult read, but money was for food and train tickets. On wiping his nose, he felt a firm tap at the shoulder.

Anybody could outrun such a granddad of a copper, if the only course was to bolt. A Woodbine packet sent spinning along the gutter by a damp wind was run over by a bus. The constable was smiling, so widely it was a wonder his false teeth stayed in. 'You've dropped your Identity Card, sonny.'

'Oh, thank you, officer. That was careless of me.'

The old fool even picked it up for him. 'Can't lose your identity card, lad, or you won't know who you are, will you?'

'Not much difficulty there.' Herbert gave the expected laugh. That bloody cold, with its runny nose calling for the handkerchief so often, had almost done for him. He stowed the card safely in his wallet and looked again at the cover of *No Orchids for Miss Blandish* set temptingly behind the glass, meanwhile waiting for the Special to turn the corner.

A mindless and happy wandering among carts and lorries in Covent Garden was ended by a violent splashing of rain. Horse piss was washed away, petrol fumes mellowed, but the wind was cold after rain, the sun fickle.

At the clarity of the air a sudden panic sent him back to the safety of the Underground, going down at Holborn and getting out at St Pancras. A shadow passed over him in the great space. He was threatened by odours of smoke and steam, wanted to flee but the street was even rowdier. What to do or where to go was the greatest problem on earth. The worst thing was to look bereft in the booking hall of a mainline station.

His heart thumped at the peculiar sensation of freedom, of having to deal with choice, take risks with reference to nobody else, lock into throngs of people who had a purpose and knew what they had to do. In a German town soldiers with rifles and fixed bayonets might surround him any moment and march him back to the prison camp. At least you'd know what was what.

The cheerful scene, even an educational experience, told him he would be safe as long as he kept moving and appeared certain of what he wanted to do. But what was that? He could only say it was good to be in England now that April was here. Instinct, welcome reinforcement to his fix, said that other people were his best camouflage, the commoner the better, so he stood at the back of a queue and stayed till an army sergeant in front asked for a ticket to Nottingham. Why not? Herbert's twenty-one shillings and eight pence was at the ready. Whoever will imagine I've gone to such an outlandish place?

There was a rush along the line to get on board and, well trained in games of murder ball, he forced his way through. A balding middle-aged man in spectacles glared as Herbert fell into a spare seat. Simpson had put the NCOs through a course of unarmed combat, so if it came to a fight he could hurl the weedy twerp through the window.

He was disappointed. A scrap would have been fun, made him feel less tight, though it wasn't on because you didn't draw attention to yourself when on the run. The pathetic man, a clerk most likely, folded his newspaper to read standing up. Maybe he had been wounded in Normandy and was now demobbed, you never could tell, which thought made Herbert give up his seat to a woman and her child.

He stood in the crowded corridor, back to *Caged Birds*, though the narrative seemed less gripping now. The train moved slowly through railway yards, and he was glad to be on his way, almost gloating. Let them find me. I'm safe for a hundred and thirty miles, unless we go into a river like the train at the Tay. Life was exciting, helped by the metallic thump-thump of the wheels. The only thing wrong was in being hungry, but that was also part of the escape. Dismal buildings bordered the line, bare bulbs glowing between in the partially lifted blackout. A man stood at one in his undershirt, perfectly still, as if watching every face in the train, like a policeman off duty.

What peculiar places people lived in. If he had to hole up in such style – he pushed a soldier away who was trying to lean on his shoulder and go to sleep – he might not like his freedom at all. On the other hand maybe he would be glad to live in such a room. He'd be glad to live in even worse at the moment, except that he had to vagabond as far as possible, go somewhere else after – where was it? – Nottingham, and lay a twisting trail to mystify and wear out the most fanatical hue-and-criers.

*   *   *

30

The market square seemed vast in the semi-blackout. But for a single trackless bus it looked like an encampment that had been abandoned to flowerbeds and low stone walls. Herbert wasn't worried about finding a place to sleep, but knew he would sooner or later have to discover a niche into which a policeman was unlikely to poke his nose. His money was almost gone, and his gas mask had been left behind, though he didn't think there could be any use for that at this late stage of the war.

Eight boomed from the clock above the Council House and it felt like midnight. On a further exhausting perambulation of the square, pausing again to look at the lions, those same old lions, he saw a pub, or rather heard it, the noise sounding as if the whole population of the town was carousing inside. He edged a way to the bar through a crowd of mostly servicemen.

Sixpences were draining away but he scorned to spend them carefully. Glancing at an old man close by, dressed in a clean blue overcoat, a cap and scarf, and with an empty half-pint glass by his side, he said: 'Have a drink on me.'

The man's look of surprise was more obvious than his expression of distrust. 'All right. I'll have the same again.'

Herbert, celebrating his escape from school, called for two, and along they came for a shilling.

'Throwing your money around, aren't you?'

'Not particularly.' Herbert refrained from sneering. Parsimony was the last refuge of – he couldn't think what. 'Perhaps I want to get rid of it. Anyway, it's a great occasion for me.'

'Is it, then? How much money have you got?'

Herbert wiped his nose, and explored the cloth caverns of his pockets. 'Another two shillings.'

'Where did you pick up that stinking cold?'

The whole damned school had had one. 'On the train, I suppose.' Colds were loathsome, only inferior types stricken – till you caught one yourself. 'It was packed.'

'They usually are. Here's to your health, which seems a fair toast.'

Wasn't there a line in Lullabalero about Nottingham's fine ale? He'd never tasted anything so good. 'And to yours, as well.'

'I'm Isaac Frost.' A frail hand was held out for shaking. 'What might yours be?'

He touched the cold fingers. 'Herbert.'

'Is that all?'

'For the moment.'

Isaac looked at him pityingly. 'I've met some funny chaps in my time, but not one that throws his money about when he's got so little.'

Herbert supposed that his lavish father would easily spend his last shilling treating someone he didn't know to a drink, especially if he came into a place like this and met one of his old soldiers – except that he most probably wouldn't set much store by this dive. He took his foot from the brass rail and stood full height. 'As soon as I've nothing left it will collect my mind wonderfully towards getting some more.'

Isaac adjusted his glasses on hearing such pretentious nonsense. 'Sounds a cock-eyed notion to me. And you're a bit too young to be a philosopher. You're from London, I suppose?'

Herbert had heard of coppers' narks, and wondered whether he shouldn't make a run from this noisy and exuberant den, though pride decided him not to. Either that, he thought, or I'm too done in to care. 'Thereabouts.'

'What hotel do you propose to put up at?'

Being laughed at encouraged him to more openness, whether the man was a nark or not. 'I'm not on the run, if that's what you mean. I'm seventeen, and want to get a job. As soon as I'm eighteen, though, I'll enlist.'

Isaac was appalled at what the war had done to the young. 'Why do you want to do that?' A tinkle of broken glass came from further down the hall, and a woman's scream was followed by such male effing and blinding as made Herbert turn his head, though slowly, to look. The smack of a fist on flesh sounded even over shouts and laughter, and a burly man in evening dress frogmarched a capless glaze-eyed soldier out on to the pavement. 'There's always a bit of that going on,' Isaac said, 'with so many women on the loose. And you know what soldiers are. But the doormen are very good here at dealing with it.'

Herbert turned to his drink as if nothing had happened. 'The army will take care of me for a few years. I need to learn how to kill properly.'

Isaac laughed in such a way that Herbert wondered if he had asthma, knowing what it sounded like because Dominic had a touch of it when he first came to school. 'You don't have to learn a thing like that. Necessity will tell you, if ever you need to. In any case, who would a nice young chap like you want to kill? There's been enough of that going on in the last five years.'

'My parents, for a start.'

'They seem to have made a good job of you.' His thin lips curved even more in amusement, as if to say: who the devil have I got here? 'You should be grateful.'

'They packed me off to boarding school from India when I was seven.' The laughter at some jokester further down the bar diminished. Herbert, not knowing the right thing to say, or even what he really believed before this sceptical old man, said whatever came to mind. 'I'd have been quite happy staying where I was.'

'I wish my parents had been able to send me to such a place. I left a hellhole of a school at thirteen to work on a market stall. And then I fought my way up, if you can call it that. Anyway, the best thing you can do is take my advice, and never blame your parents for anything. Whatever you think they did, it wasn't their fault. And whatever they did do can't be altered now.'

'Really?' Herbert hoped his attempt to resist an outright sneer would be obvious to the most imperceptive, or so Isaac surmised. The silly kid's trying to seem more adult by blaming his deficiencies and troubles on his parents.

Two half-pints, and the ever biting famishment, not to mention tiredness, made him grip the brass rail to stay upright, while trying to show interest in whatever other rubbish the little man had to say.

'I was a printer for much of my life. Now I'm retired, and live on my own. Why? Well, I like it that way, that's why. I've got a couple of beehive rooms up one of those narrow streets across the square, and as I can see you're in a fix you're welcome to come back and sleep on the floor. I won't be the perfect host and offer my bed, because I'm sixty and need it myself.'

Herbert knew he should say no, thank you very much, it's awfully kind, I must be getting on, but he put himself into the hands of this stranger because he was too much starving and done for to know what to do or where to go next.

Stars spun over the sky; he looked at pavements and tarmac to get his equilibrium settled. 'It's not good to drink on an empty stomach,' Isaac said. 'Certainly not Nottingham ale.' He led the way up the stairs of a damp-smelling decrepit building of offices and store rooms, turning from the landing to say: 'I've told you my full name. What's yours? And I don't want an alias, either.'

The question signified a Rubicon that would have to be crossed sooner or later, a turbulent river for Herbert after his determination to follow the *Caged Birds* code of concealment, but he had blabbed plenty in the pub so he decided that a little more truth wouldn't get him turned over to the law. Trust was laziness, a deadly sin, but even so he answered: 'Herbert Thurgarton-Strang.'

'One of them?' Isaac worked his keys at the lock. 'We'll have to find you a shorter monicker, otherwise the blokes in the factory will make your life a misery.'

'I'm not going to have anything to do with a factory.'

'You'll want a job won't you?'

Herbert followed him into the small room. The old man's brain must have been working overtime. 'Well, yes, I suppose I do. Or I well might.'

'You've got problems, and I'm wondering what to do with you. Anyway, Thurgarton-Strang, in the meantime, I'll cook us some chips.' He took off his hat, overcoat and scarf. 'I've got spuds, fat, and a loaf of bread, so you won't go to sleep on an empty stomach, which it looks like you've got with that bony face. There's tea and milk as well but, alas, no sugar.'

'That's awfully kind of you.' His speech sounded clumsy even to himself, as if he had landed in a foreign country with an obsolete phrasebook. 'Very kind I must say.'

'Kind is a word you don't have any cause to use,' Isaac said with a wry smile. The smell of paraffin, soap and dampness pricked Herbert's nostrils. The old cove was helpful, but as domineering as a teacher, especially when he went on: 'Maybe I succumbed in a weak moment in asking you to come back here, though I always respond to an attempt at generosity. Unless it was a subtle ruse of yours to treat a stranger to

34

a drink out of your last few bob.' He looked at Herbert, as if holding a new penny up to the light. 'But I hardly think so, if I'm any judge of character.'

The walls were mainly bookshelves, with a table close up, and two chairs of the sort used in canteens. A second room through an archway, little more than an alcove, contained a bed and a chest of drawers. 'It wasn't a ruse,' Herbert said, 'I can tell you.'

'Sit down, then, and don't be offended – while I get to work.' He filled a kettle and saucepan at a tap on the landing, and Herbert drew out a book to find that half was in a script he hadn't seen before. It wasn't Greek or Hindustani, but whatever it was suggested that Isaac, though only a printer, might be something of a scholar, and not so lowly and simple as he had thought at first. A smaller curtain in a corner covered his larder, and in a few minutes the room was pungent with the smell of frying. He must be lonely though, to do what he was doing so well, cutting spuds into chips for someone he had just met. 'I've even got a pat of butter for our bread. It's a lucky night. Every man should be able to cook, otherwise he's no man.'

Herbert sat down to the most welcome meal of his life. 'It's marvellous,' starvation diminishing with every mouthful.

Isaac ate daintily for a man in such accommodation, and Herbert saw the skullcap on his bald head as something to keep off the chill. 'Which you are too young to feel with your black thatch,' Isaac said, when Herbert politely mentioned it. 'It may well be marvellous grub, but I'll burn in hell, if there is such a place, for eating a mixture like this. However, necessity knows no bounds, with which I'm sure the sagest rabbis would agree.'

'Why shouldn't they?'

'Well, my son, I'm Jewish, and this fat is not what they would call kosher, though I get it when I have to.'

'Kosher?'

'Ritually clean, to you.'

Herbert guided a piece of bread around the plate with his fork to mop up the fat. 'Why shouldn't you eat it?'

'That – is a very long story. Very long indeed. You'll have to bury yourself in Leviticus to find out.'

Herbert felt himself to be what people meant by intoxicated, and that the beer was responsible. He was also drunk with freedom and food, for on standing up the room seemed to be without walls, and he hoped he wasn't going to faint. After being locked in all his life he belonged nowhere at the moment, no rules or walls surrounding him. Every nerve tingled with a mixture of relief and trepidation, but on the whole it was good, even better than he would ever have thought good to be. Acting out of his own will, Fate had led him to this funny old chap who for one night anyway had given him a place to sleep. What more did he need? He'd never had the chance to bump into such a person before, and all he had heard from his father about his sort was a slighting comment on one who had kept a store in Simla. How strange and wonderful life was! He sat down and said, as if to flatter him for his generosity: 'I'll bet you have lots of interesting stories to tell.'

Isaac laid the plates in a washing up bowl and set it by the door, in place of a steel helmet which he put on to a pile of books. 'I used to look a sight in that when I did my firewatching. Yes, I've plenty of stories, and I might tell you one sometime. I won't go into any now though, because as soon as I've done with this cigarette it'll be time for bed.'

They sat as if silence was part of the ritual until Herbert, confident that Isaac was to be trusted, said he found it hard to believe he had left his bloody awful school only that morning.

'In that case you won't mind sleeping rough.' He took a blanket from a cupboard. 'Though I've slept rougher in my time, let me tell you. Spread this over you when you get your head down.'

Herbert unpacked his spare trousers, jacket, shirt, underwear, socks and handkerchiefs, complimenting himself on the forethought of bringing so much. He remembered the wet tents he had slept in. 'I can hardly believe my luck.'

The response was a don't-know-you're-born look. 'There's no such thing.' Isaac called from the alcove where he was changing into pyjamas. 'Everything's pre-ordained, as you'll find out more and more as you go on.'

*   *   *

Herbert opened his eyes. Sunlight, albeit watery, came into the room. He folded his blanket with cadet neatness and cleared the space, feeling as if the awareness of freedom all through the night had doubled the intensity of his sleep. Waking up penniless gave him no worry at all.

'Borrow this cap,' Isaac said after breakfast of sugarless tea, bread and jam, 'for when you go to the Ministry of Labour, otherwise they'll take one look at you and make you a penpusher. You'll earn a lot more in a factory, and mix in better. But watch your accent. Act the silent sort, as far as they'll let you, and get a grasp of the accent as soon as you can. You'll find they're a lot more tolerant in a factory than an office. Another thing is that for a while anyway say yes to whatever you're asked to do. As for your proper name, forget it. Tell 'em at the Labour that you've just left school and your certificate's coming from Ireland where you were evacuated.'

He cleared the table and took out a box of pens and rubbers and inks. 'Give me your Identity Card.' Herbert looked at it as well, opened before them both. 'This is one advantage in having been a printer,' Isaac said. 'I'm going to alter it so that Ernest Bevin himself wouldn't know the difference.'

'Isn't it a bit criminal? I mean, what if I'm caught out?'

'You won't be.' Isaac cracked his fingers to make the joints supple. 'A little innocent forgery to fox the bureaucrats never hurt anyone. We'll make your surname into Gedling, which is a district around here. Bert Gedling you'll be, and a good honest name it sounds. If and when you want to join the army I'll change it back for you.'

Herbert wondered if they still wouldn't smell him a mile off for what he was, while Isaac sipped the rest of his cold tea as delicately as if it had stayed hot and sugar had been magicked into it. 'Now where's your ration book?'

'Ration book?'

'We might as well alter that while we're about it.'

'I don't have one.'

'You didn't bring it?'

'I never thought to. And I could hardly ask them.'

Isaac's shake of the head came from thinking what babies there were in the world. 'All right. Perhaps it won't matter. They aren't too particular these days. When you've got your employment cards, and they've found you a job, go to the Food Office and ask for a ration book. Tell 'em you lost it. Or just look as if it's your God-given right to have one. They don't let people starve in this country. At least they haven't during the war. So good luck to you, or whatever it is. I'll let you stay here two more nights, in which time you'll have to get digs. The firm you find a job with will lend you a few pounds to tide you over. That's what they do for Irish labourers who come over. And don't look so worried. I'm sure you'll be all right.'

Four

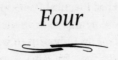

By the end of the day Herbert had employment cards, a ration book, and a job at the Royal Ordnance Factory. The wages clerk in the machine shop arranged a three-pound loan till his first wages came due. On Isaac's advice, he spent six bob on a second-hand pair of overalls hanging outside a pawnshop on the Hockley. His cadet boots would look right on any factory floor, as soon as the shine wore off.

'I knew you had it in you, after the education you've had. You're obviously from the right kind of family. But from now on, hang on to your money. Don't go throwing it about.' Isaac put the book he'd been reading back on the shelf. 'Still, it's good of you to bring these fish and chips for our supper, though you didn't need to splash half a week's rations on me. All the same,' he fussed, 'I do like a bit of sugar.'

Herbert's feet ached from walking the town all day. 'You did me a wonderfully good turn.'

'I don't want to hear any more about that, but if you really think so, pay me back by doing a good turn to somebody I don't know. That's what keeps the world a halfway decent place to live in. Now, enough of such platitudes and attitudes, and let's get down to supper.'

Before any money came to him Herbert had, as it were, to work a week for nothing, though his landlady Mrs Denman said she would board him in the meanwhile on condition that he equalized the thirty-five shillings a week out of his four pounds wages the minute it was possible.

'I've got to be practical,' she said, 'where young lads like you are concerned,' putting the kettle on the gas to make him a cup of tea.

'And I am practical, I allus was. If I hadn't been, after my Will died, I shouldn't have been running this place today.'

Herbert thought of her as Practical Penelope, though she was a bit old, being about forty, and he was to drop the nickname after a while because, for a start, she had no Odysseus to wait for, and no time for weaving. Probably no idea how to. Also, a man who was her suitor came to the house every other evening and, as far as Herbert could tell, stayed the night.

Her straight black hair was just short enough to make the face seem broader than necessary, but she had, he thought, a nicely shaped nose. A clean apron of sacking served over her white blouse and dark skirt. He also noticed her patent leather shoes which looked a bit tarty, the way they buttoned up.

'I do all the work on my own, though' – she pushed her glasses straight – 'because I never did mind it. Mrs Atkins next door said I should get a man in to help. But no fear, I did have one once, not long after my Will died, and I should have known better because he was an idle devil who only liked being at the bookies or in a pub, so I got rid of him. No more men for me, I said to myself. Well, not like him anyway. I just see Frank when it takes my fancy, and he sees me when it takes his, which suits us both. But as for having a man in the house, not likely.'

Herbert shared a room with her son Ralph, who turned from trimming a flimsy moustache to hold out a friendly enough hand when his mother showed him in. He spoke with little of the local accent, which made Herbert, already noting the cadence, determined to take more of Isaac's advice and say as little as possible until he felt easier using it.

'Hope you'll be comfortable in the other bed,' Ralph said.

'I'm sure I shall.'

'Mother's making all the cash she can.' He was surprised that Herbert had so little to unpack from his scruffy case, and Herbert picked up his embarrassment at having to share a room, which indicated that he had been spoiled. 'I wouldn't be surprised if she didn't let our beds to night workers while we were out during the day,' Ralph went on. 'She hopes to get a boarding house at Skegness after the war. Poor mother doesn't realize it might go on forever.'

'Who lives in the rest of the house?'

'Four other lodgers.'

'What do they do?'

Ralph pulled a comb through fair wavy hair. 'A couple, both men, if you know what I mean. They work in a drawing office, very hush-hush, they tell us, though I wouldn't be surprised if they didn't design bottle tops. The other two come and go at all hours, and I think they dabble in black market, which means we have bacon and butter for our breakfast more often than most, or at least I do.'

His nose turned up even more when Herbert mentioned the factory he was to work at, Ralph saying that *he* went to *business* at the office of the local bus depot – probably counting tickets all day, Herbert thought. Because of flat feet, and no doubt a few more shameful ailments, Ralph hadn't been called up – an even worse fate – though at twenty he was lucky no impediments showed.

Herbert asked about the bathroom, but it wasn't that kind of house. Mrs Denman promised to get one in as soon as the war ended. Meanwhile they could wash at the kitchen sink, and a pot under each bed saved them running down three flights of stairs and across the back yard at night. Two small wardrobes took care of their clothes. Herbert smiled: a hook and a coat hanger on the back of the door would have done for him. There was even a rickety dressing table against the wall to put things on. He'd never felt so well off.

On day three of his escape the noise as he walked into the machine shop at the Royal Ordnance Factory seemed likely to push him straight back on to the road. He shouted his question as to where the chargehand was, and barged courageously along the main gangway towards him. 'I don't know what job to give yer, but foller me and we'll find one. There's allus summat.'

Motors, dynamos and donkey engines, flapping powerbelts, the screech of steel being cut, and tools sharpening on Carborundum wheels shook his eardrums and made him want to close his eyes. He didn't know how they could talk to each other, never mind exist for more than a few minutes in this vast extension to the forge of Vulcan. Hand signals and grunts sufficed for the carrying on of work, an advantage in that he didn't have much call to open his mouth in a way that would show his posh accent.

Archie Bleasby, a burly six footer of his own age, worked on a lathe, and sat next to him on a box of castings at tea break. 'What did yer want ter cum and wok on a fuckin' tip like this for?'

The machinery still ran, and Herbert put his ear close as he bit a gap into his potted-meat sandwich, his mouth conveniently full. 'Munny,' using a pronunciation of *money* heard from Mrs Denman. The reply satisfied Archie, who was also disinclined to waste much breath on chat except: 'I don't know whether yer've cum to the right place for that, Bert.'

So Bert he was, and must know himself to be, if he wanted to be absorbed into the shop, which seemed to be happening because, on going into the canteen for dinner at half past twelve, he found that Archie had kept a place for him at the long table. 'This fuckin' grub'll kill yer, but it'll keep yer goin' till it does.'

A grunt of agreement was safe enough, as he was getting his head down towards the spuds and mincemeat, a delicious smell compared to most of the meals at school. After the pudding and coffee Archie stood up. 'Let's go outside a bit, and 'ave a fag.'

'I forgot mine this morning,' Bert said.

Men were kicking a tennis ball along the pavement, and they stood to watch. ''Ave one o' these, then. I on'y smoke Players.'

'Ta.' Herbert took one and put it between his lips. He would buy a packet and pay Archie back, but meanwhile he had to make sure he didn't seem a stranger to the habit. Archie held the light, and Herbert puffed without drawing in too much of the smoke. 'I'm used to Woodbines.'

Archie was looking at one of the office girls walking by. 'Not bad, eh, is she?'

'Yeh,' Bert took another puff of his fag, and managed not to choke.

He cleared swarf from between the machines, or lifted boxes of shellcaps and fuse cases from the gangway to the viewing benches. Archie showed him how to bend from the knees instead of the waist. 'Ye're tall and thin, see? and this way you wain't snap yer backbone. Yer wouldn't be any good at fuckin' then, if yer did that, would yer?'

Not that the labour was hard to get used to, Herbert mused, maybe due to the game and cadet scramblings on the obstacle course at school. Everything was so new that whenever he looked at the clock another hour had gone by.

In the evening he sat in his room and popped blisters with a needle heated over a match flame, dousing them in TCP, then picking brass splinters out with tweezers before they could fester. Archie was his mentor, with no asking, sharp eyes for his problems and always volunteering a remedy. 'If you don't tek care o' yer 'ands they'll get to look like tree stumps, and the women don't like that. As long as they're nice and clean they'll let you get at their knickers.'

He was clocking out when Walter Price, a toolsetter of about forty who had been lame from birth, asked if he played darts. He remembered Isaac's advice to fall in with everything. 'Now and then.'

'It's like this, yer see, we need a new chap on the team, because that bleddy fool Jack Blundell cum off 'is motorbike and broke 'is arm last week. Can yer cum to the Plough tonight, after yer tea?'

He had scorned the dart board in the games room at school, as something to amuse the tiddlers who were miserable at being away from mummy and daddy. Now he wished he hadn't, though he recalled some of the jargon. 'I'm a bit rusty. Down from three-o-one, though, in't it?'

Walter smiled like a man who only did so to hide his pain. 'That's the ticket. We'll show yer. It's the enthusiasm of youth we want on the team.'

Herbert's uncertainty was overcome by assuming that if these men could do it, so could he. At his probationary session, he tried for the bull, and though the first half-dozen went all over the board at least none gouged a hole in the blue plastered wall.

'Don't 'urry, lad. Just chuck 'em about a bit to get yer 'and in.' But after a few more scatterings Walter lost patience. 'I'll coach yer. Now, just watch me.' The disability of having one leg shorter than the other had made Walter a better player than most. 'I want a treble, don't I? A seven? Now don't tek yer eyes off me.' Lopsided he got one. 'Now a double six, then a bull – inner and outer. Y'er not lookin'! Look at me!' He got those as well. 'Now yo' ev a go, me owd duck.'

Herbert applied the rules of the firing range, while taking in what

43

he could of Walter's expertise. Legs apart and firm on the ground, arm straight and fingers holding the dart as if an extension of both, he aligned his eye along the length. Taking time, he let go, and got an outer bull. When the next dart hit a treble Walter set a pint on the table. 'Sup that. Y'er doin' well, for a beginner. I on'y 'ope it ain't starter's luck.'

He doused his chagrin, but smiled agreement with irony he hoped, at each comment. 'He's got a cool 'ead, that's the main thing,' Walter said to the others.

Herbert's long drink of beer put a fur lining in his throat. Use all the time you need, just like they're doing. Imitate, he told himself. Act. Mimic. Away from work, they knew how to go easy, from long experience. On the next run he tried for a double and a treble, and got them with two darts, though the third was nowhere.

'It's a matter o' patience, from now on,' Walter said.

'He'll do, though,' came a voice from the back.

Better to try the accent while wiping beer froth from his lips. 'Mekin' progress, am I?' The thud of steel tips into cork was satisfying, but he was happy to let the old hands have a go, since the pint might foil his aim.

People he didn't know would call in a friendly way as he walked into the canteen: 'Hey up, Bert!' His name went up on the notice board and after a few more sessions he was let in on a match, though feared he'd never be as good as most others on the team.

During an hour or so when there was no sweeping, or lifting, or trolleys to push, and it looked like someone had hammered nails against the arrowed hands of the clock face, he had time for thinking, and didn't much like it. The heavy load in his mind was asking to be sorted out, and that wasn't what he had taken a job in the factory for. A voice he didn't trust said the only course was to pack up at his digs and get on the train to another town. Life would be interesting again. The challenge of the unknown would get his blood jumping.

'Slowin' down a bit, aren't you?' Archie said.

Herbert leaned on his brush handle. 'I'm bored out o' my clogs.'

'You're gettin' used to it, that's why. But don't let it get yer down, the first three years is the worst. Just 'ave a word with the chargehand and tell 'im yer aren't mekin' it pay. Tell 'im yer've got to mek it fuckin' pay, or you'll gerra job somewhere else. Things might look up, then.'

Herbert thought it best to be inconspicuous. Another place would be just as boring, and there'd be less chance of being recaptured if he stayed where he was.

'It gets fucking monotonous working on a lathe as well,' Archie went on, 'but at least I'm mekin' munny, so it don't!'

The best way to diffuse the blues was to flash up the Stalag towers of his school. He swept a coil of swarf from Archie's lathe, like the discarded tail of a steel piglet. Eileen looked as if trying to weigh him up – what for? – and not for the first time he noted her blush as she turned away. One of the women beside her said: 'Go on, he wain't bite yer!'

He might, one day, if he got the chance, and decided to be pleasant in her presence and see where it got him. The dungarees over her bosom in no way hid the shape, and her headscarf only scantily covered glistening auburn hair. Hard to imagine there'd be much chance with such a favourite of the department, though she wasn't near as stuck up as Dominic's sister had been.

He marched across to the viewing tables, in response to her shout: 'Come on, Bert, get these boxes out o' my sight.'

The first one slotted on to the trolley. 'Tek yer sweat. You're workin' me to death.'

'We all thought you'd faint when you first come into the factory,' she said. 'You looked as if yer'd never done a day's hard work in your life.'

He leaned close to smell her powder. 'Yer was wrong. I've worked since I was fourteen.'

'What made yer so strong, then?'

'Bovril.' He pushed the trolley away. 'And Oxo,' he called over his shoulder.

Arthur Elliot went off sick, so Herbert was set to work on his lathe. 'We'll give you a day to get used to it.' The chargehand thought him a bit daft to be writing the instructions down. 'After that we'll set you up on piece work. We'll find Arthur summat else when 'e comes back.'

'Now you'll be able to GRAB!' Archie bellowed into his ear as he passed on his way to the lavatories. 'Just like me!'

Herbert practised for an hour, and next morning the chargehand came to see how he was getting on. 'Have you done this before?'

Herbert flicked the turret ninety degrees, adjusted the sud pipe, and eased in the drill. 'No, never.'

'You're on your own then, from now on. Two bob a hundred. I'll bring you a time sheet.'

To make it pay in the manner of Archie was not part of his purpose. 'Grabbing' wasn't in him. Still, he thought, if I don't make a show they'll smell me out and snub me for being stuck up or incompetent. So, a few days more and it was grab grab grab like the rest of them. Bert nodded a response, too grabbing and making it pay to take a hand off the levers and signal back, which concentration at the job no one understood better than Archie.

The result of putting on an act was that after a while his behaviour became normal, and Herbert had never imagined that life could be so easy and engrossing. For the first week his limbs ached even more by the end of the day, due to hour after hour of daunting repetition, though there was something satisfactory in that as well, proving that grabbing on a lathe was better than sweeping up and humping boxes for a living.

He looked on the machine as his own possession, with its handles and levers, and power supplied by a motor down by his feet. A clumsy touch and your hand got gouged, so he treated it much like the chariot witless Phaeton had tried to control on his feckless jaunt across the skies, pulling and spinning, easing here and there with calculated panache. If a thief came by and began to unbolt it from the base he would fight to the death to stop him.

Conceding his past, at least to himself, he baptized the lathe with a splash of milky suds over the turret, calling it Dominic, after his old chum at school. 'Hey up, Dommy,' he said every morning, ''ow's tricks today? Going to be a good lad and earn me a bob or two?' He could turn off a thousand or more pieces from clocking in to clocking out, which brought in six pounds a week. Stoppages left him with four pounds ten bob, but it was more than enough to live on. With subtle economy he was able to buy a new suit, as well as go out now and again for a pint with Archie.

Eileen was disappointed when he went on the lathe. 'I can't shout at yer any more, and I shall miss yer long face.'

'Thanks for nothing.'

'Nothing!' she mimicked. 'Where did you get that?' – a warning that he still needed to watch his language.

'I 'eard it on the wireless, duck. But I miss your nice face, as well. I'll come and wink at yer now and again.'

'Won't yer say summat, as well?'

'Course I will.'

So that was all right. Machines were being turned off all round, men and women crowding the gangways. Were they downing tools, or was it a ritual they'd been miffy enough not to let him in on? Hard to believe, because Archie, already wearing his jacket, took Herbert's from the nail and brought it over. 'Switch off, and put this bit o' rag on yer back. We're going out for some swill.'

'What's it all about?'

'War's over.'

He'd known it couldn't be far off, but hadn't assumed they'd pack in work when it was. ''Ave the gaffers said owt?'

'Fuck the gaffers. I expect they're blindoe already. Anyway, it's a national 'oliday. Churchill says so.'

The pub crawl took them into every place, a continual push through the crowds in each to get at the bar. In the singing and drinking Herbert lost his cap, but enjoyed himself to an even greater pitch when his mind flashed a picture of the chapel at school, where beyond doubt the poor sods were bellowing 'Onward Christian Soldiers' and slavering at the thought of an extra cake with their piss-like char.

Slipping on the cobbles near the Trip to Jerusalem he thumped Archie in the ribs out of happiness at not going down, and got like treatment on the rebound for what deep-buried reason neither could say. An old man with a blind drunk glitter in his eyes and spluttering into his ale at the bar called to his mate above the din: 'We beat the fuckers. Oh yes, we beat the fuckers. Didn't we Alf?'

'Yeh,' Alf said, 'but they'll be at it again in twenty years.'

'No they won't,' the old man said. Bert had never seen a pint go so quick. 'Not this time they won't.'

To the tune of 'Coming Round the Mountain' (and she'll be

wearing camiknickers when she comes) Bert took a wet-gin kiss from a woman old enough, he thought, to be Mrs Denman's grandmother. 'That's for you, my lovely handsome duck,' she said.

'Yer've clicked,' Archie laughed.

'Course he's clicked,' she screamed at them with a laugh, huddling back against her smiling husband.

'Let's run, Bert, or she'll 'ave us both.'

'She will, an' all,' her husband laughed.

In the Royal Children a girl shoved a full pint at Herbert through the fug saying she'd bought it for her bloke but he'd nipped out to heave his guts up, and what a shame it would be to waste it. The cold slurry went down too quickly, and after a further jar in the Rose of England Herbert also ran out to the back yard and threw up as if all the weary years at school were fighting pell-mell to get from his system.

Archie led him the shortest way back to his digs, Bert hardly aware of passing streets. They sang their way up the steps into Mrs Denman's impeccable parlour, from which place she hurried them into the kitchen. Bert screwed a knuckle into his eyes for clarity. A tall thin man with greying hair was introduced by Mrs Denman as Frank, her Frank, her own especial Frank (she'd had one or two as well), Frank of about forty who, the only one sober because he'd had to stay on at work doing maintenance, suggested Bert be roped to a pit prop, first to stop him falling on his face, and then to shoulder him up to bed.

'It's the best place for him,' Mrs Denman said. 'Poor lad's as white as chalk. He ain't used to it. I wouldn't trust him to keep even a cup of coffee down in that state, nor yo', either,' she said, turning on Archie. 'So gerrof home and let us look after him.'

Archie laughed – and belched. 'All right, ma. You don't need to tell me twice.'

Such speech was perfectly clear to understand, and Herbert didn't seem one bit drunk, though realized that the slightest wind would blow him down. All he wanted to know was how much sleeping time there was between the coming collapse and getting back to his lathe. The wall clock wouldn't tell him, one hand moving slowly rightward, while the angle between the two increased until his forehead hit the floor, mocked on his way down by the strident laugh of Bacchus, which seemed to come from himself, though also from those looking on.

'Ah Beryl,' and Herbert barely heard Frank's words, 'let's stomp up the wooden hill as well. You can't blame 'im, though. He won't have owt else to celebrate like this again in his lifetime. They'll be no more o' them concentration camps. Worn't it terrible?'

'Them pictures,' Mrs Denman said.

From his laid-out state in front of the fender Herbert told himself how nice were Mrs Denman's shapely legs – Beryl, as Frank called her, then felt hands under his armpits and knew he had better co-operate in standing so that they could get him to where he most wanted to be.

Archie, as if undecided about switching on his machine, came over and bellowed: 'How yer feeling after last night then, Bert?'

Herbert's head rang like a month of Sunday mornings, his feet felt shoeless and half buried in broken glass, a band of nails gripped around his waist, and his mouth tasted as if he'd swallowed a tramp's overcoat. 'Never felt better.'

Archie drew his lips into a smile, and gave him the hundred-year look – as if he had been to the same Understatement College, and considered it a disgrace not to hold himself upright no matter how much booze he had guzzled.

There were moments when Herbert felt that he had always been a workman. Or was he imagining it only in the face of overwhelming reality? It was certainly a soft and easy life compared to his previous existence. A workman lived without heartache as long as his wage packet came comfortably padded on Friday afternoon. Mr Thomas the history teacher used to maunder on about their sufferings, saying how much better it would be if nobody had to slave in 'dark satanic mills' and live in dismal slums that threatened to strangle the beauties of England with their brick and mortar tentacles. But Herbert liked the glow of homeliness in the streets, the beer-smelling fagstink of friendly pubs, and the mateyness of the blokes at work. He was captivated by the logic of machinery, of how its many parts worked, fascinated by the certainty of construction and the usefulness of its application.

By the end of the working day his dream state was dominated by cog wheels, ratchets and pulleys, which reminded him of his mother talking engine terms with his father when the car used to conk out in India.

His expertise at mechanics was widened when Sarah, a large-bosomed blonde who operated a milling machine, turned pale one morning and, overcome by dizziness, was advised by the toolsetter to go home.

'Must 'ave bin the flu,' Herbert said at tea break.

'I'll bet it's her monthlies,' was Archie's opinion. 'Not that it'd put me off. I'd swim through her lovely blood any day.'

Herbert felt disgust at this vivid picture, though was called on to laugh: 'Ah, I would, as well.'

He was shown how to operate Rachel's machine, and then told to get on with it. It was necessary to stand back and rehearse the motions, having memorized a cinematic picture of his cursory lesson. The first dozen were slow to make, but throughout the afternoon he built up speed, and turned out so many aluminium elbows in the next few days that when Rachel came back her absence on the production line hadn't been missed. 'If you stay here much longer,' the chargehand said, 'you'll be doing my job as well.'

Bert knew when he was being flattered. 'Don't worry, I'll be joining up soon.'

'Thank God for that,' he laughed, walking away.

Mrs Denman came into his room with a starched and ironed shirt in one hand, and clean underwear in the other. She slotted it neatly into a carrier bag with his folded suit, and stood by the door as if he might forget to take it to the public baths. He was trying to get the grime out of his fingernails. The other lodgers called her 'Ma', so why not him? 'Thanks, Ma.'

She stood by the door. 'I expect you'll be going out tonight?'

On Saturday afternoons he went to the baths and hoped he came back looking different. For a few pennies everybody who needed to could get clean. 'Ye', I've got a date.'

'I expected as much.'

He didn't know what she was waiting for. 'By the lions, at the Council House.'

'You're a nice lad, Bert.'

He smiled. Never been called that before. He liked it, from her. 'Don't you reckon Archie is, as well?'

She held his hand, but let it go in a moment. 'He was made brick by brick, though, and you just grew tall on your own.'

She was in a strange mood. 'Is Frank calling tonight?'

He wondered what he'd said wrong when she answered: 'What's that got to do with it?'

'I just asked.'

'We might go to't Town Arms for an hour or two.' It was the top of the list for her, as far as pubs went, but he wouldn't be seen in such a place, so dead that everybody stared at you as you went through the door. In any case, he had to meet Eileen. He sorted his money under her gaze, and when he paid his week's board she left him to his lack of thought.

If you stayed longer than fifteen minutes the attendant elbowed the door because more people were waiting, but it was enough time to wash, soap, and steam himself, a sybaritic experience after icy showers at school.

He dropped the bag of old working clothes in his room and went down to pork pie and tomato salad tea which Mrs Denman put before him in silence before going to get in the evening's coal. When she came back he asked: 'Where's the rest of them?'

'Gone for the weekend.'

'Saves yer some work then, don't it, Ma?'

'Well, I like an hour to myself, though the kitchen floor'll have to be scrubbed. That's one thing I don't much like doing.' She sat opposite with a cup of tea and a cigarette. 'I told this to Ralph once but he didn't want to know. You see, I was in an orphanage from the age of eleven, and all I remember was scrubbing floors. They set me to do it with a bucket and brush, and I had these long corridors to keep clean. I was so tired I used to do it in my sleep. I must have scrubbed miles before somebody else was put on to help me. I'll never forget the smell of that yellow soap. I scrubbed so much my hands would often be raw.'

'You've had a hard life, then,' Herbert said.

She smiled. 'You never know, do you? Maybe not as hard as some, all said and done. But I got out of the orphanage at sixteen, and went to work in a factory. Then I got married. I'm not complaining, though. Don't think that. I'd hate anybody to think I was complaining.'

'I've had a charmed life,' Herbert said, 'compared to that.'

'Well, Bert, all I can say is I hope it stays that way.'

He walked to the middle of town, losing the gloom of Mrs Denman's reminiscences on the way. At the bar of the Eight Bells, which place was like a scene from the Wild West, he called for a pint. Most were soldiers, and shorter than him, so he had a good view of their clamouring. They had no more fighting to do, in Europe at least, unless later among themselves. After his week's stint the ale went down with the alacrity of lemonade in earlier days, and he made his way to the back door. Eileen watched him swaggering mac on arm across Slab Square. 'I've bin waiting five minutes. Where'd yer get to?'

'Sorry, duck, I got stuck in a pub door and couldn't get out.'

'You leery bogger. I might 'ave known. Just because you're on a lathe you think you're the cock o' the walk.' She disliked him being so rough, sensing his different parts, the way he now and again stood at work to drink from his tea mug, or the times he forgot to snap like a dragon at his sandwich. Tonight he was imitating foul Archie Bleasby.

Herbert was amused to note that in the fog of her uncultivated mind she couldn't sort out what mystified her. He jeered, and gave a gentle push. 'It's better than bein' on viewin', like yo'.'

Her knuckles stung when she jabbed him back, but he knew better than to show it. 'I'm not on viewing,' she snapped. 'I work on *inspection*. I use a micrometer to test things. I use a depth gauge.'

He didn't particularly like himself for talking broad Nottingham, but assumed his freedom depended on it. 'I can't 'elp 'ow I was brought up.'

The July day was fresh, but the headscarf made out of a silk map kept her ears warm. 'I don't suppose yer can.' She stood tiptoe for a kiss. Her puckered expectant lips were cool, but he kept his there long enough to warm them up, the first kiss given to a girl, and he thought how he would lie to Archie in not admitting it had taken him so long. Eileen couldn't understand how somebody like him seemed embarrassed just because people gawped as they walked by.

'I don't care who sees us,' she said. 'Come on, let's have a drink somewhere.'

Her face was nothing special, that little pointed nose, the waxy skin of her full cheeks, and sharp lips, but there was a brightness in her blue-grey eyes missing from those of other girls in the factory. Even Dominic's sister Rachel – always a drifting vision – hadn't such a vivacious shine to her eyes. He gave back Eileen's affectionate smile, and took her arm like a cavalier, as if she had turned into the most desirable girl ever, which, being the only one, she had. He had to imitate the lout, but even so must show good behaviour, sensing that she would take it as a form of respect and thus become more loving and pliable, though he had to ration his sudden consideration in case she suspected he was who he wasn't supposed to be. Her sharp tongue with men in the factory was well known, as if she took it for a dead cert that all they wanted as she walked haughtily by with nose cutting the air was to slide a hand up her shapely legs.

In the Peach Tree he fed her shandies while thinking it wise to keep himself on half-pints. She talked so much that all he had to do was listen, went on about what was showing at the forty-odd picturedromes in the city, indicating an encyclopaedic knowledge of what had been on last week, what was on this, and all the coming attractions of the times ahead that she had information about. He knew of her favourite stars, and what details of their lives she had been able to cull from magazines – all of which he would have considered boring had he not thought the information might bolster his authenticity in the world.

Then she laughed at what the women got talking about at the workbench, and at how they all looked after one another, and what a good lot they were, and how she couldn't stand the women who lived in the same street at home, who were a pack of nosy bone-idle gossipers. He had to look interested, but on the other hand pitied her because she wanted to find herself in a more refined life, and couldn't because she'd never be anything else but common. Getting a word in edgeways he asked if she had ever read a book, and she said no, but her father who was a collier at Wilford Pit changed a few at the library every week, as if that more than made up for her not caring or being able to. 'Anyway, he's older than me,' she said, knowing his thoughts, 'so I've got lots of time. What about yo'?'

'Never read one in my life, and don't suppose I ever shall.' Watching her animated face made him want to hold her close and kiss her again, the music of her brash accent playing while he did. The only question was when and how. Sense told him to be subtle, to woo her slowly so that she wouldn't laugh and tell him to get lost. On the other hand maybe she was thinking him backwards at coming forwards, and wouldn't walk out with him again if he didn't do something. Archie would already think him slow in that he hadn't yet 'gone all the way'. Before the towels went on at ten he brought her a whisky, and she didn't need daring to get it down. He couldn't wait for the landlord to bawl out time and flicker the lights on and off to clear the place.

They walked with arms locked down Wheeler Gate, back towards The Meadows. On the canal bridge her peppery breath and the smell of female powder made his penis rise, and he embraced her for a kiss. She took off her headscarf, auburn hair falling over her face. 'I love you,' he said, meeting her lips halfway. 'You know that, don't you?'

'Yes,' she whispered, when he put a hand in her blouse to stroke her breasts, and feeling the nipples already responding. 'I can tell. Let's go down here.'

Steps led from the orange glow of the road to a tow path, the water dim by a facade of warehouses. He was glad she knew the way and, further from the light, she leaned against the wall. He pressed close, and when his hand was as far up as her suspenders she said: ''Ave yer got summat to tek care, duck?'

If she became pregnant and he tried to say it wasn't his she would scream so loud and long that everybody would not only know but would find out who he was, and he would be sent back in disgrace to school. All the boys would cheer because he'd put a tart in the family way. Or he wouldn't be sent back to school but would have to marry her, which notion made him screw back a laugh at the scene of his mother and father trying to fathom someone like Eileen.

She thumped his chest. 'It's nowt to laugh about.'

'I didn't say it was. I can cope, though.' He had sat on the toilet putting one on for practice, and flushed it away when he couldn't resist shooting into it.

'Spread your mac on the path and let's lay down,' she urged him.

He felt like Doctor Livingstone going into *terra incognita*, land unknown in more ways than one, with so much to explore and map. Nervousness was subdued by assuming her to be a friendly native ciceroning him through all the motions, and he was glad she knew the way when she leaned back and drew him into her heavenly softness. He muttered how much he loved her, as if he had indeed been there a few times already but the paradise of this occasion blotted the others out.

'I 'ad it last night,' he said to Archie in the canteen, though thinking it ungallant to say he had been with Eileen.

'Took you long enough. She's not a bad girl, though, is she? I've often fancied her mysenn.'

Herbert spooned into his bread pudding. 'Who do you mean?'

'What do you mean who do I mean?' At least he leaned across so that only Bert could hear. And why not? Courting, they called it. One of the men walking by shouted: 'You'll need a lot o' frenchies wi' that one, Bert.'

Herbert's impulse was to grab hold of the foul-mouth fuckpig and push his head into a bucket of cold suds and hold it there till the shit showed through his trousers, as Archie had threatened someone in his hearing, but you were expected to tolerate and even half condone such ribald joshing. If you really felt bad about it you could wait and pay him back at a time and place of your choosing.

Eileen heard it as well, her workbench close enough, though even that didn't call for a punch-up, because neither was it the custom to be a Sir Galahad, since the girl would scorn the thought that she was unable to stick up for herself. Eileen, thank you very much, could do all that with knobs on, which she went on to prove in no uncertain terms, calling out in a voice plangent enough, in spite of ear-drumming machinery, to reverberate from one end of the shop to the other: 'You're jealous, that's what yo' are, you sex-starved four-eyed wanking sight for sore eyes.' Cheers and laughs from the

55

other women at least took the vapid shine from the man's face. Bert got on with his work, having to force an impassive expression at such blistering language from a girl who on the street would look as if – to use the local term – butter wouldn't melt in her mouth.

Even on weekday nights they went hand in hand over the Ha'penny Toll Bridge (the best tuppence ever spent) and so many packets of rubbers were called for that there were few hedge bottoms around Clifton and Wilford he and Eileen hadn't snugged into. She occasionally complained that he was a bit too rough in his speech so he toned it down as much as he dared: 'What can you expect? I was dragged up in Radford, and you can't get much rougher than that.' All the same, he liked it when in her soppier moments she showed a liking for the more genteel life, though finally, like Archie Bleasby, he wondered what was the use of slogging your guts out for days on end at a machine if you had to behave yourself at the weekend. Hadn't he left all such poxy notions behind at his school?

Five

Space at either end of the long table for his elbows made sure that nobody could come too close. Electricity dried the air, and he felt at ease, readers silent but for the odd cough or foot-scrape. A young girl round-shouldered herself over an open book and he wondered whether putting on his old school voice would help him to get acquainted.

Everybody had a cold, sniffles and hacks around the compass, but compared to the factory it was a civilized atmosphere which he had to sample now and again or go off his head. He wasn't a Nottingham lad like Archie Bleasby, so could never let on to his mates about sitting in the library. Not that they would have bothered him, or been too surprised perhaps, because most of them read, even if only comics or the *Daily Mirror*, but he had to keep some part separate from his labouring status, and would have needed a stint in the library even if he had been born in the area. Coming on evenings when he hadn't enough backbone to go out with Eileen made life among the fog people more tolerable.

Fog people had never known any other area except the one they lived in, and couldn't see beyond the poor visibility of its enclosure. He remembered the glamour of India, had lived in Sussex and Gloucestershire, and made a perfect escape, like an initiative test, from the prison camp at school where he had learned more in the scholastic line than any of them ever could. The fog around him had been blown away from early days, though it would be dangerous to let the fact go to his head. Even coming out of the library with three books in a carrier bag felt like a betrayal of his own existence.

He didn't see why he should try to hide his reading from Mrs

Denman, however, and sat in her parlour with his face behind a book until bedtime at half past ten. She was old enough to realize that people could have many sides to themselves. 'It's good to see you doing summat else, Bert, except boozing with that low life Archie Bleasby, and going out with girls.'

'It teks my mind off things.'

'Frank says the same. He likes to get his head stuck in a book, as well.'

Standing in his undershirt before the wardrobe mirror, he stiffened his muscles and felt them rock hard, while Ralph dampened a finger-end and turned the pages of *Health and Efficiency*, gloating over the full and naked bosoms. 'I suppose you think you're Charles Atlas?'

'They're more like muscles than them sparrows' kneecaps yo've got above yer elbows.'

Ralph gave what he thought was a superior and enigmatic smile. 'You didn't use that sort of language when you first came to live here.'

'That were ten years ago, surry.' Talking to Ralph, he could gauge what progress he was making in the factory lingo. 'Or near enough, any road up.'

'Only a few months, if I remember.'

Herbert pulled the bedclothes up to his neck. 'If you keep on reading books like that you'll wank yourself into a bit o' dandelion fluff.' The factory was rich with such phrases, but let poncy Ralph think it one of his. 'You should get Mary to do it for you. I'll bet she'd be on'y too willin'.'

'I don't think she would at all.'

Herbert's tone was as gruff as could be managed. 'Just get 'er in the bushes, and slip it in.'

Ralph winced, and put the magazine under his pillow. 'Mary's waiting until we're married, and I must say I respect her for it.'

'If yer don't gerrit in beforehand yer wain't know whether she's worth marryin'.'

He pulled the light off, seeming dead set on sleep. 'It's easier said than done.'

Bert scoffed. 'It's easier done than said, with my lovely bit o' stuff.'

'Yes, but Mary and I are in love.'

'What difference does that mek?' Herbert sensed that some part of Ralph relished his dirty talk, so paused and put a note of menace into the tone. 'When are yer goin' ter bring 'er 'ome to tea?'

'Never. Not here. We go to the Kardomah, in town.'

'Oh, do you? Where it's all posh, eh? Don't yer want me to meet 'er, then, and tell 'er what a lovely looking girl she is?'

He felt Ralph shudder: 'There is more select company in the world.'

Herbert felt like punching him, but thought he'd rile him more by staying good humoured. 'You're stuck up, that's your trouble. I'll bet Mary knows it, as well. That's why she won't let you get yer 'and at them little pearly buttons between her legs.' It was going too far, but at the same time he sounded halfway slighted, so as to make Ralph feel even more superior and wriggle further into the trap.

'Ma told me you were reading a book the other night. I didn't believe her, but she convinced me it was true.'

Herbert sounded disgruntled. 'I ain't got no secrets. I just like getting lost in a good yarn. At least I don't read them wanking books,' though now and again he took one from Ralph's pillow to study the nudity.

'You've got a filthy mind.'

'Well, it's a mind anyway. What do yer do when you've finished wi' 'em?'

'Every so often Ma comes and takes them away. God knows what she does with them.'

'Gives 'em to Frank, I expect.' For the moment Herbert had no more to say, and then they were asleep.

French letters were free gratis and for nothing because Archie's brother Raymond worked for a dry-cleaning firm, handling officers' uniforms from army and air force camps, and searching every pocket before throwing tunics and trousers into the bins. 'He's got a cardboard box full in his cupboard, and he don't need 'em like we do.' Archie lowered his voice in case anyone in the canteen should hear. 'He hangs around the theatres to get his thrills, or he goes out with sailors. Dad ain't said a dicky-bird to him, since one of the neighbours blabbed her mouth. I don't care, though. He lets me tek as many frenchies as I like, and I need 'em to shag my Audrey. Raymond might be a nancy boy, but he's still my brother, and it's got nowt to do wi' me where he shoves his dick.'

'No, nor anybody else,' Herbert said, for which understanding remark Archie gave him more french letters than even a priapic rattlesnake could use.

'The foreman 'anded me five bob last week when I got 'im some. He's having it off with that Mrs Jennings as works a drill. She's sitting over there, eating her pudding. But don't look now, you daft cunt!'

He hadn't thought to. 'I'm not stupid.'

'I know, but 'er 'usband's sitting next to her.'

'Thanks for the frenchies, though,' Herbert said. 'I'll buy you a jar o' Shippoe's when we go down town.'

'That's all right. They're free for yo'. Just keep banging yer tart, like I do mine.'

Herbert leashed his smile into a straight face, the only way to be sure of not offending anybody. 'How old was yer when yer first 'ad it?' he asked at the door.

'Well, I musta bin fourteen.' Archie gave a marauder's grin, and pulled up his collar against the rain. 'I fucked this girl in Colwick Woods. We got down in the bushes. Lovely bit o' stuff. What about yo'?'

'About the same age, I reckon, only it was on the canal bank, up Wollaton. But it was more like she had me, because she was sixteen.'

On Saturday morning Herbert looked out of the parlour window and noted the fine spun hair and neat white shorts of Ralph's girl Mary leaning her bike against the wall before coming up the stairs to knock. They were going on a fortnight's tour of the Lake District, and Herbert envied her evident affection for milksop Ralph who ran to the door and went back down the steps with her so that she wouldn't have to come in and meet Bert the lout. He watched them walk their bikes along the street towards the station, and holding each other's hands took so much space that a milk float almost brushed into them.

Mrs Denman let the empty bed while Ralph was away to a Royal

Marine on leave, who told everybody to call him Jacko. The first thing that came out of his kitbag was an unbroached bottle of South African sherry, which Jacko placed so conspicuously on the mantelshelf that it might as well have had a big label stuck on it saying DRINK ME.

'Want a swig, matey?'

Herbert was lying on his bed for a quick read before tea. 'Ar, wouldn't mind.'

Jacko used both hands to pass the bottle, as if it was a head he'd decapitated in the scramble of battle, and Herbert, after a fair glug, returned it likewise to the proprietor, who had two bigger swallows without bothering to wipe the spout – which was noted as friendly – before putting it back on its altar.

Herbert walked the street while it was still daylight and went into a pub for a drink. His working jacket had come from a pawnshop, and he wondered who had owned it before, whether it had been sold out of destitution, or by a man who had taken a sudden step up in life. Maybe he'd even kicked the bucket. He thought a good story could be written called 'The Adventures of a Jacket', but spat the thought out as he pushed tall and upright to the bar and called for a pint to chase down Jacko's oversweet sherry.

Individual voices were crushed under the singing, and such din, mostly from women and soldiers, cheered him after being at tea with lugubrious low-browed Jacko, who tackled Mrs Denman's food as if she was trying to poison him. Though he normally enjoyed staying in a crowded pub, where no one could possibly care who he was, he suddenly sensed danger among such numbers, as if a banshee message was trying to tell him something. His pint only half gone, he turned and saw Dennis, one of Mrs Denman's other lodgers, a tall and thin man with a Ronald Colman moustache.

'Thought it was you,' Dennis said. 'Have one on me.'

'Ain't finished my own yet.' He held it high. 'Then I've got to go. I've a nobble on.'

Dennis called for a whisky. 'I've just put my woman on a 39 bus. She lives in Radford, and she's got to get home before her husband comes in from his shift at the Raleigh. Sure you won't have one?'

'Thanks. Another time.' A clatter of chairs sounded, and then a scream as the door all but burst its hinges. 'Eh, fuckin' 'ell,' came a shout. 'What's all this, then?'

Two six-foot policemen pushed with no messing through the crowd. Dennis turned away. 'Watch yourself. It's Popkess's lads, come to pick somebody up.'

They could be checking Identity Cards, and Herbert wasn't yet eighteen. He'd be yanked off for being under age, and charged with having a forged one. Then he'd be sent to Borstal, though maybe he wasn't as frightened as he should have been because one of the lads at work had been in Borstal and according to his account, the regime sounded more easy-going than the one at Herbert's school.

Speech and laughter corroded away, and the coppers got hold of a man a few paces along the bar, fixed him in a half-nelson when he tried to dispute what was said of him, and walked him out with his feet hardly touching the floorboards.

The pub was soon back to singing and talking, but more relaxed than before, as if those unmolested by the police were glad they'd been spared – this time. 'It was Alf Morley.' Dennis knocked back another whisky. 'Still, it could have been anybody. As they say in this town: every copper's got your number on the underside of his left boot. Old Alf will be back in six months, though, mark my words. It's just that he gets a bit light-fingered now and again. Careless, if you like.'

Herbert now thought there was something to celebrate. 'I'll have that drink you mentioned, after all.'

When he went to change out of his overalls Jacko pointed sternly at the bottle, indicating its contents down to the halfway mark. His eyes seemed closer in, and the trenchlines across his forehead made him look uglier, if that was possible. 'Have you been helping yourself to my sherry?'

Bert fastened his waistcoat buttons. 'I don't do things like that, shag.'

Jacko was convinced by his hard look. 'Well, somebody has, and no mistake.'

Only one person could have taken a secret drink, unless Jacko, who maybe was still shell-shocked, had sleepwalked it down his gorge. 'Too much like piss for me,' Bert said.

'Piss, you say?' Jacko poured halfway up his Navy-issue mug. 'Let's drink most of it between us before any more goes.' He held it out. 'I'm sorry I asked if it was you, shipmate, but I had to make sure.'

Unsociable to refuse, it went down like a rat on roller skates. Jacko drank enough to leave a quarter in the bottle. 'It'll help us to enjoy that stuff she puts on the table. What's it called?'

'Shepherd's pie.'

'Yes, I wouldn't like to know what part of the poor fucking shepherd it was ripped out of. She must be Sweeney Todd's widow.' He had the saddest face Herbert had seen, and he had passed a few on the street these last few months. In Jacko's case such an expression could turn mean rather than easy-going, as was proved when he put the catch on the door and with his back to it slowly undid his trouser buttons, keeping the bottle in his other hand. A glaze came over his eyes at such a malicious notion of justice. 'There's only one way to deal with this situation.'

Herbert assumed that was how rum-poachers were dealt with in the marines, which made him glad he intended going in the army, as he watched Jacko piss the level of the bottle back to halfway before setting it again, none the worse for colour, in its place.

Yet Herbert, being the age he was, had never seen anything so funny. He opened the window and let out such a bellow of laughter over the backyards that a turbaned woman pushing a kid in its cot stared as if he had gone clean off his rocker. The kid began yelling, and she hurried along in case the madman at the window decided to jump overboard and splash her flipflops with his life's blood.

He drew his head in and thought maybe it wasn't funny at all, as Jacko the Beast calmly laid all items of his kit out on the bed as if the CO would pat him on the back when he came marching through.

To warn Mrs Denman of her peril could be to accuse her prematurely, because it may not have been her at all, though if not, who else? He wanted to describe the intriguing problem in a letter, but didn't know who would be interested. His father, certainly not, nor his mother. They'd be disgusted, and who wouldn't? Yet Barney the English master used to say that a sense of humour was the first sign of intelligence, and he should know, because nobody had ever seen him laugh.

Herbert couldn't pen the Sherry Saga to Dominic Jones either, without blowing the gaff on his town of refuge. If he'd still been at school he could have concocted a moral issue out of the case, though Barney might not have liked such an essay, saying he had made the yarn up, and that if he hadn't it was not a fit topic for a composition, though the boys would have laughed over it for a few days.

Feeling it a shame to waste such material he sat in Mrs Denman's parlour on Sunday afternoon while she was in bed with Frank, and wrote a letter to himself, no less a story than when the head and tail had suffered the fate of Procrustes' bed. He called Mrs Denman Mrs Penman, and related how he had seen Jacko, now Mungo, go through his motions with the bottle, as if to make the alcoholic whizzbang stronger, or maybe even to take care of some ailment he'd got. All he had to do now was put the story aside and wait for the real-life ending.

Another way of keeping contact with the hidden part of himself was to call on Isaac, shed some of the person he had become in the factory with each step up the wooden staircase.

He carried a loaf and two pounds of potatoes, a tin of condensed milk and a few apples from a corner shop, as well as a twenty-packet of Senior Service which Isaac liked. A bag of sugar for five bob came from one of the viewers whose father worked at the refining factory near Colwick.

'Your accent's changed,' Isaac said, though not disapprovingly.

Herbert found it comforting to use rough speech, while knowing he could go from the hot tap of the local argot to the cold faucet of his school any day of the week. 'It 'ad to, in the factory.'

'As long as *you* don't. At least not radically.'

He forked up his chips, knife held too close to the blade. 'I can't do that.'

Isaac put on an ironic smile. 'Your table manners have altered, as well.'

'You do as others do.'

'I know all about that. But keep yourself intact, all the same. Your own soul, I'm talking about.'

'I can't do owt else, can I?'

Isaac put tea on the table, and they lit cigarettes. 'You've taken to that factory like a duck to water, Herbert Thurgarton-Strang. Or should I say Bert Gedling to a quart of Shipstone's ale? It shows you've got character. I expect your parents have, too.'

'Don't mention them.'

'Still like that, is it?'

He felt no need to be on his guard with Isaac. 'Nar. I want the credit for myself.'

'Nothing wrong with that, I suppose, but you've got to think of people's feelings, and write them a letter now and again.'

He'd sent one since arriving in Nottingham, telling them he was working in Stoke on Trent. Archie had dropped it in a box when he'd gone there to see a girl. 'Anyway,' Isaac said, 'thanks for the sugar. Mine went days ago, with my sweet tooth.'

Herbert, drained for words due to the intensity of his life, or that's how he put it to himself, sometimes liked sitting in idleness and silence, and though he did not much care who he really was – whether Bert or Herbert – it brought a sense of peace that was vitally needed if he was to carry on any life at all.

Isaac took down one of his strangely scripted volumes and read with head going faintly back and forth as if wanting to sing the rhythms, while Herbert in his chair faded around the edges of sleep, visions fastening on to him brought about by Isaac's mutterings. Maybe Isaac was saying a form of prayer, not the sort they were drummed into mouthing at school, but one which put him into a trance, and brought dreams for Herbert of being back in India and walking behind an elephant, huge plates of grey excrement flopping from between its rear legs, his mother and father laughing from their chairs on the veranda of the bungalow. Where did that come from? The same place as the meteorite nightmare above the jagged skyline of mountains, split in half by a scimitar of lightning. Back at school he was running along a lane in vest and shorts, coming into the gate after a cross-country run. The runner, who was somebody he didn't know, turned out to be an old man, drooling and dying as he fell into the bracken. You needed a dirk to pin such fuzzy pictures down, because when he tried to re-run them on waking they slipped away like mercury.

'You're looking a bit serious for a chap of seventeen.' Isaac broke into his exhaustion. 'Let me send you back to your digs with a drop of whisky. I've got a secret bottle, for times like this.' He took wet glasses from the sink. 'I think you must have had a hard week.'

'I suppose they all are in the factory. But I'm used to it by now.' Nothing easier. An hour or two could go by at his machine and he marvelled that work got done with no variation in the measurements. Had it been sleep? Cleft in two, part of him dreamed, part of him worked. He lived as different a life in those lost periods as he had just now in Isaac's room, and would never know what was pumped into him because it was impossible to understand. Not that he cared to, for you didn't poke your nose where it had no use being, and where nothing of interest could be explained even if you took the trouble to wonder.

Isaac held up his glass. '*L'chaim*!'

'What does that mean?'

'Long life, to you. It's Hebrew.'

The promise of longevity seemed superfluous to someone who assumed he was going to live forever, or as close as dammit. Nevertheless, Herbert said '*L'chaim*, then,' and took a fiery swig.

He thought the sherry in the bottle had gone down by half an inch, but couldn't be sure, despite the glitter of certainty in Jacko's eyes as he packed his kit for departure. 'I wouldn't say she liked it, but I wish I could have seen her face. Made her look prettier, maybe.'

'She's a good sort.' Herbert defended her. 'And I'll bet she used to be very good-looking. I like Ma.'

Jacko stared at him, unbelieving. Such an uncertain end to the Sherry Saga was hardly worth either story or letter, but Herbert noted Mrs Denman's glare from the window as Jacko, who left the bottle behind, marched smartly away with his bag and case to the station.

Having much on her mind Mrs Denman hurried to scour the room before Ralph got back, and maybe to work off her indignation at such a vile trick, though perhaps after a sip she assumed the doctored sherry had gone sour of its own chemical will, thinking no evil of Jacko at all. Herbert saw the emptied bottle in the dustbin and, however it was, tore his tale into shreds for fear Mrs Denman would read the papers with disgust on finding them under a shirt in his room.

Ralph pushed his bike up the steps, through the house and into the shed, limping as if he had worn his arse out on the saddle. He'd probably stood up in the train all the way from Ambleside. Herbert watched him fix the padlocks on his bike with a grin he hadn't seen before. He couldn't make it out, but thought he'd know before long. At the welcome home tea they were shown Ralph's map and the routes he had pedalled with Mary, a maze of pencillings and arrows and circles. Mrs Denman fussed about what a long way it was, and I'll bet you was tired, and it's a wonder you didn't get lost, and I'm sure you both slept like logs at night.

Herbert's suspicion that Ralph was keeping something back was confirmed when they were in their beds and before the light was put out. 'She let me have it.'

'What, yo'? I don't believe yer.'

'Oh yes, she did. Coming down from Helvellyn. And again near Keswick. And then near Ambleside, and then in the bushes near Langdale youth hostel – after supper.'

Herbert imagined penpusher Ralph putting a map on the wall and sticking pins in every place he'd had his oats, till it looked like the Lake District was doing to close down with a smallpox epidemic. 'And you're still going to marry 'er?'

'More than ever. I told you, we're in love.'

She's probably in the club by now. 'I'm dead jealous.'

He pulled off the light. 'Knew you would be. Good night.'

There were times when Herbert thought he had landed in as compact a prison as the one at school. He was lucky, but discontented, knowing that his present state would have been less of a prison if he'd been able to write to someone and tell them about it.

The walls were made of everything well worth describing, which heightened his perceptions and rattled his nerves. He wanted to write something about it, anything. Curiosity was spoon-fed without asking, during every hour but those passed in the dead land of sleep, where too much was minced into his dreams to sort out.

He also knew that his aching to write to someone was an impulse to betray himself and make a glorious failure out of his enterprise. The scale of the fall was tempting, but a sense of self-preservation veered him from the course of Lucifer hurtling through space, or Phaeton glorying in a smash up of universal proportions.

The police raid on the pub worried him more than it had at the time. A partial blackout had been useful on getting to Nottingham, but the war was now over and the streets lit – though not as bright as pre-war, Mrs Denman said, what with rationing and call-up still going on.

The end of the war against Japan in August made him feel still more visible. He couldn't otherwise explain his anxiety, as if a curtain was slowly lifting between him and the world he had abandoned. To be clawed back into the life of school was such a prospect that he would sooner sling himself into a vat of acid. Here was where he belonged, because he had made the place his own and was familiar with everyone. There were times when he couldn't understand how it had been so easy. Maybe he had been to a good school after all, because what other could have trained him to fit in so well? If they caught him he would break out again, just like the chaps in *Caged Birds*, who had escaped time after time, and hide himself even more where they would never think to look.

All the same, in spite of his fears, he would not walk the street except openly and with the expected workman swagger. He would go into a pub if he felt like it and have it with Eileen whenever they went out together. To lessen the chances of being found and forced back to school he decided to volunteer for the army a month or two before he was eighteen so that there'd be less questions asked than enrolling under conscription. After all, he told himself with a pride not altogether trusted, he was Thurgarton-Strang, and the longer he was free the less likely was anybody to find him.

Six

From the heights above the forest a dusty mist lay like a pancake over a thousand lights trying to pierce but merely glowing through. He walked down the slope from the bus stop with Eileen, and Sheila her workmate, into the sodium atmosphere of frying and candy floss. If there was a place where nobody would be able to pick him out it was among the jam-packed crowds of the Goose Fair, yet in such pushing phalanxes he felt perilously unsafe, couldn't explain why every glazed look seemed like a threat to his wellbeing. It was illogical, ludicrous even, and he forced a smile of protective inanity back on to his face.

Eileen on one arm, and Sheila taking the other, he guided them among the roundabouts – wondering what his school chums would say if they saw him now – and pulled them up the steps on to the slowing caterpillar. When the hood went down he'd be able to kiss them both, but would Eileen allow it? Well, she didn't stab at his bollocks with her elbow, though maybe she was too dim to cotton on to where his hands were straying, and she laughed with the rest of them as long as he let his fingers creep in her direction now and again.

He threw a penny to a couple of kids who were begging, and bought sailor hats to amuse the girls before pulling them in for a circuit on the ghost train. On coming out, it was as if an invisible cloud of depressing gas flowed between the Saturnalian wailings of delight, and the rhythmical thump of traction engines. He had caught a fit of anxiety full blast, stood as if pinioned by the different coloured lights maggoting at his eyes, and by the people pushing around him, some malign force dividing him more than at any time since running away from school, as if a patient and eagle-eyed Inspector Javert in the crowd had been set on to get him.

Such paralysis couldn't be explained, and fear even less. 'Come on, come on,' Eileen said, 'get a move on, slow coach. What are you standing there for as if you've lost your way? We want to go on summat else, don't we, Sheila?'

One moment lost beyond any hope of getting his senses back into the atmosphere of the fair, the next he felt the usual grin forcing its way on to his face, as if someone pulling strings had him under control. He lifted a wrist to sniff at flesh, as if the swarf smell of the factory might still be there, which it was, in spite of the thorough White Windsor swill he had given himself at the sink. The thrill of being at bay buoyed him all his waking hours. Even when unaware it fuelled his senses and fed his alertness.

They got into a swingboat and, pinned a moment at the top, Herbert saw the whole area of smoke and lights, the tents for a king and his army celebrating a victory over some nation only a little less barbaric than themselves. Then down went the swingboat, and up again into a whole sky of shrieks which made the scene more eerie. Back on the ground, Sheila jerked forward and was sick. Disgusted, he stepped away rather than ask if she was all right and mop her chalky brow, though not before a splash of vomit spewed over his shoes. To prove she was again ready for anything she led them on a climb up the helter-skelter, and they followed on the sedate corkscrew down. Herbert began to hate such spinning and jolting, but when they'd handed their mats back forced himself to say: 'Now let's go on summat else. I can't have enough fun like this.'

'You're spending too much munny on us, duck,' Eileen said.

'That's all right.' Thank God it was only once a year. Anyway it was his money to do what he liked with. Did she think he was going to save it up so that they could one day get married? Not with anyone, and certainly not with trash like her – which sentiment shamed him, and he immediately sent it back to where it came from, though she had mentioned too often lately that another of her friends at work had got engaged.

He occasionally had a horror of sinking among them forever, as if he had lived years in the last three months, school so far away it might never have existed. And suddenly, as they stood at a stall eating brandy snap, he felt he had come out only for a night and would be going back next morning. Such vacillations of mood were alarming, more dangerous than he liked. The screech and rattle of the fair seemed a threat from which he must escape, just as he had from school. He was a caged bird wherever he was.

Eileen tugged his arm. 'We ain't bin on the cakewalk yet.'

He wanted to say fuck the cakewalk. 'Let's go to the pub, and I'll buy you some drinks.' Standing erect, the most confident smile irradiated, he put thumbs firmly in the pockets of his waistcoat. 'I'm parched. I want some ale.' To be skint for the rest of the week was a small price to pay, and the girls must have read his thoughts, they were good at that, on their own level anyway.

'Only a few more rides,' Eileen said. 'We'll fork out for 'em, won't we, Sheila?'

Sheila nodded, but after another go she was sick again, a signal that they'd had enough of roundabouts, so went up Radford Road to the Langham, where the first pint of the evening took Herbert out of his puzzling insecurity and into a roistering Bert whose thoughts were his and nobody else's.

'I don't know who this bloke was,' Archie said as they walked into the canteen, 'but yesterday he asked about you. He wanted to know how long you'd worked here.'

'What did he look like?'

'How would I know? Just a bloke.'

He kept down the fear that went through him, half forgotten since the Goose Fair, just as lively, however, on coming back at Archie's revelation. 'I mean, did he look like Charles Laughton? Was he a beanpole with a mardy face or just stubby and miserable?'

Archie picked up a dinner from the counter, and laughed. 'Bit o' both, I suppose.'

'And what did you tell 'im?'

'I towd 'im the truth.'

Herbert sorted through the gravy to get at his pasty. 'That's all right, then, but what was that?'

'That yer'd started 'ere the same time as me, when we was fourteen.'

'Did 'e say owt?'

''E just pissed off. He sounded like a copper's nark. If 'e'd asked owt else I'd a cracked 'is shins wi' me boots. On the other hand he could have been a chap from the offices wanting to mek sure yer insurance cards was up to press.'

Herbert pushed the rest of his food away. 'It tastes like shit.'

'It allus does,' Archie said, 'but I enjoy it because I'm hungry. As long as you shake lots o' pepper on it. Do you know, Bert, the first thing I noticed when I came in this canteen at fourteen was that they had pots o' pepper on the tables. We'd never 'ad pepper at home. We still don't. I didn't know what it tasted like, but I love it now.' He leaned across the table, voice turned lower. 'What was 'e after? Did yer do a job? Are you on the run?'

Herbert smiled. 'Ar, course I am, from a wicked uncle.'

'Yer can tell me. I shan't nark, not me. I 'ate coppers.'

'I know yer do. Same 'ere.' Herbert considered packing up, going to the station and getting on the next train to anywhere – but decided it was safer and more comfortable staying where he was. It wasn't done to panic, or change plans till you had to. 'I absconded from school. It was more like a borstal, though.'

'I thought it was summat like that.' Archie winked. 'You'll be all right with us, Bert. Tek a tip from me. If anybody asks yer owt, just tell lies. That's number one. Lie till ye're blue in the face, and they'll end up believin' yer. I'll back yer up if yer need me to, though I don't expect yer will. People allus want to believe yer, even when they know you're tellin' lies, as long as yer go on long enough wi' a straight face.'

Herbert pulled the plate towards him, finished every stain and crumb. Work called for all the food he could get. Telling lies was wrong, even cowardly, done only by inferior people who were afraid. So he had been drilled into thinking. He felt uneasy at his ready agreement with Archie, who wasn't cowardly or inferior at all. Herbert's life at the moment could be considered one big lie, but it was no more than an actor's performance on stage who for two hours was entirely in the skin of someone else. And if you do it for two hours, or even for a year, what's the difference?

'Another thing,' Archie came back with pudding for them both, 'why don't you introduce me to Sheila? The four of us could go out for a drink.'

Herbert pushed a hand forward for his spoon. 'Yeh, that's a good idea. I'll talk to Eileen, and see what she says.'

'We can go to the White Horse on Saturday night. They've got good ale there, and you can sing if you like.'

People coughed their way to work through the first frosts of October, an enclosing visibility giving Herbert more confidence in his role as a man on the run, except that he would rather die than run. He walked quickly, however, all-round glances keeping watch at every angle, obtuse or acute, thinking that if anyone followed they'd need to be fit to maintain his rapid pace, and that if anybody tried to get him on the street he would kill them as they deserved, using the strength put into his arms by lifting and carrying in the factory, and the survivor's force grown in him since birth.

Such reflections, he felt, were risible, knowing that he was often split between desperate speculations and a delightful sense of having no cares in the world, and that at Mrs Denman's he was one of the family. He was safe, and looked after in a way beyond his experience. How she made any profit on his few pounds bed and board he couldn't fathom, but Archie said that was her worry, and he should bless his luck at having fallen into such a cushy billet.

Her friend Frank was more often at the house now that the war was over. He worked at the tobacco factory as a machine supervisor, and Mrs Denman told Herbert he had 'lost' his wife from cancer ten years ago. She met him in a pub when he was trying to swamp his bereavement in too much poisonous booze, and when he took a fancy to her she got him to put a stop to it.

Herbert wondered whether Frank was to be trusted, but knew he was because he didn't ask personal questions. His talk had a serious side in that he could go on about books by H. G. Wells, Arnold Bennett, and John Galsworthy, to name a few. He was also a firm Labour Party man. 'I know everybody's having a hard time these days, though nobody's as badly off as before the war. It's going to be a long struggle but I know we'll win through with Labour, don't

73

you worry. We'll end up living in a country with more equality in it than there's ever been. It's marvellous to think we'll both be able to see it, Bert.'

Herbert agreed, and felt privileged to hear such views, though wasn't sure about equality ever being possible, or even whether he wanted it, knowing he had always felt himself different from everybody around him, to which Frank said with a laugh that he hadn't lived long enough yet to know that, basically, everybody was more or less the same in that they all had a right to happiness and a roof over their heads, something Herbert had no option but to agree with.

As well as politicians Frank showed an intelligent interest in the war, maybe due to his having missed active service by being in a reserved occupation. This was more to Herbert's taste, who could enthuse about the Battle of Britain, Stalingrad, D-Day, and the Battle of the Bulge. Mrs Denman was happy to see them huddled by the fire – 'talking the hind leg off a donkey,' she said, setting down cups of tea.

They were still talking when Ralph came in, fagged out and shifty-eyed from seeing Mary. 'Still getting yer oats?' Bert said, when they were in their room.

'It seems to upset you.'

'Well. I always reckon it's too good for some people.'

There was a catch in Ralph's voice. 'I'm not getting anything, as a matter of fact. I can't think why, all I know is she doesn't let me do it in Nottingham. She says it's too common to do it here, that it isn't right.'

Herbert knew that his laugh would be loud enough to wake Mrs Denman, or even the dead, so Bert had to manage with a snort. 'You mean to say you've got to go all the way to the Lake District for a bang?'

'Maybe. Seems so. But it's more romantic up there. Well, that's her daft idea, anyway.'

'Your lady-love don't seem very accommodating. What do you think it's going to be like when you're spliced? She'll twist you round her little finger.'

Ralph's laugh was sinister. 'No, she won't. I'll have her when I want her. I'll get my own back. I'll make her sit up. But in the meantime, I love her, and I don't know what to do.'

'Well, I can't tell yer.' Bert got his head down for sleep, after murmuring that if he was in that situation he would read the Riot Act, and no mistake.

After a darts match one evening Archie supposed, when they got to their pints, that the factory would be needing less hands now that the war was over and done with. Young 'uns like them wouldn't find much work when they and everybody else came out of the army. 'It'll be like before the war, if we aren't careful, back to the dole, no matter what government we've got in.'

Herbert passed his cigarettes across. 'Nah, we'll be working flat out for years on reconstruction.' Every time he called at the library he read *The Times* and the *Daily Telegraph*, a habit not lost from his interest when they were laid out in the reading room at school. 'The Labour Government'll keep everybody at work, don't you worry. They're pledged to it.'

Grumbling went on all the time, and though Herbert listened, and sometimes took part because much of it was humorous, he couldn't basically see what anyone had to belly-ache about, unless they did so because otherwise they would be silent, and that such talk was a device for helping them to breathe. It was one grouse after another, about work, rationing, the weather, the government, the gaffers at the factory, but the patina of liberty made everything palatable to Herbert.

Work took the strain of what he saw as his previously unreal existence: the rations were enough, and the weather – foul though it mostly seemed to be – enclosed him with friendliness and protection. He was clad in an old army topcoat dyed navy blue to keep himself warm, and out of his earnings bought a utility-style suit for second best. He had a roof over his head, as well as a girlfriend who let him have it whenever there was an opportunity. What more could he want?

Mrs Denman even turned her back when he led Eileen up to his room on Sunday afternoon, a safe enough time because Ralph made sure of being at Mary's house while her parents were out visiting family. Herbert pictured him on bended knees in the parlour pleading with her to let him get it in while he – Bert – was having no trouble banging away, and telling Eileen not to cry out so loud every time she came.

All in all his existence was as great an advance on former times as could be imagined. At the factory he was liked because he mucked in with everybody else, and grafted willingly at his machine. The chargehand would be sorry to lose him when he got called up, and said they'd be sure to keep a job for him when he came home again.

Nobody expected to go on living in the same way forever, and that was a fact, and Bert knew his present status couldn't last because neither had the first easy part of Herbert's life in India. Soon after the New Year he took the morning off, put on his suit, and got on the bus for the recruiting centre, to breathe the full extent of his chest, piss cleanly into a jar, cough successfully, and see his foot shoot into the horizontal when tapped with a rubber hammer. 'You're A1,' the MO said, so he signed on for the duration of the present emergency as an infantryman, and after a few more questions was told to go back to work and wait for his papers.

'What did you do a daft thing like that for?' Archie wanted to know. They stood, before switching on for the afternoon stint. 'The army's worse than Borstal. I'll only go at the last minute. It's fucking useless. In fact, they'll have to drag me in.'

Herbert had expected biting anger, and got it. 'I want to join up of my own free will.'

'Free will? What's that? The only free will I know about is to fuck off somewhere where they can't find me, and not go. War's over, in't it? Blokes like us don't have any free will, anyway. We get fucked from pillar to post and the only thing we should do is punch 'em in their four-eyed phizogs when we get the chance. Smash their bleedin' teggies in.'

Herbert smiled. 'Yeh, you're right.' His only exercise of free will had brought him here. Now he was on the threshold of another go, and wasn't sure where it would land him. Archie said the war was over, and so it was, but the war would never be over, because wars never were. Conflict was a factor of human nature, so there'd always be a call for soldiers. Even if wars were finished on land and sea you had your own personal war battling on in yourself, which inner contest he felt had been wearing him away since birth. 'The sooner I go in the army the sooner I get out,' was his poor excuse. 'Anyway, what's a few months more or less?'

Archie had to think about such a serious matter, though his mood was relaxed. 'Look at it this way, Bert. Say it's three months. Well, three months is ninety days' boozin', scoffin' and fuckin' time, in't it? And grabbin' at your machine as well – and doing what you like after clocking out at night. It's a lot better than being a bag o' shit in the army and getting barked at all day.'

People complained eternally because they didn't have the mental flexibility to see into the future. Such an ostrich-like attitude, Herbert thought, must have come from being at home all their lives. On the other hand, maybe Archie's views were the only ones worth believing in. His basic sense was undeniable. Herbert, being two people, doubted everything at times, though he still wasn't so fixed into the present that he could settle his mind about it. 'You can do those things anywhere.'

'Yer think so?' Archie shook his head. 'Yer know, Bert, sometimes I can't mek yo' out. You must have been brought up different to me.'

'Maybe I was, but not all that much.' Herbert looked at the big white face of the clock, the same dictator in everybody's life, and pressed the button to start his machine. 'There are times, though, when I can't mek myself out, I'll tell you that.'

'Well, that 'appens to all of us,' Archie laughed.

Seven

In weapons training at White Down Camp Herbert had the Bren gun stripped and together again quicker than anybody else. It would have been too boring not to.

'Have you done this before?'

There was a lot Herbert didn't know, but this he did, and he was surprised at how much of the old cadet knowledge came back. 'No, Sergeant.'

The bullshit was no bother, either, not difficult to be smart beyond the demands of reason. Part of himself that relished freedom slipped awhile into abeyance. The men belly-ached in the first week or two but Herbert supposed it was because they had never slept from home. Having nothing to envy them for, he could only feel contempt, and keep as much as possible to himself.

Nor was the usual larking around any bother to stay clear of. Smart bastards just one notch down from sadistic made apple-pie beds, tied bootlaces together, soaped a patch of billet floor so as to watch others go arse over tit as they came in from tea, nicked kit one day and put it back in place the next – or didn't.

Barraclough from Merseyside was a past master, and Herbert wondered where he had picked up the facility. Maybe it came to him instinctively, as with someone born evil, until he heard him let on in a boastful voice that his brother was a regular and had put him wise to what went on in recruit training – or perhaps what ought to.

All in all, Herbert thought it just like early days at school but, seeing Barraclough about to half-inch his toothbrush, spun him around and pulled him close, to face the sort of black look Archie would have put on, but which came readily enough. 'That's mine, snot chops,' Bert said.

'Can't you take a joke, then?'

All the venom in Herbert's expression was brought out for use – and with interest – after the merciless torments rained on him at the age of seven. 'When I want to, shag, I'll let you know.'

Ashley Pemberton, a fearful and diffident youth, came from somewhere in Hampshire, and should never have found himself among such a rough lot. In spite of his grammar school background he hadn't been considered as officer material, and Herbert could see he wasn't fit to be a private soldier either. Probably his parents were glad to get rid of him, hoping the army would settle his ever-shifting expression and turn out a new man for them. He was knowledgeable and somewhere intelligent, but slow because he had to question the reason for everything. Herbert halfway pitied him, while smiling at his predicament.

Ashley was tormented more than anyone else because, unable to see the reason for it, he was helpless against bullying. Tall, though thin, he could have been a match for anyone, but didn't have the spirit to resist or fight back. In the army it was the survival of the fittest, Herbert saw, sink or swim, no fucking nonsense, as he watched the lads punching Ashley against the billet wall because the imperfect layout of his kit for inspection had got them all a bollocking from the sergeant-major.

A belly blow sent him across the bed, and Barraclough jumped on him. 'Let's have his bags off, and blanco his knackers.'

A timid uncomprehending scream came from Ashley as the operation began. 'Leave the poor bugger alone,' Fraser called from up the billet, but went on reading his comic.

'Let's have the blanco, somebody,' Barraclough shouted out of the scrum. Herbert paused in polishing his boots, to pick up the tin of Cherry Blossom from his locker and make a way slowly through the onlookers. They parted willingly enough, thinking he only wanted to see the fun, or do the plastering himself.

Using the whole force of his arm he pulled Barraclough upright in one swing. 'You can't do a thing like that.'

'What?' Barraclough saw the opened tin of black polish and

79

laughed. 'You mean you want to do it with that? I didn't think of polish. That'll make him look a right arse-hole.'

'No, I'm asking you to stop all this.'

'Oh, are you?'

'He's a soldier. You can't do it to him.'

'Can't we? Well, you just fuck off, and mind your own business.' He turned to the others, and made to get on with it. 'We'll do what we like, won't we, lads?'

Barraclough was a tough bastard, but there was always a weak place in a bully. Thankful of his time in the factory, Herbert yanked him up again, unable to bear Ashley's pleas to be left alone, which seemed to humiliate Herbert even more.

He pressed the full tin of black polish hard over Barraclough's spud-like nose, ashamed at the enjoyment it gave him. Ashley gathered energy at last, and sprang from the crowd only interested in the fight that was bound to follow such a rash action. He fastened his trousers and walked calmly out of the door.

Herbert stood, on the other bank of the Rubicon, in the clear space of the billet, refusing to consider the fact that he was no doubt a soft head for having interfered. Barraclough came at too much of a rush to do himself much good, and Herbert's experience at boxing helped to send him down with little damage to either. A horseshoe of spectators limited his advantage of manoeuvre, and a fist that was difficult to avoid drove at his stomach, such a deliberate foul that he got a blow in at Barraclough's face, blood streaming through the black smear. After a while of dodging and ducking, Barraclough's retreat ended, and he came back to aim a paralysing kick.

Herbert's instinct, honed for unarmed combat, twisted the leg with all his strength and, ignoring the scream of pain and surprise, sent his opponent sliding along the polished floor, breaking through the group of onlookers as if they were a posse of skittles. When Barraclough tried to move he kicked him in the ribs. 'I never fought like that in the ring, but if you come at me ever again, or do anything to Pemberton, I'll break your back.'

Some shouted that grub was up and it was time for tea, and at the loss of interest in anything but that, Barraclough pulled himself up, and hobbled after them. Herbert felt more alive than he had since leaving the factory, and wanted to say something conciliatory, but because Barraclough might take it as a weakness, he turned instead to Ashley, who had come back in to thank him. 'You'd better stick with me, though I don't think they'll bother you again.'

He didn't mind that he was disliked, couldn't or wouldn't play such tricks, or even laugh when they were done to others. Stand-offish and unpredictable, too keen at his training, an untouchable know-all, even the NCOs looked at him warily. They couldn't place him, unable to find enough fault to get him on jankers. He knew exactly what expression to assume on being sneered or shouted at. The only person to beware of was his platoon commander, Second Lieutenant Snell, who at nineteen had been in the army a year longer than the rest. Because the officer plainly came out of a public school Herbert had to play the roughneck factory worker in case he should be sniffed out as being in any way similar. Luckily Snell couldn't care less about being in the army, and was forever shooting off towards the delights of some popsy in London, happy at the wheel of his little Morgan. The men sensed his incompetence from the start, and with few exceptions referred to him as a bag of shit, with which judgment Herbert silently agreed.

When he applied for a day's pass halfway through training the orderly sergeant flicked a mote off his row of medal ribbons; he had dandruff. 'Your name, I knew a Thurgarton-Strang, in Burma. Any relation?'

Herbert regretted asking Isaac to rejig his Identity Card. 'None, Sergeant.'

'A real bastard, he was. But fair, very fair.'

A bus over the Downs took him to the bookshops of the south coast. At four and sixpence a day he could afford to be served with egg on toast or a cake on a plate in the tea shops of Chichester. On the way back he got off the bus and walked a mile or two along the footpath, to sit among the silent sheep and watch ships passing like ghosts in the misty Channel.

Far to the west beyond the green folds lay his first school, though he supposed the buildings were used for a different purpose now. Or they had fallen to pieces through ivy and neglect. With a notepad on his knee he wrote to his parents, telling them about his life since leaving school, knowing it was too late for his father to prise him from the drab khaki of a private soldier.

Eight weeks of summer training turned him into as good a soldier as he had been a machine-operator. When the sergeant-instructor went for a piss one day he came back to see Herbert showing slow coach Ashley Pemberton how to put the Bren together. He must have watched from behind a bush, Herbert surmised, who had not only named the parts but explained their function as he slotted them into place.

'You know the lingo, as well,' the sergeant said, as Ashley now assembled the gun with no trouble.

In a few weeks his lance-jack's stripe came through, and he didn't care that it distanced him even further from anyone who might have been friendly. Accustomed to being two people in the factory, he had turned more solitary now that he was one again, and he liked the feeling that relinquishing his guard separated him even more from those roundabout.

The others were surprised however when he joined a darts game in the NAAFI. The click of steel tips hitting grid wires was a sound hard to resist. Pint in hand, he watched for a while till a private said: 'Fancy a throw, Corporal?'

'Down from three-o-one?'

Barraclough sat nearby. 'Watch he don't cheat.'

'I never do that.' But he left him alone.

He won four games out of five, and rather than walk away with a pound in his pocket spent it on beer for those he had defeated. 'Pints all round. Have one as well,' he called to Barraclough. 'No hard feelings.'

'Ah, all right, you bugger.'

Halfway pleased at having broken through his guard, they wondered where a toffee-nosed hard case like him had learned to throw darts with such accuracy.

The few bob a day made him abstemious, verging on niggardly after his easy-going factory time. A few pounds saved out of his pay, and from his wages before enlisting, gave enough to lodge at Mrs Denman's on his first leave, and to take Eileen out as well.

She loved her soldier Bert, who was more unlike one of the factory blokes than ever now that he had joined up. The loudmouth pose had never seemed natural to him, and now he was quiet and even polite, which led her to think he really loved her.

Herbert found it easy to get her up to the bedroom while Ralph was out at 'business'. Disembodied from the everyday world, a feeling almost of sin at all other men being at work, he drew the curtains, took off his clothes and watched her do the same. She had pleaded a day off, but at other times she would rush from the factory in her dinner break to pass half an hour in his arms, no opportunity to eat anything before getting back to the factory. 'I can live on love,' she said.

He marvelled at the pale delicate skin of closed eyelids when she gave herself to him with loyal passion, and afterwards hinted at how their intimate courtship ought to become more formal now that he was a responsible adult in khaki. This turned him back into Bert, though only to himself. Not bleedin' likely! He sensed in his deepest gut what she wanted. She craved that their togethering would go on forever, for them to be hugger-mugger in bed all night and every night, a situation in which he – her Bert – would get up, as he should in the morning, make his own breakfast, and go out to work, while she languished an extra half-hour because of her swelling belly. She would stand like a proud *Daily Mirror* mum with other women in the grocer's queue to buy the weekly rations, then go back home to make the beds, wash up, and cook some slop for their supper. She could tek a running jump at herself – though he had to admit it was impossible not to believe they were profoundly attached, he in love with her, if she liked to put it that way.

And yet, like a blade of light straying around their most delicious joinings, he recalled his hopeless juvenile yearning for Rachel, saw her oval peach-coloured face and large blue eyes from behind the topiaristically sculptured bush and across the 'Dig For Victory' lettuce patch as she strolled so unwillingly with Dominic and her parents. At times he imagined going softly into her, in the depths of some wood on a hot summer's day, she lying with legs as open as Eileen's and giving kisses as welcoming. He would shudder into an ejaculation sooner than intended, but felt such a fantasy was worth it, and in any case not much time went by before he could rise again.

A long-term plan for seeing Rachel came to mind. She had pushed out a lizard tongue of contempt that first time, but almost seemed to like him after he had forced that little runt Dominic to make an introduction. She would be taller now, with shapely legs, and nice breasts (though not as big as Eileen's) and would hold his arm in the most adoring way as she talked about paintings and the latest books he would by then have read. She would admire his quotations from Ovid, or look adoringly as he modestly related his adventures after coming back wounded – though not disabled – from some jungle or desert skirmish. The idea of never seeing her again made his heart ache miserably, putting him for a few minutes through a whirlpool of emotion he had thought himself too adult to bother with but which was relished for old times' sake.

He certainly didn't intend sinking as far down into the life of a factory chap as to marry Eileen, warm and wonderful though she was in bed. He anchored his expectations, and therefore hers, from one day to the next. Whatever notions she had of their future were no concern of his. He ignored her hints, open and more plangent towards the end of his leave, except for vague agreements as to the kind of life she longed for. Being silent but polite was the best way of getting her into bed without too much awkwardness, and at such times, which she mistook for the possibility of acquiescence towards his responsibilities, her simplicity and trust was guaranteed to give him a good time and, he was sure, to go by her cries and behaviour, satisfy her as well. He teased her about the dreams she related, long and tedious narratives that got nowhere.

'I like to dream,' she said. 'Dreams mean summat, that's why I tell 'em yer. Last night I dreamed you and me was looking at a house to live in.'

She wanted him to say how nice. 'Lovely, duck. I dreamed I was walking over a frozen lake, and the ice gave way. It was 'orrible.'

'Yo' would, wouldn't yer?' But he couldn't deflect her. She was, what was the word? – irrepressible. 'I read horoscopes every day in the paper.'

'And you believe in 'em?'

'Course I do. They often come true. It might sound daft, but I like to.'

He didn't care what she dreamed, or what she read, only wanting

84

her to be happy in the way he wanted to be happy. She mostly was, or seemed to be, seeing that if not she might drive him away. He envied her, living on the edge of her nerves – and her experience. When she couldn't help but be moody his annoyance was marked by an even deeper silence, which brought her to earth more quickly than any argument. She then tried to be more cheerful, assuming he was discontented at being a soldier, and at having to leave her when his furlough came to an end – just as any young man would be.

Archie called, his battledress bearing the shoulder flashes of the REMEs. Near the end of his leave and halfway bored, Herbert was glad to see him, and sat him down in Mrs Denman's parlour. 'Have a fag.'

'I will but I've got this terrible thirst.' He was slimmer, and there weren't so many blackheads on his skin. In spite of his grousings about going into the forces he was as smart a soldier as drab khaki would allow. 'The sooner we whistle up a drink the better.'

'How you getting on in the army?'

'Army? I'm back at school, learning how to mend fuses and roll telephone wire all over the shop at Catterick. I took a test to go on the course, and somebody said I must be intelligent when I passed. Me! Well, it ain't too bad, a bit of a skive, though it might be useful later. There was nowt doing in camp this weekend, so I flitted for thirty-six hours. As long as the redcaps don't stop me on the street and ask for my pass.'

Herbert hoped he was wrong in assuming that Archie had gone AWOL. 'You're going back, though, aren't you?'

'Of course I bleedin' well am. King George wouldn't like it if I didn't.'

They went to Yates's Wine Lodge and found a table in the gallery. Archie fished for his paybook and unfolded a paper. 'I've got a leave pass, because I slipped one o' the bone idle orderly room penpushers half a crown for it. But it needs somebody's signature, otherwise it ain't valid.' He passed it across. 'Just sign it for me, Bert. I'd do it myself, except the red caps 'ud spot the writing of a numbskull like me straight away. Any road, you're a lance-jack. You know how to do it.'

Herbert drained his jar to gain time. 'I don't suppose you'll get stopped. It'd be a million to one chance. Another pint?'

'Yeh. But it'll look better if it's signed. Just put RSM somebody or other. I'd never nark if it got twigged.'

Herbert came back with the drinks, set them down, and took out his pen to scribble his father's name on the form, demoting him to the rank of captain. 'How's Sheila, these days?'

'Sheila? Going back a bit, aren't yer? I've got somebody else now.'

'How's that?'

'She wanted to get engaged. Went all mam and dad on me. So I towd her to piss off.'

Herbert laughed. So that was how you did it.

'She said she'd wait till I got out of the army, but I towd her I worn't interested. What's the point gerrin' married?'

'None at all,' Herbert agreed. 'Let's 'ave another.'

'Any time. But drop me a line now and again.'

'Sure. I'll do that.'

The names of wild flowers came back to him from school, but there weren't so many around Nottingham, being shy in chill July. He told Eileen what some of them were, when she asked because she didn't know what else to say as she warmed her failing spirit by pressing against his shoulder. They walked down a lane and into a field, on the last day of his leave.

'It ain't the end of the world, duck.'

Nothing he could say would help because for her it was, or she thought it was, which must be the same. She had hardly noticed flowers before except poppies, which wanted to reach out to her from an age when she had caught sight of them with such delight on a school outing ten years ago, and had run from the bus to pick one by the head, blood red and fragile till blown into the grass where she let it be. 'I could kill myself, I feel so rotten.'

We'll go back to the river, then, and you can jump in, if I don't throw you in first. I'll light a cigarette, and stand under the trees to watch you sink. Why can't you live from day to day like me and just enjoy the good fucks we have now and again?

A carpet of morning glory covered a hedge with white trumpets, some open and others closed, so maybe there's a chance of no rain, he thought, if that's what it means. The edge of the field was their horizon, but they stopped under a great elm. 'Don't think like that,' he said. 'You'll have me crying in a bit, and soldiers aren't supposed to.'

'But I love you,' she told him, 'and soldiers go away, and get killed.' A lime-green and black dotted ladybird settled on her lip. She brushed it away. 'Or summat else 'appens, and they don't come back.'

Here's one that won't, if you go on like this, and if I have any say in the matter. 'Of course, soldiers come back. I will, you can bet, and you know why I will?'

'No, I don't.'

He unbuttoned his battledress and lay it on the grass for this princess of the workbench. Walter Raleigh had nothing on him. 'Because I love you, that's why. You mean more to me than anybody else in the world.' Pushing out all the pretence of Bert Gedling, he gave in to a feeling of luxury, and spoke as the words came out of his heart. 'I've never been as close to anyone as I am to you, and I never will be. I know that. You're the best person in the world, not one better anywhere.' He couldn't stop himself, didn't see why he should, because every word was true. 'I loved you the first minute I saw you in the factory, and I love you now a hundred times more than I did then, if that's possible.'

No effect. It was a more solid sign she wanted, a tawdry pawnshop engagement ring sliding on to her finger. Even if he had one he wouldn't know which one to put it on, thought of walking away, the tragic swain rejected though all his poetry had been spoken. His feet wouldn't move, and he didn't want them to. 'I love you. I can't say any more than that.'

So many tears that the shoulder of his shirt was wet. The tap runneth over. Her eyes were illuminated with misery and determination. 'If you love me. Is that all?'

'I'll be back, you know that.'

She sat down, her legs shaking, the skirt lifted to show shapely white ankles. 'I took the day off work specially to be with you.'

The ultimate sacrifice. He passed a clean handkerchief. The ring could wait. Words would be enough. No one was going to control his fate – if he could help it. 'I'm glad you did. I appreciate it.'

A fist struck at his leg, hurting her more than him, he was sure. 'Don't talk like that. Appreciate! Appreciate! You don't mean it, I know you don't, using words like that. Who *are* you, anyway? You don't talk like anybody else. There's summat fishy about you.'

Not me, duck. You're Pisces, and I'm Taurus. He wondered if she hadn't cooked all this up as a way of getting shut of him, a cunning route through the jungle of her self-preservation. The thought chilled him, for a moment. To tell somebody to push off for good all you had to do was disagree on a basic issue, such as liking a different film star, or another sort of food, or saying you didn't care for a certain place, or even a particular colour in a dress. That way you also gave whoever it was a reason to get rid of you. With primitive people of inferior intelligence you had to agree with everything, otherwise the union wasn't viable.

If he sank himself into the foreordained scheme of marital captivity he would give her a few kids and abandon her in five years, really ruining her life. The very picture made him want to say yes, let's get engaged and then married and we'll find a room, a flat, a house with a garden, and after the army I'll pack it in at the factory and get a cleaner job elsewhere and in a few years I'll love you even more and you'll change so completely by being with me that people will think we came out of the same drawer. Then I'll light off, beat it with spectacular suddenness, utterly unexpected, and it'll be a lot worse if we've had kids because you'll never hear from me again and you'll be scrubbing floors to feed them.

Perhaps she picked up the best of the reflections, for when he sat down all hope left her and she held him in a burning embrace, and they made the best love ever, he decided, at the crying out when she came.

Looking up, he saw the large melancholy head of a cow with big purple eyes fixed on them from over the hedge. Definitely not, he said to himself, unpeeling the frenchie before turning to help her, though minutes passed before he could stop her crying.

Back in camp a letter was waiting from Brigadier Thurgarton-Strang, in reply to one Herbert had written on joining up. His parents were on their way home by troopship and would get to Southampton in a month. As soon as Herbert could wangle a forty-eight hour pass they would like to see him and talk things over and please find the cheque inside for twenty-five pounds – a month's wages at the factory, and about three months as a soldier. He smiled, looking at it back and front before slotting it into his wallet for use in an emergency, though thinking he might not cash it at all.

Strangers were demanding his reappearance in a stage play he had walked out of years ago. What did they want to see him for? Who were they, in any case? Who was he, come to that? He felt a mix-up of curiosity and resentment, at the idea of meeting people who had abandoned him for seven years. He wouldn't even know what they looked like, nor they him, as if arranging a rendezvous by a lion in Trafalgar Square with someone you'd never seen, so that you might stand a few yards apart fruitlessly waiting for hours. Lord Nelson high above would recognize him before they did. Still, they were his parents, or claimed to be, so he had to respond to their curt summons, acknowledging that at least the cheque had been generous.

But should he go? Hard to say. In Nottingham he could have talked the matter over with Isaac, though in the end the decision would be his and nobody else's. It wasn't worthy of a grown-up to be uncertain when a brigadier wants to see you. There was nothing to do but, as with headmaster or foreman, do it with neither thought nor malice.

London was familiar, and he walked as if the streets belonged to him. You could still tell the place had been bombed, odd corners roped off, brambles proliferating behind wire fencing. Gower Street was shabby, but he supposed it always had been. Smells of petrol, coal smoke and plaster dust enriched the air. At eighteen he felt superior to everyone, a soldier with creases as sharp as his reactions in dealing with traffic when crossing the road, disdaining green lights and Belisha beacons. Boots were blackened to the utmost shine, gaiters blancoed, and a belt buckle that winked at whatever young secretary, darting from a door on the way to get her sandwich for lunch, might glance back at him.

The Underground train rattled along to Notting Hill Gate. He stood without strap-hanging, well enough balanced and controlled to stay upright at the stops and starts. Most of the people looked worn out, so closed in on themselves he wondered if they weren't, in the words of Mrs Denman, sickening for something.

He found the place easily on his map, a small but three-storied cottage kind of house in a street south of the main road. Within the railings two wooden tubs stood by the door, each holding an evergreen. Herbert adjusted his cap – though there was no need – to conceal his hesitation, not willing to put a hand on the knocker. He saw himself walk smartly away, a jolt to the heart at such a move, for he would never afterwards make contact. But they'd know where to find him, so escape was impossible. It would be easier and more sensible to meet them.

He detected regret in the man who opened the door, at not having a skivvy to do the job. Times had changed. There were no servants now, at least not in this country, unless you were a millionaire or in the Labour Government, his father's expression seemed to say. Herbert was led into a parlour whose bay window fronted the street. 'Maybe we'll have someone to look after us when we get back to the old place in Norfolk.'

'When will that be?'

'I'll be out next year. And then we'll see. Meanwhile this doll's house costs ten pounds a week. Sit down, my boy, and let's have a look at you. I hope you don't mind sandwiches for lunch?'

Herbert's head was level with that of this erect oldish bloke of nearly sixty who claimed to be his father, bald but for a few grey strands, a returning trace of rubicund in his face after the sea voyage. He removed his beret and stared into his father's grey eyes. 'Not at all, sir.'

Hugh smiled. Mufti or not, you could tell he was a soldier, straight and slender, head seemed more inclined to the ceiling than to anybody else's level. He held Herbert's right hand with both of his, instead of returning the handshake that was offered. 'Do you know, my boy, we were never worried when you bolted.' He spoke as if the escape was yesterday, though maybe it was to him. 'We were surprised at first, a little annoyed, I won't say we weren't, but that was about all. I always dreamed of doing it from my school, but never had the initiative to carry it out. It was good of you to let us know so soon, though. The first thing I did was write to your school and tell 'em they weren't to go after you. Don't suppose they liked it, but they must have known better than to argue.'

Herbert smiled, at what must have been the longest ever speech from his father. All his fears about being caught had been for nothing. Bugger it! – almost came to his lips, though he considered his chagrin unjustified because, on looking back, it seemed he had rather enjoyed being a fugitive. 'It was good of you to take it like that.'

They sat as if both were too big for the armless chintz-covered chairs. 'Well, I didn't think it would do you any harm, especially when you wrote and said you were working in a factory. Everything helps to make a man of a boy as long as he puts his back into it.'

Herbert struggled for a moment to keep his accent from straying. 'I liked the life.'

'I'm sure you did. A lot of my chaps came from such places in the Great War, as well as in this one. We had a few bad eggs, but most of them did well. And when they did well, there were none better.'

Expecting a shouting at, he felt at a loss, glad when the half-shut door was kicked open and the woman he supposed would turn out to be his mother came in with a tray of cups and saucers. Thick grey hair was tied back, showing her strong profile, and a string of brown beads fell over the white blouse covering a sloping bosom.

She must have known he had been in the house five minutes already, so had been waiting to compose herself for the moment of reunion or, more like it, hadn't thought it necessary to break off what she was doing; the latter more likely, because pride grew out of her bone marrow.

'I even have to learn how to make coffee – though I always could, you know.' She set the tray on a shining walnut wood table between them. The crockery rattled, a sign of nervousness at the longed for meeting, he could only suppose. 'How are you, Herbert? It's been so long, such a dreadful time, not being able to see you. You were quite a small boy . . .'

'Hadn't started to grow,' Hugh laughed.

He had already stood up, as you did when someone came into the room. She grasped his forearms, and he was embarrassed at the fervent kiss, at her eyes glistening with love and recognition, a definite tear in one of them. He hoped she didn't notice the drawing back in his heart and hands. Could he believe she had dreamed of this reunion for years?

'I can see you're well,' she said, 'and I can't tell you how glad I am that you are. Apart from the height you've not changed a bit. You're the replica of your father when he was your age. Isn't he, Hugh? Just look at him.'

'Is he?' He smoothed his moustache, the first real pleasure he had shown.

She touched his arm. 'How much sugar, Herbert?'

'Two, please.'

They sat without talking for a while, so much to tell that nothing would come out. Maud knew it wasn't done not to say a word or two. 'You look a very smart soldier, but I do wish you'd go in for a commission, Herbert. It would be natural for you. You're our only child, and we want you to do well.'

'We'll have lunch, and talk about that afterwards.' Hugh dangled his watch, spun the chain around a long finger, then threaded it into his waistcoat. 'I suppose we can fix him up with a show this evening? That's what I always liked to do in London.'

Maud picked up the *Daily Telegraph*. 'There's *The Gang Show* at the Stoll. Not very much really. What about *Song of Norway*?'

'Bit musicky, isn't it?' Hugh said.

'Well, there's *Caesar and Cleopatra* at the pictures. Shakespeare, Herbert?'

'Expect you got that rammed down your throat at school, didn't you?' Hugh winked.

He smiled. If they sat in the cinema it would be two hours when he wouldn't need to talk. 'Well, yes, but all the same I'd like to see it.' He turned to his mother. 'That'd be fine.'

'All right,' Hugh said. 'Might be just the thing.' He stroked Maud's wrist, and Herbert noticed his loving smile. 'Vivien Leigh's damned good to look at.'

'That's settled, then.'

Herbert knew he couldn't berate them any more for shovelling him into those dreadful schools, but neither did he feel any flush of returning affection. He'd have to go back too far for that, to his infancy in India when they mooned over him with so much pleasure and, he now realized, spoiled him rotten. His heart was like a stone, as if he'd just come back from its funeral. 'I don't intend to sign on in the army,' he told them at lunch. 'All I want is the experience for two or three years. After that, I'll decide what to do.'

Hugh's fingers drummed some garbled message on to the table, while Maud worked at her beads, looking to the window as if a solution to the situation might show itself in the glass. 'I suppose we can at least be pleased at the way you seem to chew things over before you speak,' Hugh said.

She stacked the plates to clear the table. 'Well, that's just like you, isn't it, dear?'

His father could be as sarcastic as he liked. Nothing would alter his mind. Not that he knew what his mind was. He didn't much care, being on Fate's conveyor belt, and he could do nothing about that even if he wanted to. Neither, therefore, could they, which suited him fine. You could hardly expect such old parents to understand. At the same time he was beginning to feel so much part of them that there was nothing more to be said or done, except do exactly as he bloody well liked. Time in the factory had strengthened his will against intimidation. If they thought to change his mind later about their ideas for his future they would be thwarted because a troopship would soon be taking him to he didn't know where, a place he hoped would be as far from them as he could possibly get, Japan for preference.

Eight

He walked across the deck for a change in the view, bracing a leg at each step, to find that the opposite horizon had the same aspect of violence and colour, coming equally close at the tilt of the ship, but he felt the world to be his, and that he was part of it, feet solid on the wood, in harmony with the world on water, body invulnerable. He had never felt better, or more himself or, more to the point, that he had no interest in who he was, merely that he was separated as far as could be from his past yet was part of a moving organization in which he had for the time being found refuge.

A light from France flickered white as the troopship made a long turn towards Biscay. 'We're on our way,' Pemberton said.

'I'm glad. You?'

In the last months Pemberton had lost the oversensitive uncertainty of his mouth. The light had gone out of his eyes, the quick movement that remained due more to self-preservation among the mob than from any kind of fear. 'All right. Neither good nor bad, philosophically speaking. Things just are.'

Herbert smiled, and asked if he wasn't leaving a nice girl behind.

'You don't meet girls when you're swatting for Higher School Cert. The girls in the office were difficult to approach, though there's one I write to. We're just friends.'

'You mean you've never had one?'

'Had one?'

'Well, I think if the fucking boat turned a somersault, and a fish floated up with your number on it – would you be very happy knowing you'd never shagged a girl?' Pemberton looked blank: what you hadn't had you can hardly regret. 'Though I suppose', Herbert

94

went on, a stiffened arm stopping him getting cracked ribs at the rail, while Pemberton weathered it with some fancy twitching of the feet, 'that if you have had it you regret dying even more in knowing you'll never have it again.'

'I imagine that's the case,' Pemberton said. 'But I'm going down to find my hammock, before I start to feel queasy.'

Herbert was also sad to be leaving, so could relish the best of both states. He took Eileen's letter from his battledress pocket for another musing read. Now that she hated him, and wished he would – as if such a journey would somehow scare him – 'go to bleeding hell', he imagined himself still half in love, though no more so in yearning for her warm body and cow-like generous trust to be with him now. Maybe he would get a reply off at Gibraltar, asking her to think again, wait for him, even to forgive, though he didn't know what for.

A shudder of regret was meaningless to the waves, which was no bad thing. He was on his own at last. The opposite rail started its exorable lift, beams and girders taking the strain. Rain hit the portholes like gravel, peppering the superstructure. He put the letter into his notebook and, before it could get wet, slotted it back into his pocket; then zigzagged into the dimly lit other ranks' saloon.

Bumping between the crowd showed no place to sit. For a while he stood with his legs apart to counteract the swaying. Fag smoke and diesel smells weeded out all but the strongest stomachs. Barraclough put down his unfinished half-pint and, with muslin features, pushed by on his way to be sick.

When the sun shone from a clear sky off the coast of Spain he sat among hundreds on the open deck to relish the cruise. Passing Cape Trafalgar, a sandy-looking bluff in the distance, he opened his notebook to write up the log of his travels. A copy of the farewell missive from Eileen rested there, as well as his reply. He pulled both out and tore them into the smallest pieces possible, and watched them blow away from the stern like snow, a confetti that disappointed the gulls. She had callously reminded him of what he didn't need to know, that there were a lot more pebbles on the beach. Being compared to a pebble irritated him beyond endurance, especially since he was one of a thousand on this three-funnelled troopship heading for some outpost of the Empire.

The Med was stormier than Biscay, and his stomach wasn't too steady, so he was glad to clatter down the companionway to the bottom of the ship for bulkhead duty, a paperback snatched from the library in his back pocket. So far below, he was clear of the sea-howl, stew-reek and diesel stench that thickened in the air of upper decks.

The steel doors either side were to be rammed shut if a mournful death-in-the-heart signal indicated that the sea had broken in. Very comforting, he thought, but practical. The bottom length of the ship was divided into compartments, each to be made separate and watertight so that if rock was struck or a stray mine left from the war brought in the floor the vessel would stay afloat. Crippled but viable, it might even make a few knots, which kind of mechanics made firm sense. The sergeant of the watch came striding in. 'Not supposed to have your nose in a book when on guard, are we?'

'Sorry, Sergeant.'

He winked, passing close. 'Don't do it, or you'll get me shot with shit. If you hear that klaxon it's not because Sheffield Wednesday's scored a goal. Just wind them doors shut, or we'll be floating like tiddlers in a bowl. Your reading days will be over if you don't, and so will mine. What's it called?'

He turned to the front page. '*A Room with a View*, Sergeant.'

His pale face came near to laughter. 'No fucking view down here!' And went on his way.

Dereliction of duty – damn it, he murmured, getting the book back from his pocket. He wouldn't let the novel be invaded by his present situation, had stopped regarding himself as the perfect soldier since forging his father's name on Archie's pass. Every spin of the ship's screws was taking him forward on a mystery trip, but wherever it ended up he would still be himself. A burst of sea water into the bulkhead suggested panic if he allowed the possibility, though as far as his mind went it was easy to control, the mind being like the ship itself, unsinkable, kept going by its many lockable compartments. If something threatening rushed in you could shut it off, and live in those that were clear of disturbance.

All the same, maybe there was something behind the closed doors that he didn't know about but should. Any door invited opening. You couldn't batter it down to find out – cut your way in, claw steel and shavings away. Such bulkhead doors, or doors of the mind, you had to wait for them to give way or open up of their own accord to reveal the mysteries. No room with a view in the bowels of the ship. The sergeant was right. There was no fucking view anywhere, until you got clear and made your own.

By the last hour of the watch in the dimly lit depths he knew that the terror of what wasn't yet known was only another manifestation of normal life, inflicted by the imagination in the stifling warmth. Strict control of the brain was as much necessary as guidance from the bridge keeping the ship from all obstacles, whether on the surface or half-sunken. Jonah in the whale could only keep calm and wait.

'That grey blob over there must be Pantelleria.' Pemberton also had a map. 'It certainly doesn't look up to much.'

It had, at one time, to Herbert. 'Maybe there are some nice girls there, though, and a lit up café, with a band outside playing stirring Italian music.' Steaming by the island before, he had wanted to throw himself overboard and swim there, or drown on the way, having been told he was to be left at school in England. The pathetic little boy in short trousers sobbing at the rail was an image best forgotten, and he wondered why it had come to undermine him as he turned to watch a school of dolphins making scimitar curves out of the water, the boat track no doubt crossing that of Aeneas on his way to found Rome after leaving Dido to her fate.

'Sounds good,' Pemberton said. 'Maybe we'll end up in an even more exotic place, holding the fort somewhere in the Far East, a real Joseph Conrad backwater.'

But after ten days steaming from Blighty they were stepping down the gangplank on to a lighter at Port Said, going ashore with the rest of the regiment. Talk of a Cyprus posting left Herbert discontented, galled at cheers from the ship as it weighed anchor and steered off down the ruler-straight waterway for India and Singapore.

The close, unforgettable odours of the ship were changed for the sun, sand and sewerage smells of a transit camp near Ismailya, a two-month limbo of waiting. Set to guard an enormous encampment of stores, Herbert one midnight prodded a ragbag thief into the guardroom at bayonet point. The man was shivering with fear, and rage at having been caught nicking what he looked on as belonging to him by birthright, hardly able to lift the motor tyre he'd tried to purloin, which Herbert made him carry.

'Another bugger,' the redcap sergeant behind the desk said. 'That makes three tonight. God knows what they do with 'em back there. Give 'em a bloody good pasting and let them go, I shouldn't wonder. You can't stop it. There's five born every minute in this fucking country, and each of 'em's got ten thieving fingers.'

From then on Herbert let marauding shadows slide away on velvet feet, and took no action.

There was nothing else to do but put up with boredom beyond all experience, even to the stage of a cultivated emptying of the mind in the hope that time would take off its clogs and whizz along on bare feet. Pemberton passed him a magazine of current affairs called *Compass*, read and re-read till it fell from Herbert's hand in light-brown flakes.

The sea was calm on the short run to Limassol. Disembarked, they sat in a lorry, kit and rifles heaped by shining boots. The exhaust marked a track from the port, through town and across a dusty plain, much honking around bullock carts, and drab-garbed women in the middle of the road who took little notice. From a bend Herbert saw the mountains had come closer, green with groves and orchards, streaks of snow still on the summits, light green on nearer spurs, a jumble of re-entrants. The view was like paradise, but halfway towards it the driver took a fork and brought them back to a vast area of tents not far from the coast.

When the six hundred men were moved from place to place, an exercise of seeming pointlessness, all complained at being fed up, fucked up, and far from home. The eternal grumbles were raved out with melancholy humour, better that way, Herbert felt, because otherwise they would be inclined to go out on a binge of mayhem and murder, and so would I, he mused, knowing himself better off for being in tune on that point at least.

More training, though with less obvious bullshit, and more sentry-go, all compounded into more and more boredom, unless he laid hands on a paperback book or two from a stall in Nicosia, detritus from those who had already come and gone, not even to be haggled for, thrown across for a few of the local akkers. As the weeks slid by it seemed as if the colonel was going mad with the map, shifting them here there and everywhere. At least the landscape changed, though the island wasn't so big, and eyes soon lost their sense of wonder. Moving numbers to more purpose would call for the unravelling and joining together of subtle organizational threads beyond their capabilities, though much time was devoted to trying, with a talent that in Herbert's view never seemed more than mediocre.

At times he wondered whether he wouldn't have been more content as a commissioned officer, but soon enough doubted it. Being that much singled out had no appeal for him, and to land himself closer to the scene of control would have made him even more exasperated and contemptuous. He lacked the tolerance to understand how time could be squandered and energies blighted. The more hours NCOs spent in offices performing their administrative duties the more was life made dull all around.

Yet he was happy enough being a soldier. His limited experience of other states told him this one was one of the best, interesting, exciting even, when waiting didn't milk the élan out of the platoon's morale. Existence came close to real life, and was a lot improved when echeloning up a hillside between black goats whose neck bells told the umpire over the rocky crest that they were on their way, all surprise gone. Moving at speed between the trees was also mindless, but it was better than sitting around a lorry in the wrong gully, that the driver had brought them to because he couldn't read a bloody map.

They infiltrated remoter parts of the mountains looking for no one knew what, a sense of realism provided by living off what they carried, and occasionally for a day on almost nothing because no lorry turned up at the rendezvous. When there was a lorry they were glad to sleep by its huge presence, as if the vehicle was alive and would give comfort and protection. 'God knows why we're doing all this,' Pemberton said, spreading his groundsheet.

'Best not to wonder.'

A wind flipped through the branches of the pines. 'I can't help it. The people here want *Enosis*. They want to belong to Greece. They'll be fighting us about it one day – in a few years. I'll bet Byron would be on their side.'

'You don't say?' He wanted to laugh. 'You mean "The Isles of

Greece", and all that Missolonghi stuff? Well, Byron's dead, and it's different now.' He had read in a pamphlet that the Phoenicians came to the island first, followed by Greeks, Egyptians, Persians, Romans, and then Turks who had lost it to the British. 'Anyway, what difference would it make?'

'It'll mean a lot to them,' Pemberton said, 'the people who live here.'

Months passed in eating, sleeping, reading when you could, smoking what fags were available, doing your duty with as little effort as possible, and saying nothing. 'Let's get our heads down. We have to relieve the others in a couple of hours.'

When under canvas, or at the NAAFI at some base near a town, or in hutments if they were lucky, he leaned with notebook on knee and recollected his Nottingham period. The year, in memory so rich, had elasticated into a decade. A good time, now that he looked back. All good, not a day dead, more at home than he had been anywhere – at least since leaving India at seven, and that didn't count any more. On his last visit Maud had come out with the phrase 'wage slave', and though he was glad she had been human enough to let the term drop against her intention, he thought it much better to be a wage slave than a soldier – though however you were occupied he supposed you were a slave to whoever paid you. Soldier or wage slave, it was certainly better than being a slave to your own confusions, during these long bouts of idleness and waiting, though you might just as well accept time on its own terms and go with the drift. In the factory there was little tolerance for such uncertainties and quite rightly, because you were sweating to fatten your pay packet which, while you were at work, was all that mattered. Existence then was as close to perfection as it was possible to get, because it was so plain and simple, and only a fool could imagine there was any state on earth that could be called perfection.

Pemberton plonked himself down and opened his book. 'Hope you don't mind.'

'Push off. You're breaking my train of thought.'

'We're on War Department property. I can sit where I like.'

'Any news this morning?'

'Nobody tells you anything, and when they do it's an unfounded rumour. Those who start them have weird imaginations. I've stopped asking when we're moving.'

He counted six birds in a row along the telephone wire. 'Maybe they know something.'

'Shouldn't think so,' Pemberton said. 'All I know is we've been here six months, and that leaves us with another year before humping it back to Blighty.'

'Back to the office, eh? Carry on penpushing.'

'Suppose so. I don't think my parents will be glad to see me. They hope I'll stay in, in fact. I had a letter from my mother this morning and, wait for it, my parents are getting a divorce.'

'Lucky devil!'

'After twenty-five years, though. Would you believe it? My father's the manager of an insurance firm, and apparently he's been carrying on a bit too long with a popsy who works there. Mother has lost patience at last. And it's not the first time he's been at such tricks.'

'I suppose in some way you might say good luck to him.' He couldn't tell whether Pemberton was sad about it or not, though supposed he ought to be, somehow. Such news wouldn't have affected him one bit. His parents seemed as if crayoned on to cardboard, his last visits completely unreal, when they should have been defining moments of his life. In their last letter his mother asked whether he wouldn't like to do something or other at Oxford when he got demobbed. What would he do at a place like that? Do nothing at all. Get into trouble, and go to the dogs. She must have thought he'd just sit there and knit.

Hugh's view, in a later letter, was that while it might be a good experience for him to be getting some experience in the ranks, he wondered if he wouldn't sooner than later like to have a commission and make the army his career. He'll never stop harping on it, Herbert thought, resenting the fact that it made him angry. He pictured his mother going over his father's letter and putting it in such lucid terms. They were a conspiracy sent on earth to give him life, and then try everything to ruin it. He could only go on respecting them if he didn't let them do it. He saw no future in the army, and in his reply mentioned neither of these possibilities, thinking it strange how little they knew about him even though he was their son –

and how easy he was able to put them out of his mind for months at a time.

Pemberton looked up from his book. 'Maybe I'll stay in the army, though. I'm getting to like the life.'

'Why not? You could even get a commission.'

'You think so?'

'No one more suitable. You had such a horrible beginning.' They laughed together. 'You're a funny old sod, Ashley. I can't understand why you joined the army in the first place. You'd have been better off with the Brylcreem Boys.'

'I did get called up, you know. There was no choice.'

'Got any brothers or sisters?'

'No. There's only me.'

'Hard luck. Same here. Let's go inside for some more coffee.'

Of all the duties the one he hated most was guarding the camps of the Jews, who were being prevented from going to Palestine. Destiny was keeping him in a grip which there was no possibility of breaking out of, but he did not want to be a gaoler, or a policeman. A soldier had to feel as well as know who an enemy was, and nobody thought these people were. All they wanted to do was go where they weren't allowed, and it made no sense to stop them – though it was no business of his. It was a duff job, being a guardian of the Empire, to which no real soldiering was attached at all.

Routine was the enemy, an unending roster of sentry-go that corroded the spirit, made you feel dirty and useless, an automaton. One day he had to deliver a wad of lists to the administration office, and the sergeant made out a pass which allowed him to go through the camp itself. He walked at his smartest, one of the elect only because he wasn't a civilian, and this was an unexpected effort because he was escorted by a cloud of flies. They landed on him everywhere. They were all he saw, all he felt. They tormented him like the Erinyes. He wanted to murder them, hoped they would magically perish, thought a giant mobile Flit-barrel of deadly gas was about right, except that it would be too good for them. He could only pity the tens of thousands in the camps who had to endure such a plague all the hours of daylight.

It was eyes front as if they didn't exist, difficult to look at anyone if he was to keep his stance and not run helplessly off course from the continual thousand-Stuka raids.

After delivering the papers and when halfway back, he stopped by a door as if to adjust his cap, unable for a moment to go on, and not being too sure of which direction to go for the main gate. A woman called to him from inside the hut, and turning gave another excuse to brush off the flies which seemed to be eating him alive. 'Come in here,' he heard.

One step backwards, and quickly into the hut, which seemed free of flies, but was no miracle because the reek of DDT almost pushed him out again. The walls were lined with bunks, from floor to ceiling, as he had seen in the pictures of German concentration camps, but these were clean and in smart enough order, though for the moment unoccupied. 'The people are out in work parties.' She had read his mind. 'Putting up tents for others.'

In the light, so much dimmer than the glare outside, he saw a slender fair-haired woman of about forty, with dry brownish skin, sitting at a cardtable. She folded the papers of a letter. 'Can I trust you?'

He smiled at a question no one had ever asked so openly – you might say brazenly – before. He hoped it hadn't been because they were afraid to get the wrong answer. No fraternizing was the regulation, but instant obedience had been forgotten in the pragmatical world of the factory and its surrounding life, and it hadn't yet worn off. In any case, no was beginning to seem like yes to him. 'Of course. Why, though?'

She licked the envelope with a precise little tongue, and looked up, saying in an accent he assumed was German: 'I'm going to ask you to post this letter for me.'

'Can't you do it yourself?' Maybe they weren't allowed. He'd heard something about it. Or their mail was opened and read, which he thought nobody had a right to do in peacetime. Anyway, you couldn't argue, because if a woman asked you to do her a favour you did it, unless it was to commit suicide. 'All right. Of course.'

'There's no stamp,' she said, as if it were a matter for bitter regret.

Perhaps they had no money, though that was unlikely; or no way of buying them, which was possible. The place wasn't provided with a nice clean post office, flowerbeds all round, and that was a fact. Since coming into the hut he'd felt a mad wish to laugh out loud. 'Don't worry about that. I'll stick one on. Where's it to?'

'Palestine.' The address was in Hebrew as well as English. 'But will you be sure to do it?'

Impossible to know what made him say yes, or why she had chosen him. In the lottery of passers-by he'd been the one, he supposed. His eyes stung from the disinfectant, and he wondered how she endured it, and hoped she wouldn't think the tears at one of his eyes meant he was upset about anything. Nothing on earth to get upset about – and even halfway through the gesture he felt a strong urge to change his mind because it might be taken by her as demeaning – he opened his cigarette case and passed three across, while taking the envelope from the table. It fitted safely in his pocket. 'I'll see it gets there.'

A gold tooth showed when she smiled. 'Thank you.' He turned to go. 'And also for the cigarettes.' At such politeness he went back to the table and, seeing one already between her lips, laid a box of matches down. Another insane action, felt himself colouring from shame at her having to accept them. He wanted to say '*L'chaim*!' but didn't because he would be embarrassed at seeming to get too familiar. Instead he gave a sloppy kind of salute, which brought a look of amazement – or was it amusement? – to her face already half obscured by cigarette smoke. Then he swung on his heels and went back to the flies and sunlight.

He stood at the door for a moment to orientate himself towards the main gate. A sergeant came by. 'You been talking to the people in there, corporal?' he said, though in a not much caring tone.

Bouncing between euphoria and undeniable pity, he kept a hard face. 'Somebody called out.' He held up his wrist. 'Wanted the time of day.'

'And did they thank you for it?'

'You're kidding. Told me I was a swine, and so was the whole British Army.'

They walked on together. 'And what did you say to that?'

He waited till a pair of low-flying planes had got into the distance. 'Told 'em to fuck off.'

'That's the ticket. We've just got to do what we're told, and they don't allow for that.'

'Can't, I suppose,' Herbert said, wanting to laugh.

Off duty in the evening he walked a mile to the village, a glass of resinated red his intention. Opposite the café was a post box, which reminded him of the letter. He took stamps from his wallet and put it, with one for Archie, into the slit. Had he done it because he wanted a pat on the back from old Isaac? Certainly not. He would never mention it, even supposing he ever saw him again. You didn't want approval for any such deeds. Not done. Not easy ones like that, anyway. Nor did you angle for disapproval of the bad deeds, either. Maybe it was a letter to her husband, or to a young man bewitched by her.

Other units were given the job of guarding the camp, and life was more interesting again, at times even pleasant. Cyprus was a neutral ground where he could think of the past without rancour, and the future without anxiety. He spent his leave on a camp on the Troodos Mountains – four beds to a room, plain walls, and plain service. But there was solitude, and paths between the tall pines to walk along. He took a packed lunch, and no map, and lost his way, but instinct for the lie of the land always got him back for dinner.

On a day when he stayed in the complex to read and rest he was disturbed by Mrs Plater, who ran the place. 'When you first looked at me, as you passed on your way to the huts after booking in, I could see you holding your nose in the air, as if you thought I might try and pick you up.'

'An involuntary scratch,' he said. 'It was rather the other way round, I think,' though it hadn't been, and she may have been right, if anything had been on his mind at all. He couldn't remember. In the NAAFI at Berengaria he'd heard a Brylcreem Boy of the air force, with a signals flash on his shoulder, waffle out to his mates over some issue or other, that he 'couldn't care less'. He said it several times, as did the others. It seemed their favourite, most well-used phrase. Once Herbert's contempt at such an attitude had dissipated he knew that beneath his disciplined attachment to duty he felt much the same, in everything, though it was not a philosophy, he realized, that any Thurgarton-Strang would want to be caught dead with.

It was the middle of the morning, and he sat in the canteen with a pint of orange juice. Mrs Plater, a cigarette smouldering, came back and put her coffee on the table. 'Still don't mind if I join you?'

'Of course not, Mrs Plater. I'm honoured.'

Her throaty laugh echoed around the room. 'That's the sort of welcome I like to hear. Call me Alice, though.'

'I mean it. Life gets so dull.'

'You could go for walks. They're lovely around here.'

'I've done them all.' He had also been to Othello's tower in Famagusta, walking the battlements and looking with pleasure at ships in the harbour, sitting to eat his sandwich, and read about the place from a guidebook Pemberton had found on his assiduous browsing. 'Busman's holiday, walking. In any case, I thought I'd save my feet today.'

A hand was close to his, too blatant, he wanted to pull away, but couldn't cause offence. Then it wasn't blatant enough, and to withdraw his hand was unthinkable. He didn't know what took place in that converting moment, only that, when her periwinkle blue eyes looked at him, litmus paper flared between them. A fly alighted on the sugar, set for a feast, but he waved it away, though it was awkward bringing up the other hand from the side of his chair. She smiled when he met her eyes. Two soldiers at the end of the hall argued as to who should read what part of a newspaper. 'Life would be boring for me too,' she said, 'if there wasn't so much work.'

The image of straw came to mind, a Home Counties corn dolly, except there was something refined in her features. She had worked in Cyprus with the camp organization for three years, and whatever the problems it was far better than being in dreary old England, with rationing and all that. Agreement came easy on such a score, and he found himself enjoying talk with a worldly woman of thirty. 'You should be in an officers' billet,' she said, after he had mentioned his old school. 'I spotted it straight away. And then your name, of course.'

The usual thing. Only the other week his platoon sergeant said: 'You strike me as being a bit of a gentleman ranker, Strang. A perfect candidate for signing on and getting up the ladder a bit.' The sergeant, a few years older, seemed so far ahead in age that acquaintance of a sort was possible, but not friendship. 'I'll have to think about it,' Herbert said.

But a woman of thirty was close enough to his own age, and their talk made him feel friendly towards her, like her, in fact, so that he kept any trace of the old Bert well hidden – not difficult these days. She must have felt something for him because otherwise why should she have sat at his table? 'You've got a girlfriend, I suppose?'

'Not me. People like me don't have girlfriends.'

She drew back, a deliberate gesture meant to be amusing. 'You're not queer, are you?'

He laughed. 'I don't keep 'em long enough to have as a friend, is all I mean.'

'Let's see how we go, then,' her fingers touching his wrist and then pulling away, an unmistakable signal.

Chitchat was what he wanted. He settled down to the luxury of benign thoughtlessness, a state of calm without worry, and let things take any direction she cared to go in.

She was like nothing on earth, or in his experience at any rate, a whirlwind who knew what she wanted and so made every move. For that reason the affair lasted little beyond the weeks of his leave, scorched itself out. Regret, surprise, the ditcher ditched, he assumed she had found somebody else. And why not? Yet there was a wound, and it ached, the only consolation being that he learned to separate the heart into compartments, as he had earlier surmised he would before having good reason for it. Like the bulkheads of a ship, if the flood of salty despair broke in, you could shut the watertight doors and keep the rest intact so as to prevent the whole bloody vessel going down into the dark. Life was too short not to write people off now and again, or be written off by them.

Nine

He stood at the door of a shed on the quayside while an RASC fatigue party loaded stores into the lorry. Time for a fag before seeing it back to the rendezvous in the mountains. 'Have a drag, Ashley?'

'Thanks. Looks like a troopship's in.'

Among the pink-knees coming warily down the gangway Herbert spotted an awkward chubby figure, then the unmistakable gait and face of his old schoolmate Dominic. 'There's someone I don't want to see.'

He dodged into hiding. Hallucination was the order of the day. But no, the sky was clear blue, the group illuminated, filing towards the next shed. Dominic stumbled under his kit. It was him all right.

'Pay Corps wallahs,' the driver said. 'Our money'll be fucked up for months.'

Another clandestine gaze through the slit of the door, and Dominic waited in line to board a gharry. His face had hardly altered from what seemed all those years ago, the last person Herbert wanted to see. Take a long time to get his knees brown. 'Have they finished loading our gear yet?'

'Another twenty minutes,' Ashley told him.

The new Pay Corps arrivals sat in their lorry, silent and sweating. 'Where do you suppose they're going?' Herbert asked. 'Some cushy job at headquarters, I expect.'

Ashley put his paperback away. 'Same road as us. I asked their driver. He's browned off because he waited for them all morning.'

Dominic must be happy to be on such a ripping adventure, but Herbert thought that if he had to put up with his questions on all that had happened in his life since lighting off from school it would be positively sick-making, at the best tedious. Anyway it was no bloody business of his that he had spent most of the time working in a factory which he, Dominic, would consider a bit of a come down after all that stuff out of *Caged Birds*.

Stores loaded and roped on, Pemberton climbed into the cabin of the fifteen-hundredweight. 'Get going,' Herbert called. 'We'll go back through Omodhos.'

The driver unfolded his map. 'Take a bit longer.'

'Why not? I like that road.'

'You're the corporal.'

Carob trees flicked by, long brown beans gangling in the sun like withered turds. 'Turd trees,' the driver hee-hawed, gunning along the flat and not bothering to slow down, though he almost twitched a sleepy old donkey into a ditch.

Herbert wouldn't bump into Dominic, no chance of it, and the Omodhos route attracted him in any case because on an exercise around the village, between urging his section to take cover, and getting on through the vineyards, he had seen a young woman hanging sheets on a line. She wasn't long in his view, but the picture stayed with the clarity of the design on a postage stamp: a pallid oval face, black hair lengthening behind, dark brown eyes, and white headscarf. An arm reaching up to the clothesline elongated her bosom under a flowered blouse, though it was hard to be sure how much detail his lascivious imagination etched in later. 'Did you see that woman?' he asked Pemberton at the time.

He'd been half-asleep, as had most of the others. 'What woman?'

'In the vineyard, back there.'

'You must have a touch of the sun.'

She saw him, and smiled. He settled into his outpost on the hillside for a few hours' sleep by his well-oiled Bren, and dreamed about her. Heat in the rocks cooled after dusk, aromas of thyme and juniper drifting on the breeze. When on the march, incidents from the factory were his favourite recollection. Faces invaded space without warning, wanting to take over his soul, solidly and forever. He preferred to be colonized by an obsession with the woman than be a victim to anything from the past.

The sight of her made him wonder what he would do when he

left the army, where to go, what caged bird refuge find. In a few months he would be on his way out, and the smile on the woman's otherwise placid features turned away the thought of going back to Nottingham and immersing himself in the rattling machine music of the factory. Better to make his way around the world on a merchant ship, or try a job in London and know what it was like to be an ant among millions. The idea of having to make up his mind was anguish, and he even considered staying in the army for seven and five, though he preferred the heady uncertainty of not knowing what he was going to do till he did it.

At the warehouse a piece of grit had forked into his left boot, which helped the next few miles on the road to weary him even more, so that all he ached for was to see the woman and talk to her. Water still ran in the river, though it was June, and the road snaked between taller trees, their driver wrestling the wheel as if with a dragon whose head he had at last got down on the ground. Herbert envied him the combat, anything but sitting still and watching the all too familiar landscape go by, which only another sight of the woman could bring to life.

The pebble in his boot was easy to ignore the closer they got to the village. Brooding over the girl showed a sickness of the spirit, he was sure, a threat to himself he could do nothing about, a gun to the head. He didn't want the vision to melt, though wondered whether Pemberton or the driver could detect the thickness of his obsession.

The undulating scrub of heather and olives, and then scattered tall trees whose shade flickered the windscreen, gave off a dry luxurious scent, fresher than at the coast, deepening his foolishness in love, at chasing a picture which had snared him on to a fateful road. Useless to choose it by hoping to avoid that idiot Dominic, the chances being they would meet in any case. He would have been a bigger fool to think it unlikely. Only the woman – though a cooler voice said such revelations never came twice. Even so, he must be driven through the village to prove it true or false.

If he saw her he would wave and get the lorry to stop, stroll between the trees and talk to her. She would smile again on seeing him. But how would he talk? His Greek was less than basic. He knew the alphabet from school but not much beyond a few travellers' phrases, and how to count – a large percentage more than most but hardly

110

fluent enough for courting. On the other hand maybe she was a schoolteacher who knew English, and had come back to be with her family for the weekend.

He would marshal up words and signs to charm her till she agreed to meet him a few days later. After a few occasions of stumbling communication in the vineyards, or by the house she lived in if he was lucky (perhaps he would meet her like Rebecca at the well) he would take her to the cinema, even though tall moustachioed brothers came as chaperones. Laughing at his gauche mistakes with the language she would teach him, till he could unravel affectionate thoughts for her wondrous approval. He was nineteen, and she maybe a few years beyond, but how could it matter? After a while they would get married in whatever church she named, buy a house for a few hundred pounds and, on his discharge from the army, he would land an easy job in administration so that they could live happily ever after.

Human intercourse would be difficult at first, on all sorts of levels, but exciting; she will have no preconceptions about my past, he thought; I'll have no clear notion about hers; therefore we'll have the romantic experience and even difficulty in getting to know each other, which may take years, but so much the better because it'll be an adventure, since there'll be more than a lot to learn.

Eyes ached at following the descent of one in ten. The road zigzagged up again, terraced vineyards to either side. He gobbed all that was dusty in his throat out of the window, as if to let the bus struggling behind tread down such pathetic ideas. Crumbling stone walls bordered the road, divided groves and terraces. When caged birds weren't escaping, or preparing to, they were the victims of romantic dreams, he mused.

Milky cloud covered the descent into Omodhos. A building was marked with an Enosis sign. With such a big difference between ideas, language, race even, no woman would be seen with a British soldier, smile though he might, hope though he would, so he'd have to get used to the impossibility – unless she was Aphrodite or Circe or Oenone, for whom such trivial considerations wouldn't matter. And yet, if they were made for each other, as he knew they must be, she would come to him in whatever manifestation because she had, after all, smiled at him. She could be married, but he wanted her with an excitement that wouldn't leave him alone.

After the large monastery they drove through the packed houses of the village. Men stared from the café, and the lorry had to wait until an ancient geezer on a donkey turned into a side street. Women on stools in the doorways clicked sticks to make lace. Clear of buildings, there was no young woman for him to get down from the lorry and walk towards over the stony soil.

Chagrined, he looked at the village with the eyes of a soldier: the closely grouped houses on the bend would control the road if fortified both ways. Dispositions were noted on his map for artillery and crossfire, the siting of Brens and mortars, so that he momentarily forgot why he had made the driver bring them on this bleeding-heart roundabout track which Archie Bleasby (or even Dominic, had he come this way, or whenever he did) would say was a more than useless carry on.

He peered at every tree and wall, but the grove had been magicked away, no woman there. Or he couldn't say where the ground had been. Terracing was at all angles, trees differently spaced. A blackbird flew across the windscreen. Beyond a house-to-house search, or a battue through outlying land, there was nothing to be done. She was gone, never to be found – as he had feared would be the case. A faint whistle of breath indicated marks for trying, and now it was back into himself, though with the certainty that the dream would haunt him forever.

Swivelling at a bend, the driver swore blind at what only he saw, spun from one side of the road to the other to avoid killing a woman who suddenly appeared carrying a load of wood. Such a hit would bring the population down from the village intent on stringing them up, and who could blame them? Carelessness was unforgivable. The problem was avoided, but Herbert knew they'd had it. Or the lorry had. Something was bound to happen, and he braced himself for the impact. Doors and bumpers hit a bridge, scraping masonry. Pemberton stayed silent and upright. They bounced back across the road.

All so slow. When was the loony driver going to bring it under control? Herbert called out as much, though didn't know why. Inevitably the lorry jumped a culvert, slow it seemed, spun through pine trees.

You could count them and the seconds it took for each to go by, if the heart let you.

Heads went down, and he sensed their progress in vivid colours, heard the grazing of sultry trunks, scraping and turning, the driver fighting with the strength and skill of a demon who wouldn't be cornered. They landed precariously on a ledge lower down and, on thinking they were safe at last, the wheels slipped.

'No!' Pemberton shouted.

Herbert's last hope, a crushing pain in his leg, was that they didn't have enough petrol in the tank to catch fire – before the lorry went three more somersaults and smashed against rocks by the river.

He was sure he had been tied up and thrown on to a bed of pebbles. Some were sharper than others, though only when he tried to move. They were cooking him, and he couldn't understand why. 'What had he done to be treated thus? If you want to know he'd offended us.' Bloody silly words streaming again and again through his brain.

He wasn't even hot, or uncomfortable in his dream, but would be if he woke up. Would they eat him when they'd finished? Where they were he'd never know, too sleepy to care. One pebble grew to enormous size, and was sliced in two hemispheres, each shining grey as quartz as both parts wheeled off on separate trajectories into space. He hoped he hadn't screamed, would be ashamed if he had. Every nightmare was only the same in that none lasted forever, though he swore the knives and forks had been real.

A clown face showed through clouds of disinfectant, recalling the Jewish hut in the refugee camp. Maybe he was sweating the stuff. He'd been knocked about. The bite of gangrene came and went.

'You've got a Blighty one, corp. Half a dozen, really. The army won't want you any more.'

Nor did he want to see that Beano face again, with its typical RAMC wide-lipped cackle, now that I know I'm not blind or deaf, he added to himself. As for the rest, maybe the MO would enlighten him – if he could get away from putting his hand up the nurses' skirts. He vomited at the pain when he tried to turn to a better angle of comfort. The needle of the ward sister felt like the cut

113

of a scalpel, and an enormous soft pillow muffled him back into oblivion.

'We thought you was for the black pyjamas,' the male orderly said, spooning slop into his mouth for supper. 'Your driver only had a few bruises and a headache.'

'Thank God for that.' The croak came from inside his armour casing. He had never slept so many aeons. 'How long have I been here?'

'A week ago it happened. We laid bets when you was brought in.'

'I hope you lost.'

'Nar, I won five akkers. I just knew you was a hard case, though it was hard to read it on your face.'

All your life was said to pass before you in the moments before death, but it hadn't with him because he had come out alive. The Technicolor flash-bang of the collision drummed around, and he wondered if he would ever get free of its endless tentacles of flesh and metal.

'The shock's wearing off,' he was told.

His body was shaken to pieces, bombarded by stones, in a barrel corked and locked at both ends. Nightmare was more the name. He dreamed of being sawn in two across the waist, but the fatal separation didn't happen. The two halves came closer in fact, and he awoke – though still in the dream – into a miracle of flying above mountain peaks that were swathed in snow. A jagged piece of dead wood ripped into his face again and again.

'We had a little old woman from the town stitch your flesh together,' the MO said. 'A dab hand with a rusty needle she was. Still, we'll have you out and about in a few months. You'll never know it happened.'

He flew to another world, saw people, everyone he'd ever known but in no order, from all over the place, laughing or warning or commiserating. Hugh and Maud told him they were dead, not him, but he wasn't to worry. Things would sort themselves out. What others said he couldn't remember – drugged up to the eyeballs, he thought.

The major laughed when he came for a look, at the peepshow for the whole battalion. 'You'll live, Corporal, but I don't know whether you'll like it. Pity about the other chap. Things always happen to my best soldiers.' A jovial, hard-hat, thinking what were a few wounds to a soldier? The trade had its ups and downs: ribs cracked, leg broken, one arm likewise, head bumped around enough to leave a permanent deep scar down one cheek. 'What other chap, sir?'

'They haven't told you? Kind of them, I suppose. Pemberton. Brain-dead when they got him in. Nothing they could do. These bloody roads are a nightmare, though why you took the one through Omodhos I'll never know. Just as much traffic as on the other. I've brought some fruit. We've told your next of kin there's nothing to worry about.'

Sleep was peace. Those who die will be the lucky ones, he recalled from *Treasure Island*. Poor old Pemberton had jumped the gun, died the death. His folks will love him now he's dead. No use worrying about that. He did, and the blackest gloom settled, because if he hadn't chased that chimera Ashley might at worst only have been in the next bed, a leg equally angled.

They had both died, but he had been born again, or that's what it seemed, all he could tell himself, out of action, in traction, and birds beyond the open windows whistling him into a summer mood, a cosy lull that let the days go by as if on casters, all worries of the past drained away in his weakness and sorrow and then, after God alone knew what process, blown back for him to put into their proper slot.

The ward maid had black hair pulled tightly back, and a comfortable bosom under her white apron, doing things for him no one should have to do for another, in a regime under which pride fragmented, but out of which manhood had to grow again, for what it would turn out to be worth. At least she wouldn't be following him into civvy street to shout about the baby and booby he had been, which buoyed him up in darker moments.

He came out of his afternoon nap to see Archie sitting by the bed, and thought the accident was getting to his brain at last. Dominic would have been worse to dream about. It was Archie because the voice was real. 'You look like an old man of forty. I walked past yer bed, till the sister pointed you out. What a bloody mess, though.'

'What are you doing here?' He wanted no one to witness his

115

downfall, his helplessness, but regretted the harsh tone, and smiled. 'I'm glad to see you.'

'I asked for you at your camp, and they told me where yer was. Here's some fags. Me and a gang came down from Blighty a fortnight ago. We've got to wire up on one o' them new bases for National Servicemen. It was bleddy marvellous coming on the aeroplane. All in one day! I loved it. They even gen us a meal, and it worn't the usual army slop. We'll be finished though next month, and I'll be sorry because I love it here in Cyprus. We get pissed every night. What 'appened, though?'

Herbert told what he could. 'And my mate got killed.'

'That's a bleddy shame. Got his number on it, I suppose. Anyway, I hope you aren't going to lay on yer back much longer, yer bone-idle bastard.'

Herbert laughed, the first time since when? – though the pain was no incentive, and he had been told to avoid it for the fear of splitting the stitches in his face. Nor was it easy to talk. 'I won't be here a minute longer than I've got to.'

'Ar, I know yer won't. Yer'd better not. Yer was lucky, though, coming out of that. I'll tek yer for a pint of the local spew when you're out, to celebrate.'

Which, Herbert thought, would be one in the eye for the woman of Omodhos. 'I'll keep you to it.'

Archie leaned close. 'I met a bint the other night in town. Lovely she is, black hair and dark eyes, and very nice tits. Trying to teach me the lingo. I was doing all right, as well. I told 'er I'd come back and marry her when I got demobbed.'

'What an awful lie.'

'Me? A liar? Not me, our Bert. I shan't marry her, though. She's too nice for that. I'll do her a favour. She deserves a lot better than me.' He stood. 'But I've got to 'op it. The blokes can only cover up for me a couple of hours. I'll see you in a few days, if you aren't out by then.'

'I might be. I'm already hobbling to the lavatory.'

The MO said he would need a few weeks yet, but he willed himself to mend, to become viable by his own effort, walking up and down the ward all day and every day, and wandering the grounds in his hospital blue like a bent old man. A glance of his figure in a shining window forced him to straighten, and go at a faster rate. He drew the pieces of his body bit by bit together. In the evening he sat by his bed, aloof, unwilling to talk to the man next door who was writing poems which read like the worst of Patience Strong. Herbert read one out of politeness, and said it was good, and that he should persevere, which made the man happy. Herbert did all that his brain allowed him to, which was pull the copy of *Caged Birds* out of his small pack and comfort himself with the same old story.

Shaken from sleep at five in the morning of a day before Archie could call on him again, he was told that a signal ordered him home. 'Blighty, that's what, lucky swine. I'll give you a hand with your clobber.'

An ambulance screamed all the way to Akrotiri, a fine fresh day beginning, though Herbert within his deadness knew he was glad to leave. Helped up steps into a capacious York transport plane the smell of pear drops, furniture polish and petrol had a touch of civilization about it. Four engines roared at the end of the runway, and soon the nearest silver wing floated by the mountains. His face burned at the memory of his passion for the unknown woman of Omodhos, who had killed Pemberton in mistake for him, the goddess-madonna who seemed to be shadowing him even as a coastline was left behind which he hoped never to see again.

A few bumps before getting to twenty thousand feet caused an RAF bloke behind to use his sickbag. Herbert supposed they were far over the sea when weird snowy continents of cloud spread below, an antarctica of topographical complexity looking cool to walk upon – with the nightmare sensation of falling through and down to annihilation on the earth. Wanting to tell Pemberton (he couldn't for some reason think of him as Ashley any more) to put his bloody book away and look at such marvellous and fantastic scenery, the pang struck that he no longer existed – except in memory. Immortality was a confidence trick of the church, because you only lived as long as anyone alive could remember you. But Ashley, an unexplainable image, was close because Herbert still lived. Maybe I'll write to his

117

folks and tell them what a good chap he was, either to twist the knife, or make them grateful.

He pulled a copy of *Everybody's* from under the seat, and in an hour had done the puzzles and read every crass piece. The pilot announced they were overflying Crete, of which only a few ashy peaks showed through a gap in the weather. The meal finished, he leaned his head back, senses culled away by the noise of the engines.

A medical orderly going home on leave had been seconded to watch over and generally help him, but his head close to a Paul Renin book kept him silent most of the way, for which Herbert was thankful. Being talked to or at would be like having a bandage continually put on and torn off. Every wound was a low-grade ache, more than enough to make the temper surly. To be sealed into himself was the only possibility of ease; no longer interested in the cloud scenery. Nothing would fasten his senses into concentration, he was embroiled within, unanchored, disembodied, couldn't even envy those with the whisky flask in a better sort of class nearer the crew's quarters.

Malta, George Cross Island, part of the real world, recalling the thrill of its last-ditch tribulations heard about on the wireless at school, far back in history it seemed. The place looked arid, till they went grandly over the harbour, and he could peer down at greenery between the walls as the huge plane turned for the airfield.

With half a dozen others he shared a hut at Passenger and Freight Services, night-stopping before the last leg to Blighty. A meal of soup, pork chops and tinned pineapple was too much for him to finish, and he went to his bed more worn out than if he had been crawling over the hills of Cyprus for a week, knowing nothing till the orderly shook him to get dressed because it was morning.

The coast of Sicily came in sight. Two more hours and he saw the north-east shoulder of Sardinia, then Corsica. Cutting the shoreline into France, cloud assembled, and nothing was visible except murk when over the Alps. A Penguin Life of Shelley called *Ariel* kept him going until, without any reason looking from the window, he marvelled for the first time since leaving Cyprus at being eighteen thousand feet above the earth, and at the four Rolls Royce Merlins with their sturdy but invisible propellers made in Derby speeding them along at two hundred miles an hour. Bundled into the plane from the hospital, he had felt only numbness, but now he opened his map to surmise their route, as if an inner light was bringing him back to life.

Lyons, Orleans and, after five hours from taking off, the orderly elbowed him to say they were over the English Channel. Herbert woke to changing pressure as the aircraft decreased height, and saw the coast by Portsmouth. The orderly's head was between him and the window, as if he had never been to England before. Sheep spotted the pale green spurs of the Downs while making their run in. To turn his neck was painful, but worth the wrench. 'You're not supposed to do that,' the orderly said.

A mouthful of the foulest language came easy to his lips, which caused him to smile at realizing that the factory was again close enough for him to use it, though he checked himself, saying merely: 'Well, I've already done it, shag, haven't I?'

Down to earth, the therapy of recovery went on for more weeks than he cared to endure, until all limbs were in good trim and the MO said he was as fit as when he enlisted. He could be demobbed and returned to civvy street while still twenty. His parents wanted him to come and see them but he considered himself old enough not to bother, wouldn't call until mood or circumstances allowed him to without endless worrying about the decision. For the present he had firm control over both, though on one of his trips into town he posted a letter saying he would come as soon as was convenient.

A real man should have no parents, he thought on his way back from posting the letter, taking his way through summer woods on a back route to the hospital. You can't begin to feel a man till you have broken from them in body and spirit. A man with parents, who cannot for that reason act as he would wish, is in no way a man, that is to say independent. And yet he didn't feel at all bonded to them, so what was he going on about? Unless by thinking this way he wanted to be influenced by them, obliged to them – which he couldn't imagine to be so at all.

The further you got from their petrifying orbit of control the freer you were, was all he knew, and the freer you were the more were you at the behest of the unexpected, which force of change or fate provided the only possibility of living your own unique life, of having your life altered in unexpected ways, and of eventually advancing into a sphere so exalted that you could look down and wonder at the petty lives your parents had led, and realize how insignificant your life would have been if you hadn't fought free of them.

Finally he could only say aloud, as he paused while wading through swathes of tall bayrose willow herb blocking part of the path: 'Nah, I just don't want to be bothered with them,' not unhappy that he had reasoned the matter through only after going to the pillar box and not before, and knowing that working in a factory would be just about as far from them as he could get.

Part Two

Part Two

Ten

He stood by his case and cardboard box of demob clothes in the corridor of third class. The livid leftside scar gave him a look of surly violence. From trying to solve the crossword in a folded copy of *The Times* he glanced at patchwork fields and woods conveyed along half-open windows, scarves of engine smoke waving a welcome, he hoped, from the city he was bound for. A younger soldier stepped over the demob box, and Herbert, back from overseas and no longer feeling young – if ever he had – sensed his envy and respect.

A refugee from the land of the dead seemed his normal status, and going back to a familiar bolt-hole rubbed out any ideas of retrieving that part of himself left behind at school, or taking on the life his parents wanted for him. Maybe he had been altered by his accident, though he hoped that after a year putting himself solidly together in the factory he would know more what he wanted to do. Besides, he had no qualifications for any other work. Mrs Denman had written to say she would be happy to give him full board after his convalescence.

Going home again, he walked from the smoke of the station and inhaled the air of the streets. No other place had given such strong memories. The road was wide, and he crossed against the traffic of lorries and green double-decker buses. His case felt full of stones along the wide avenue of Queen's Walk. He'd sauntered by the taxi rank at the station as if to become Bert rather than Herbert as quickly as possible. It was a mistake, five minutes took twenty. A train drummed under the railway bridge and, stopping to change the weight to his other arm, and covering the weakness by retying a bootlace, paving stones shimmered as if he was about to faint. No you don't, not with me. He stared at them till they behaved, picked up his luggage and walked as if it weighed nothing. Low cloud held in sombre hootings from the engine sheds, at which earthy and melancholy sound it seemed as if he'd been away a very short time indeed.

'I never thought I'd see you again.' She opened the door to the parlour and told him to sit down. On the shelf were the usual small white jugs, pots with gaudy coats of arms, a photo of her dead husband, and one of Ralph and Mary when they got married. All the old gewgaws, as well as the same furniture, polished and well kept as if it was going to last forever. 'You look pale. I expect you've bin through the mill, though. Soldiers do. Archie sent a postcard telling me what happened. The army must have made a better man of him, anyway.'

Grey in her hair: amazing how long people lived. The light was too dim; he would like a bulb to shine two hundred watts. 'I'd rather sit in the kitchen.'

'You've changed, the way you talk.'

He laughed. 'You mean I've got posh?'

'A bit.'

'You do, after a few years away. I'll soon get the lingo back.'

Such an intention seemed to her liking. 'I'm sure you will.'

But he wouldn't if he didn't want to, the accent not being so necessary now. 'Cigarette, Ma?'

'Thanks, I will.'

He pushed his legs full out from the armchair. 'How's Frank?'

'Same as ever.'

No one changed, not here anyway, and why should they? Nearly three years was nothing to people who never left home. 'I expect I'll be seeing him.'

'He'll be thrilled to death. The Prodigal's coming back, I told him last night. That scar meks you look rough, though. But then, you allus was, especially when you went out boozing with Archie. I expect he's about to be demobbed as well, in't he?'

Such a prospect eased his gloom. He nodded at the window. 'You've put up new curtains.'

'You *do* notice things, then? I took the old ones down to wash 'em, and they nearly melted in the water they was so worn. Frank managed to get me some new ones, no coupons and no questions asked.' In the kitchen she took a pork pie out of the cupboard. 'I got this specially for you. I remember how you liked 'em.'

He didn't ask where she got it. The days of austerity and hard rationing seemed to go on forever. She cut a large wedge, and poured his tea into a cup instead of the usual mug. The meat was rubbery and overspiced, not much improvement on Spam, but being so hungry it tasted delicious – knowing he must stop looking back on the variegated menus of Cyprus.

'Now that our Ralph's married you'll have the room all to yourself.' Not only spliced, but he had two runabout sprogs and a ducky little bungalow at Bramcote. 'You'll be the only lodger, but I don't mind. I often think I've done enough work, and I can manage all right now.'

'What about that guest house at Skegness? Ralph told me you were very set on that.'

Her smile coated a nuance of regret, as if she had failed somewhere in life. 'What would I do in a place like that?' she said in a tone superior to self-indulgence and disappointment. 'I like it too much here in Nottingham.'

He followed her lovely legs upstairs to his room, thinking what a pity old people in their forties couldn't buy new faces from the Co-op. Still, Frank kept his hand in with her. 'He papered it,' she said, 'every wall as you can see. And I put new curtains up at the window as well. I bought the bedspread from a pawnshop.'

Garishness was never more homely than these heavily flowered walls and deep orange curtains. 'Looks wonderful. All I'll want is a table to read and write at.'

'There's one in the shed. A bit of elbow grease, and we'll soon mek it shine. You and Frank can get it in tomorrow.'

'I don't want to put you to any inconvenience.'

'Inconvenience!' she scoffed, giving a very leery look.

Too late to recall his stupid remark, he knew it was always best to show no warmth, lest you betray yourself. The personality he was to regain should merely have given a nod, or a look of understanding, or even incomprehension – it didn't matter. Posh reactions to kindness on anybody's part would only delay settling back into a sense of reality. You had to come down from the clouds in a place like this.

Glad to be alone, he took off his boots and lay on the lumpy bed, as exhausted by the half-day as if he had sweated a fortnight at the lathe he would soon go back to. Lulled into oblivion by friendly shouts from the backyards, the uncertain acceleration of a motor car in the street, and Mrs Denman banging washed pots back on the rack in the kitchen, he dozed in the luxury of his return.

The MO said a couple of weeks cycling was the surest way to co-ordinate arms and legs. He ran a finger along the frame of a secondhand five-quid grid, chained up outside the shop, painted black so many times he wondered what pitted rust lurked underneath. The shopkeeper wouldn't look at his cheque, and it took half an hour to go into town for cash. Maybe the bike was nicked, though the man gave a receipt. Trying it out, a green double-decker ran him into the kerb. The brakes were good, and so was the steering.

After getting a job the bike would pay for itself, by saving on bus fares. He pedalled to the toll bridge, and for a penny at the gate rode over the Trent. He looked at every woman in case she was Eileen, thought he had spotted her a time or two but felt dead towards her when it wasn't. He wanted someone new, in any case, with free and intelligent ideas, not the old cloying courtship which put you on to a bleak and dead-end road.

He'd only biked before around the leave camp on Cyprus, so wobbled a bit through Wilford, frequently stopped to adjust the brakes, pump the tyres, check the steering, tighten one of the cottapins, soothed by so much mechanical fussing. Following the country breezes to Clifton, a long and at times painful slog uphill drew him into a freewheeling stretch to Barton-in-the-Beans and the placid river again. For twopence an elderly Charon, his pipe smoking like a chimney connected to the punt itself and providing the power, ferried him and his bike to a cindered track on the other side leafy with privet and elderberry. Tyres bumping along the riverbank after Attenborough was better practice than cycling on tarmac.

Soon enough knackered he lay on the grass to watch the manoeuvres of uxorious swans, and fishermen coming out of their statuesque pose only to cast their lines. A hundred pounds back pay and demob money would let him drift, before offering his sweat to a factory. He liked the thought, and feeling an unmistakable spit from watery clouds biked to the nearest pub, the taste of local beer locking nostalgia into place with the scenery outside.

Varying the exercise, he put on boots and walked the town. With the map main thoroughfares were avoided as far as possible, as if road blocks had been set up for him alone. Leaving the Park area of big lace manufacturers' houses whose leafy quiet he enjoyed, he angled through the straight and barren streets of Lenton, working a route by the cycle factory and into the maze of Radford. The new and geometrically laid-out estates didn't tempt him, so he re-entered the countless streets and became wilfully lost, till finding his position again by the map.

The complex layout of the town was knitted in his mind so that if necessary any pursuer could be lost in it, though who would want to chase him and why was impossible to say. He noted all terraces, the various yards and offshoots of twitchells and double entries, as well as the landmarks of factories, cinemas, churches and, especially, the pubs and their names. People he found in them when stopping for a drink were good to hide among if he was going to be here for the rest of his life. It was as well to know the place.

But why was he still in hiding? After school he had been on the run, or thought it necessary, and now, out of the army, all he wanted was to conceal himself in a life and locality that wasn't his. Water always flows downhill, his father had contemptuously said when Herbert, on his last leave before going overseas, told him that he might go back to the factory after demob. A young man with your background should have a destiny, was the inference.

Whatever he did was his destiny, but madness seemed to be stalking him these days, because halfway along a street, dreading to meet whatever lurked around the next corner, he quick-turned back to the junction, and launched himself along a corridor of similar houses, moving as rapidly as if a malady was eating his life away and he had to get to a secret refuge before it killed him. Going at the double left everyone behind on the pavement but, he thought, my own self most of all. He timed his rate of walking and found it to be a hundred and thirty-seven paces to the minute, as if chasing an unattainable vision of heaven, retreating from the possible horrors of hell, either of which his blank and steely mind could put a picture to.

Grimed with sweat after uncounted miles, limbs racked and the scar on his face sore, he went into Yates's and drank a pint to get cool, comforted to find a point for homing on, especially the long bar that had furnished his first roof in Nottingham.

Early evening, the place was quiet and familiar, a few drinkers further along minding their own business, an air of preparation however before crowds came in later. Herbert recalled with embarrassment his time as a school kid ordering half a pint, and the naive effrontery in asking Isaac to join him, a man almost old enough to be his grandfather. The four years stretched back like forty, and the time since India seemed centuries away, but Isaac was a more recent human landmark, and must still be where he had always been.

On the pavement he adjusted his mackintosh and pulled the cap down as rain blew across the flower beds. Workmen on their way from factories were criss-crossing the square to change buses and go home. He climbed the stairs wearily and, no response to his knock, tore a sheet from his notebook to say who had called. He pushed it through the slit but, when he was halfway down the stairs to the outside door, heard bolts drawn and locks undone. 'Come back up,' Isaac called. 'I thought you must be one of *them*.'

Herbert followed inside. 'One of who?'

'The landlord's men.' He looked much harassed, hands shaking as he relocked his fortress as if the crown jewels were inside. Thinner than before, and more bald, he buttoned his dark blue overcoat. 'Am I glad to see you, though.'

He didn't eat regular meals, had become pasty-faced, waxy almost. 'Why, what's wrong?'

'People come up here and threaten me, hoping I'll pack up my tranklements and leave. They want to do the place up and let it for a lot more money. So these bloody oafs say they'll kick me in if I don't skedaddle. They don't know me, though. I like this place, and I'm sticking.'

A cold wind rattled the window, and Herbert passed over his packet of cigarettes, fighting down the words that came to him, wanting to say them but knowing he mustn't, words such as admiration for Isaac's courage and independence, and in living the way he did, regard for his qualities as a human being, respect for his knowledge and experience, and even awe at his age. It all added up to the nearest he could get to affection for someone other than a woman he was going to bed with, and even then the sum of his feelings might not amount to half so much. 'What time do they come?'

'Hmmm – Players. Where did you get these?'

'They had some in Yates's.'

Isaac washed cups, fingers chapped, heavy grey veins on the back of his hands. 'One of 'em was here an hour ago, about half past five. But you don't need to get mixed up in it. It's none of your business, sonny boy.'

'I can think about it, though.'

He opened a cut loaf and buttered the slices. 'There's even some sugar in stock. I got my rations yesterday.' A pigeon warbled on the window ledge facing the narrow street. 'Sometimes I think I'm going to start eating them, except I don't see why they should pay for the sins of the world. Now sit down and tell me what you've been doing since I last saw you. Your postcards were welcome, but they didn't say much. How did you get that scar, for instance? Makes you look a bit of a devil.'

Up Wilford Road he turned right into Goodhead Street. You never went to the front door because the parlour was often somebody's bedroom, or was used only on Sundays. To find the right house from the back meant counting doors along the street from the entry way, and then going behind and ticking them off again.

The rabbit hutch in the yard was empty, and a bike leaned against a bath big enough to wash the baby Hercules in. A girl of about fifteen came to his knock, a pair of curling irons in one hand and a fresh cigarette in the other: Archie's sister Janet. The homely smell of toast drifted from inside. 'What do yo' want?'

'Is Archie in?'

He noticed the delicate tits pushing out of her thin blouse, wanting to put a hand on them, except she might turn him into Polyphemus with the curling irons. She glared, went back inside, and he heard her say: 'It's somebody as wants our Archie, Dad.'

Herbert was amused at the disgruntled voice of doom: 'Tell 'im 'e's still in the fucking army.'

She came out again, and managed a smile to meet Herbert's halfway. ''E's in the army.'

'When's he coming out?'

She turned and bawled: 'When's 'e coming out, Dad?'

'How do I know? Nex' week, I think.'

'Are you his posh friend, then?'

He put on his most atrocious accent. 'I don't know about posh. Just tell 'im Bert called.'

She nodded. 'Yeh, all right' – and banged the door to.

With Mrs Denman's sandwiches in his saddlebag he set off north to explore the county as far as Worksop, wanting to know the region as if he had been born there. He pencilled the routes to be covered on his map, but found the tarmac dull under his tyres for the first few miles, fields dead and woods deader, the cold shoulder given to dismal villages and worse towns. He didn't wake up to the beauty until well towards Edwinstowe, fighting off questions as to why he was where he was because there was no answer to what you could do nothing about. To murder someone and get hanged was one solution to his uncertainties, suicide another. Both options stank of romantic defeat, but he'd always wondered whether the life of the criminal wasn't more to his style than any other.

In each town there was a library, church, schools, a cinema and meeting halls, from which he felt himself as definitively barred as from the world of his parents, from any world perhaps except that of the factory and the pub. The long main street of Worksop seemed like the end of the world, busy and exclusive, so he turned from halfway down to avoid coal smoke and diesel fumes and pale faces, and rode south east towards the Dukeries.

The straight rides hid him and became friendly, took him in, a silent biker pedalling through the glades, no longer feeling isolated because, without people, he had become himself again. Standing on the bridge at Hardwick Grange, by the absolute peace of the lake, he watched the effortlessly floating mallards, part of the willows drooping over cloud reflections, as if this had been his birthplace, or maybe a sign that he was being born again. Not even memories of India, returning in colour and clarity since his accident, but only as if he had read about them in travel books, could nudge aside the healing tranquillity.

The scene was hard to leave. He could grow old, hands splayed on the sandstone balustrade, never moving again – until a postman rode by on his bike and stopped his whistling to call out: 'Hey up, duck! Nice day, in't it?' the tyres crunching gently along under his weight.

Herbert waved, and told himself that all thoughts were irrelevant, that it was what you did that mattered, though if harmony of thought and action was the ideal he must lift up his arms and get back to town, and patiently wait for that blessed state to come full force and take him over, after one last look at the sluggish water of the stream.

He worried about Isaac, and called on him again, thinking that if more than one of the landlord's thugs showed up at the same time he would have a struggle to deal with them. On the way he queued thirty minutes at the coke depot and bought half a hundredweight in a sack borrowed from Mrs Denman's shed.

'They haven't called for some time,' Isaac said, suggesting that his tormentors were either on holiday or occupied with some other elderly tenant. 'Which means, I suppose, that I can expect them any day. I'm ready for them, though.'

Herbert held up his sack.

'What's this, then?'

'I owe yer summat.' More than anyone else, he thought, untwisting the strand of wire from a bundle of sticks and laying them on crumpled paper in the fireplace.

'You don't have to speak the local lingo to me,' Isaac said, holding his hands to flames that waved in the grate.

'I'm practising the accent for when I get a job next week.'

Isaac took books from the table and slotted them in the shelves,

131

then washed his hands at the sink. 'I always thought you were a funny chap.' He pushed his false teeth back to the roof of his mouth. 'I can't think what you'll end up doing with your life.'

'I'll cross that bridge when I come to it, and if I never do, it'll be all right by me.'

'Aren't you going to stop for some tea?'

'No, I'm off to the library for an hour. I'll call in a couple o' days.'

Archie beat a man and his fancywoman to a table, the Peach Tree was crowded as usual. The army diet had thinned him down to a well-toned six-footer, made him healthier than when he'd gone in. His demob leave had started but he was still in uniform. 'There was talk of us staying on because of the Russians trying to grab Berlin. They wouldn't have kept me, though. Not that I hated it any more, but I'd had enough. I spent half my fucking time on jankers this last month. Sometimes I thought I'd ram one up the spout and tek the sergeant-major with me. Even the officers got my number. So no more army for me, unless it's two years on guard outside the Eight Bells with an allowance of ten pints a day and all found. I start back at the factory next week. I've got a nice married woman on the go, so I need to earn some money.'

'There's a little job I want yer ter gi' me a hand with first,' Bert said.

Archie stopped the jar halfway to his mouth. 'Anything, my owd, except I draw the line at robbin' a bank.'

'No, it ain't that yet,' though the adventure of a big snatch and well-managed getaway, all planned to the off-chance of a dropped pin, and no violence unless called for, went through Herbert's mind as a good scheme for a stood-down infantryman, except it would be like the pictures where everything went wrong. He told him about Isaac's trouble with the rent man's bullies. 'All we have to do is be there when they call, and frighten them off, or kick the shit out of them if they don't get the message.'

Archie laughed. 'Yer don't need me. Just show 'em that scar on yer clock, and they'll run away screamin'. Only don't let my new woman see it, or she'll want me to buy one as well. I was frightened to death when I saw it in Cyprus, but I didn't say owt. All yer need now is an eye-patch and a wooden leg. Yer look as if somebody's comin' through that door to get yer, and ye're wonderin' whether to knife 'em or strangle 'em.'

'These are hard men, from what I've heard. It might not be easy.'

'All the better,' Archie said. 'It's at least a month since I 'ad a set-to. I've got itchy knuckles. Is the old man a relation o' yourn?'

'A sort of uncle.'

'That settles it. I'll get bullshitted up for the fray.'

'We'll have another,' Bert said. 'Then we'll do a recce and plan it all out.'

Archie would be posted across the street, and stalk the men two minutes after they'd entered the building. Bert, already in, and waiting at the top of the turning stairs, would have the advantage of height and be hidden from Isaac's door. He and Archie decided to wear their uniforms, on the assumption that a couple of tall swaddies couldn't but seem more threatening to a pair of bastards who had no doubt been deserters all through the war.

'A pincer movement', Archie said, 'by the First Battalion Stalks and Wanks. When's the day?'

'Next Monday, I hear, after the landlord's been for his rent. We'll just go over it again, to mek sure we know our stuff. We won't disturb the old man, though.'

Archie stood to empty his jar. 'I'll be off to see my woman, after that. Her husband's on nights, and I've got to mek hay while the sun shines, though it looks as if it's going to chuck it down in ten minutes.'

Green double-decker buses circled Slab Square, the biggest market place in the country, or so Archie had informed him, as if he had designed and built it himself, or was glad to tell Herbert something he didn't know. Cement block borders lined the pavements and flowerbeds which in springtime blossomed with comic book colours. Archie also told him that if you stood between the lions in front of the Council House for an hour a week everybody who lived in the town would sooner or later pass by.

Not that Herbert wanted to see anyone at all, why he was idling there was hard to say, unless wondering whether to go back to his room, or spend an hour in the library before closing time. He lit a cigarette, envious of people who knew without thinking what to do and where to go. A woman togged up with wire glasses and false teeth, flaunting a gaudy headscarf and puffing a cigarette, dragged a grizzling kid with one hand and bent towards a baby reined into a pushcot with the other. A few paces by, she stopped and backtracked till level with Herbert.

'Oh, so yer've come back, 'ave yer?' She jutted her face at him, speaking with such venom he almost lost balance. 'I'm surprised yo' 'ad the cheek, after all that. I thought I'd seen the last o' yo'. I don't know how you could show your face in this town agen, after the trouble yo' caused.'

'What do you mean?'

'What do you mean what do I mean? I suppose you thought you'd changed so much in three years nobody 'ud reckernize yer? Some bleddy 'opes, mate. I'd know yo' any time, even with that scar down your fancy clock. I expect some 'usband slashed yer. Serves yer right, if he did. He shoulda bleddy killed yer!'

He could only smile, and wonder what villainous sod she had mistaken him for. Maybe she was a bit off her head, or came out every day to pick on someone at random for a bit of fun, and she had fixed on him because he happened to be standing there. Quite an adventure, really. But look affronted, he told himself. Look shocked. Look as if ready to do her in if she doesn't stop her senseless ranting. Look as mortally insulted as you're beginning to feel.

Yet her misery was real, and cut through both the Bert and Herbert layers of who he was. The voice behind the diatribe locked into harmony with her raddled but still young face, and he leaned half fainting against the stone lion. 'Eileen!'

'Oh, so yer know me, do yer? Yer've got my name wrong though, that's all. I'm not Eileen, but I suppose she was just another of the women you took down. I'm Betty, and yer bleddy well know it. Don't even remember my name! That's the bloody limit.'

Thank God for that. She wasn't Eileen. A middle-aged man and woman stopped to enjoy the entertainment. The child in its pushcot tugged and screamed. 'I've no idea who you are,' Herbert said.

'Look at *him*, then' – she jabbed a finger at the kid. 'Go on, look, because he's yourn. I was pregnant when you went off in the army and left me all on my own.'

Unless Eileen's middle name was Betty she was barmy, she had a screw loose, was all he could think. He'd used the best frenchies, and three months had gone by between fucking her and getting on the boat, and she hadn't blabbed a word. If she was Eileen the kid was obviously somebody else's. Even though it couldn't be his he considered taking a quid out of his wallet and pushing it into the child's hand as a gift, but resisted because that would be admitting responsibility. She knew very well it wasn't his, and shouting was her idea of getting a bit of her own back on the world. It was sometimes hard to remember who he had fucked during those heady days when he was seventeen.

He hurried away, and the extra decibels of abuse weren't even muffled by a downburst of rain. The stiff upper lip came in useful, yet he regretted not cursing back even louder. Not to have done so was out of character, or was it? It was always best to give jeeringly better than you got. In the face of injustice you carpet-bombed. If not, you betrayed yourself, and might be sniffed out for who you really were, which might not be altogether a bad thing because then you'd know who you were yourself.

The disturbance brought on hunger, and he sat on a high stool in a milk bar looking at his scarred phizog in the wall mirror while eating a cheese cob. Scarface – no use not liking what he saw. He was lumbered with it. It was totally him, scarred outside and blemished within as well, which he had always known. No hardship living with both as long as he grew to forget them. What's more the face was worth a smile, being accused in no uncertain terms of fathering a bastard. He finished quickly and, back on the road, cut through to the library, hoping to find a seat in the reference section.

He took down a gazetteer with an atlas at the back, but soon got bored thinking of places he would never see. The woman who had assailed him by the lions needed writing about. The incident wouldn't leave him alone, so he unscrewed his pen, opened his notebook to find pages not damp from the rain. She wasn't Eileen, but he made her Eileen so as to see her as more human than the drab with the kid. He wrote until the usher came round at kicking-out time, page after page recording what thoughts she must have had behind the wails of distress. He outlined her appearance, where she lived, and had once worked, and by the time he walked back to his digs she was so real in all dimensions that he no longer needed to feel guilty about her.

Two tall soldiers, buck swaddies bulled up smartly, polished and blancoed and in top fettle, met by the closed door of the Eight Bells. 'Shame it's too early for a pint o' jollop,' Archie said, adjusting his beret.

'Time for one or two when we get back. The place'll be jumping by then.' Bert led the way up Wheeler Gate and by Slab Square, his scar drumming with an ache that had been with him all day, the world on his back seeming a weight too hard to bear even with a grin. Why such a coal-heavy burden he didn't know, though it was a fact that the grub at his digs was worse than in the army, that the backyards stank like shit when people boiled their sprouts, and that he'd seen too many stone-age faces walking the town.

Archie fell into step. 'I didn't get it in last night. You'll never believe this, but Janice's husband – or is she called Janet, I get mixed up sometime – forgot his sandwiches, and the starvo-fuckpig came back for 'em. I just had time to skedaddle out of the front door when we heard the latch go click. Bang went my hearthrug pie. If he'd caught me I'd have slung my boots at him – they were still in my hand. It's left me with a very nasty ache in my fists.'

He positioned himself in a doorway across the street as arranged, while Herbert, back in the mood of a Thurgarton-Strang, and mind emptied but for the prospect of a justified set-to, went quietly up to his place at the top of the stairs. He was concealed, but able to observe Isaac's door through the dusty wooden slats of the banister. He sat on the top step, head almost touching the skylight, though he would make no sound getting to his feet when the time came. He felt as if hidden by a fold in the ground, two people in one body, the mutual antagonism producing a high tension of electricity, so much enclosed force that he was able to wait patiently, calmly, and without regard to time.

A bird hit the grimy glass and went like a falling aeroplane across the street to make an emergency landing on the opposite ledge. He smiled when the two men began to climb the stairs, their laughter sufficient to cover the sound of his standing up.

The tall thin man in front wore a raglan overcoat, open to show a three-piece suit. A close-eyed expression of anxiety could look menacing to anyone he wanted to frighten. I'll call him Dandyman, Herbert decided. 'It's time we chucked a few of his things out o' the winder.'

They didn't care who heard. 'I'm game. One bash and the door's in. The gaffer wain't pay us if we don't do it this time.' Herbert dubbed him as Beer-barrel, middle height and stocky, looking feckless but confident at the job in hand. First across the landing, he sent a solid kick at the door. 'Come out then, Dad. We know you're in there.'

'You've no right to come here,' Isaac called through the door. 'I pay my rent.'

'No right!' They laughed at that. 'We'll show you what rights are.'

'I've got a butcher's knife,' Isaac shouted, in the voice of a much younger man. 'The first one through that door gets it in the stomach.'

Herbert almost laughed. Isaac was too peaceable even to think of such a weapon, so his bluff would be no good. The others thought so even more.

'He's bluffin',' Beer-barrel said, loud enough for Isaac to hear behind his door.

'You just try. I'll cut you to pieces.'

Bert, recalling his purpose on being there, clattered down the stairs and shouted in his roughest voice to Isaac, heightened by as much as could be mustered of a sergeant-major's parade-ground bellow: 'Yer don't need to do that. I'll tek care on 'em.'

He stood two steps above, outlined against the skylight. He was tempted to laugh, but that would mean ruination of the scheme, so kept a sharp rein on Dandy the hard man, fixing them. The beret folded into the shoulder strap of his battledress might have told them he was out for business, as should the long scar turning

137

more livid at his face. 'Get back to where you come from, and leave him alone. He's my uncle. We aren't looking for trouble, but if you don't clear off I'll put your arses where yer fuckin' 'eads should be, and yer'll never know what kicked 'em,' a threat heard from one man to another at the factory gate.

'It's like that then, is it?' Dandyman turned to Beer-barrel. 'Come on, Charlie.' They turned to go, but it was the oldest ruse in the world. Any actor could spot that retreat wasn't in their faces. Charlie Beer-barrel turned, and came on like a cannonball in a hurry. Bert's shining boot caught him full smack at the shoulder, while his fist at the face of Dandyman was dodged. Then Bert had something to avoid but didn't.

Dandyman came forward, and lightning was only just good enough. There were no rules as in boxing at school. This was behind-the-garden-shed stuff. Fighting dirty, filling the gap between Herbert and Bert, he used his soul's venom to smash father, mother, schoolmasters, shitbag officers and gaffers, even the old clergyman who had given him money.

Dandyman was no fool, and Herbert felt a blow, staggered, then Dandyman was pulled from behind by gleeful Archie and belly thumped, doubled up and breathless, to the landing below.

'We know who yer are now.' Bert drove Beer-barrel with a few aimed punches at the chest to join Dandyman. 'Cum 'ere again, and yer number's up. We know where you live, and what pubs yer get pissed in.'

'I ain't had enough yet.' Archie stroked one fist with another, but they gave no reason for him to have more, and his face looked even uglier, a self-defeating expression he could do nothing about. All in all it was still only a scrap rather than a real fight. 'I'd know 'em anywhere, though. Two ragbags from Sneinton.'

Isaac, sensing the fracas was finished, opened his door and came on to the stairs holding a large black-handled two-foot butcher's knife. 'I appreciate what you've done, but they would have got this if they'd come in and I'd been on my own. Nobody persecutes me and gets away with it.'

Archie laughed. 'Nar, Dad, yer can put that away. It's only fists they appreciate. Next time they'll gerra real pastin'!'

'Now you know the score,' Bert told them. 'So fuck off, and pick on somebody else.'

Beer-barrel had given up, but Dandyman, an eye bruised and his overcoat torn, was about to say something. He caught sight of Archie's moiling fist and thought better of it. They weren't in the game for a fight to the finish.

Bert and Archie followed them to Slab Square, then turned downwind for the Eight Bells. 'Are you all right, then?'

'One of 'em got me in the ribs,' Bert said, 'but all I need is a drop o' Shippoe's oil. Then I've got summat to tell yer.'

When they were seated by their drinks Archie asked what it was. 'But let me sink this pint, and then I'll listen.'

'I was standing by the lions the other day and this tart I thought was Eileen started yammering at me. At least I think it was Eileen. I couldn't be sure. She said one of the kids she'd got with her was mine.'

Archie leaned back, laughing. 'Yer'll have to get used to things like that. It 'appens all the time. If it *was* Eileen, though, she must a bin having yer on. Our Janet says it was Pete Scrimthorpe who knocked her up. Then Jack Wiley married her. He's as happy as a pig in shit, Jack is. Thinks the kid's 'is. Everybody knows except 'im, the dozy bleeder. I expect somebody'll tell 'im one of these days, and then he'll cut 'is throat. Or he'll 'ang issen in the shed to save shittin' on the carpet.' He blew smoke rings towards the bar, unable to hold down his merriment. 'On the other 'and, the kid could be yourn.'

''Ow do yer mek that out?' he asked, putting on as near a smirk as he could manage. He wondered what went on in Archie's mind: only what you heard and what you saw gave any clue. No cunning, subterfuge, or power of ratiocination, that's what he loved about him. But Archie leaned close. 'Well, you know them frenchies our Raymond lets me have? A couple of his pals at the cleaning factory got their tarts in the family way, so one day a chap blew one of 'em up, and saw pin-holes all over the place. Nearly killed our poor fucking Raymond. Some wicked bastard must have known what was going on, but fancy playing a trick like that. You was in the army by then, but you might 'ave 'ad one o' the early models. It's like that old joke, about a scaffolder putting up some big name, letter by letter at the

139

top of a building. Well, 'e slips, don't 'e? And falls through the big letter O and gets killed. There was a joke and it ended summat like: "He went as he came, through the 'ole in a letter!" So let's drink to it, Dad!'

Bert laughed, to show that such humour was right up his street. The publican looked up at the noise of two local swaddies of the same tribal family on a night out that promised to be very good for trade.

Eleven

Drills, milling machines and lathes buggered the hands back to what could only be regarded as normal: calloused, scarred, yet each day becoming more flexible for work. In cap, jacket and overalls he jinked his way along cobbled streets, or swerved around corners on his bike, to gaol himself at his appointed spot and be lost in nobody's aura but his own, except at tea break and dinner hour. Bashing out energetically on piece rate, his earnings climbed in a few weeks to give a Friday pay packet nicely padded with a dozen pound notes and a few bits of change.

Sweat was cheap at the price but he worked with dogged contentment, no truck nowadays with the darts or any other team. He could laughingly tell people to all but piss off without fear any more of giving himself away or being thought stand-offish. He was an old hand again.

In the evening after a wash and his sit-down tea he went upstairs and beamed light on to the mirror. With scrubbed fingernails, a fresh handkerchief and bottle of TCP he cleared whatever blackheads had formed on cheeks and temples from too long standing in an atmosphere of suds and metal dust. The fight against spotted skin was never-ending.

As a pastime it amused him to scribble whatever came to mind about people at the work place, easier when feeling clean. He unscrewed his pen and hovered it over lined paper, never able to decide on the exact moment it started to move, nor why. A few pages took on the shape of a story, till he felt like a spy in wartime France collating reports on resistance and the moral state of the inhabitants, certainly fancied himself at this early stage as an observer, perhaps the smaller part of himself, looking on the world from the outside. It was the ideal viewpoint from which to write, and if he didn't sit down every night or two with his pen the factory existence would become so intolerable he would have to flee from it.

The effort of staying in a situation he didn't altogether want (only to avoid one even worse – though he couldn't imagine what that might be) led him to try thinking clearly in the hope of finding an answer as to why he must ask the question at all. The result was that there were no answers, only thoughts that chased each other around in the same circle. The inner strength of his upbringing sustained him in the way of life he had chosen, so he must resist abandoning the factory for fear of turning into a faceless deadbeat shambling from place to place for the rest of his life. Happy or not, it didn't matter, as long as he could tolerate the present, live from day to day, become stable and content, and carry on as if working in the factory and living at Mrs Denman's was half his natural state, the other part putting up with what he had become, looking on it with tolerance and, when necessary, keeping an excess in check.

Existence was easy when such brooding spared him. At dinnertime he would finish his sandwiches and guzzle off his tea in ten minutes and, if the pavement was dry, spread a *Daily Mirror* to sit on, and lean against the factory wall with the latest Penguin or Everyman classic. Cap low over his eyes, a posture in no way strange for a workman, he opened the book so as to hold it in one hand, and read till the hooter called him in at two to continue the day's stint.

Wood from packing cases splintered in the factory yard was sometimes thrown aside as scrap, so he tied up a bundle and took it home as kindling for Mrs Denman. Another time he humped a load through town for Isaac, and on his way a man asked where he'd got it, wanting to buy some himself, for the air was icy, and fuel of any sort hard to find.

Isaac wore leather gloves, a trilby hat, and a heavy woollen scarf inside his overcoat. 'My last lumps o' coal went yesterday, but it's not the end of the world, to be without a bit of fire.'

'Gorra chopper?' Bert split the wood into smaller pieces on the landing. The room was cubby enough to warm quickly, and with cigarettes on the go as well he asked if there'd been any more bother from the landlord's men.

'I ain't heard a dicky-bird. Seems you and your friend discouraged them. In fact a woman from the Council was here yesterday, and said there's a chance of me getting a small flat, with central heating. It might not happen for ten years or so because of the housing list. But I appreciate her giving me something to look forward to.'

'Sounds good.'

'Doesn't it? I might even be sorry to leave the old den.'

Bert slung his nub end into the embers, and split more wood for another transitory blaze. 'I've got to scram, or I'll be late for my tea. Mrs Denman don't like to be kept waiting with her burnt offerings.'

'Just a moment, then.' Isaac turned to the bookshelf. 'Perhaps you'd like to read these. I've been meaning to give you them.'

'Dickens?'

'They'll keep you going for a bit, *Our Mutual Friend* and *Bleak House*. Come back if you want any more. I don't suppose you read such entertaining novels at your posh school.'

'We had Kipling, and Rider Haggard, and all that stuff. Not that I didn't think they were wonderful, especially Kipling. Hard to remember some of them, but they kept me going at times. We mostly had the classics rammed down our throats, and I'm glad we did.'

Isaac rummaged further along the shelf. 'Take this Bible. It's a Jewish one, without the New Testament, as your sort call it. Stick your nose into it whenever you get the urge. They could write sublimely in King James's time.'

He needn't return the favour of the firewood, but always did in some way, so it would be churlish to say more than: 'Are you sure?'

'They're not things I'm short of, as you can see. When I first came here I had a bit of extra cash, so splashed out at the secondhand place down Wheeler Gate.'

Herbert sat again. His supper could wait. Generosity of spirit, one of Isaac's built-in virtues, was to be marvelled at. A smile and a mordant few words might be the response if he mentioned it, but Herbert still thought it a miracle that he had been rescued by him that first fateful night in Nottingham. The more time passed the less the event receded, came starkly into focus in fact, distilling juvenile horror and despair at the idea of Isaac having been absent from the pub that evening. 'How did you come to live in a place like this?'

His smile was of the wryest, hiding a more bitter response perhaps. Wrong again, Herbert heard:

'Like all long stories it can be told in a few words. My wife died, after twenty years of marvellous devotion, on both sides. It was quite sudden, and when she went I wanted to, as well. But I couldn't commit the ultimate sin of suicide.'

Herbert nodded towards the framed photograph on the bookshelf: a placid yet vulnerable face, dark hair drawn back from pale cheeks. Thin lips fixed in a half-smile suggested she endured life rather than lived it. 'Is that her?'

Isaac indicated that it was, as if to speak would bring tears. 'I took to the road. Gave up job, house, family, everything. It was just before the war, and I was on the tramp for two years. I went as far down as any man can, or so I thought. Up in Scotland I was taken into prison for vagrancy, but an elderly chap on the street, who saw me marched off, came to the court and handed in the ten-pound fine, saving me fourteen days in prison. Who he was I'll never know. He just saw me, and did it. Scottish, Protestant, I suppose, and charitable. Can you beat that? It brought me back to my senses, and I went down to London, to my daughter's. She wanted me to live with her, and I did for a while, but I couldn't get on with her husband. When I left she gave me some money, and I ended up in this place. I've been here nearly ten years, and don't think I've ever been happier. I like being alone, and I manage with my pension. It's surprising how little you need living on your own. She sends me a quid or two now and again, for they're doing quite well. Keeps promising to come up and see me, but I put her off.'

True, it wasn't so bad. A lot of people put up with worse. You could call Isaac lucky, living absolutely the way he liked. Herbert thought that if he could afford to give up factory work he would be happy to pass his time reading, or cycling, or walking the town, and writing when he felt like it. Such a dream life would need a few hundred pounds a year to bring off in comfort, however, because Isaac's near poverty wasn't at all to his liking.

His jacket soaked by driving sleet, he held the books close to his chest to keep them dry. Mrs Denman grumbled at the late hour but laid out a supper of warmed-up Spam fritters and fried potatoes. 'You don't look after yourself. See how wet through you are.'

Never speak with food in your mouth. But he was famished, and being Bert he could say so what to manners. 'It wasn't raining when I went out.'

She reached up to the mantelpiece. 'This came for you today.'

His mother's writing, not the first letter asking him to visit them in Norfolk. He knew he should call, but didn't care to squander a weekend. What would he have to talk to them about, in any case? Everything they would say to him he already knew, or thought he did, and his temper was too short these days to do much listening.

'If I got a letter,' Mrs Denman said, 'I'd open it straightaway.'

He didn't want to snap back and offend her. 'I know who it's from.'

'I dare say you do. Your parents, I suppose, like all the others.'

'They want me to go and see them.'

'I'm sure they deserve it. Don't you want to make 'em happy?'

'I'm not sure I would.' She was more than right, and her advice softened his feeling of being pestered by their letters, though he hoped she would now keep quiet about it, for if he felt too guilty he might tell her to mind her own business. 'I will one day.'

As if knowing his thoughts, she altered tack in any case. 'You look like a drowned rat. I'll light the geyser so's you can have a hot bath and get warm.'

Splashing in the carbolic steam he wondered where Isaac went for the same luxury. Always clean and dapper, he must use the public baths. He lifted himself out and got dry, putting on two jerseys to face the room. Supper weighed heavily as he closed the door, and drank the mug of tea from Mrs Denman before cold reached its core.

Flakes spinning down the panes in slow Catherine wheels seemed to have eyes that looked at him, so he drew the blanket-like curtains, and lit a cigarette to warm the end of his nose, or staunch the mucus trying to fall from it. He'd had more colds than he could count since leaving Cyprus. Questions as to what he was doing here only came at such times of reflection, and even though unanswerable he supposed they were necessary for what he wanted to do.

Bert's life had to be written about, and that was a fact, but it could only be done when he said bollocks to questions and side-stepped into being Herbert, the query ritually answered on setting himself at the table to begin an inky scrawl across the page. Herbert and Bert were two ends of a magnet, each competing for the iron filings of other people's misadventures. One end of the horseshoe had to be Bert, but the other was labelled Herbert so as to make the style clear, and in the hard body of the metal they became one, and words meshed craftily to make sense of the story.

He was closed into a baffle of Third Programme music – anything classical would do – from his fifty-bob secondhand wireless. Archie connected the transformer and fixed an aerial out of the top bedroom window, on a pole that pointed like a finger at the sky as if hoping to draw nothing but the best from God. Music was both an inspiration and a screen, sounds to be enjoyed but for his mind to fight against, the balance opening a space for whatever came.

'You write because you didn't want to perish,' he put into his notebook. 'Dreams and fantasies hold back spiritual disintegration.' Pegging dreams into the logic of reality was as much a part of him as it must be with others. Everyone working in a factory was afflicted by dead limbs at the end of the day, and the only way to know the extent of this was by working there yourself; impossible to write about it except by turning into one of those people and doing it.

He was split in two, like that great sphere dividing one half from the other in the old nightmare of infancy. Somewhere spinning and dispensing terror, the trail it left provided a light and showed which words to write and what yarn to spin. After a few pages the impulse burned itself out, and all he could do was go down to the warm kitchen and smoke his last cigarette of the day, bent into a calamitous state of exhaustion.

Mrs Denman, her bed-time curlers in, sat by the fading coal to sip her night-owl coffee, as she called it. 'I don't know what you do in your room all these hours.'

What did she think, in her secret heart? Wank himself to a cinder? 'I read.'

'You must be freezing. Why don't you do it down here, or in the parlour with an electric heater?'

He wanted to be in his own four walls, with the door shut, private, often not aware of the cold. She was used to his silence at her questions, thinking him a funny lad, but then, weren't they all at that age, come to that? 'I'll mek yer a nice mug o' cocoa, so at least you'll go warm to bed.'

You had to say something to show thanks at such concern, whether you believe it or not. 'I don't know what I'd do without you, Ma!'

'Ah, well, somebody's got to look after you, since you can't seem to do it yourself, working all day in that factory. Not that I don't know why not. But it's allus bin like that, and allus will be, I suppose.'

He wasn't unhappy, languishing under her platitudes like the helpless booby he knew he was not. It was the role of the common workman to accept it as his due.

'You should go out more,' she said. 'Find a nice young woman.'

The response to such concern should be to reach out and squeeze her hand, with the jocular remark: 'Nar, I've got yo', ain't I, me duck?' – but he could only say: 'I'll have to see about that.'

'You ought to go and visit your parents, at least. It's a shame to lose touch. You might need 'em one day. It'd do you good to be away for a weekend, anyway.'

''Appen it would,' he said.

Feet up on the range after the day's sweat, just as he'd thought his metamorphosis to a workman was as complete as it could be, he reached for Mrs Denman's *Evening Post* and saw that a public lecture was to be given at the Mechanics Institute by the author W. J. Hawksworth, winner of last year's Windrush Prize. A little gingering of the intellect might improve his perceptions in general, though he was doubtful that such testing would occur. In Cyprus he had taken Hawksworth's *Glebe Farm* from the camp library, telling about a woman who had to run farm and family on her own because her husband had gone off to the war. A third the way through he left it on his bed to go for a shower, and came back to find it nicked, which led him to believe it may have been better than he'd thought, but a few days later the book was back on his bed, and pencilling on the inside cover said: 'Bloody trash.' Herbert had to agree with this criticism, and didn't go on to finish it. Still, even a mediocre novelist might be amusing to listen to.

Midweek or not, the occasion called for a more than thorough wash and shave at the bathroom sink. He put on his best shirt, cursing the recalcitrant collar studs and cuff-links, which wouldn't go through the holes made too stiff by starch. Buttoning the mackintosh over his best suit he walked up the street and leapt on a trackless into town.

He spotted a chair near the back of the packed hall, on the edge of a row. A youngish woman beside him had dark ringletty hair and a thin face, all that he could see of her before the curtain opened on W. J. Hawksworth sitting at a table on stage. A man to his left talked a few minutes about how good Hawksworth's novels were. So many people loved them because they could see themselves mirrored in the characters he wrote so well about. Not the fucking people I know, Bert said to himself.

Hawksworth twiddled a watch chain across his waistcoat, touched up his grey crinkly hair. The human pen was nervous at least and, glad to hear the last of his introducer, he got up as if it was the last thing in the world he wanted to do.

Herbert noticed that one of his legs was twitching, out of nervousness, or exhaustion, or from too much booze, though perhaps it was to put rhythm into his cadenced and well-rehearsed sentences. Hawksworth went on for nearly an hour about how he had become a novelist, told them how he wrote (he held up his fountain pen), what his first story had been about (himself), explained that he was careful to type all manuscripts neatly (double-spaced with twenty-five lines to a page), and expatiated on how he had sent the first stories out to various magazines (with stamped self-addressed envelopes for their possible return). He then sat down to wait.

The stories came back but, playing ducks and drakes with them (his phrase) he skimmed them out once more on their travels. One was accepted and published. Encouraged by this (and the sum of five pounds) he wrote a novel, and he described the process of doing that as well, detailing the work stage by stage, almost thought by thought until, like a car being bodged to life at a garage by a totally incompetent mechanic listening to 'Music While You Work' on full blast, he knew it was fit to face the world. Or he hoped so. The book was turned down half a dozen times, but eventually someone had the good sense to see what a talented work it was for a young man of twenty-five, and a lifetime of producing novels began. He went on to talk about the great modern novelists such as Waugh, Forster, Huxley, D. H. Lawrence and Graham Greene, implying that it wasn't necessary to add before such an intelligent and discriminating audience that he was one of them. He's an old ham, Herbert thought. He must have given this talk dozens of times already. The woman by his side was writing notes, and between gales of splintered clapping at the end Herbert asked if she was reporting the lecture for a newspaper.

Her laugh was the kind of merry expressive tune he couldn't remember when he'd heard last. Perhaps she was flattered, but had to say no. 'I want to remember some of the wonderful things he came out with. I love all his books.'

He was careful to assume the sort of accent a local worthy and not a factory worker would use. 'My favourite is *Glebe Farm*. I couldn't put it down.'

'Well, it's good but have you read *Bird of Paradise*?'

'No.'

'Or *Life on the Heaviside Layer*?'

He made space for her through the crowd on the institute steps. 'I've been trying to get that one for months, but it's never on the shelves.'

'What about *Never Say Never*?' she asked. 'Have you read that?' She knew them all. 'He's written a lot. There's *Fires of Love, The Far Side of Heaven, The Lady from Leatherhead*.'

'I'll get them as soon as I can.'

'You must. He's so good. Better than J. B. Priestley.'

They walked slowly, crossing the road at the lights. She must have read all twenty. Or was it forty? He agreed that W. J. Hawksworth was a great writer, and would she like to go into a coffee bar where they could talk about him some more? Maybe she was married, but he thought her too special to worry about that. Anyway, he couldn't see a ring.

Her yes encouraged him to think that he interested her. The dragon hiss of jets steamed from behind the counter, and to see her shapely little nose twitching at the reek of bacon cobs told him it was an unusual place for her, which was even more promising. The cream silk scarf at the opening of her white blouse made it hard to gauge the size of her breasts, or even their shape. He also noted her soft suede gloves and leather handbag, as well as her fashionable New Look coat, and stylish shoes. Who, he wondered, did she think she had taken up with?

After his working day, and the effort of absorbing all that might be useful from Hawksworth's chatter, he was happy to let her continue with glistening eyes about novels he would never read while there was still so much good stuff to catch up on. At a convenient break he stretched his hand across the table. 'I'm Herbert Gedling, by the way.'

She unravelled thin fingers from the coffee mug to brush a ringlet off her cheek. 'I'm Cecilia Colston. But how did you get that scar?' – as if it was something to pity him for. 'I'm dying to know.'

'Cyprus, in the army.'

'Were you wounded?'

'A piece of shrapnel got me from a bomb. I looked up too soon.'

She said what a pity, and asked in the same breath where he worked. He told her. 'In the offices?'

'If you like.' Let her sort it out. She was puzzled, for he could have sworn she caught a whiff of disinfectant suds. You were never free of it, even after a bath. 'And where do *you* work?'

'At Clapton's, the solicitors.'

'In the office?' Giving no time for an answer he said: 'I've done some writing of my own. Just bits of things. Stories, a few of them, or near enough.'

'So that's why you came tonight?'

He nodded.

'You want to be a writer?'

'I don't know. I just scribble a bit. A sort of hobby, you might say.'

'You're too modest.'

'I don't know about that,' not caring what the penpusher thought. The tightrope of his deception swayed, till he resumed full control.

'Descriptions of people,' he said when she asked what they do with their lives.'

'Can I read some?'

'More coffee? Sometime, maybe.'

She indicated no, brown eyes looking as if to find out more about him than even he could possibly tell. He met her gaze unblinking, knowing that since it wasn't done, not in her terms, to get her under the table and fuck her there and then, as Bert might try, or at least Archie would, he'd have to stare her haughtily down as Herbert, and take the risk of her getting up to walk out. It was evidently the right way to behave, and when she looked down he knew he would have her sooner or later if – as Bert would say – he played his cards right. 'I'll find some pages to show you.' He remembered Hawksworth's advice. 'They're not typed yet. I don't have a typewriter.'

'Well,' she said, 'you'll have to buy one, won't you?' – as if they grew on trees, all waiting to be plucked as she was plucking down Herbert's heart, nuances he detected with no bother. He'd never thought of becoming a real writer but if by pretending to be one he could get more quickly into her New Look knickers he would take on such a role any day.

Twelve

The train puffed and banged its way along the track out of Norwich. He seemed to have been travelling all day, but it was only a few minutes after noon. Mrs Denman had packed him off with enough food to get him to the South Pole and back. 'All that way? You'll be hungry. I would be. As soon as the train's over Trent Bridge I have to eat a sandwich.'

Why his parents had cut themselves off in this remote corner of Norfolk he couldn't think. Nottingham was a metropolis, and he felt vulnerable as the line descended the valley of the Yare. More like the *yawn*. He closed the map.

Still, he felt something pleasing in the landscape, as if he'd been here before. Perhaps in another life he had. His mother's lot came from this way, likewise old Uncle Richard at Malvern who gave him the pound notes that paid for his escape from school.

As the train turned northerly he felt human again, more relaxed than in Nottingham. Being on the move was what did it, but he didn't trust such a feeling of wellbeing. He liked it, but something was wrong. The man opposite looked at him too closely. Herbert thought that if he had a knife he would aim the point at his throat. Such a lunatic picture forced his gaze out of the window.

Woods and fields were soothing, though why should he struggle to stay calm? Small motor boats lined the river, and he imagined living on one. Any small cabin would do, equipped with books, some food, and lots of fags. In the evening he would find a snug pub and drink himself into a haze before weaving back to the boat for what sleep he could get.

He didn't know why he was on the train, felt unstable, free-floating

152

in a way he didn't like. The man opposite – stout, rubicund, tie bowing out of a Fair Isle sweater, wearing a hacking jacket, gleaming brown brogues, and with half a whistle on his stupid lips, which might any minute turn menacing – seemed too interested in Herbert's state of mind, which Bert thought was none of his fucking business. 'Why are you looking at me like that?'

The man smiled, for want of anything else appropriate in such a situation. 'Looking at you?'

'Yes, me.'

He had what Herbert supposed was an East Anglican accent. 'I wasn't.'

'You were.'

'I was looking out of the window, since you want to know.' He was being friendly, which made his former attitude insulting. 'Not much to see, though, is there? It gets even less picturesque soon, depending on your point of view.'

Herbert heard himself, saw his own face from the opposite seat (though not as accurately as in a mirror, and even that couldn't be an exact image) was unable to hold back: 'You were staring at me.' He was afraid, couldn't stop his useless twaddle, felt sweat on his forehead. The words cartwheeled out, words nevertheless precious because he had to stand by them, back them up loyally though he couldn't think what with.

'I really wasn't.' It was the man's turn to be afraid, locked in a compartment with no way out except on to the line and break a leg. 'I never stare at people.'

'You were staring at me.' Stop it, stop this, he told himself. What's happening to you? He heard the voice from a distance, looked at the man, but couldn't stop the voice even when trying to nail his mind into place with thoughts of Cecilia. He'd see her again soon: easy to get Colston's number from the book.

'I know you were looking at me.' That's enough, then. But it wasn't. Cecilia faded. He couldn't get her coat off nor her blouse. 'I'm a stranger in the land.' Why did he say that? But it prevented him saying any more for the moment.

The man hoped to head off another barmy accusation: 'That church over there is Westwick.'

'I dare say it is.'

'Are you going to Cromer?'

Perhaps there was a lunatic asylum there, and he was coming back from leave. His mother had died and they'd let him go to the funeral. 'What's that to you?'

'None at all, I know.'

Herbert was calm, the storm gone. What was that all about? Why had he terrorized the poor bloke? He was afraid, wouldn't let it happen again. 'I'm going to Worstead.'

'Next stop, then.' The man smiled, his best news of the day. 'You'll be there in a few minutes.'

A series of white humpbacked clouds formed an escort to the road. Herbert hurried towards the village, needing a drink to drown the Devil within. Something had got into him today, and he prayed the pub would be open. The lane followed the railway line a few hundred yards before turning east. At not quite two o'clock he saw the pub near the church.

He carried his beer to a table by the window, away from the clutter of people at the bar. They were expecting him for lunch, but he couldn't care less. Didn't they realize how many changes of train he'd made to get there? He was more tired than if he had been at work, the scar sore, and thought that everyone stared at his Cain's mark. In Nottingham he would have punched them in the face, but then, they didn't stare at you in Nottingham. Or they did it when you couldn't possibly notice. They knew the consequences. He went to the bar, and asked the way to the Old Hall.

Another mile. The autumnal grass smelled sweet. A pigeon on a gate post rattled away as if aware of his murderous thoughts. Beyond the last house of the village, forking left between the fields, the east wind drove at his face. An isolated cloud was flying by, tatterdemalion white against surrounding blue, heading for companionship towards a more solid bank in the west.

Blue vetch half hidden in the hedge. No other person in sight, his freedom was threatening, too much like isolation, no compensation for the effort of going forward. He thought of his room at Mrs Denman's, and peace when sitting at his table to read or write, wondering why he had put himself beyond its range. The factory, even more protective, was pushed out of mind to avoid sprinting back for the train on hearing its whistle.

The words 'Old Hall' on the five-barred gate at the end of the gravelled drive had once been white but were now half-covered with mildew. Getting too old to keep the place in order. He lifted the latch and jammed the gate back against the bayleaf bush, leaving it wide open for a quick escape. A few sheep ran from the fence on either side, and in the garden area before the house his father poked a hoe into a flowerbed. He must have heard my footsteps. Or maybe the man at the pub had phoned to say I was on my way. Or the man on the train had called from the crackers hospital in Cromer.

'Herbert!'

'Hello, Father.' He put out a hand, but Hugh pulled him forward. 'I'm glad to see you, my boy, very glad.' He was strong, and bony, and reeked of the tobacco he began loading into his curved pipe. 'We did hope you'd get here for lunch. Couldn't wait, though, or it would have gone cold. It was a leg of best lamb – mint sauce and all the trimmings. Your mother had Mrs Sewell cook it. Still, there's plenty left. We even put out a bottle of wine, though there's beer if you want it.'

Hugh changed from boots to shoes in the conservatory. 'I wanted to visit you in Nottingham but your mother said you wouldn't like that, though she needed to see you more than I did. She seems to know you better.'

Herbert felt horror at the notion of such a visit: 'This is my landlady, Mrs Denman. She mothers me a bit too much, I'm afraid. And this is Frank, her fancyman. Yes, it is a small room, but it's all I need to sleep in, and when I come back from the factory, or totter up to bed half-drunk on a Saturday night. I'm sorry, Mother, but for that you'll have to go downstairs and across the yard.' 'It wouldn't have been a good idea.'

'Why ever not?'

'I only have one room, and it's hardly the place to entertain anyone, believe me.'

'That's nonsense, and you know it. I wouldn't have cared if you were living in a cave. You should have seen some of the mud holes I had to live in for weeks at a time in Burma. If my mother had been able to call on me I'd have welcomed her with open arms! You're a grown responsible man from a good family, and you know perfectly well how to go on.'

The row had started earlier than expected, his father wanting to bluster him into the ground. Herbert felt awe, even a shameless fear, stepping back to knock against a column of telescoped plant pots. He straightened them. Bert gave Herbert a nudge, stiffened him not to be afraid of the old bastard, told him he could even be conciliatory. He envied Archie having a father who didn't know when he was coming out of the army. 'I'll get a flat soon, then it'll be marvellous for both of you to come and see me.'

'That'll be a move in the right direction.'

Herbert looked at him, getting towards seventy, frailer perhaps than he thought himself to be. It wouldn't do to feel pity, though a tinge went through him, and straight out again. Better if they were to go into the house where his mother might soften their talk, but Hugh stood upright among the potted plants and puffed away as if to gas them both with his smoke. 'We don't see you from one year's end to another, and I know your mother suffers from it. She doesn't say so, but when she suffers so do I, which is totally unnecessary.'

A knife for cutting string lay on the slatted table, and Herbert turned his eyes away, disturbed at such a murderous thought. His father only missed him because his mother did. If she wanted to call on him alone in Nottingham it would be all right, though the thought of them walking up Mrs Denman's staircase was intolerable. He re-harnessed his self-control. 'I'm sorry about that.'

'Well, never mind. Let's go in. You didn't come here to cross swords with me.'

He should have expected they would be more concerned about him in their retirement, been old enough to realize their cloying wishes for his wellbeing, but if guilt was all they could make him feel they could get stuffed, especially when Maud showed him to a large room on the first floor looking across the paddock and orchard, a vague hint of metallic sea in the distance.

He took in the commodious luxury, the perfect appointments of a double bed, a wardrobe, two tables, an armchair, a large sink with steel taps, and heavy pelmetted drapes to close off the world, as well as a bathroom for himself alone next door. 'It's yours, whenever you come to see us, though we'd like you to live in it all the time, no questions asked. Me and your father have talked about it. We'd make you an allowance. And if you want to cut yourself off I can get an electrician to put in a kettle. You'd be quite cosy in here. I know you would be.'

It was the ideal refuge, perfect and long wanted. 'Thank you, Mother.' He could sit in peace and write, totally cared for while heaping up the pages of a novel. 'Scribbled much today, you dark horse?' one of them would enquire, not knowing that the other had said the same an hour ago. He would be an infant again, till they arranged for men in white coats to come one morning and cart him off. You only went home again when you died, not at twenty-five. So the room wasn't for him. Nor could it ever be, with his parents so close. Would Isaac have called him a fool to refuse? No doubt about it, but a fool was always the master of two imperfect worlds, saw neither clearly but survived the perils of both. 'I'll be going back tomorrow.'

She sat on the bed. 'Oh, Herbert, so soon?'

'I must be at work on Monday morning.' He hardened himself against her wanting to make him cry tears of chagrin for the way the trap was closing. If he stayed an extra twenty-four hours he might hang on forever, and the thought made him so blindingly angry that he had to fight off his berserker mood. Easy. Huge efforts were no efforts at all, but the minor annoyances were dangerous.

'But why do you work in a factory, Herbert? I don't understand it.'

He preferred to pity her rather than shout, which made him say, the first time loud and clear to anyone but himself: 'I'm thinking of writing a novel about it.'

'Ah! I see.' The knowing smile told him he'd said exactly what would satisfy her. A report of it might even mollify his father, which made him regret having spoken, since he didn't know whether he would ever be able to make the claim good. Lying to make someone happy was a crude ploy, and he wished it unsaid. If he didn't want it to be a lie he would have to write the bloody book, which would give them some control over his future. He wouldn't put up with that.

157

Only if they were dead could he follow his path with a quiet mind, but they seemed so full of life he was sure they would live forever.

'And after you've written it?'

He laughed, glad now that the idea had shot up from more or less nowhere, while knowing there could be no such place. 'No use thinking about that. It takes years to write a book. A good one, anyway. Another thing', he went on, 'is that I'm working in a factory because I feel easy being among machines. It's my métier, it seems.'

'I've always loved machines as well,' she said, 'right from when my father bought his first motor car. I still tinker when I can. If the lawnmower goes bang it's always me who mends it. I suppose that's where you get your fascination from, which is very gratifying. I understand perfectly well but, all the same . . .'

They were so close in spirit that she knew when to stop talking, and he realized how pleasant it was to be with someone who sensed your thoughts as much as you were aware of theirs. 'Let's go down and have tea.' She sprang from the bed like a girl of twenty. 'Your father likes it exactly at four, and so do I. Mustn't disappoint him.'

'I have to wash off the grime of travel first.' He loved her now, with no vicious afterthoughts, and gave her a few minutes to go down and repeat what he had said to his father so that there would be less pain and mystery as to why he had immersed himself in a factory, though he hoped they would not make his stay comfortable enough for him to regret leaving.

There were so many flowers surrounding the Old Hall that, looking down from the window, their various scents and colours – bees working among roses, honeysuckle, lupins and bougainvillaea, and many whose names he didn't know – gave the impression of being in a vast undertaker's parlour.

He wanted the visit to be over, though couldn't decently depart for another twenty-four hours. Every minute was torment, and ought not to be, he knew, if only he could learn to accept being there. It was hard not to look every few minutes at his watch. This itching to get clear, to flee along the lanes and back to the train, was against his deeper grain, an unnecessary burden, and especially irritating since the St Vitus yen existed only on the surface, a weak mesh of impulses dominating the stronger part of him which was capable of enjoying the stay and being made much of. If they hadn't been his parents the problem wouldn't exist, and anger at the inability to overcome his aversion made it even more difficult to do so.

Having recognized his disorder he went downstairs feeling more calm, yet was embarrassed at the homely and affectionate way they were so absolutely at ease with one another, at seeing how his father adored his mother, and she him, as if they had met only weeks ago. After tea in the lounge Maud said: 'I do wish you wouldn't puff all the time at that pipe, my dear.'

Hugh reached over to smooth her wrist, and gave a great laugh. 'When I give up smoking, my love, call in the doctor, though there won't be much he can do for me then.'

'And Herbert's smoking, too.'

'So I notice.' Hugh winked at his son. 'I have a couple of cigars for us to demolish after dinner, the last of my Burma cheroots. I came back with boxes and boxes. Then again, though, there are those Havanas you found for me last Christmas.'

'Oh, so I did.' She smiled.

Herbert, remembering, took a piece of orange cleaning cloth from his jacket pocket and unwrapped a highly polished brass lighter. 'I meant to give you this, Father, a present I cobbled together at my machine in the factory.'

Hugh rolled it over in his big hand and then, flame first time. His features gave off a mischievous flicker at Herbert's siding with him against Maud. 'You made it all on your own?'

'Absolutely.'

'Beautiful. A bespoke lighter. I shall treasure it.' He pressed it twice more to get a flame, before slipping it into his waistcoat pocket, then stood from the deep armchair without using his hands as support. 'Excuse us, Maud, I shan't keep him from you for long.'

'And where do you intend dragging me to?' Herbert smiled, also standing.

Hugh did a 'With my head chopped off, underneath my arm' walk to the door. 'Come up to my study, and you'll see how I spend a lot of my time.'

Glad to avoid a stultifying melt into nothingness, Herbert followed, his father's back as upright as ever, though his tread up the stairs was slow enough. He had been through trench warfare in France, and fought in the jungles of Burma, leading his battalion and later shuffling the wreck of his brigade against the Japanese to great effect. He envied him for having done so much, wanted to take all his experiences into himself.

The table was covered with overlapping maps, some neatly folded in stacks, others opened from rolls and pinned down by piles of army notebooks. Wads of yellowing papers, ragged at the edges and stained with mud (and maybe even blood) were not yet arranged in any order. 'Don't tell me,' Herbert said. 'You're writing your memoirs.'

Hugh leaned against the enormous glass-fronted bookcase. 'It was your mother's idea. Well, I always knew I would, one day, but I let her think she set me on to it. If I don't do them for publication I can give all this to the Imperial War Museum. Or to you eventually, if you're interested.'

He realized he was. 'I'd be glad to have them.' Yet would he? They'd probably get mildewed in Mrs Denman's shed, until forgotten, or the ragman carted them away – a prospect that gave real pain, however.

Hugh unfolded a map and bent over, lowering his magnifying glass to the close brown contours, then shifting its circle to the yellow of cultivated areas. Herbert smoothed over the exquisite colours with his fingers. 'What a lovely map.'

'Of course it damned well is,' Hugh snapped. 'Don't you know that the British soldier always died on the best of maps? But look at it closely, though, and you'll see what abominable country we had to scramble about in.'

'I don't see any roads,' Herbert said.

Hugh ringed a ford and a hamlet with a soft black pencil, stood up straight. 'Roads!' He let out an expressive guffaw. 'There was never any such thing. It was a hundred degrees up from awful. Mud tracks for donkeys, if you were lucky.' His mouth came close to Herbert's ear, who had the presence not to move away. 'When you get married,' Hugh whispered, 'as I'm sure you will one day, always keep your wife happy. Let her think everything that's good about you is because of her. In my case it happens to be true, but even if it weren't that's what I would do. Another thing is, though I don't know whether I need tell you, is that you never, never, never ever say any of the bad things that come into your mind, either about her or about anything, but especially about her. Only the good things, and even those you must think about carefully in case they can be taken wrongly. A wife is the most precious thing a man can have, and if you live by that, or make the attempt at any rate, your wife will think the same of you.'

'I'll try to remember,' Herbert smiled.

'There are so many difficulties in life that marital discord ought not to be one of them.'

He stood away, and looked again at the map, gazing with affection and appreciation, as if all his speculations about human nature had their origins in his ability to relate the contours of a map to the shape of the land itself. 'There are less paved roads in that kind of terrain than the other, except those perfectly paved ones that you make yourself and spend your whole life maintaining.'

Such longspeaking indicated to Herbert how difficult being married to his mother might have been. Some of the times in his father's life must have been absolute boils and blisters. A photograph of Hugh and his staff showed them standing by a twin-engined transport plane, a row of palm trees behind. Hugh, taller than the rest, was grinning as if he owned the aircraft as well.

'I'll remember all you say.'

Hugh put an arm on his shoulder. 'I'm sure you will. You've always been a sensible chap, and we won't bother you in your life. Everyone has to make his own way, and we're sure you'll do well in the end.'

It was a strange world, where only utter agreement made everyone happy, and all was in terms of 'we'. Whatever the old man said could make no difference. He walked downstairs and into the garden, scent from rose bushes taking him to the grounds of his first school, the perfume of gratuitous cruelty rushing back, though too much in the past to be more than a reminder of days which led to him being where he was and even possibly how he was.

A track led across the paddock to an orchard where a branch had been split off by the weight of large reddish apples, some pecked by the birds or bored into by wasps, but most ready for picking. The one he ate was a blend of tart and sweet, and he tossed the core up towards heavy clouds sending down the first drops, soon steady enough to enrich the smell of bent-over grass between the trees. The whole place wanted going over with a lawnmower.

Not visible from the ground floor of the house, he let the water flatten his hair and run down his face, saturate his jacket, get through to the skin, an icy clamminess connecting him to an area of the sky from which a real self looked down on the marionette specimen he felt himself to be. Such rain made tears invisible, unnoticed. He shivered with exhilaration – regarding the elements as nothing compared to the volcanic compound of misery and defiance inside the armour which no downpour could penetrate. The experience was perversely enjoyable, a dose of self-induced reality, and however long he stood in the rain he would stay no other than who he was, no matter how many spirits attached themselves to him.

'Herbert!' Maud's cry splintered him back, and he saw her in oilskins and wellingtons, basket over arm and parting the brambles. 'I need some apples for a pie. You must take some back with you, unless you catch pneumonia and have to go to bed for a month. I say, you're soaked.'

'Am I?' He took the basket. 'Let *me* do it.' When it was filled she gripped his elbow and guided him to shelter in the house. What a peculiar idea, he thought, imagining someone like me getting pneumonia, recalling summer days in the factory when he had walked out into the breeze soaked in sweat.

A bath freshened, and cleansed away his uncertainties, till he felt as if he'd lived in the house all his life, hadn't left it for a day. The Rayburn dried his clothes, and upstairs he took off his father's heavy checked dressing gown before putting on a clean shirt for dinner.

When he walked into the lounge, Hugh came from behind his *Daily Mail* to offer him a sherry. The tall old man stood stiffly with the decanter and poured a tumbler three-quarters full, Herbert deciding that the best way to get through the evening was to soak in as much as was given him to drink. 'It's good,' he said, after a slug of the golden liquid. 'Dry.'

'Can't stand the sweet stuff.' Hugh poked at the logs, though the room was warm. 'Your mother tells me you're writing a book.'

Another swig lightened the seriousness of the issue. 'Well, you can say it's in the planning stage.'

'Not an easy thing to do.'

'I'm going to do something that hasn't been done before: which is write about people who work in factories. Do it properly, though, from the inside.' The words rolled out, oiled by drink. 'I know them so well by now, there's nothing else I really can write about.'

Hugh refilled both glasses. 'Are they worth it, do you think?'

'Everybody is.'

'I expect you're the best judge of that.'

Maud looked at them as they linked arms and walked in for dinner. 'How much sherry have you two had?'

'A couple of little ones, but we'll go easy on the wine.'

They did, though all three went back to the lounge afterwards and drank several Martell brandies, so that by ten Herbert could decently say he was tired, and would they excuse him if he went to bed?

The silence of the dark was unnerving. If he put on the light the ceiling would revolve. An owl struck the night with its note, and he felt apprehensive, as if the room had no walls. He put on the light and read a few poems from *Other Men's Flowers*, but one that was anti-Semitic reminded him of Isaac, and he put the book away.

He would wait for the dawn, though it was only eleven o'clock. The floor was cold to his feet and, wearing the all-embracing dressing gown of his father's, he opened the door so as to make no squeak at the hinges. Sliding a finger along the wainscot to keep a straight course, he navigated towards a splinter of light, at the other end of the corridor. No one could accuse him of sneaking about, because he was going downstairs to stand in the fresh cold air and get some of his drunkenness blown away.

He was not a prisoner, in any case, and put an ear to the door through which light showed. 'Nor me,' his mother said, 'but I'm sure he won't turn out to be a bad egg.'

Poor things had no one else to talk about. His father's study was just as he had seen it in the afternoon. In the attic he found a fort and fire engine broken and dusty, toys from his childhood. Finding his way in darkness to the kitchen, he hated the night. Night was inhuman, antipathetic, no good for him. After five minutes of fresh air he made back for bed, his only refuge. Night was a black cloth covering all romance, and he slept as if utterly worn out.

When he woke up bits of dream were stamped on by the boots of daylight.

The morning was dry and blustery, and at breakfast Hugh said they would go out with the Purdys. 'See if we can bag a rabbit or two down by the river.'

Energized, ready for anything, Herbert chose a pair of wellingtons from the hall by the kitchen and, with a bandolier of cartridges hanging from his shoulder, and the gun pointing down, followed his father to the lane. Like two soldiers on patrol, Herbert thought.

High stinging nettles bent over the track, a thick hawthorn hedge and a ditch on the other side. The carmine blue and gold of an overflying painted lady stopped Hugh for a moment in his stalking, and Herbert all but ran into him.

By a pink blaze of rosebay his father signalled for stealth, which put both at the crouch and immobile. He straightened, gun at the same time coming to his shoulder. Herbert went down with equal slowness on one knee to take aim, and the question came as to whether he should put a stop to his father now, in the back, at ten yards range. He pressed off the safety catch, stroking the cold trigger.

Two mature and confident rabbits came from under a laden bramble, furry snouts at the twitch, facing each other as if for a round of boxing before loosing themselves for breakfast in the rich pastures. A large white butterfly made a hypotenuse up from his sights, and he lined his gun on the left-hand rabbit, assuming his father would take the other.

For no reason he could think of Archie's face printed itself on his mind, enough of a glimpse to make him wonder if such a powerful almost sexual urge to blow a hole in his own father should for a moment be morally contemplated. He decided that Archie was too primitive and too civilized even to think of such a murder, and in any case so was he.

The rabbit spun over, and he hit the other before it could run. A third report from a higher elevation brought a wounded pigeon flopping on to the Pliocene soil. He was astounded that his father had not all along intended to fire at either of the rabbits but had left both to him, confident of being understood.

The shots alerted wildlife for miles around, so that in spite of another hour's tramping and a few wasted shots, they downed nothing more. 'Two rabbits and a pigeon ain't bad,' Hugh said. 'That was a good bit of shooting, by the way.'

'So was yours.'

They stood under a half-shed chestnut, Hugh wielding his pipe for a well-earned smoke. 'I have so much faith in this little lighting-up machine you made at your factory that I didn't even carry matches this morning.'

He said 'Your factory' as if Herbert owned it, which for some reason pleased him. Light brought out autumn's colours, a blade of sun catching a clump of Scotch pines. Herbert liked the sound of birds embellishing the day. His father leaned, holding a flame over the bowl. 'Do you remember that cheque for twenty-five pounds I sent you? It was years ago.'

'Yes, Father.'

'Why didn't you cash it?'

Why ever not? He'd long forgotten it. 'I was waiting for a rainy day, which hasn't come yet.'

'Well, in my youth I'd have made the bloody rain pour down so that I could have had a whale of a time on it. So cash it. Stop waiting for emergencies.'

'I promise I will.'

They climbed the stile from the lane in silence, then Hugh laughed as he opened the gate to home. 'Ah! I can smell something good for lunch.'

Maud drove him to Norwich in their Vauxhall Velox Saloon so as to shorten his journey home. 'I wish you would make your home with us, though. Or in London, at least. Your father could get you a job in insurance, or shipping. You must have enough material for your book by now.'

The prospect of being alone in the train lured like a gleam of paradise. 'Not quite.'

She overtook a farm wagon on a bend. Another such manoeuvre, he smiled, and all our troubles will be over. 'I'll need a year or two yet.'

After a mile of ointment-quiet she came in with: 'I can't think why you torment yourself so. It's not like either of us.'

Luckily the engine drowned his sigh. 'It's how I am.'

'I know. But I worry about you.'

He touched her hand at the wheel, a natural almost loving gesture that felt strange to him, though there was nothing behind it but the action, which made him free of her as well. 'You don't need to, believe me.'

'All right, I won't. But write now and again.'

'I promise.'

'And come whenever you like.'

He wouldn't, unless some reason hard to imagine impelled him. 'I shall.'

He had an impulse to sling the bag of apples out of the train window, but decided they'd make a present for Mrs Denman. She liked fruit. At the station there was time to send a postcard to Isaac, as proof that he had done his duty.

Thirteen

Mrs Denman thought the excursion had done him little good, wondered whether he had been to Norfolk at all, but had gone instead to London and fallen into bad company. As for the apples, he could have bought them at a stall, though in the end she had to believe him, since he was too proud a person to tell a lie. 'Was your parents well?'

'Yes.'

'What do they do?'

'They're retired.'

'They must have a nice garden.'

'Not bad.'

'I expect they were glad to see you.'

'I think they were.'

'I'm glad you went, though.'

He raised his eyebrows, and smiled. 'Yes, so am I.'

She didn't think the trip had made him happy, which disappointed, almost irritated her. He seemed to have a ghost before his eyes every minute of the day, one that he saw all night as well in his dreams, to judge by his expression when he came down for breakfast.

There was something swinish, he knew, in disappointing her, but what could he say? It was harder to come back than it had been to go. Pedalling his bike to work was a relief, part of an ongoing donkey circuit keeping him on course to where he would eventually get. If I unlock myself from such a totally absorbing existence, he thought, the language of his schooldays coming back, as if there was no other way of saying it, I'm lost, so here I am and here I shall stay. Life's too short to worry about anything other than work and shelter.

A blindoe drink-out with Archie was necessary before he could relax within the palisade of safety, and write a letter thanking his parents for their kindness. Pepper's chip shop on Alfreton Road was crowded with people just out of the boozers, clamouring for mushy peas and cobs, fish and pickled onions and mugs of well-sweetened tea. Archie elbowed his way to the counter, Herbert in a moment by his side: 'I'll have the usual.'

'Fish, chips, cobs and teas twice,' Archie bawled.

'Tek yer sweat, then. There's others before yo'.'

While waiting Herbert said: 'I need to get myself a typewriter.'

'What do you want one o' them for?'

He would pay for it out of his father's old cheque. 'Just to play around on. I want to learn how to tek one to bits and put it together again. Whereabouts would I go to get a good 'un?'

Archie's brain seemed to be working at the back of his eyes like the spinning fruitwheels of a one-armed bandit. 'Here's the grub. Let's get stuck in. Don't go to one o' them secondhand places. You'll only get done. I'll bring one to your room as soon as I can. It might tek a month or two.'

They moved to a corner, away from the crush. 'That's all right. I'm in no hurry.'

Herbert leaned his workaday sit-up-and-beg against the parapet of Trent Bridge and looked towards the War Memorial, along the sweep of the embankment steps where people were getting into boats for an hour's pull at the oars. His promise of a mystery trip had called for some attention to the map, until a breeze ruffled inconveniently and he folded it back into his jacket pocket. 'Not too far, though,' Cecilia had said. 'It's at least a year since I was on a bicycle.'

High cauliflower clouds operated in the west so it looked like a day of dry grass. The quickest way out of town took them along nondescript Wilford Lane and over Fairham Brook. True country began when he navigated into Clifton Grove only if they ignored the new housing estate through trees to their left. He felt something magical and Grecian in the long avenue of beeches, oaks and elms, though he couldn't let Bert make such a comparison to Cecilia. Shouldering his bike over a dead tree, he went back for hers when she couldn't lift it and avoid nettles at the same time.

She looked fresh and athletic in her white blouse and jersey tied to hang over her shoulders. A grey skirt and laced shoes set her up for a day in the country, which put her almost on a par with Ralph's bint when they had set out for the Lake District years ago; but in spite of her provincial confidence there seemed something lost about Cecilia. She was like Mariana out of Tennyson, waiting for who could tell what? Otherwise why would he have latched himself on to her if she hadn't been waiting all her life for him?

He laid her bike against the tree and reached for her arm, and took her over by the waist. Such courtly treatment was rewarded by a slight pressure to his hand. Beyond the village he steered by her side, playing the cavalier who guarded her from a brush by traffic, hoping the gesture wasn't beyond notice. The difficulty made him wonder why they used such a plebeian mode of transport – as the swinging of a car passed too close to his elbows. Watch where you're fucking going, he wanted to shout.

He judged the contours, and chose the road to Gotham rather than Barton because the hill was less steep. Even so, she found it hard to keep to the saddle of her new Raleigh. 'Gotham is where those funny yokels tried to rake the moon out of a pond,' he said.

'People still do,' she smiled. 'They're always fishing for something they can never get.'

Was that a hint against what she must know he was after? If rain threw it down – which didn't seem likely – and they sheltered in a barn he might get at her buttons in the hugger-mugger. Or he might not, would have to be subtle and slow, but it would be a pity not to try because she might be dying to get the old mutton dagger inside her. With such a woman you never could tell.

Stopping by a gate, he took the top from a lemonade bottle, and passed it for her to drink, deciding to put on a bit of the old Herbert. 'People fishing for something that turns out to be impossible can at least get the thrill of realizing how stupid they are. There's always something to be had in fishing for the unattainable.'

'You should be an actor, the way your accent changes when you try to say something interesting.'

169

'Ah, I could have been a lot of things.'

'I think there's more to you than meets the eye.'

'I can only hope so.' His father's advice, to make the woman imagine that all the good in you came from her, seemed apt at the moment. 'I listen to the BBC, and get influenced, because I think you would like me to.' Back to Bert, he spat out a mouthful of the vile and oversweet lemonade, and screwed the top back on as if to strangle the bottle. 'I'm for the road. Are yer fit?'

She found him stiff, and awkward, though not detecting any definite fault only added to her confusion as to the real quality of his character, especially as she hadn't actually known whether she wanted to come out on such a jaunt and be exposed to its full force. Cycling was more difficult than she had thought when, holding hands on the table in the café, he had so eloquently told her how pleasantly liberating a bike ride would be to the body and spirit. At such times he spoke like someone whose mind was halfway into another world, one she would be more comfortable in yet could hardly understand. He had a persuasive way of stating all arguments clearly, setting one against the other, but finally coming down on the one he wanted to win, and in such a way as to make you imagine you'd outlined it yourself.

He reached across and touched her hand, pointing to Leake Hills a mile away. 'Just look at those splendid woods over there.'

'I'm glad I came,' she said. 'It's wonderful to be in the countryside.'

'If I could ride close enough, and be in no danger of knocking you off the bike, I'd get a fan and keep the gnats off you.'

'They're not too bad.' He could be gentlemanly and polite to an extent she never found in any of her previous boyfriends, who hadn't shown a fraction of such finesse. But when he came out with: 'After we get to Leake I think I'll sink a pint or two in the pub. It's thirsty work, this bikin'. As for yo', duck, yer can 'ave a glass o' shandy,' she wondered where such habits and manners came from, and why it was, after saying something gallant, he immediately suggested an action which showed he was ashamed of having tried to be nice. Such switches of personality – or whatever it was – added to her mixed feelings, an anxiety latent at the best of times. She felt close to tears. He was unknowable, unreachable, unfathomable, and there

170

must be something in him as hard as nails. Either that, or he was incredibly stupid, perhaps even cruel.

On the other hand maybe his frequent lapses into the demotic merely indicated his snobbery in wanting to make fun of the common people, but if that was the case how was it he did it so well? He had obviously picked it up from the pubs, and on the street, and being a good mimic knew how to make it sound genuine.

That, he thought, was what she would like to think, and he could only hope for her sake that she did. He came back with crisps and shandy from the bar, and a pint for himself, relishing the trip with this young woman who vacillated between the suave and the highly strung. Twelve miles out of the city added up to hardly enough time to be with her and get all he wanted, though if they did much more cycling she would no longer find it pleasant, he gathered, because her legs ached, and her behind was getting sore.

She seemed to be in the ladies for an hour, though it could have only been a few minutes. All the same, her absence went on long enough for him to think that if he couldn't seduce her on this outing he wouldn't bother to meet her again. He'd pack her in, to quote Archie. In fact the chances of getting so far looked in no way promising, and he wondered what would happen to her if he wasn't there when she came out of the ladies, if he mounted his bike and rode alone to Loughborough, to see what he could pick up there.

The longer he sat thinking about such a good idea the greater was the chance of her seeing only the back of him as he vanished through the door. Dwelling enjoyably on such a picture delayed him until she came smiling into the bar. His standing up to watch over her sitting down was seen as another example of perfect manners, but then he had to spoil it by saying that since he was on his feet he might as well go to the bar and get his glass refilled.

Outside, noting that her tyres had not been firm since Clifton, he pumped them up, but even ruined that considerate service by adding: 'You feel the bumps, and that's what's making your arse sore.' He talked about continuing the ride as far as Nanpanton in Charwood Forest. 'Maybe jolly old toothless Nancy Panton will have a cup o' tea and a charcoal sandwich ready for us!'

Such a total run of forty miles would be impossible for her, though nothing to him, and to persist in the idea would be cruelty, so like the reliable consort he was called on to be, he confessed to a little tiredness, and said maybe they ought to wend their way back, providing of course that she didn't mind. 'I love you,' he said, 'in any case, and wouldn't like either of us to get too exhausted.'

She put a hand on his, eyes lovely with relief. 'Yes, we can turn round. I don't mind.'

'Whatever you like, sweetheart.'

She had hoped for a pleasant meadow by the roadside on which to eat lunch but, a little ahead in Gotham and without saying anything, he forked left on to another track. Ascending the hill she felt the bumps as painfully as ever, so manoeuvred her bike on foot, until he took both machines and pushed them easily along.

She could imagine being married to him, for he thought of kind things to do almost before they came into her own mind. On the other hand he could be disturbingly unpredictable, at times like someone on the verge of mental illness. Or perhaps she was exaggerating, having often been wrong in differentiating the rough parts from the smooth, which led her to question the workings of her own reason, something she didn't like at all, since it came too easily even in matters of no importance. No one had ever made her doubt herself more than Herbert, so that it was difficult to get the right advice from her instinct in dealing with him.

The slope steepened, awkward off the track to hold the bikes and guide them upright between tussocks or grass. She followed, willing him to stop, heard him call back after a rabbit skipped panic-struck towards the woods. 'That's where we're going.'

To be fair – and she liked to be fair – she could never find the final damaging evidence that he was no good for her. Something always surfaced to make him likeable, so she assumed it would be all right to go on meeting him.

He stopped, and let her catch up. 'You wanted to get as far away from the city blight as possible, so I did my best.'

He remembered everything, which was good, but only to use it against her, which wasn't. His enthusiasm led her uncomplainingly to the line of woods, where he found a smooth place and spread his cycling cape like Raleigh his cloak so that she could sit in comfort.

'We're about three hundred feet up. See how many villages you can count.'

'As if it matters,' she said. 'Stop treating me like an infant.'

He walked along the edge of the wood to find a way inside, where their snogging could take place more privately. He found it easy to get in, but knew it would be impossible to coax her under the barbed wire. 'If I'd known about the fence I'd have brought some wire-cutters. I don't like being kept out of places.'

The picture of him, like an ant gone wild, destroying with glee the fence which a farmer had spent so much to erect, disturbed her. It would be wrong. 'You'd be breaking the law.'

On his own he would have cut a wide enough gap for a tank to get through. 'You don't believe I'm daft enough to do it?'

'I don't know. Do you know the difference between right and wrong? I sometimes wonder.'

So did he, feel the guise of Herbert getting away from him, slipping – sloping almost – over the horizon, and too far off ever to be brought back, a dim unreal person set apart, a pair of muddy heels vanishing in the distance. He found it frightening, fragmenting, but the fright coming and going like one of his other selves. It wasn't always easy to feel convinced that he was who he was supposed to be at the moment. Often it was hard to tell even when he thought he most certainly knew. He came back to Herbert sufficiently to say: 'I absolutely am aware of the difference between right and wrong. But anyone who does wrong not realizing that he does so is a fool.'

She thought better of continuing the sort of argument he would never let her win, and to divert him mentioned a burglary they'd had at the office a few nights ago.

'Did they get much?'

'Oh, some stamps. But they took two typewriters, and an adding machine.'

He looked into the sky, thinking he might have to call Bert back. 'Nothing's safe, I suppose. Life's an ongoing guerrilla war between the rich and the poor.'

'Well,' she said, 'we're not rich, and I'll bet they're not poor. So it's wrong, whatever you say.'

Nor did *he* feel it was time for an argument. 'I suppose you're right, if I think about it.'

They ate sandwiches, corned beef for him, and lettuce and cheese for her. He drew her down on to the cape and kissed her, as gently as he hoped would be preferred, lips roaming to her forehead and eyes. She liked it, and put her arms around him in a relaxed way. They lay as if half-asleep and, it seemed to him as well as to her, perfectly harmonized with the smell of warm herbage and the rustling from trees behind.

'I love you.' He omitted the word 'duck', his love only true as far as the scorching desire of his groin. 'I'll never forget today,' he murmured, warm breath caressing her ear. 'Our lie-down together on the Gotham Hills will stay in my memory forever.'

'I love you as well, but my arm's going dead.' He moved, an opportunity to readjust so that his hand could reach her ankle. He stroked the lisle covering between kisses and, crabwise, finger by finger, but in the slowest motion, inched as far as her calf, then let the hand rest awhile. She seemed unaware of his purpose, or at least she said nothing. Perhaps she liked the perspirational closeness, and enjoyed what he was doing, as long as he did it with gentleness and consideration. He assumed she wanted him to go on, so resumed the sly and tactical creep, her skirt ascending with his hand.

He toyed in the silky cavern at the back of the knee, and felt her passion increase, though perhaps it was only in his own mind. Motionless together on the hillside, like an outcrop of two bizarre rocks, he felt himself close to victory as the sweet and lingering kisses were returned.

His eyes were fully open before the final advance when, looking beyond her shoulder, he saw an animal fifty yards away, which he at first thought was a large dog, and wondered how the hell it came to be there. A reddish pelt glowed in the reflected sun, its long nose sniffing the breeze for prey. Clean and sturdy, as if fresh out of creation, an elect ruler of all it saw, the still pose seemed fixed forever: a fox.

For Cecilia to see it would be a unique treat, except that by pointing the scene out he would have to shift his besieging hand, which had gained its position after so much pertinacity. Telling her would make their hillside idyll even more memorable, an unforgettable prelude to the fucking she was going to get, and her gratitude would be everlasting, but he became Bert and Herbert both, and gloried in the fox whose resplendent orange brightness against dull green joined the two parts of him together. They had never been so close, and he took a lesson in the fox's stillness to say nothing.

The encroaching hand under her skirt had a mind of its own, even so. Nor was the increasing pressure between his legs any help towards a decision. Under cover of a series of softened kisses his hand went higher, till a stiffened finger touched the rim of her knickers, and felt for a glorious second the texture of hair.

She moved. 'Do you want all of Nottinghamshire to see what's going on?'

He wouldn't have cared if Leicestershire and Derbyshire were getting a look in as well. Nobody was visible, as far as he could see, and if some modern chiker had invested in a pair of binoculars to further his foul ends good luck to him – though if he caught anybody doing such a thing he'd pound them to blood and gristle.

At her movement the fox melted back into the woods, and she would never be aware of what, by his unity with the animal, he had allowed her to miss. He looked at his watch. 'We'd better go, if we want to be back by dusk.'

She stood, and held him close, and he knew that the wrench away from loving had been as hard for her as for him. 'We'll do it soon, darling. I want it too, but it really wouldn't be good to start anything here.'

Pride made him say it didn't matter, and kiss her tenderly, telling himself that soon had better mean what it implied or he wouldn't bother wasting much more time on her. Love ought to have some substance, and the wetter the better. His pocket hadn't been lightened by the weight of a single french letter. Luckily he didn't have cold rice pudding down his leg, though the tumescence was plain for her to see.

While reading *The Times*, clandestinely acquired with the *Daily Mirror* on his way through town that morning, he was disturbed by Mrs Denman calling that Archie was on his way upstairs. Bert put the newspaper under his pillow, and swung round to undo a packet of cigarettes.

Archie smiled forlornly, and put a weighty package on the bed. 'I got this for yer.' He wore his weekend suit, with collar and tie, though such a smart rig did not take attention from his black eye and scuffed face.

'What 'appened to yo'?' Bert said.

He sat on the spare chair, head down as if to hide the worst patches. 'Got my comeuppance, din't I?'

'It bleddy looks like it. What 'appened?'

'The other evening it was. Cherie and me was all set for a bit of delicious hearthrug pie when her 'usband comes back to the house with some of his pals. One at the front, but two at the back. I ran straight into the two at the back, the cunning bastards. Then all three set on to me. Some fucker must have shopped us.'

Bert grinned, the only response being: 'Shall we go out and get the fuckpigs? Give 'em a real pastin'?' Such an offer of assistance was all that could be made, after the hastily considered and rejected alternative of taking the mickey out of Archie for his misadventure. The problem was that after taking the mickey out of someone like Archie there wouldn't be much left to take. Should Archie feel the consequences of such an emptying, which he probably would, being more sensitively acute than many, he might go into a berserker's fit and take the house to pieces. Mrs Denman wouldn't like that. Nor, thought Herbert, would I.

Yet there was always more to Archie than anyone would suppose. 'You never know, Bert,' he said. 'Maybe one day I'll get a scar as bad as yourn, then I'll 'ave all the women I like – maybe even a posh whore will fall for me. Anyway, I'll get 'em sooner or later.' He stood to unwrap the parcel. 'Let 'em stew a bit. It's the luck o' the game, anyway.'

'Where did you get this?' A neat little portable typewriter lay snug in its shining black case. Herbert put it on the table and clipped it open, all keys and tappets shining, a black and red ribbon already installed. He hoped it wasn't one of those taken from Cecilia's office, though it was too late to worry about that. In any case, they didn't use portables in offices.

'Search me! It was just about to fall off the back of a lorry, I expect, and somebody – don't ask me who – caught it in time and stopped it smashing to pieces.' Archie stroked his battered face. 'Ain't she a beauty? I still can't see why you want one, though.'

'It's summat to keep me out of mischief. I don't fancy gerrin beat up like yo'.' He slotted in a sheet of paper, and ping-ponged his name. Then he did Archie's, both exquisitely printed. 'How much do you want for it?'

'They said twenty-five. Is that all right?'

'I shan't argue.' He smiled: good to think of his father coughing up for such a potent tool. 'Can it wait till the weekend? I've got a cheque to cash.'

'I suppose so. But no longer, or I'll have to volunteer for Korea. Them lads want their money quick.'

'I shan't let you down. It's worth a fortnight's wages to me.' He craved to see some of his handwriting in print, but could not dismiss Archie so soon after he had brought the machine. As consolation he clacked out both names again, and thought how distinguished they looked. He turned to Archie. 'You'll have to stop going with married women.'

'Not me,' he said. 'I love married women. They know so much. And they're grateful when you mek 'em cum, especially if they're married to a numskull, as most of 'em are. Can't think why. Anyway, let's go down the road for a pint, and seal the deal. Bruises like these make you thirsty.

Fourteen

The wall of the restaurant was mostly glass, making two of everything and everyone, which suited him fine: a double ration of his own face each belonging to the other. One sort was all Thurgarton-Strang, roman-nosed and verging to swarthy, and a cicatrice whose up and down soreness acted like a barometer for his spirit. Then there was the brighter and more accepting version of Bert Gedling, out for fun rather than mischief, and not giving a toss for anyone in the world, not even for himself should he need to fight his way out of a perilous fix.

How the place with such mirrors had got through the Blitz he would never know, but a surreptitious side-on view of all the Cecilias, whose eyes were preoccupied in other directions to avoid his scar – because it wasn't a pretty sight tonight, or even at the best of times – showed how tragic her aspect could occasionally be. Maybe he and she were made for each other, though he rather thought not. Her laughter always seemed as much a punctuation device as cursing did with those in the factory, because there was nothing humorous about their glum meal. She seemed sad, and distant in thought. 'Say something,' he told her.

An obliterating glare dissolved, as it should from a carefully brought up young woman. She smiled: 'I liked your short stories.'

His thank you came with a sneer, hard to say why.

'They're typed very well,' she said. 'Not a mistake anywhere.'

He objected to her thinking he'd make a good clerk, or pen-pusher, but let it pass. 'I got a book out of the library on how to touch-type.'

She drank her coffee as if it were brewed from superior acorn dust and, forgetting her determination to make him break silence first: 'They're very vivid. But why do you write about people who swear all the time, and do terrible things to one another? I mean, they're always getting drunk, and being sick all over the place.'

He pulled himself back from laughing. 'That's the way they are. It's no good playing it down.'

'I think you play it up, though.'

'I appreciate the criticism.' He didn't. She could at least say she was entertained, or amused, or had learned something about people she didn't know. Or she could just say his stories were wonderful, and shut up. 'I'll have to check what you say, and then maybe I'll do better by making things a bit more subtle.'

'There must be other subjects to write about.' She was encouraged by his attitude. 'People just don't drink and fight all the time.'

She didn't mention the fucking, of which there was quite a bit, though it must have been in her mind. It was certainly in his, but he wouldn't bring the matter up in case it delayed him getting such a nice middle-class woman into bed.

'What's more,' she went on. She didn't, presumably, know when to stop. 'You are not like that.'

'Thank you very much.'

His table manners and behaviour tonight were impeccable, even to someone who had always found such fault with the clerks who had taken her out that they soon gave her up for a girl who would provide unstinted love and approval. None had come close to the perfection of Herbert at his best. 'You aren't, though, are you, darling?'

Certainly not, but the Bert in him regretted not wearing overalls and having a spanner to brandish. 'I couldn't write about such frightful people if I was. Nor would I care to.' He mimicked a public school accent with sufficient accuracy to stop her suspecting he had at one time used it. Nor did he want her to think he was mocking *her* accent, of the local but clearly enunciated sort. He was far enough into alien territory to feel irritated and uncomfortable, and to realize he should be on his guard. It was hard enough fitting into one sort of life, and here he was jinking among three.

His obvious hedging and dodging put a flush into her delicately boned face. 'You should read more books by Walter Hawksworth.

He's good. You'd learn a lot from him.' He wondered if she had ever been to bed with Hawksworth, the way she went on. Hawksworth was a good writer, she said. He wrote about those whom any sensible person would want to be like. Even if people in his books happened to do something bad they did such actions later on that they ended up good. Hawksworth didn't write about those common people who lived all around us, and who didn't care about the difference between right and wrong. The people all around us, well, you knew how they lived already, in any case, so you didn't need to read about them.

She was so delightful it would be easy for him to relinquish the role of Bert Gedling, or enough to give that impression. His defences fell flat when he was only vaguely aware of the rough side of himself and could be mostly a Thurgarton-Strang, a part in the play of his life which seemed to charm her, though he couldn't really care whether it did or not. He could, after all, be who he liked whenever he liked and behave in any way he cared to, having had a good education and come from the sort of family that she would never know about. He had just spent a good part of his week's wages paying for their dinner and she hadn't even had the grace to thank him. She wasn't always aware of the change in his accent, and whatever was in her mind he could only hope it would snare her into doing all he wanted her to do, though as soon as this looked like coming about – and his villainous faculties, he smiled, would tell him precisely when – he would revert positively to Bert Gedling in the hope that her ant-like restless desire would let him do what he liked no matter who he felt himself to be.

'I'm going slowly through the Everyman Library.' One of the books Isaac had given him had a full list at the back. 'I'm on Joseph Conrad at the moment. *Lord Jim* was terrific. Jim is a ship's officer who jumps overboard when he thinks the boat's going down, and leaves all his dago passengers to drown.'

'What an awful thing to do.'

'It makes a marvellous novel though. And he pays for it in the end. You'd like it.'

'He should have stayed on the ship and looked after them, or gone down with it.'

Maybe he shouldn't have been on the ship at all, just as Phaeton ought not to have driven his father's sun chariot across the sky. Look what trouble that caused. Most come to grief when they overreach themselves, though if you don't overreach yourself you'll never know what you can do. And if you come a cropper it doesn't much matter as long as you're still alive. And if you aren't still alive your worries are over.

'Then there would have been no moral in the story.' He reached for her hand. 'Conrad does rather put old Hawksworth in the shade, though. I think you ought to tackle a bit of grown-up stuff now and again. Maybe you should start with Evelyn Waugh. He's very good.'

She smiled. 'I do find you difficult to understand.'

Nor do I always understand you, and I don't care to, but what does it matter anyway? You only need to understand about someone when you're writing about them, and if it's someone you've never met that's even better, because then you can make it up, which comes out just as good if not more truthfully than if you had really bumped into them. 'It takes a long time to understand a person.'

'You don't tell me anything about yourself.'

Her twinge of complaint was difficult to forgive, since not only did he know so little of himself but her pathetic attempt to find out more than he even knew made it seem as if she was starting to nag.

'Let's go for a walk, my love.' He manoeuvred her through a crowd at the door waiting for a table. 'I've told you my life-story already.'

'Yes, but it was a very skimpy one.'

Let her settle for that, and wonder about the inconsistencies, in her old-maidish droning. He held her by the waist as they walked towards Slab Square, her arm over his shoulder being a slight advance up the ladder of affection. The human warmth was good for him. He needed to have a body close to his own, and none could serve better than hers. However he thought of her, he wanted to hear that she liked his writing, but the sparse comments so far could perhaps be put down to the bottle of wine which had tasted like sock-juice, for which he couldn't altogether blame her. The next hope was for her body, but all he'd had up to now were a few kisses verging on the passionate from him and the hard given from her while saying good night at the gate of where she lived in Mapperley Park. 'Very skimpy,' she repeated.

'I'll write a novel about it one day, so's you can have a good read. I can't explain things to you in speech.' He let Herbert take over again. 'I find it extraordinarily difficult to say what's on my mind, probably because I'm so fond of you. The ardent desire I feel for you puts me off. On the other hand, you haven't told me much about *your* life.'

'I did, but you weren't very interested.'

'I didn't want to be nosy.'

'Are you only saying that because you don't want me to go on about you, and *your* past? I know you aren't who you say you are, but I don't care. I like it that way, in fact. I knew who my other boyfriends were, only too well, and they bored me to tears. I don't care where you came from.'

'Well, I respect that opinion.' And he did. 'But I still don't know much about you,' which he realized was more of a lie than not.

'I think you do. Anyway, not much happened in my life. I went to Mundella Girls till I was sixteen. Then I went to work. My father could have kept me at home, but he told me to get a job, so that I'd know what it was like to earn a living. Not that I minded. What would I have done, staying at home?'

He wondered how many men she'd really had. She was at least thirty, but he thought there couldn't have been many. When he asked she said it was no business of his, and he had to agree that it wasn't, because she didn't want to know how many women he'd been with. In more ways than one she seemed older than himself.

They walked up gloomy Mansfield Road, all shops shut, and few people about, though with fists clenched he marked each shadow until it had gone by. They turned off by the cemetery. 'I'm on my own in the house for a couple of weeks,' she said into his ear. 'Mum and Dad have gone on holiday to France in the car.'

His heart went bump in the night. 'Really? Where to?'

'They're staying a night in Paris, then going down to Nice.'

'That's really good news. Thanks for telling me.'

She looked at him as if he were a fool – as he'd supposed she would. 'Why not? I only hope their travel allowance lasts out, and they don't come back too early.'

'Your father must have stuffed his back pocket with five-pound notes, you can bet.'

She pulled her arm away. 'He'd never do anything like that.'

Oh, wouldn't he? She had no right to be so naive at her age. He really was a fool. She only meant you never *said* that kind of thing.

The large house had its own space, lilac bushes and trees heavy from rain, a damp soil smell reminding him of muddy and murderous rugby matches on the playing fields at school. 'I'd like to see inside. I don't think I've ever been in a big house like that.'

She squeezed his arm, at being able to grant his wish. The kitchen covered the same acreage as Mrs Denman's ground floor, but the decoration reminded him of his clergyman uncle's place near Malvern, all pine wood and marble top. 'What sort of work does your father do?'

'Work? He goes to business. He has property. Shops in town. Things like that.'

He watched her make a pot of tea, so prissy and precise with the doses of leaf it was bound to be as weak as gnat's piss, but at least she did it with her coat off, a white blouse over slender bosom from neck to wrists, all done up, with beads as well, which made her look, as Archie would have said, like lamb and lettuce. 'What's upstairs?'

Her smile of amusement was real, though time would tell whether it was because she had already arranged everything. 'Just bedrooms. Why?'

'Can I see?'

'If you promise to behave' – a positive laugh this time.

'Of course I promise.'

On the landing at the top he said: 'I suppose you have a woman in to clean all these carpets?'

'Oh, I vacuum them sometimes, on Saturday afternoon.'

He put both hands forward over her breasts, finding some shape after all. Encouraged by a trembling hand at her shoulder he kissed the ringlets from her neck and licked the warm skin, a hard-on pressing into her skirt. 'I'd love to be intimate with you,' he whispered, on an all or nothing course.

He expected to be pushed away, but she turned, and he tasted the cachou breath around her mouth. 'Can you cope?'

If he answered yes she would take him off for a rake who had a dozen women on the go. But if he said no she might write him off as inexperienced, such virtue not doing him any good at all. Remembering the triple-packet of frenchies in his left waistcoat pocket he had to say that he could.

He knew he would have to take special care with her delicate body, in any case, otherwise she might break up under his bit of rough stuff. Another thing was that a pregnancy would be fatal, the baby so big it would end up having her. He felt as if he had never before been in such a situation, that his time with Eileen was puppy love from another age, almost from another country, which with fiery Alice in Cyprus it had been, though their love had been full-blown, and he hoped Cecilia would come up to it; but going into the furnace of a new affair cut off the others as if such phases of his past life were like the carriages of a train, each abandoned to rot in a siding when done with.

He stood by an armchair as she took off her clothes, needing minutes to come down from three-o-one with so many pearl buttons to her blouse. Her brown eyes glowed, and a faintly modest smile made her look like the whore of Babylon, apt for the moment, but something she could never otherwise be as she unclipped her pretty white brassiere and gave her tits a stroke before attending to her stockings and skirt. Had she put on her best underwear knowing how the evening would end, or did a woman like that always wear such clean and flimsy stuff?

The light was clinical, which must be what she wants, he thought, the full-length mirrors of the white wood wardrobe doors seeming to multiply the dazzle. She neither wanted to hide the slight wrinkling of her mouth nor diminish the intensity of his scar. Her figure was thin but not inelegant, and he lustfully noted her charming breasts with their delicate carmine nipples. Seeing her whole nakedness appear, though she was no Aphrodite parting the waves and coming into land, he noted how shapely her legs were now that he could see them all the way up, and robust as well, as if made for a fuller figure than she had, and which some day she might grow into. Dark ringlets turned her into a houri, out of an illustration in some fairy-tale book he had once seen.

'I always knew you were beautiful.' He smoothed a palm down the neat bush of pubic hair. 'But you're far more so with no clothes on.'

She blushed almost to her shoulders. 'Thank you. I like looking at myself in the mirror, as I'm doing now.'

'Do you do it often?'

'Why not?' She drew back the covers of the bed, and their first tentative slow-motion movements hardened him more. He had taken the precaution of being already sheathed and, by midnight, three well-blobbed specimens lay discarded around the bed.

'Weren't you good?' She seemed an entirely different person to him now. 'Don't you think it was worth waiting for?' Her smile was brief, faintly teasing, which he liked because it drew them even closer together. 'I think it was, certainly,' she went on, wanting him to agree, while he could only wonder that she saw an altered man in him as well. 'You'd better flush those things away, though, and be careful not to spill anything.'

She was nothing if not practical, influenced no doubt by reality, which he couldn't care less about at such a time. He bombed them into the toilet bowl, each making a satisfying splash, as if retaining their individuality to the end, then pulled the chain, but even after a ton of water one of them surfaced like a poor benighted jellyfish that didn't want to go into that bourne from which no traveller returned. He waited for the cistern to build up, and tried again, but the same forlorn homunculus spluttered up and eased its bulbous tail out for another circuit. The head of number two peaked from under the porcelain lip to see how his brother – or sister maybe – got on. Two more attempts, but number three still wanted to survive. Herbert didn't fancy plunging a hand in to drag the recalcitrant bleeders out and throw them from the window for fear Cecilia's parents would think a funny bush had grown in their garden during their time away.

She knocked on the door. 'Are you all right, darling?'

'Yeh, fine, coming.' Another massive flush sent the final unwilling spunk bag to its doom – or he hoped so. Maybe it would surface in the morning for a final pathetic look at the sunlight coming through the mock stained-glass window, and only then do the decent thing and drown itself. At least he wouldn't be there to hear her comments if the bloody thing didn't succeed.

On the way home he told himself he was in love, said it over and over on the long depressing stretch through town, not even complaining at the thought of having to be in his overalls by seven. Words, however, were not rivets to fasten his emotions into place. He loved her compliance, and the pleasure of going round the world on her body again and again on her parents' great bed. If he saw no more of her he would surely miss such delectable copulation. It was not, on the other hand, the profound and life-long love he ought to have felt, for it didn't have that rootish tug of the heart, the all-enveloping sinking into the depths as between him and Eileen in the old days, which memory surfaced after his flesh to flesh fucking with Cecilia as if it had been only yesterday – though when seemingly flying home he felt no reason for complaint.

On Sunday morning he saw Archie and his pansy brother Raymond out by the shallows of the Trent near Clifton, both in their waders and hoping for a bite from fish that had just about had time to congratulate themselves at escaping the peril of the weir. Raymond went off to moon by himself, and Archie complained to Bert that the pair of them hadn't been out for a booze-up lately.

'It's all right for you,' Bert told him. 'You can see your women in the week because they're married, but me, I'm courtin', and I can only meet my tart on Fridays and Saturdays.' After a genuine no-nonsense berserker laugh, he added that his backbone was turning slowly, almost without him knowing – though he would most fully by the end – into a string of shiny Wollaton Park conkers.

Archie sat on the bank to watch his float. 'Who is she, then?'

About to blurt out the truth, honour forced Herbert into an account of how he met a young woman called Joanna on his way back from guzzling a jar or two in the Admiral Rodney at Wollaton. He described how he sat next to her on the top deck of the bus, rain peppering at the windows all the lumbering way uphill and down into town. 'I didn't know how it was. We just got talking.'

Archie soaked in the account, enjoying the story whether true or not – though Herbert realized he took it for gospel, because why shouldn't he? What you said to people they believed, as he would have taken in a similar story from Archie. 'You clicked good and proper.'

'Yeh, we talked the hind leg off a donkey. Then we got off the bus in Slab Square, and went for a drink in the Old Salutation. Lovely, she was. Dark hair, and a nice slim figure. She towd me she worked in an office and had a room of her own at West Bridgford, in a house owned by a Polish bloke.'

Archie clapped him on the back, saying what a ram he was. 'I'd like to meet her sometime.'

'Fuck off!' Bert said. 'If you did you'd only tek her away from me. I'm keeping her to myself.'

'No, not me, Bert. I'd never tek my mate's girl. I don't need to do that.'

He returned the thump on the back. 'I know you don't. I was only jokin'. Look, yer float's bobbin up and down.'

Three weeks after their first session of love Cecilia told him, with much regret, that her parents would be back next day. Herbert wasn't worried. They had fucked as much in that time as if they had been married for six months, and a rest before he melted away would be no bad thing. They smoked the usual cigarette over a mug of coffee in the kitchen after their couple of hours upstairs. 'We'll go on seeing each other, though?'

'Whenever we can. You make me know who I am,' she said, 'and I love you for it.'

His high opinion of her changed from that moment, to something of what it had been before their bonus of a honeymoon, because he couldn't think much of a woman who didn't know who she was every minute of the day and night, and who put the responsibility of defining herself on to someone like him. She had a year or two's advantage in age, so such a statement made her seem almost childish. On the other hand he knew that his juvenile denigration had to be set against the intensity and delight of a passion never to be obtained from such as Eileen, a sort who knew herself to the core and would spit in anybody's face if they tried to tell her who she was. She also never wanted to try any position except the hydraulic up and down.

Maybe Cecilia was flattering him, and knew very well who she was, and if so that was even less tenable. She was secretly smiling because he was younger and, rarely being capable of deciding which of these states she was in, hinted that even he did not know who he was. She wasn't to know that the only time he did was while sitting in his room to write, and he saw no reason to tell her.

Nor was that entirely the case, for in his dark thoughts he knew

187

to the marrow and back again who he was, certainly in a more complicated way than anything she could mean. He was two people instead of one, and knew them both intimately, even if only because they were so widely separated and he could see them from every angle. You couldn't be more deeply aware of yourself than that.

The advantage of such thoughts was that before knowing what part of the town he strode through he was almost home, having hardly noticed his part in the real world at all.

The word love came up all too often in their encounters, especially after they had been together in his room, which she liked even less than the district roundabout. She sat on the bed fixing her suspenders. 'Where do you think all this is going to lead?'

His mood hardened. Not another discussion about that. 'What do you mean?'

'Well, are we just going to go on like this forever?'

He opened the curtains and looked out over the dismal backs, not a good sight for his morale. 'What would you like us to do?'

'If *you* don't know, how can I?'

She was proposing to him, but wouldn't come right out with it. He put on his jacket, fastened the top button. 'I like things as they are.'

'Oh, like, like, like,' she cried out. 'I don't care what you like. That's not what I mean.'

He passed the ever clean handkerchief from his lapel pocket, in case tears were close. 'I love you so much I want it to go on like this forever.'

'Well, I don't know.' She sniffed into his linen. 'I don't, I really don't.' And threw the handkerchief on the bed. 'You can see me home now.'

Her kisses were just as passionate at the gate, and he was more than in the mood to match them. Quarrels were meaningless when they were finished. Let things go on forever, until for some reason they stopped. Marriage to her or anyone would be a loss of freedom, and as serious as suicide.

They said they loved each other, genuine sentiments on either side, though at times he thought guiltily that they couldn't altogether be so on his, otherwise he would indeed have known there was somewhere to go from where they were now. To latch himself on to her style of life would mean climbing the ladder to where he came from, which was unthinkable. Maybe their love in bed was only so satisfying because they disagreed on almost every issue, the one pleasure that stopped them running a mile from each other.

Having written down his thoughts on the matter, and put the papers into a folder for possible use in the future, he yawned and got into bed.

Fifteen

Herbert was happy to see steam coiling from the chimney of Wilford pit, and hear the jangle of laden coal trucks in the shunting yards. 'Work, you bastards, work!' he made Bert shout. 'Flat out, day and night! Work! Keep at it!' – then pulled him to rein but not before he had pictured a cartwheel, and a maniacal laugh with a thumb at his nose.

He passed through the area to reach his favourite strolling ground by the sluggish but insidious Trent, under towers of humming transmission lines, where surveyors were checking levels and mapping the alluvium to make roads and lay out factories.

The city spread its buildings for people to enjoy, better dwelling places than those on the crummy acres of the Meadows where Archie lived. The new estate across the river caused arguments when Cecilia said what a shame it was there'd soon be no countryside left. Her complaint reminded Herbert of tedious belly-aching books by D. H. Lawrence and others, who wanted people to live in cottages without bathrooms but with the Greenwood Tree at hand to dance around at the weekend; while at night they would read those same writers' books by oil and candlelight. He erased the picture, and walked more quickly, glad when he was beyond all sight of the city.

A notebook on his knee, he sat by the weir at Beeston, green water sliding over the lip as smooth as paint. In the warm sun, when the breeze slackened, smoke from his cigarette kept off the midges. Instead of stories and sketches he thought he would use his experience of the last seven years and write a novel. People on the street and at work, and his digs, led intense and unique lives. They did everywhere, but few seemed to realize that they did here as well.

Everyone he knew thought themselves the centre of the world, as far as they were concerned. Burdened in the morning with fatigue, headaches and unresolved dreams on their way to the factory, they were quick to be offended if anything unexpected was put in the way of routine, not wanting to work but knowing they must to earn a living. Only when fully awake in the middle of the day, and aware that all they had to do was endure until evening, could they afford to be cheerful. They slogged home at half past five, as if having stood so long at a machine had solidified legs and feet into lead. Yet when a sluice of water had gone over chest and face, and they'd eaten a tea of the cheapest food, the daze cleared from before their eyes, and what seemed like the length of another day opened for them to do what they liked in. Eight hours of sweat had been traded for eight hours of freedom, and everyone was different in the use they put it to. Likewise with Bert, who Herbert at times knew better than himself. The permutations of stories from such existences were endless, and even incidents out of his imagination could be described in sufficient detail to seem credible. He mulled until clouds darkened over the eddying water, giving reason to hurry home and make a beginning.

The typed sheets lay on his table under a folded shirt, a secure enough hiding place, he had thought, until Mrs Denman said one day at supper: 'I didn't realize you were writing a book, Bert.'

He cut a sausage in two, dipped one half in a pool of sauce. 'What meks yer think that?'

She let the newspaper fall. 'I can't see as Archie will like what you say about him, true or not.'

'It ain't Archie,' he said gruffly, reaching for the bread. 'And if it was he wouldn't mind.'

'I only found it because I wanted to wash your shirt' – not caring, he assumed, to be accused of snooping. 'As for that woman you write such things about, well! I suppose she's that nice dark one you tek to your room.'

'No.' He didn't see why she should feel like a criminal or, worse, a sneak. 'It's completely made up.'

'So you say. But there's me in it, as well. I've got black hair, though, not ginger.'

'It's all right, Ma.' He could only laugh, and touch her arm. 'I'll alter it before it's finished. You won't know yourself when I've done with you.'

'That's a fine thing to say!' Which remark he couldn't decide how to take. Perhaps she was amused at the description, and wanted him to leave it be, for she smiled: 'I allus thought there was more to you than met the eye.'

Within three months he had written the novel again, sucking so much ink into the rubber sack of his fountain pen that he wondered if for the rest of his life he would use sufficient of the blue-black liquid to drown himself. Changing people so that they couldn't be recognized, yet not distort the sense of their reality, or their appearance to the world, seemed hardly possible. The best he could hope was that – if by a far off chance anyone in the district read it – few but scattered qualities of various people they knew would be detectable. He wanted to make the book readable and convincing mainly for himself and for whoever didn't know how industrial workers lived.

Every day in the factory, as each finished artefact fell from his lathe, he wondered what vocation he might otherwise have followed in his life. He could have been a soldier, certainly, perhaps an actor, even a confidence man, not to mention a mechanic that half of himself had become, but he was turning most of all into a thief of broken dreams, or a cat burglar of other people's lives. Switching off, he tidied up so as to leave the lathe and its surroundings clean for the next morning's start. The lathe had been the only thing in his life he could go back to, but now he had something else, his spirit floating like a compass needle in alcohol as he reached for his jacket, haversack of sandwich paper and empty flask, and collected his new Raleigh from the cycle shed. He rode away from the factory like a somnambulist, and when he got home washed himself at the kitchen sink and sat down to a silent supper. Afterwards he went upstairs and closed the door to his room. Eight hours of pandering to the mechanical part of himself called for a refuge in which he could fit his daydreams together like the scattered pieces of a Meccano set. Phrase by phrase, he was assembling a version of himself, but not turning into a Bert or a Herbert, rather someone a little of both but unique to neither. Such a way of finding out who he was gradually revealed that no one ever discovered who they were, at least not to the depth and unity he had formerly hoped was possible.

The cold emotion felt while writing told him that he was reconstituting himself, whoever he was, by using the people among whom he lived. From Phaeton driving a disintegrating chariot across the sky he was putting the pieces back and fixing them together while the vehicle was still in motion.

A dark cloud, shaped like the top half of South America, drifted across scintillating Ursa Major. While saying a passionate goodnight to Cecilia at the gate of her house he noticed a man smoking a cigar come on to the pavement, and look up and down the road as if wondering what rent he would charge if he owned the houses on it, or as if to make sure that no roughnecks from Radford or the Meadows were swarming up in the darkness with knives between their teeth to take his posh villa to pieces: her father.

Cecilia broke free, and forestalled him. 'Hello, Dad.'

'Thought I saw you. Is this your young man?'

Herbert objected to the description, it being a long time since he had thought of himself as young, and in any case he didn't care to be lumped with any group of the population by such a slob. But for Cecilia's sake he held out his hand, moodily shaken by a short, compact, bald-headed man who all but ignored him by saying sharply to Cecilia: 'You'd better get in. It's late.'

Herbert appreciated the kiss on his cheek, but was annoyed at such obedience from a woman of her age. 'Good night, then.'

The large front door thumped to. 'You seem to be courting my daughter.'

Bert opened his packet of Senior Service, and took time to light one. 'You could say as much.'

'I hope you're not stringing her along.'

What kind of world was he living in? 'If you believe that you'll believe anything.'

He scuffed the end of his cigar into the pavement. 'Have you got any long-term plans?'

'What's that supposed to mean?'

'I'm not surprised you don't know. Future intentions – you know very well what I'm getting at. I'd be interested to hear your views.'

'So would I. When I have some you'll be the first to know, after Cecilia, I expect.'

'That's straight enough. She deserves well.'

'I couldn't agree more.'

'Make sure she gets it, then.'

Herbert's supercilious smile was wasted in the dark. If I loved her I'd be polite, because of his age, which is supposed to give him wisdom and knowledge, but who can say he's wiser or more knowing than I am? He thinks all the advantages on his side give him the right to test my seriousness with Cecilia, but I stopped taking tests when I left the army. He clenched his fists at having been forced into reflection, ready to knock the self-important little tyke down if he said much more. 'Are you threatening me?'

'You told her you worked in an office.' Coming closer, Herbert gave him top marks for guts. 'But I happen to know you work in a factory.'

'She's aware of that.'

'I don't think she is.'

'She should be by now. In any case,' the full public school accent took him over, 'it's none of your business. So if you'll excuse me, I must be going. I have to get up in the morning and do a day's work.'

'If you think I don't work, you're wrong.' Herbert sensed the man relenting towards him, maybe because of the accent, which made him angrier. The pathetic swine wanted a good pasting, but there was no point squandering time. 'I'm not implying anything, old boy. I'm just trying to tell you, in no uncertain terms, to get off my back.' It was satisfying to see him walk away so quickly.

It had to be done somewhere, so why not in his room? He led the way step by step, between wallpaper that must have been there since before the Boer War. Likewise the shabby carpet. Cecilia wore the usual mock-thoroughbred expression at muted bruto noises from the backyards, and turned up her shapely nose at the sparse economy of the furnished room, heavy with odours from train and cigarette smoke, and diesel fumes from the buses, not much improved when he closed the window and curtains. A good half of him sympathized with her, which didn't please him, so he said: 'If I bump into your old man again I'll black both his eyes, and break one of his arms.'

She laughed as he closed the door. 'Oh, darling, you made him hopping mad. I promised faithfully not to see you any more. Don't be angry, though. He was only trying to look after me. He still thinks I'm a young girl. There are times when I don't like it, but I know he'll never grow up and treat me as a woman, and I'm twenty-nine.'

'Doesn't it bother you?'

She sat on the bed. 'I'm used to it. I can always pacify him, and get what I want.' Does that mean, Herbert wondered, that she thinks she can do the same with me? He undid his belt. 'Take your clothes off.'

'You know, I don't much like doing it here.'

He drew her forward for a kiss, and managed it delicately. 'It's just as sweet as anywhere else. I feel such love for you. Come on, sweetheart.'

The encounter reminded her of one they had seen in a French film of before the war, so she loosened her skirt, and lay on the bed. He manoeuvred a warm shoulder out of her blouse, much appreciating that she accepted his squalid digs as an adventurous place for a fuck. His kisses sent her into such rapture that soon it didn't matter that they weren't on the brightly lit bed at home. He couldn't be sure to what extent she had climaxed, because a train whistle sounded at the same time.

'You keep promising to let me see your typewriter,' she said, arranging her clothes. 'But you never do.'

We've just made love a couple of feet above it, he wanted to say, having wrapped it in a piece of blanket and shoved it under the bed. Not that he was convinced the machine had been stolen from her office. 'One of the letters went phut, and it's away for repair.'

'Oh, what firm do you use?'

What indeed? 'I take it to a bloke up the road. He knows all about them. Used to work at Barlock's.'

'I really must see it, one day. I can't wait to read your novel, either, when it's finished.'

'Nor can I.'

'Well, you know what I mean.' She didn't want to stay long after making love, as if everyone in the street had their ears fixed against the wall. The French film effect had worn off. The room was cold, its window rattling at every breeze. She wanted to be walked back to where steam pipes were hot to the fingers.

She came out of the love-making mood before he did, though he was happy enough to shift, even to walk in silence through the same old dismal town, rain blowing against their faces.

'Let's say goodnight at the end of the road in case my father's waiting. No use antagonizing him unnecessarily.' Another reason was the ever present violence in Herbert which, though it had some attraction, made her afraid for herself as well as for her father. It was too easy to imagine them getting into a fight. She would like Herbert to have more control, and not be so self-indulgent. He was often touchy for little reason. Her other young men had put on a show of respect for her father, but Herbert relished no such laws, and her father had ranted only that day that he wouldn't trust him as far as he could throw him.

They met less often, she making excuses for staying at home, which he didn't question, using the time to work on his novel, whose progress she no longer asked about, indicating that she had lost interest, which at times suited him well, while at others it increased his sense of isolation.

He persuaded her to go to the pub on Wilford Road, thinking she might like to see a scene from one of his chapters. He led her along dark streets to get there, which route, apart from tiring her, put her into a gloomy state, especially when the devil was in him to rile her more than usual. The saloon bar was disappointingly empty. 'You haven't been in a dive like this before, I suppose?'

She smiled, knowing his game. 'Is it just another of your planned adventures? It's called slumming, isn't it? If so, I can do without it. Pubs like this aren't places a well brought-up woman would normally go into.'

'A good upbringing should allow one to go anywhere.'

She sipped her brandy as if the rogue factory worker before her would belt her one if she didn't appreciate it, or he would look askance if she drank it too quickly. Like everything about him it was hard to tell. 'You ought to get a room in a better district.'

He only annoyed her to make her more lively, unless it was an underhand way of increasing the liveliness in himself, which thought brought on momentary shame at such meanness, though in revenge at her making him feel it he said: 'You've told me that a hundred times already.'

Her face flushed with excitement, as if every quarrel took them further into the unknown. 'I'm telling you again.'

'There are two reasons why I don't,' he said calmly. 'One is that it's cheap where I am, and the other is that it's close to work. Another thing is I like the woman who runs the place.'

She retied the pretty coloured scarf around her neck. 'But you're a writer, aren't you? And you work in an office, don't you? You could surely get a nice flat.'

He swallowed half his pint, wondering whether to belch. He didn't, though if this was taking place in a story he certainly would have. 'I've slaved on the shop floor since I was fourteen, except for a few years in the army.'

'Oh stop that stupid talk. You know very well what my father told me. I suspected as much before, anyway. But why did you try to deceive me?' She was close to tears. 'That's what's so unforgivable.'

If things had gone that far between two people it was time to end the affair. He grinned, as widely as he was able to stretch his lips without the help of his fingers. 'I didn't deceive you, duck.'

'You revelled in it. And in any case I've always known you weren't what you said you were.'

He respected her, and maybe loved her too much even now to let rip the full power of his assumed personality. 'You just try to guess everything, without coming out honestly and asking to talk it over. You don't know anything about me.'

'But if you loved me you'd have been open with me.' She was ready to let the tears fall. 'Why weren't you?'

She guessed he had been searching for a reason to stop seeing her, and realized that she wanted to stop seeing him as well. Her legs supported her in standing up, though it was hard to stop the shake at her ankles. 'You're sly and deceitful, and mean. You're afraid of the world and everybody in it. You don't know anything about human beings because you're not human yourself.'

The words came out hard, like a machine gun firing dumdum bullets which ought to have chewed his guts to mush, and would have if they'd meant as much to him as they obviously did to her. Real life again, he smiled. She had come alive at last, at the very point when he was intent on ditching her. To tolerate such yammering he drummed up more Archie than there was even Bert Gedling in himself, and no attempt at control could stop him. 'You're a sour old maid, a bleedin' snob, as well, and all because o' the work I do.'

Further words were stopped by her brandy splashing his jacket and shirt. 'Don't expect to see me again.'

The drops that hit his scar stung like acid, and if she hadn't gone quickly he would have smacked her between the eyes. He had often wondered how it would end, and now he knew.

'I think you asked for that,' a man called from the bar, seeing his shock and rage impossible to hide.

Bert, realizing the procedure in such a situation, said that he supposed he did.

'That's a lovely scar you've got, though,' the man said, stricken with admiration and envy. 'Did *she* do it?'

'Good Lord, no,' Herbert smiled.

'She gave you what-for, though, didn't she?'

Herbert admitted that she had indeed, but said it wouldn't be the last time such a bust-up would happen to him. He hoped not, anyway, otherwise what was the point of being on earth?

'You've got a point there,' the man said, and went on, cheerfully enough: 'I've had six wives, if you want to know.'

Herbert didn't particularly. 'Six?'

'Well, women, you might say. Three of 'em I left, and the other three left me. Not bad, eh? I can't wait to find another, but I'm having a bit of a break at the moment.'

'I'd say you deserved it.' Herbert strolled across for another pint. The occasion of his rupture with Cecilia called for a swagger. He seated himself beside the Lothario, though he hardly seemed that, with his fat slack body and worn features, pasty skin and grey but alert eyes.

His navy-blue three-piece suit was of good quality, his collar and tie impeccable, as was the trilby at a confident enough angle. Even the stool he sat on seemed to feel the privilege as he swivelled to face Herbert: 'No use crying over spilt beer, that's what I always say.'

Herbert denied he was made that way, though knew he had lost her right enough, deciding never to get rid of anyone so unfeelingly again. In other words, have even more self-control over his mouth than heretofore, and watch his behaviour every second. That way he'd get what he wanted and stay sane as well – and you couldn't have it better than that. As for happiness, if you thought about having much of that you would really end up to your neck in shit.

'You know how to keep a woman happy?'

The man seemed to be intercepting his thoughts, but Herbert appreciated being amused by this funny little chap who claimed to be so irresistible to women. 'Give 'em a good fucking every night?' Bert said.

He laughed. 'Yo' young 'uns! Nothing so crude as that. I've worked it out like this: every time you feel happy, give her a good hiding; every time you feel rotten and down in the dumps, make her feel as if she's the queen of the earth. Can't lose, because that way neither of you can take each other for granted, or get fed up.'

'How come that three of your women left you, then?' He called for another pint and sat on a stool to listen.

'I'd better start from the beginning.' The man sipped at whisky that the publican had put down without him even having to ask, suggesting that he was trying to drown his sorrows in drink now that his peculiar system had fallen apart at the seams.

The longer the rigmarole went on the more dismal it became, a catalogue of tricks and woes spun out in monotone, with a lack of art that Herbert found depressing, boredom only offset by pint after pint until both of them were blindoe and incoherent. It was a story no one either sane or drunk could make head or tail of, and the only happiness of the evening was when he reeled into the street at kicking-out time, finding the way back to his room as if radar had drawn him to it.

Sitting alone he realized the truth that Cecilia had walked out on him, and who could blame her? With another woman it might only have been a step to a more realistic relationship (albeit of unbearable cosiness) though with her it was final because he had so blatantly let it happen, had even been gentleman enough to engineer it in his own particular way.

Consoling himself, before getting out of his clothes and falling into a dreamless sleep, he thought of Aeneas leaving Dido at Carthage, and couldn't imagine that Aeneas had felt very good about it either as he sailed away over the cerulean briny. Like Aeneas too he felt beckoned on to higher things, while not caring to ask himself what they might be.

Sixteen

He lit the Rippingill heater, and the bubble of paraffin going down into the reservoir under the wick was a comforting sound on cold nights. Though heavier curtains made a womb to sit in, both glass and cloth seemed merely conductors to let the freezing fog inside. He wore two pullovers as well as a jacket and a pair of mittens, less willing to shiver than in former days, when he had undressed and jumped naked into bed. Now on icy nights he undid belt and all buttons, braces and bootlaces, and had his pyjama top to hand as soon as shirt and vest came off, and the bottoms pulled on the moment he was out of his boots. Socks were left till the bedclothes were drawn back and he could get in to generate warmth. Every winter seemed closer to the one before, each useful for writing his novel over and over again in an effort to transmute people so that not only would they find it difficult to spot themselves, but would also get some feeling as to their relationship with earth and heaven.

Mrs Denman's had been his refuge longer than any other place, and he occasionally felt, as at the climax of one of those penny-dreadful comic books sometimes read at school, that the walls of his room were closing in, and would crush him to death. The hero-victim inevitably found a way out, but Herbert saw no exit except by keeping a wary eye on the walls' position – and endurance. The dulling sunflowers of the wallpaper urged him to write for them as his first audience, as if they monitored every sentence even before it came into his mind; and when he was out of the room they would put on flesh and blood, to check with big brown Cyclopean eyes what he had written.

He needed some other brain to imbibe what he had done, even

if only to tell him he wasn't on a slow boat to madness, or that the accumulating pages in the cardboard box under his bed weren't merely the evidence of his splintered mind. Perhaps it didn't much matter, for he had no fear of madness as long as he felt the anguish of uncertainty about what he was doing, but he needed to know whether the writing would engross others to the extent that he was mesmerized on reading it himself.

Cecilia had long since gone – been dumped, he now knew – which could be a pity, because she would have commented in some way, even though the collected works of Hawksworth clouded her paltry mind. He couldn't show his secret writing to Archie, and that was a fact. If Mrs Denman took a look now and again she didn't say, though even she must have lost interest because he could never find any disturbance to prove otherwise. The only person he could think of was Isaac; he put the typescript into a carrier bag, and walked with both burdens into town.

Isaac was thinner and more frail. Every few months showed a difference, eyes shining through the papery skin of his face as from a lantern, false teeth too big for his diminishing features. But the same gimlet light came into his eyes. 'You haven't called lately. I thought you were chasing the girls.'

'I wasn't sure I'd find you. I thought you might be in your council flat by now.'

'That's cold – as they say round here. Maybe I never will be. Old folks like me come last on the list. Still, times are a lot easier now that rationing's a blight of the past. Not only that, but my daughter sends money every month, to bolster my pension.'

'Maybe her conscience has started to bother her.'

'I don't mind what it is,' Isaac said. 'If you begin questioning people's motives when they do good deeds there'd soon be no virtue left in the world.'

Herbert thought he might work such a statement into his novel – and laid the bag of typescript on the table. 'There's this to take your mind off things. Have a read, when you can find the time.'

'I wondered when you were going to let me see what you'd been up to.' Isaac washed his hands at the sink, then spread the papers to separate the first chapter. Over seventy, he moved slowly as he sat down to read. Herbert stood by the window, a rank smell rising from the narrow street. Even the pigeons in the opposite guttering looked drab and fed up as they nudged each other aside for a better view of the chimney pots. Noises of approval and understanding from Isaac caused him to sweat with embarrassment, and regret that he had given his underground work to the mercy of a man who hadn't been young for fifty years.

Not knowing how long it would be before Isaac grew tired of the story, and came back to life saying what absolute rubbish, or maybe even how marvellous, or merely how interesting (since he wouldn't know what else to say), Herbert pulled a book from the shelf called *Guide for the Perplexed*. The title seemed right for him, and his eyes fixed on:

> If there were two Gods, they would necessarily have one element in common by virtue of which they were Gods, and another element by which they were distinguished from each other and existed as two Gods; the distinguishing element would either be in both different from the property common to both – in that case both of them would consist of different elements, and neither of them would be the First Cause, or have absolutely independent existence; but their existence would depend on certain causes, or the distinguishing element would only in one of them be different from the element common to both: then that being could not have absolute independence.

He went back and forth over the complex netting of words, played at interchanging God for Man – and even man – so that he understood that you could use the word God in any way you liked, because the concept had after all been invented by human beings, who must have known themselves as such, while hammering the idea out on stone, or scratching it on animal skin.

God was just as much split in two as Herbert most of the time felt. In the contest between nihilism and a code of morals he was most comfortable with the former, since it allowed him to enjoy doing more or less what he liked, or as much as he could get away with. While he had to control his actions his thoughts could go free, and the gulf between thought and action was a power house that fuelled his double life, and was vital to his writing.

Spanning both states, he acknowledged the need for morality or fair play in the world (he wasn't a Thurgarton-Strang for nothing) while knowing he was a savage compared to Isaac. For Herbert to lead a good life would fetter his intuition and, even more, his imagination. Not only that, but a virtuous stance on everything might make his views more rigid and therefore less interesting. The fact that Isaac, being the epitome of rectitude as far as he could tell, lacked no human qualities, convinced Herbert of his unique spirit.

Isaac's voice startled him. 'Looks like you've stumbled on Maimonides. I never could get through all of it.'

'It's interesting.'

'Do you want it?'

'No.' He slid the book back. 'I've read enough. How about my effort, though?'

'Well, it's not a bad read. You ought to think about getting it to a publisher.'

'It doesn't need redoing?'

'Not as far as I can tell, though there's no reason why you shouldn't think so. It reads as good as any novel I've taken out of the library lately. Go over it once more, then send it to London. With a bit of luck you may shake 'em rigid!'

A pale evening sun made the walls of the newspaper offices glow red, the muted noise of machinery sounding from inside. He was glad to get out of the airless library, after copying publishers' addresses into his notebook. His aim was to go through Slab Square and back to his digs, but by the Peach Tree he bumped into Archie, eyes seeming closer together than usual, indicating anger for some reason or another. 'Yer look pale,' Bert said. 'Did another 'usband put the shits up yer?'

His laugh was that of an unhappy man as he gripped Herbert's arm and drew him towards the pub door. 'Not likely. Come in for a drink, and I'll tell yer.'

Hunger for his tea was made up for by the comforting smell of ale. 'What's it all about, then?'

'You know this fucking trouble wi' Egypt?' Archie said, when two cold pints were on the table.

Hard not to. A real killpig. They'd grabbed the Suez canal, and Israel had kicked their arses all the way across the desert. It was in every newspaper, but he wondered what world affairs had to do with Archie.

'Well, I might get called up.' His face was crimson at such injustice, as if only he had been singled out. 'They've put me on standby.' He showed the envelope. 'But I'm not going this time.'

'I ain't got mine,' Bert said, 'and I'm on the reserves as well. Maybe there's some mistake.'

Archie laughed. 'You're later in the alphabet than me. Anyway, I heard on the wireless they'd be wanting some of us back. Not me, though. I don't have a uniform any more. I was looking for it yesterday, and Mam towd me she'd gen it to the ragman. So I can't go, can I?'

'I don't suppose I'll mind all that much.'

'You wouldn't, you daft bastard. You're a gentleman-wanker who's got no fucking sense at all.'

'Well, don't despair, Archie, my owd.'

He guzzled, and took out a handkerchief to wipe his mouth. 'Despair? Not me. Despair's stupid, and I'm not fucking stupid. All the same, just think of it. It'll be jump to attention again, and polish yer boots, stand by your beds, and all that bull. They're either a bunch of fucking Hitlers, or a pack of useless shitbags. It's all right for you, Bert. You was made for it, though I'll never know why.'

Herbert, as if Archie was looking over his shoulder, was almost ashamed at the pleasure of being wanted for service again. Even Mrs Denman said: 'Good news, Bert?' when he opened the little brown envelope.

He wondered what use he would be. 'I've been called up. It's that Suez thing.'

A new television set had been pushed under the table until Frank came in after work to do the installation. She stroked it, could hardly wait to see the pictures. 'What a shame. It ain't right, is it, that young chaps like you have to go.'

Archie walked to the station to see him off, helping to carry his suitcase and kit bag. Half an hour to go, they sat in the refreshment room of pillars and plantpots, one of the more elegant places in the middle of Nottingham. Tea and Mars bars were set on the table. 'I think they forgot about me.'

Bert slipped his folded beret under a shoulder strap. 'They'll get you, don't worry.'

'No, they wain't. Maybe they don't want any electricians, only infantry. If they do want me, though, it'll tek a long time for the redcaps to find me. As for yo', Bert, you could have swung the lead, and towd 'em yer can't walk because of the smash-up in Cyprus.'

He could, but wouldn't. The injuries, such as they were, had never relegated him into the ranks of the unfit. Pain in arms and legs had long since gone, which pleased him, because he thought it the lowest form of life to be useless either as a workman or a soldier. When he mentioned the breakages on getting to the depot the MO merely asked if they still bothered him.

'No, sir.'

'It wouldn't have made any difference,' the sergeant said outside. 'You're for the Canal, like the rest of us.'

Few cared for a soldier's lot; it was so long since the war. The blokes were more bollocky than before, and who could blame them? It was Archie's good luck not to be called, but Herbert was exhilarated at being in khaki again, and hoped the war in Egypt wouldn't pack in before he could add the experience of battle to his life – as he put it in a letter to his parents. His affinity with the ways of soldiering was proof, if it were needed, that he wasn't as cut off from his old school self and the notions of his father as he had imagined. Heredity never relaxed its power, and within a week he felt he could stay in the army forever.

The men of his platoon were disgruntled rather than grumbling, near mutinous at times, though Herbert assumed that even the married ones would be all too ready to take such resentment out on the Egyptians. Getting the lads to let go on the range with the Bren was a fiasco at first, half of them not on the list till he noticed and made it right.

Rain splashed down as they marched across the airfield for embarkation, visibility almost nil. Basic kit was already on board, and transport

206

planes waited to fly them to a staging post in Cyprus. He wondered would he see that beautiful woman who had worked in the vineyards – or her younger sister by now? Best to hope not, and to avoid her vision even in daydreams, because maybe she had been Lady Death, hiding behind a rock and luring him and Pemberton into the lorry crash. It was easy to cut her out. He was more powerfully himself than in those days. The copy of *Our Mutual Friend*, bookmarked halfway through, jutted from his trouser pocket, and he only wanted to get on board the plane and carry on reading.

A headlit jeep swung into the dispersal point, and the RSM climbed down with a signal to say it was no go. Lorries would take them back to barracks. Everything was at full stop, just as they were about to go out and clear the mess up forever. A cheer spread along the lines, but the ground missed a beat under Herbert's boots at being robbed of a chance to blend the disparate sides of himself in the most perfect way. The meat-skewer bayonet would never come out of its scabbard. No use spitting tacks, or even cursing. Despair, as Archie said, was a sign of stupidity. Maybe he had wanted to be killed in a blinding whirl of heroics before lights-out, so that only in death would his two selves be united.

He gobbed into the sud pan, pressed the button, and adjusted the machine to the job in question. Gratitude would have been the order of the day, at being so valued by the firm that his place had been kept open which, at fifteen quid a week, was worth having.

His hands had become soft while he was in the army. Amazing how little time was needed. They blistered from pressure and repetition. The skin grazed too easily and was prone to splinters. Brass was the worst, bits that festered like mad till he got them out. Archie said steel was *his* curse, and Herbert supposed it depended on the preference of your flesh, or even some temperamental make-up that couldn't be analysed.

Resuming work was harder to slot into than when, scarred and broken, he left the army after Cyprus. Motivation now seemed lacking, and tedium reigned for the first few weeks, an inner voice suggesting it was time such labour came to an end. He was getting too old for it, the bolshie tone went on, had done as much of a stint as any man needed, and certainly enough to write about it for the rest of his life. He was bored more often than he could tolerate, at times bored almost to death, though knowing he must continue until he could move into another existence without destroying himself in the process.

You should never complain, though he was beginning to, in the silence of his mind, considering it lucky no one could know it. Muscles ached, but he struggled on till the morning tea trolley showed at the end of the shed door, steaming as if in imitation of Stephenson's *Rocket*. After the scalding liquid had gone down and the sweet bun was scoffed he was lured through the day by the promise of refuge in his room, where he could write in spite of the muted yacker of the television from the kitchen.

He tried to describe how a man felt when at work in the machine shop, or in the sand foundry, or when stuck at the pressure die-casting machines. The aim was to tell it without the distortion of sympathy, but the accounts were even so a world from reality. What did words know? Though if they couldn't, what might? Every word was a label for something, or an action, and enough permutations barely existed to use them as they had never been used before, while too much trying would make for a heavy and stilted style, debasing the inspired flow of what had to be told. Best to let rip, and tinker later, let blocks of action, varied by badinage and laced with glum but often feverish hopes, make an account fine-tooled by his experience over the years.

The process wasn't so different from that of taking a piece of angular steel and, with the aid of a blueprint, shaping it at your machine till a pristine object of exact utility lay fashioned and almost finished on your bench, but which still had to fit into an overall pattern with other pieces.

His writing was considered in this way also. Three months absence made him happy to go back to it, but some time passed before his eyes could focus and make the mass of words coherent. He had to be sure that every phrase was where it ought to be. Time was, as they said, no object, but as a wage-earner he longed for the day when he could tell himself the book was finished, and send it away as a parcel. If too frightened by the risk he could put it back in the drawer till driven to take it out for another re-writing. And if a sense

208

of its uselessness overcame him he would go through his notebooks and muse something else into shape.

His scarred hands were cramped, stiff fingers barely able to grasp the pen as he read the opening pages again, of two brothers fishing from the canal bank. Circular clusters of white elderberry flowers concealed them from the lane, and the steamy summer heat over the water kept the coloured stripes of their floats perfectly still.

They biked the countryside through pastoral scenery which he tried to describe with the purity of *The Eclogues*, a memory of school even more pleasurable when lines came unexpectedly in Latin.

The brothers went back to their labour on Monday morning, and Herbert laid the raw alternative of the factory against the succulent peace of the countryside. He made a theatrical stage out of the shop floor and lifted the narrative into a three-dimensional experience of stench and noise which, he hoped, would keep a reader turning the pages to find out what was going to happen to the people he wrote about.

He told that such toil was a normal and not too disagreeable way of earning a living: all components of the factory's activity, the hundreds of different jobs, the inner musings and outer mouthings of those who sweated there, all living in and moving through the mansion of his novel, so that by the end something had happened to them, not in the apocalyptic way of earlier versions, but as fitted with the easy-going morality of the times.

Should Archie and his brother Raymond, or their mates, or their sisters and mothers even, ever pick up the book they might speculate as to who the people were, what street they lived in, or what place they worked at, while they would be seen as complex and interesting by those who hardly believed such characters existed.

In ten years Herbert's soul had been captured as surely as if a net had been thrown over him by a gladiator in the arena, and the long fight to get free from its entanglements had led him to know more about himself than if such a fate had not ensnared him. He posted *Royal Ordnance* to a publisher and, when it came back with no comment, sent it out again.

* * *

He closed the typewriter, feeling neither Bert nor Herbert, and far from a solid mixture of both. A booze-up with Archie might bring one of them into focus and ease his spirit, but Archie was nowhere to be found so he forced himself out of the house and quick-walked into town.

Standing at the bar of the Eight Bells, he saw a woman even Mrs Denman would have looked at sideways and leerily. Fair and dumpy, big tits and beehive hair-do, high heels and brandished fag, a slight gap between her upper teeth that promised mischief, the photo-flashed picture was one Bert Gedling liked. 'Drink up, duck.'

'Give me a chance.'

Down it went. So did his. 'I had to get out of the house tonight or I would have gone barmy.' At least you could say what you liked for the price of a drink. They sat at a small round table in the corner.

'Like that, is it?' she said.

It was, though no longer. 'I couldn't write any more. My pen nib went rusty.'

'Was yer writin' letters?'

'I allus am.'

'I wrote one yesterday, to my sister in America. She got married to a Yank ten years ago. I went to see her last summer.'

'How did you get on?'

'I loved it.'

'I'm not surprised.'

'It's smashin' over there. They've all got fridges and washing machines and cars . . . how did yer get that scar on yer chops?'

Always a good talking point. Her name was Denise, and she worked at Chambers in Stapleford packing pencils. Like all of them, there was more behind the eyes than you thought at first. 'Why is it a nice girl like you don't have a young man?'

'Where's your young woman, then?'

'She packed me in,' he said. 'Or we fell out, you could say. It happened last night, so I forget.'

'My young man was married to me.' She shaped her lips to indicate he hadn't been up to much. 'We'd only been together six months when the police called and took him away for burglary. After he came out we had a bust-up and he left me. I'm lucky we never had any kids. This is the first time I've been in a pub in months. I just wanted to get talking to somebody.'

Even if she had been on the batter since leaving school he would have liked her. 'Well, we've both got company tonight.'

She was easier to get on with than Cecilia, and that was good – almost like being seventeen again, except it took time and a few drinks to lighten the deadness in them both.

He knew they were drunk by the time they got back to the house, and felt the old rough Bert topside over Herbert. Standing on the doorstep he put his fist under her nose. 'If you make any noise getting up the stairs I'll crack you one.'

With a scar like that he might even try. 'Bleddy masterful, aren't you?' Too merry to care, she squeezed his arm, and he kissed her saying: 'I love you, and want to get you into bed.'

Her mood changed like the flip of a penny. 'You ought to show it, then.'

'I will.'

'I love you,' she said, 'whoever you are.' Her smile showed a vulnerable, more sensitive face. With love and care she could be beautiful, but he had no wish to do a Pygmalion, especially when she added: 'At least let me get my hairnet off.'

He put his key in the door. 'Shurrup, though, like I towd yer, or there'll be trouble.'

'You're frightened o' waking yer mam, is that it?'

Rage blasted his nerve-ends into darkness. He wanted to get his hands at her throat because she wasn't Cecilia. The doghead of himself had got rid of her, for nothing, for no reason, to destroy himself, to drop himself into the mire, then out of it and beyond into something he must have wanted but was too scared to think about. What an idiot he'd been.

'Oh, don't you have a nice little room?' she said, when he pushed her inside.

Nice? He wondered what sort of squalid den she lived in, what rat-hole space she shared with a score of others. Maybe she shared a house with her ageing mother, as decent as they came except for an occasional night out like this. He could ask, but it didn't matter. She stripped in practised fashion, skirt down, suspenders undone,

211

stockings off, roll-on unpeeled, blouse and bra on the floor – good clean underwear she'd spent money on.

She spread her white and robust figure on the bed, pubic hair sprouting as if to wave him in. Glad the light wasn't too bright, she was half gone anyway, make-up smeared from kissing on the stairs. Smile at north and south, she beckoned him to get a move on, telling him not to spill his cocoa. He was too drunk to do much, barely able to get hard enough. In a sober corner of his mind, a recurring and suicidal fantasy, he wondered what it would be like to stay with her for the rest of his life. By laughing it away he was able to use her. Even so, he was too quick, and had to play her by hand.

They were soon asleep, and in a dream he was standing by a large tropical bird of red and yellow and royal blue. He was affectionately stroking its warm vibrating plumage, when the Bird of Paradise lost its friendliness and, mindlessly, viciously, pressed its razor-sharp beak deep into his hand and wouldn't let go. Blood spurted out, so to save his limb and possibly his life he squeezed its neck with the other hand, using all his strength until the feathers were bloody and ligaments began to separate till the bird was dead.

Tall thin Frank bent over the stove to fry their breakfast. Traffic noises beyond the windows were muted by rain. 'It ain't right,' he murmured. 'It ain't bleddy right.'

'What ain't?' There was no sign of Mrs Denman, and no place set for him, so he took plates and cutlery from the cupboard.

'She's having a lie-in this morning. But you know she's not well, don't you?'

He didn't, but thanked the Lord he had got Denise out into the street with no noise. She'd been too sleepy to care, because it was only half past seven. 'I at least expected to stay a bit longer,' she whispered at the door. He pushed a pound note into her hand. 'Your taxi fare.' 'Oh, ta!' she said, happily enough.

'Why, what's wrong with her?'

'She keeps complaining about her stomach, and won't let me get her to the doctor. She gets these terrible pains. I phoned Ralph last night and told him about it, but the bogger don't seem interested. He said she'll see a doctor when she's good and ready. I tell yer! His own mother!' He put tomatoes and bacon on the table. 'But will she see a doctor? Not her. She's as stubborn as the bleddy Hemlock Stone.'

Herbert had thought she had looked all right to him. 'Maybe she's overworked.'

'You think so?'

'It wouldn't surprise me. She needs a week at the seaside, just sitting around all day or strolling along the front. She'd feel better then, I'm sure.'

Frank ate bread and butter with a shaking hand. 'I'll try her. You could be right. It's the pain, though. She gets pole-axed, and it breaks my heart.' He began to cry, and Herbert couldn't wait to get out of the room.

The drill snapped, and a piece gashed his right arm. A short cut through carelessness. There was no such thing. He had done it himself, because the chuck hadn't been tight enough. Blood marbled into the vat of milky suds, filtered away between coils of shining swarf. Toolsetter Paul, who knew Bert wouldn't slacken without good reason, came to look. 'That's nasty. You'd better go to the first aid and 'ave it seen to.'

He felt close to sleep. The wound began to burn. 'What did you say?'

'Your arm. Looks like an 'ospital job. Are you all right?'

The ragged pomegranate split would need stitches – another scar to show. 'It's hard to say, at the moment. I have to be off now.' The accent made Paul think he must be far from his old self, imitating the bloody BBC. He ought to be in the concert party.

Walking through the open gate of the hospital with his arm in a sling, he went at an unaccustomed slow pace down the street towards Slab Square and the bus stop. Cecilia was walking on the other side, by the eighteenth-century houses, in one of which Byron had lived, though she wasn't talking about that, but saying something to a tall smartish man – good-looking in his clerkly provincial mode – who rounded his shoulders to hear her words. Bert assumed he could pass unnoticed wearing cap and overalls and clomping along in swarf-dull boots, but she saw, and expected him to give no sign. The shape of her lips would take a decade to analyse, but the impression he got was of regret, panic, damaged feelings and, finally, unmistakably, relief that he had caught her signal, and would pass as if they had never been acquainted.

He owed her that much, though the thought of assailing her as Bert, crowing: 'Don't yer know me, don't yer know me, don't yer know me, then, – duck?' caused no inner laugh or gloating. Turning her prospects, even happy ones, into entrails of misery, was no part of him.

Putting out his left arm for the bus, he spewed contempt at the idea that his heart was wounded but knew it was true enough. He hadn't been sufficiently adult or loving to hold her, or sufficiently mature to want to, though it was good that he hadn't, since if they had married the inevitable parting would have been more destructive. The sense of loss reminded him of childhood, though he no longer blamed anyone for what he might have suffered then.

The bus on Wheeler Gate was slowed by the crowds and traffic at dusk. He scorned the bite of regret over Cecilia, though wondered whether it wasn't time to flit from this town of romantic agony.

Mrs Denman and Frank were sitting by the range reading the advertisements in the evening paper for boarding houses at Skegness. She got up to ask Herbert what had gone wrong with his arm. It was plain she'd been ill for weeks, to go by the deep blue moons under her eyes. He hadn't noticed, and now that he knew he must act as if she wasn't. 'Just a scratch. Industrial accident, it's called.'

'It's only an excuse to stay off work,' Frank said.

She reached for a letter from behind the walnut wood clock. 'This came for you.'

Frank sat in the rocking chair to sip his tea. 'We're going to Skegness for a fortnight. And after we come back I'm going to make an honest woman of her.'

'I should think it's the other way round.' Herbert, half fainting in the haze, put the white envelope into his pocket, and took Mrs Denman's hands, drew her close for a kiss, noticing her carmined face above the pastiness of illness. 'Congratulations, Ma. I'm glad.'

'Me and Frank have known each other so long I think we can stand living together.' She sat in her usual armchair by the fire. 'I'll still be here to look after you, Bert.'

'That's all right, then.' He went slowly upstairs, as if the ache of gash and stitches ascended from each foot and ended as needles stabbing at the brain. Such a small room, no more than a cell it seemed, had been a life-long comfort, but he felt intolerably boxed in and wanted to put his coat back on and run as far as he could get into the countryside. Coming to a dense wood he would find the middle, fall asleep in the undergrowth, and hope never to wake up again.

Even the energy to reach the front door was beyond him. Bert couldn't get up to save his skin, and though Herbert might manage it he would be neither better off nor wiser if he did. He unlatched the buckles of his overalls with one hand, twisted them free and loosened his bootlaces. The wardrobe mirror gave back a perturbed mask, as if he hadn't looked into it for years. His father's features showed more clearly. You're the image of Hugh, his mother would say, as if to drive him round the bend and two-thirds up the diminishing zigzags. He had struggled free by becoming who he was not, and in spite of the battle found himself more than halfway back to being who he really was.

Dark hair, straight nose, forceful chin, and the cul de sac of a scar showed a self-engrossed though raddled aspect. A smile gave the image a facile supercilious charm which would deceive nobody, certainly not him. He was amused that *cul de sac* backwards produced (more or less) *cased luc(k)*; which sign caused him to hope that the cul de sac he was caught in would turn into an open street, on which his luck would begin to change.

The mirror also reflected how his face might seem to others, because all the people he had ever looked at were in some way embedded there, which made it more of his own face than ever. Such switchings of template took place without his awareness, and turning his head from side to side, as if to discover how and why, was a gesture which further emphasized who he was.

The reflected image was made up of too many faces because the one that indubitably belonged to him had behind it all those people who, in his novel, had been through happiness and sorrow due to his god-like devising, though the basic aspect was as much under his control as the chariot of a Phaeton arriving successfully at the end of the day.

If his face seemed a mass of contradictions at certain moments there was a discipline within which could always bring it back to one he recognized, because whatever he cared to read there showed it could be no other than his own face, whether the roughneck Bert Gedling or the superior Thurgarton-Strang. Only a member of the elect could look in a mirror and realize there were many versions of his face instead of, like any oaf of the common run, thinking it complete and in no way puzzling.

He wrapped himself in the cold bedding and reached for the almost shredded copy of *Caged Birds*, to indulge in a soothing read, until his eyes would no longer obey his will, and he was so warmly asleep that he failed to hear Mrs Denman calling him down for supper.

Part Three

Seventeen

The publisher's letter said they would appreciate him calling, at a mutually convenient time and date, when they might, after some discussion, be prepared to make an offer on his book. During days of fever the words shot and spiralled around his brain like fiery arrows, always reforming at a distance his arms couldn't reach nor his eyes decipher. When his mind cooled back to equilibrium he thought that whoever had dictated such stilted language must have been to a similar school to his own. But then, maybe they all had in that particular trade.

Knowing the letter by heart, he sent every bit from the window while passing St Albans, and opened the *Evening Post* to gloat over Cecilia's marriage to her middle-aged company director. Director? As they said about one who strutted around the factory, he couldn't direct a trolley from one end of the firm to the other without getting lost, unless it was loaded with bags of somebody else's money and he was going in ever-diminishing circles in the hope of reaching an exit.

If you looked at the photograph one way the man was handsome and self-assured, while squinting at it with one eye closed he seemed furtive and lecherous, and well on the way to being sent down for embezzlement. At the risk of thinking himself mean and despicable Herbert finally considered the man to be a type eminently suitable for Cecilia who, in her virginal wedding dress, would no doubt become a fitting partner for him.

A woman opposite, who he was starting to see as the spitting image of Eileen's apparent reappearance by the town hall lions after he came back from the army, disturbed the recollection of his perfect afternoon with Cecilia on the hillside near Gotham, which had culminated in his sublime eye-contact with the fox. He saw again the clean orange flame of its pelt framed in green, snout to the wind and turned towards prey. Yet its instinct had been defective in not spotting the entwined bodies of two lovers. Even a fox made mistakes.

'What time does this train get to London, duck?'

'How do I know?' Bert snarled.

'Sorry, I was on'y askin'.'

So as to look more like Bert Gedling than Herbert Thurgarton-Strang he stood before a glass at St Pancras to set his cap at an angle, though not too much in case he appeared a caricature rather than dignified. The white silk scarf around his neck was barely visible when his jacket was fastened. A tall thin man of twenty-nine, he sniffed the worldliness of the air outside, mackintosh open and showing his smartest suit, a clean haversack settled on his shoulder. Fingers poking from the arm in its sling were available for adjusting his tie or dealing with trouser buttons. He took care not to look like one of the walking wounded back from a hard campaign of whippet breeding in the North.

The eternal pigeons circling Nelson's head spiralled down in clouds to scavenge crumbs and corn. One settled on the thatched napper of a five-year-old boy with sparkling blue eyes who held a piece of bread in a still hand hoping a bird would come off its perch and eat. Bert smiled when one did. On his way through the same square from school, so long ago, identical pigeons had brought him luck, reinforced him with their powers of intuition and self-preservation, and sent him on a circuit which had brought him back. He waved to the kid's young mother, and set off towards Covent Garden.

A streak of white shit struck the peak of his cap, from a Heinkel pigeon-bomber following along the street. He looked up at the plump-chested bird on the window sill turning its head this way and that, as if looking for another pigeon to blame it on. He slotted the map into his haversack and pressed the bell with the same force as starting a machine at work. Some Mrs Mop had not long scrubbed the step, but he scuffed his fag and leaned on the white button again. Maybe they were on holiday, though the date had been unmistakable. Or the letter had been posted from Mars and had been a hoax, in which case he would jump on the next train back. A busty woman in her twenties pulled the door open. 'What do you want?'

'I've got an appointment to see Mr Humphries.' He turned his scar away, and tried a half-cock grin to put her at ease.

'Come in, then.' She showed him to a small office, treading backwards as if he might lunge forward for a kiss.

He wondered how long she had taken to nurture her posh accent from the glum corner of the country she had grown up in, and noted her diamond-shaped brass earrings, the string of black beads over her grey striped blouse, and a rosebud mouth with just the right curl for scaring callers away. Bert felt like belching in her face. 'Worked here long?'

'Longer than you.'

Sharpshit. He took his cap off. 'It doesn't sound long to me,' Herbert said, in his most polished accent. 'I'm rather surprised you can't be rather more polite to an author. If it weren't for someone like me you wouldn't have a job.'

'Think I'd care? They pay me next to nothing.' She looked for something on the desk, which he thought might be a perfumed clothes peg to put on her snout, then fastened a few papers together. 'What are you going to see Mr Humphries for?'

You may be Bert Gedling, he thought, but you don't have to think like Archie Bleasby. He went up close. 'It's about a novel.'

'And you have an appointment?'

'I wouldn't be here if I didn't. Bert Gedling's the name.'

'Oh.' She pressed a button on the intercom, and a Donald Duck squawk came back. 'Sit down.' She pointed to a chair, as if he was blind. 'He shouldn't be long.'

He preferred to stand, sniffing the dusty upholstery of the sofa while relishing a whiff of the girl's scent. To bolster the role of Bert Gedling, which he must put on in no uncertain terms, he recalled acting in the Ovid play at school. Now that he was on a real stage the experience would be put to more practical use, though the encounter with a publishing firm was a come-down compared to Phaeton's fatal drive across the universe in the Sun God's horse and cart. Life and death stakes weren't on the cards, but if this wasn't a metamorphosis he didn't know what was.

Perhaps the file box under Humphries' arm was to give the idea that he was hurried, the ruse wasted on Herbert, who saw him as ordinary enough in that he only had one side to his personality, and wouldn't be difficult to deal with. If he was a worried man he was the sort who had been born that way, and so was able to put on a smile of pretending to be at ease, betrayed by lines across his brow as close as contours defining a steep hill.

He looked at Bert from the doorway and, twiddling a watch chain across his waistcoat, came forward to shake his hand. 'Humphries,' he said, unable to meet his eyes. He led the way to a large office on the first floor, the stair walls decorated with framed photographs of authors who looked as if they had been to the same school as Herbert Thurgarton-Strang.

They sat at opposite ends of a leather-covered couch. 'Well, Mr Gedling,' Humphries said, still hugging the file box as if his lunch was in it. 'I don't see any point in beating about the bush. We've read *Royal Ordnance*, and we're very impressed. We want to publish it.' He paused for a look of surprise, or even pleasure, but Herbert, knowing it was called for, and in spite of a bumping heart, gazed across at a shelf of novels, deciding it was unlikely that he had read books with such gaudy spines.

'Mind you, it's an unusual piece of work, and there's no saying how well or otherwise it will sell, but we'll certainly do our best to push it. I don't think there has been a working-class novel quite like it, though I'm afraid you might have to alter a few of the more explicit words.'

'Oh, well, 'appen I will,' he grudged. 'People'll know what I mean, anyway.'

'No doubt about that.'

Above the bookcase stood a large framed photograph of a school cricket team, and Bert walked across as if interested in the books. 'You published all these?'

Humphries laughed. 'Oh, many more than that.'

'It's a lot.' He managed a look at the photograph and saw, among the lines of faces, his old adolescent self, not as he would like to have imagined – head half backwards, with a sneer at the world, or at least an aspect of Byronic contempt – but as a sixteen-year-old with a look of trepidation, he would almost say fear, certainly anxiety, unease, a nervousness at the lips and a stare showing how at bay and unhappy he must have been. To cover the shock and before turning round he took out a packet of Woodbines. 'Fag?'

'No, thank you. Are you all right?'

'I was only thinking I ain't read any o' them books. I've got a lot to mek up for.' The cigarette hid his face in smoke. Isaac's advice had been to let them do most of the talking, but it was necessary to emphasize his identity as Bert Gedling, so he couldn't stay dumb.

'I don't suppose you've had much time.'

'True. I've slogged my guts out in a factory since I was fourteen, but at least I learned how to write a novel about that life.'

'You certainly did. Do you still work there?'

Thoughts and talk lived on different levels, and he decided it was best not to speculate on how the photograph of the old cricket team came to be in Humphries' office. 'I've got to earn a living, 'aven't I?' He looked around the room. 'There are worse places.'

'What about your family?'

Bert's impulse, which Herbert trod on, was to tell him that his family was none of his fucking business. Instead he decided he would be more convincing if he didn't clip off too many aitches. 'Mam and Dad was killed in an air raid, so an aunt took me in. When she couldn't stand me going out to pubs and coming back kay-lied she threw me on the street and I 'ad to live in digs.'

A real son of the people. Amazing. Humphries shook the money up and down in his left trouser pocket. 'How did you learn to write so well?' – not a grammatical slip anywhere, and the neatest-cleanest typescript I've seen for a long time. They'd even wondered whether it wasn't a novel cooked up by some university chap pulling a fast one, but it was far more authentic than that.

Bert smiled. 'Easy. I read a lot o' books. Then again, I went to a good school till I was fourteen. If yer didn't spell right yer got bashed.'

Humphries stared, as if not entirely believing that he had before him an all-round twenty-two carat, totally unspoiled self-taught novelist from the working class. Bert gave the stare back, then crumbled his expression into the cheery open-hearted smile of a workman which, he knew from much practice with the mirror, would make him look like a berserker only halfway gone from self-control. Humphries cleared phlegm from his throat for a further question. 'Where did you acquire that scar? And the sling? You seem to have been in the wars.'

Humphries felt free to ask about the scar because he looked on him as from a lower sort of life. He may not know why he's doing it, Herbert thought, but that's how it is. If he took me as one of his own kind he would have waited for me to tell him about it. The trouble is he doesn't even know he's being supercilious, and because I do, and because I want him to think I'm somebody I'm not, I won't give him a mouthful of well-delivered execration, but get back to being Bert.

'I was. Life's a battlefield where I come from.' He lifted the sling an inch or two. 'Industrial accident, this. As for the scar, they're a rough lot up north. I offended a bloke in a pub, but don't ask me what I said. Maybe I only just looked at him, and the ponce came for me with a knife. Got a swipe in before I could dodge. He thought he'd frightened me off, but nowt frightens me. I had my boots on, so I went straight back in and kicked the knife out of his hand. Then I cracked 'is ribs to stop his complaints. He didn't look very pretty after I'd done.'

He flipped his cigarette end into the empty fireplace, as if ready to go out and manufacture another fracas, or give a performance on the spot, should there be any sign of trouble.

Don't overdo the Bert bit. Pull back. Yet it was irresistible, because playing the role was as near as he'd get to driving a chariot across the sky – better in fact because he wasn't as daft as Phaeton, so it wouldn't be fatal. Functioning through the eyes, brain and heart of Bert made Herbert wonder how long he could keep up the stance, a long part to play, and not always easy, calling every moment for care and dexterity. It was hard to understand how Humphries was unable to penetrate such an everyday person and see the real man within. Had he led such a sheltered life? Still, didn't Archie always say that if you live a lie you become the lie itself, and didn't feel you were living a lie at all? He was acting out of inspiration, and knew it was safe to carry on. 'I enjoy a bit of a bust-up on a Saturday night.'

He should be on the stage. Humphries offered a cigar from his leather case. It's even better than too good to be true. They smoked in apparent peace. 'Well, Mr Gedling – or may I call you Bert?'

Herbert nodded. 'Any day.'

'We'll draw up a contract and make an advance of two hundred pounds. Half now, and half on publication.'

'For ten years work? Is that all authors mek on a long book like this?'

'You'll earn more when the royalties start coming in.'

Bert detected a fear on Humphries' part that he might reach for his novel and march off with it elsewhere. 'That's only a promise, though. You can't live on promises.'

'It's more than that, I think. Do you have an agent?' – as if he could deal with him or her more easily.

Ash fell from Bert's cigar, such a good Cuban it didn't break on impact but lay like a turd on the carpet. He put his foot on it for luck. 'My lawyer will look at the contract. He knows all about book advances. But I did think five 'undred would be nearer the mark.' Herbert could live a year on that, with care. 'That's what he said when I showed him your letter.'

Humphries put the ashtray between them. 'Has he read it – the book, I mean?'

'Loves it. Reckons it's as good as owt that moaning minnie D. H. Lawrence wrote, though I suppose he was having me on.' Herbert could see him trying to decide whether he was bluffing or just being naive. Dense thoughts were struggling around in the compost of Gedling's brain, which made him unpredictable, untrustworthy.

Humphries wondered with a *frisson* what F. R. Leavis would say to his views on Lawrence. Though clearly from the boondocks, Gedling was no fool, and in spite of the clarity of his writing there was something sly about him, which may be no bad thing when, Humphries thought, we put him through the publicity machine. 'I'll tell you what we'll do, Bert. As a gesture of confidence and goodwill, and to show our faith in you, we'll make it three hundred – if I'm able to square it with the other directors, which I think I can.'

Herbert had hit as much of a jackpot as the one-armed bandit could deliver, but it was even so beyond what he had hoped for. He asked, as if still not satisfied: 'When will you publish the book, then?'

Humphries barked into an intercom for a sheet of schedules. 'I want you to know, Bert, that we have a policy here of treating our authors with decency and respect. We look after them, but expect loyalty in return.'

A better-looking girl than the female Cerberus on the front door came in with the schedules. 'Thank you, Deborah.' He flipped through the papers. 'We'll bring *Royal Ordnance* out in the autumn,' he told her, 'which gives us about six months, plenty of time to get advance copies to the reviewers.'

'Deborah, eh?' Bert said, when she had gone. 'A bit of all right, in't she?' Cool and haughty Deborah in her purple blouse, with a nice golden trinket between her tits, had given him a quick look, and assumed it told her everything about him, but once outside she would realize that such was not the case. If – no, when – he met her again that kind of uncertainty would give him half a chance.

'She's one of our up-and-coming editors,' Humphries said.

The curt tone was a good reason for Bert to frown: 'Autumn's a long way off. I was thinking a couple of months would do the trick.' He stretched his legs from the sofa, and blew a perfect smoke ring towards the fireplace. 'I might 'ave another done by then.'

'That's all right. We can bring it out next year. Do you have a title?'

A photograph of Rodin's *Thinker*, seen in a book at Isaac's, showed the attitude to take, until the words flashed into his brain. 'Ye', I'll call it *The Other Side of the Tracks*.'

'No resting on your laurels, eh? That's good. And in the meantime you'll go on working in the factory, I suppose?'

The country house he'd buy would have a well-shaved lawn you went on to from French windows. There'd be a table, and a sunshade under which he'd scribble tales from the factory on to a foolscap pad so that the sunshine breeze couldn't flush the papers away. A middle-aged motherly housekeeper would disturb him with the musical tinkle of a tea tray, or perhaps wake him from an illicit snooze. Maybe his good luck and swelling fortune would run to a flat above the National Gallery, with a view almost level with Nelson's melancholy phizog. In the morning he'd amble across the Square in his dressing gown and carpet slippers to eat breakfast in Joe Lyons, a friendly nod at the policeman who'd soon get used to such eccentricity: 'Nice morning, Mr Gedling!' 'Would be, if I hadn't drunk so much last night.' 'Ah! You authors!'

On the other hand maybe he'd live half-starved in a furnished room for the rest of his days, and struggle with the poverty he'd read about in George Gissing's books. 'The factory's all I know. Unless I pack it in and get a job as a clay-kicker down the pit. The money's better there, better than writing novels, any road up.'

Humphries clasped hands, and Herbert could never see such a man feeling contrite at the thought of a writer on his uppers. 'I don't think you'll have to do that kind of work much longer.'

'I hope not. I've done my bit.'

'Before you go, though' – he pressed a button – 'I'd like you to meet my chief editor, who wrote such an enthusiastic report on your novel.'

Herbert lay back, uninterested, smoking at his ease, when who should walk in but that wanking little blighter Dominic Jones, who had been his best friend at school. Bert considered himself to be in the shit bucket up to his neck, at the same time realizing that publishing was just the sort of occupation in which to find someone like Dominic. So, he told himself, get deeper ever deeper into Bert as quickly as you can, though even Archie's skin might not be thick enough to hide in.

'Dominic, I'd like you to meet Bert Gedling, who wrote *Royal Ordnance* that you admired so much.'

Bert uncoiled himself to greet this pink plump man of middle height, already slightly bald, but spiffingly dressed, as they would have put it during those long ago days at school. 'Hey up, Domino.'

The same old baby face, but turning to petulance. 'Dominic, if you don't mind.'

It was him, right enough. Bert corkscrewed so deeply into Gedling that his own mother wouldn't have known him or, better still, he wouldn't even have spotted himself walking along the street. 'Sorry, I thought it was Domino. They 'ave funny names down in London.' He used the grip of a million handlepower, so that Dominic needed all his spartan school upbringing not to flinch at the pain. He couldn't possibly connect Bert with the Thurgarton-Strang whose contemptuous handshake had never been more than the extension of one finger, and who he had last seen playing table tennis in the games room more than twelve years ago. The scar helped, as did the muffler, the calloused hands and hardened face, the half-closed eyes, and one or two blackheads cultured for the occasion.

Dominic backed a pace. 'It's certainly a good novel. Unusual, too.'

'That's high praise,' Humphries said, 'coming from him. It's only the third book he's accepted since the new year. What did you say about it?'

'A real achievement, both as art and realism.' He looked at Herbert, but then, he would, wouldn't he? Herbert felt the horizons spinning, the room in a flux, as if he had put back six pints of Younger's Number One, and never drunk anything more potent than cocoa before. Bert was reluctant to come up and help keep the perilous world at bay, but Herbert kept him up front by the scruff of his neck.

'I was talking about it with someone at Penguin's yesterday,' Dominic said, 'in Chez Victor's.'

'Were you, then?' Humphries leaned against the desk, hoping his chief editor would have enough diplomatic sense to handle the kind of rogue element carefully that neither of them had met before. 'They'll have first refusal on the paperback rights, but only if they're quick about it, and if they come up with the right price.'

'Penguins!' Bert exclaimed, in control again. 'I thought they on'y touched classics. I've read all of them, though.' The more mystified they were about his ability to produce a book from such a background the less they would imagine him to be who he really was, in which case Herbert could afford to throw out a few hints now and again as to how cultured he was. 'I'll 'ave to be off soon. I want to get back up north before my lawyer shuts 'is offices.'

He felt absolute joy, walking arm in arm with Bert in the sunshine up St Martin's Lane, both too full of their success to get straightaway back into the Underground. Such freewheeling happiness made his strides seem ten feet long, no one nearby coming up to his measure. 'We did it, old boy, we pulled it off,' Herbert said.

'Fuckin' did,' Bert crowed. But a cloud went over his face: 'What about that snotchops who looked a bit funny when 'e saw yer, though?'

'Oh, you mean that little twerp Dominic? Don't worry about him. I'll deal with him when the time comes.'

'Yer'll have ter watch 'im, is what I think. Trouble is, 'e in't as daft as he looks.'

'I assure you, he is. I know him from a long time ago.'

'Do yer? Where was that, then? You aren't 'oldin' summat back from me, are yer?'

A steely tone came into Herbert's voice. 'That's none of your business. Don't get too uppity with me, Bert Gedling, or I'll close the lid on your box.'

The doppelgänger had worked overtime and been convincing, and would stay in control only as long as he needed it. No doubt Dominic would say to Humphries that Bert Gedling put him in mind of someone at his old school. 'So much so that it's damned uncanny, though of course it can't be him. It's impossible, unthinkable, idiotic to suppose so' – which would set Humphries laughing so loud and long as to bring on an epileptic fit.

Eating a dismal sandwich in the station buffet, Herbert's elation declined. His apparently successful deception seemed to have cheated him of a proper achievement, and he wondered what the result would have been had he called on them as Herbert Thurgarton-Strang, and haw-hawed with his old public school swagger.

Such metronomic moods never let him enjoy anything for long, so he slept all the way back, the ordeal having been more exhausting than he could have imagined.

He poured from the half-bottle of White Horse. 'I'm a working-class novelist to them, you see, and they only know me as Bert Gedling.'

'Instead of someone of impeccable military and clerical descent?' Isaac put water into his glass. 'It's a bit too strong for me.' He sipped. 'I don't see the problem, though. You've made your bed, and now you have to lie in it. What's wrong with that?'

'I'll get used to juggling the pair of us, I suppose.'

'You've done quite well so far.'

'But why do I suddenly feel uneasy about lying?'

'Success brings its uncertainties. It needs more strength of character than failure.'

'Maybe I should have been an actor.'

'You'd have been a bad one,' Isaac said, 'because your life wouldn't have depended on it. Not like your writing.'

Herbert slowed down on the whisky, not caring to get Bert pie-eyed – though he felt like swigging the lot. 'You probably know more about me than anybody else.'

'Perhaps, but don't worry about it.'

'You should have been the writer, not me.'

Isaac took a clean handkerchief to his spectacles, of the sort made from wire and always about to fall to pieces. 'I couldn't write to save my life.'

'Well, you're acute about other people, you've read far more than me, and you know a lot about human nature.'

He smiled. 'I knew you'd make one sooner or later, though. You've got everything it takes: education, confidence, experience, imagination, and a split personality. You seem to dislike most people, except those you write about, which is one way of saving your soul. Anyway, we'd better read that contract, clause by tricky clause, so that we can make sense out of it, and see that it's all shipshape and correct. Open your Bert Gedling writing pad, and we'll get cracking.'

Eighteen

'Are summers longer than winter?' Archie said.

Diagrams of astronomy were drawn across Herbert's mind from school: the earth rotates on its own axis in a left-hand annual orbit around the sun; but he'd forgotten the dates of the equinoxes. 'Maybe just a bit.' He smiled. 'The days are longer, though, especially in the afternoon.'

'I know that,' Archie said.

'Does it bother you?'

'Well, today I don't want it to get dark, but some days I can't wait.'

'You're a dirty old man,' Bert said.

'I'm not, I'm a dirty young 'un. I will be a dirty old man, though, when I'm old.'

'You're hopeless,' Bert twitted.

'I know. It's lovely. I like meeting a woman in the dark.'

Chitchat against the wall, the same as ever, not many variations but it carried the time along between canteen and hooter. With hardly a cloud in the sky, the yards and sheds of the factory seemed to function better in the sun than under the mists of winter, when it looked what it was, a slum that should be swept away. The signal went for getting back to work. 'I sometimes think that if I hear that moaning minnie one more time I'll go off my head.'

'I'll live to see the day,' Bert said. 'Come on.'

He had been given lighter work because of his injured arm, which wasn't yet healed. No one doubted when he told them, though it was true enough. He serviced other people's machines, pushed trolleys up and down the gangways, and checked finished material before it was taken away, feeling at times as if he had never written a novel, or been to London, as if the life of writing couldn't possibly be part of him. Such blank moments worried him that he might sink into being Bert Gedling and no one else forever. There were times when he hated the name.

Nor was it encouraging when the men and women bantered him as to how he had landed such a cushy job for his convalescence. While the flesh of his wound coloured back to normal he spent a fortnight sharpening tools, finally put back on his lathe though the scar was still raw enough to give pain when he knocked it against box or turret. Galling though the work was he forced a smile and stuck up two fingers to the heckling so that the others could say: 'Good old Bert! He's back on form!'

Walking home in the warm evening uplifted the spirit, a happier mood after spending his energy for eight hours. The short future of some spare time made life tolerable, and in his room he massaged all fingers into sufficient flexibility to put a few paragraphs on to paper. Any old words to which he could attach the grandiose label of thought. From lathe to typewriter, one machine to another, seemed not too big a difference.

Archie called on Saturday morning: 'Come outside, and see what I've got.' He and Raymond had bought an old banger of an Austin between them for seventy quid.

'How long yer bin drivin'?'

'A couple o' months.'

'I suppose you've got a licence?'

'What's one o' them? Course I 'ave. I took the test last week; passed first time.'

'Is it taxed?'

'What do you think that is on the windscreen? A Guinness label? Come on, and I'll tek yer to Aspley for a run round the estate. If Macmillan says we've never 'ad it so good I want to 'ave it good as well, if not better.' He opened the kerbside door for Bert to get in. 'When I see somebody in a posh car who's rich I don't want to nick his money – I just want to be rich myself.'

Archie the demon driver bawled at the dilatory, and cursed the speed mongers until he had passed them as well, his reaction micrometer-tuned.

Bert felt no anxiety that he would chock or be chocked. He would certainly make a good job of driving the sun chariot across the sky.

'My motto is,' Archie's eyes gleaming at a straight bit of road, 'nobody in front, and nobody behind. If you see somebody in your rear mirror, it don't matter how far away he is, he's right behind you.'

Beyond the middle of town Archie got out and tied L-plates back and front. 'Come on, Bert, there's no traffic here, so it's your turn to have a go at the wheel. But whatever you do,' he said, showing the gears, 'don't drive like me, or you'll never pass your test.'

'I never like to tek tests.'

'Nor me, but this one you'll 'ave to, sooner or later. Don't worry about it, though. You either get through, or you don't, and if you don't you can allus tek it again.'

'I suppose so.' Archie was more locked into the world and its ways than Bert ever could be, Herbert thought, because he never had to question who he was or continually mistrust himself. He was solid enough to show such confidence in a friend that he could even offer him the wheel of his car, which was as close to love as any two people could hope to get.

One machine was much like another. At the controls it was a matter of synchronization, the only difficulty being that man and machine moved at the same time, which Herbert soon got used to because Archie was a patient instructor. Bert enjoyed driving so much that Herbert wondered why he hadn't bought a car years ago, in which case he could have driven to London and impressed that fuckpig Dominic even more with his proletarian dexterity.

The galley proofs of *Royal Ordnance* came with a covering note from Dominic. Herbert tackled the tight knots of the string, no problem to industrialized fingernails. He got it off in one length because Mrs Denman kept a drawer full, having the habit, even so long after the war, of not wanting to waste anything.

The long story was so enthralling it seemed to have been written by somebody else. All was clear, everything was in place, as he read from sheet to sheet, though by the end he sensed it might not be so, and a second reading showed printing errors missed on the first time through.

The dedication page was blank, no name, no words of memory or appreciation, nothing to thank anybody for. He wanted to write: 'To Bert Gedling, without whose labour and life's blood this book would never have been written.' Or maybe: 'To Herbert Thurgarton-Strang, without whose help this confidence trick of a novel could not have been cobbled together.' But such notes would betray him to the wolves, who would rip him even further apart than he already was because of the stunt he was playing on them.

His sense of loss seemed beyond a joke, knowing he should dedicate the book to Cecilia because writing it had cost him her love. The fresh clean sheets were soaked in the invisible ink of shared memories, which he wanted to retain for his own special hoarding till the emptiness in him was filled with something else – or he became bored and no longer interested in picking up bits of the book at random with which to torment himself.

The sheets were needed urgently, the slip of paper said, and so, turning back to the dedication page, he wrote: 'For Beryl Denman', then posted the package back, by which time he felt almost the same enthusiasm for the book that Humphries had shown.

Archie navigated him over the Trent and into a maze of lanes beyond the Fosse Way. A haycart or occasional tractor held them up, or a dozen cattle being shifted by dog and man to another field. Wheeling and turning through villages where hardly anyone seemed to live gave safe practice at the controls, so easy for Herbert till for some reason he saw beyond the windscreen the climbing of the lorry into the mountains of Cyprus. The woman in the vineyards looked at him, and he felt the same agonizing pull, seeing the curve of her breast as she lifted her arms, the houri eyes, the benevolent and promising smile.

Sunlight flooded the turning, and a tree came towards him, arms of privet and hawthorn ready to embrace him for a meal. He swung the wheel, slid along the bank and let the skid carry him till he was able to straighten out. Heartbeats pounded to his head as tyres scraped the verge, missing the tree and almost hitting another.

Archie, unnaturally still, said nothing. Herbert stared ahead, back to more measured driving. 'That was careless. It won't happen again.' Such a near call unsettled him, seared his throat, and maybe Archie's, since he indicated the way to a snug pub at Cropwell Bishop.

When cool beer and salty crisps were on the table, Bert said: 'What's up wi' yo'? Ye're too bleddy quiet for my liking. You've hardly said a word all evening.'

'Tek yer sweat. We'll have a sup o' this first.'

I've more than enough material, but something's eating him, so I have to listen. Convinced he knew everything already, Herbert considered it time to quit. He'd soaked up people's troubles like a sponge, and felt he was sinking under water.

'I'll tell yer.' Archie flipped open a packet of Senior Service, smoke soon drifting from his lips. Herbert saw him as a much regarded man of the local world, dovetailed into every square and circle; whereas he, Herbert, had problems only death could settle, though he expected to keep it at bay for the usual three score and ten. 'Go on, then, tell me.'

'Can't yer guess?' Archie leaned across, as if walls still had ears. 'I've got a girl up the spout.'

'You've what?'

'In the club, on the tub, a bun in the oven, preggers.'

'So what? She's married, in't she?'

'Is she fuck.'

'Yer didn't use owt?'

His bitter laugh suggested he had turned at last into a victim of Fate. The following smile indicated that he did not altogether dislike the fact. 'I'd got a frenchie in my pocket. I allus 'ave, you know that, but summat stopped me bothering. We was in her house on a Saturday night while her mam and dad was out at the boozer. I didn't think I'd get it in that night, but she looked at me, and I looked at her, and suddenly we was latched on. I went in raw. In no time at all we was going at it like rabbits in a thunderstorm. Never known owt like it. Fuckin' madness! She's a lovely girl, long red hair, and tits like a statue's. Only nineteen, as well. I must have bin in love with her. I still am. I can't stop thinkin' about her. When she says she loves me I believe her. She says it every time we meet, and I love to hear it, just as she does when I say it to her. It's marvellous. Such a nice girl, as well. She's a Catholic, at least her family is, mam and dad Irish. She wants a lot o' kids, but we shall have to see about that.'

He knew Archie would make a superb father. 'Then it's no problem, is it?'

'I suppose not. I'm thirty, and I've 'ad a good run for my money. It's about time. I'll be all right with her.'

Herbert could only think of saying: 'We've got to grow up sooner or later, Archie, my owd.'

'Yeh, but I can't see yo' ever doing it.'

He's right. I'm as grown-up as I ever will be, Herbert thought, or will ever want to be, or will ever need to be for what I want to do. I was a grown-up me from the day I was born, and growing up's got nothing to do with it, in any case. I don't have any wish to kill myself in that way, and never will have. Growing up is for the others, for those who can't do anything else but live dead, or for those who go on living for people who write to show the living dead that they might not be as dead as they feel. 'Yer can't?'

'Well, yer don't show any sign of it. You're a funny bogger, though. I never could mek yo' out. Ye're just like one of the lads, but sometimes there's a posh bogger trying to scramble out. I've allus known it, but I've never said owt. A bloke can be what he likes for all I care, as long as he don't think he's better than me, and I know you've never thought that.'

'You're right there, Archie.'

The pink of the setting sun deepened against the window, and the steady expression in Archie's grey eyes seemed to need the kind of answer which would soothe them both, and fuse them together into one brotherly flame, or at least find an explanation for the intolerable burdens that had bothered them since birth. 'You're not the only one who's puzzled,' Herbert said. 'Sometimes I can't even mek mysenn out.'

'For instance,' Archie said, 'you could have bin a chargehand at work, but yer've never wanted to get on. Another thing is, yer've met some nice women, but you've never said owt about getting married.'

Bert banged him on the shoulder. 'Come on. Let's slop another one down, then we can get back. I'm beginning to feel knackered.'

A pall of dusk lay over the fields, films of mist permeating the greens and browns till next morning. He knew Archie too well to judge him, which may have been a limitation when writing about such people, but the fact was that Archie's sins were also his, otherwise he couldn't have written *Royal Ordnance* at all. Under a microscope rather than a magnifying glass, he recognized the eternal turmoil of unrest, indicated by lines across Archie's forehead, the down-curving lips, and the occasionally twitching fists when speaking of real or imagined injustice. Perhaps it was only a phase in life which he, as well as those written about, would one day leave behind. Such feelings had become his own, which neither he nor Archie were ever likely to relinquish.

They leaned on a gate, staring at a dim light from a farm across the dip, and a cluster from the village like white spots surrounding a mysterious rural rite they could never be part of. Archie's voice startled him. 'Work tomorrow. Never stops, does it?'

Archie knew nothing of his novel. No one did. Maybe they would one day. He wanted to tell him, but didn't in case the confession broke their notion of equality and trust. Whatever happened, he needed the friendship of his life to be safe, though the test would come later, which Archie would pass as easily as he had that for his driving licence.

'Tek the wheel on the way back as well,' Archie said, 'to mek sure you get over that near miss' – his first reference to it.

Herbert decided that his work in the factory must come to a stop. It would be too easy to stand rooted to the same spot forever, and go on till his life was washed away like milky suds flowing over shaved steel. 'I'm packing it in,' he said, when they were going over Trent Bridge. 'The firm, I mean.'

Archie handled the window down to bawl at an old man in a new Ford Popular who was too slow getting away from the lights. 'I've been expecting it,' he said. 'You should 'ave done it years ago. What shall yer do, though?'

He stopped for a Belisha beacon, so enclosed in himself, so dead selfish all his days that he hadn't realized how intensely Archie must always have thought about him – even though such thoughts had been made plain enough in his book. 'I'll go down to London, be on the loose for a while. I'll have to get a job sooner or later, I suppose, but I've got enough dough for a month or two. Give me time to look around.'

'Good luck to you, is all I can say. Let's not lose touch, though.'

Bert turned into Waterway Street. 'We'll never do that.'

He wiped his hands on the sud rag, and walked along the gangway to the plate-glass office. A week's notice was the formality. 'That's a shame,' the foreman said. 'We thought you'd be with us forever. You're the sort of bloke we can't afford to lose, with these new export orders coming in.'

Good of him to say so, but all he could feel was a sadness that had no sorrow in it, because the world he half knew already was dominating his expectations. 'I'll miss the old place.'

'If it's the wages, I can put you in for a bit more.'

'I've got a job in London.'

'Ah, I wondered if it worn't summat like that.'

On the last afternoon he wiped his hands, looking around as machinery fell silent and sweepers came in to clear up. Overhead belts squeaked to a stop, dynamos whined into their weekend rest, and men reached for jackets and knapsacks, put on caps, fastened bike clips, and set out on a quicker walk than most had shown coming in. Waiting in groups, they clocked off, the ding of each buff card pushed down into the available slots making a monotone song of release that set Bert whistling as he made for the gate.

He pushed his card down and bent it – Gedling, Bert – not sorry to walk away from a part of his life he could now afford to let go of. Men began running for the exits to be first at the bike sheds, and some who had cars were already revving up along the street. Archie waved, and offered to drop him off at his digs.

'It's all right. I feel like walking. See yer in the Eight Bells though later on.'

Archie wound down the window. 'I'll be there.'

* * *

The flowered dress, as she stepped from the ambulance that had brought her from the hospital, draped the stones in weight that had been taken away by her illness. 'There's nothing more they can do for her,' Frank wept in Herbert's room, handing him the clean towel brought up as an excuse. 'If God would take me instead of her I'd be the happiest man in the world.'

'It's never like that, though, is it?' was all Herbert could say.

'I've never believed till now, but you've got to have Somebody you can pray to in a case like this.' He straightened Herbert's pillow, as if caring for him also might bring a miraculous recovery for Mrs Denman. 'Tell her you'll come back and see her, though, won't you, Bert? You see, she still thinks she's going to get better.'

Another week and he would be gone. He couldn't wait, though wanted to see as much of her as possible. 'I hope so, too. But we'd better go down. I don't think she ought to be left alone for long.'

'I shall miss yer, Bert.' The snuffle in her voice embarrassed him into feeling pity, contemptuous of himself at not being able to help her. One of the last people he cared to see waste away and die, she would turn into a memory like all the others he would say goodbye to, and while she went on living she would turn him into a memory as well, which he hoped for so as to get the weight of the intolerable past off his back. Something would fill the space, but he was too weary of the present to wonder what it might be.

Despite her frailty and pain she stood up to set out his tea. Frank signalled with his eyes that they weren't to stop her. 'Will you be going home to your folks?'

Some were afraid to go home again because they dreaded the womb of milk and comfort, and would face anything rather than risk annihilation, but the stronger the fundamental tug, the more energy was generated in resisting it. 'I don't think so.'

'I'm sure you've got a lovely home to go back to,' she said, 'if you want to.'

A decent response, in words of Archie's calibre, would be humane, but no lightning bolt of emotion came to melt his rigid control. 'No, Ma, I'm off to live in London,' was the best he could say.

'I don't know why you want to leave here at all.'

'It's only that I think my life's got to change.'

She sighed. 'It must be marvellous to be young, and hope for summat like that. Are you going to get that book published?'

He hated to see tears in her eyes. 'If I do you'll be the first person to get a copy.' His tone was such as to stop her asking more, because a proper explanation of his departure would take years to write, a job to be set aside for some later date, and from a different person. 'I'll be back as often as I can to see you.' He wasn't sure how he could. 'You can rely on that.'

The factory had taught him to waste nothing, a place wherein energy was sweat which you couldn't afford to lose, where you needed to conserve if your backbone wasn't sooner or later to melt. Economy of effort had been the order of all days, and time meant money in your pocket to pay for booze, or to treat a woman, and to live as well as you could.

He had learned a lot, the long way and hard, much that was impossible to quantify, though with little awareness of the struggle because he had been young. To slough off the invisible skin of overalls would need long exposure to different qualities of air. Certainly it would take time for his body and the roots of his hair to discard more than a decade of imbibing disinfectant and the atmosphere of iron and steel. From having been a workman for so long he felt a *frisson* of excitement at the prospect of change.

Nineteen

Not quick enough to count the girders, he worried at losing his speed of perception, a bad sign when heading for London. Thirty years old was over the hump, the highway to decrepitude – if you didn't watch it. A green and sluggish Trent slurried the past away, not forgetting to take his guilt at deserting Mrs Denman, though he supposed such a feeling to be on the plus side, having admitted it, and left a suitcase to signal he'd be going back. Abandoned as well were oil-soaked overalls, dulled boots, cap and knapsack, for slinging in the dustbin, or handing to any ragman who would take them.

'I understand how you feel,' Isaac had said. 'Fate likes to work its little coincidences. Doesn't it just? Anyway, she might live longer than you think, or longer than either of us, for that matter.'

'All the same, I'm a real shit.' Herbert stacked the books he had borrowed on the table. 'She's been absolutely first rate, right from the beginning. You could say she's made me halfway human.'

A doubting smile formed on Isaac's thin lips. 'Send her a copy of the book.'

'Oh, I shall do that. There'll be one for you, as well, someone else I don't like leaving.'

The sentiment was waved aside. 'You mustn't worry about that. I'll live forever. Or until God says so, which has to be the same. Just come back and say hello when you can spare a moment from the fleshpots of London. There's no place like it in the world. I loved it in my youth. What happy days!'

A first-class seat had never before been indulged in, but his status as a possibly successful writer while standing in the queue brought out the demand – from what part of himself he preferred not to know

– for which he got a 'sir' with his change. Two suitcases snug on the rack were as heavy as if packed with stones, one more piece of luggage than he had gone with, yet they were mostly books and papers, and hardly equal to the sum-tonnage of experience gained.

Despite strong arms the pull was hard, lugging them into the streets of St Pancras. He crossed at a light on red, and a gravel lorry hogging by splashed his turn-ups. The anonymity of London to bask in buoyed him on to a spring-heeled track, but when rain drummed on his mackintosh he went into the first bed-and-breakfast place and paid fifteen bob for a night in advance. The man spoke Greek to his wife as to which room was empty, and Herbert supposed they were from Cyprus but, because of the present troubles, thought he'd better not tell them of his time there with the army. A subtle smell of olives and resinated wine followed upstairs when the man showed him into a room with immaculate sheets. The curtains wouldn't keep out much light. Or dull the noise: traffic was continuous. He left his cases and went to find somewhere for lunch.

Three days at the hotel would rush him as much as a week's board in Nottingham. Real life had jumped him at last, economy with money helping him to become more of a man of the world. In the coffee bar he smoked a cigarette while culling the *Evening Standard* for advertisements of furnished rooms. A quick move was necessary, even if only to escape the squeals and moans of the middle-aged couple next door, who jumped around at night to make the best of their clandestine tryst. At breakfast the man, obviously from the North, called to Herbert: 'Do you make model aeroplanes, chum?'

Herbert smiled at such a strange idea. He didn't.

'What a shame!' The man, only trying to be friendly, went back to his plate of kippers. 'Just wondered if you might.' His wife (or whatever) a fragile woman, sat with one big blush on her face, avoiding all eyes.

Isaac had mentioned an area of cheap rooms south of the Elephant and Castle. He spread the town plan, pencilled streets on which vacancies were indicated, and found a box on the main road to make phone calls. London air is different, he had been told. Wind never came from where you expected because of so many buildings. Multiple winds, some more subtle than others, brought grit rather than homely smoke, making him feel scruffy instead of plain worn out by work. He came up from the underground and back into the air, a coating on the skin that would wash off at night and leave no trace in the morning.

Mr Glenny the landlord sat outside the address in a Rolls Royce, and came on to the pavement to shake hands. He wore a boiler suit and was hard to place, though Herbert didn't think such a rig was meant for labouring. His tie and pin were precisely fixed, and gold cufflinks shone from the sleeves of a laundered purple shirt with a white collar. Maybe it was the closest he could get to a de luxe prison garb, which he'd one time been used to. On the other hand a squashed snout suggested experience at prize fighting, while his accent seemed local enough. 'What's your line of work?'

Herbert felt he could be as direct as to tell only half a lie. 'Publisher's office.'

Glenny didn't believe him, but because he distrusted everyone it made little difference. 'Want it long?'

'As long as I stay.'

'Have a look, then. You might not like it.'

'Who else lives here?'

'Riffraff. But they pay me.' He pushed the door open against a wedge of letters. 'They're all right, though. As I said, you might not want it.'

Meaning it might not be good enough for him. It was. Preference had nothing to do with the matter. Any simple billet that stopped rain splashing on to his head would do, and no fortnight's rent passed more willingly from his hands. The room was larger than Mrs Denman's, two windows instead of one looking on to the street. The ghastly shit-coloured wallpaper could be ignored. Compared to Isaac's cramped accommodation it was a clover field, furnished with a hot plate and small sink, lavatory and bathroom down a few stairs, all for fifty bob a week. A stink of beer and sweat lingered like poison gas from the last labouring occupant, but by keeping both windows open the place soon freshened into the faintest mixture of train smoke, car fumes, and skirting-board dust.

When the hunger clock struck he burnt offerings of sausages, in a pan bought from a junk market for sixpence. An orange, or a banana sandwich, satisfied for dessert. There was ample cash for food, and though the shopfronts of London were lavish with temptations, especially to someone living alone, he didn't eat more than was needed, or snack between meals. Walking everywhere kept him thin.

An hour passed, blank, musing, contented, pleasurable to be on his own, footsteps along the street not even causing him to wonder where they were heading, nor care, since they could have no connection with him. Laughing to break the spell, he cleared the table except for the red enamelled mug of scalding tea, whose handle was bound with post office string, otherwise it was too hot to lift with softening fingers.

Two hundred pounds in his account was enough for idling away without anxiety. When down to his last fifty he would scout for work, as if the novel was already dead and buried. A month was to elapse before copies could be in the shops, and he refused to rely on earning more. The ever wise Isaac had told him there were always jobs going in London, but Herbert decided that if nothing interested him he would go back in the army and do some work or other. Standing at the window, mug in hand, fag in the other, he optimistically felt that the more uncertain the future the more promising it would be. In no way would he take on work that dirtied his hands.

Hungerford footbridge was his favourite way into the West End. Clouds lifted from the wide expanse of water, a long way up the sky above the City and St Paul's. Excursion boats of late summer tracked in and out from Charing Cross pier. Responsible for no one but himself, he felt as rich as if all he could see belonged to him, as if he had rented it out and was waiting for the leases to fall due. If he stood on the balustrade and opened his arms to fly he wouldn't have to fight against the crowds to get from point to point, though among the mob he felt both his personalities merging into one. More people looked at him than they ever had in the runnels of Nottingham, as if by some magic he had become unique enough to be noticed.

In a fortnight he would have to pass himself off as the unregenerate Bert Gedling, so had better get even more firmly back into the old pit-prop guise or it would be a case of the impostor of the age being out on his arse. Meanwhile he could give in to the luxury of being

Herbert Thurgarton-Strang, the only way to tolerate anonymity in a conurbation of eight million.

Dusk was the time of doubt and loneliness. Gedling told him not to be mardy, while Thurgarton-Strang scorned to be influenced by such failings. He wrapped up complimentary copies of *Royal Ordnance* to Isaac and Mrs Denman, as well as one to Archie (not forgetting another to his parents) as careful with each bundle as if they were packets of sugar in the days of rationing.

The Jaffa-orange of the landlord's bulb gave little light, so he changed the wattage for a hundred, which spread a satisfactory whiteness over the table and outlined every inked word of his letters. Glenny called in to collect the rent at half past nine on Thursday evening, as if he had a girlfriend in the neighbourhood, or was trying to dodge the income tax man. 'Settling in, Mr Gedling?'

'Yes. Suits me fine here.' Glenny sat in the best chair of the two, so there was no option but to ask: 'Would you like coffee?' To Herbert's surprise he said yes, as if raking in rents was his only social activity. He dashed some Nescafé into a glass. 'Do you have many properties to call at?'

Glenny seemed to like the question. 'Half a dozen round here. It keeps me going. What would I do otherwise? I started my life as a porter in the markets.'

'Milk and sugar?'

He did.

'You're a bit of a dark horse, aren't you?'

Herbert couldn't fault the man's direct style. 'I worked in a factory up North for ten years.'

'Looking for something different now?'

'I might be.'

He sipped his coffee. 'You been in the army?'

'I did three years, some of it in Cyprus.'

'I suppose that's where you got that decoration on your cheek?' Glenny, a big man, tilted the chair, but came forward when a crack sounded somewhere in it. 'Do you want to do some work for me?'

'Doing what?'

'Getting in the rents.'

'Is that all?'

245

Glenny coughed. 'There's one or two undesirables I need to deal with.'

'Sounds good.' Life was scattered with signposts, the right or wrong one lightly followed. He saw himself as an ex-service thug with his own gang, hired by anyone who needed rough stuff to increase assets or further their careers. Any reinforcements he could get by asking Archie and a few others down from Nottingham. The picture wilted. 'The only thing is I'm waiting to hear about another offer. Comes up in a fortnight.'

Glenny shook his head, disappointed. 'Shame. Let me know if you think about it and change your mind.' His laugh was dry. 'You'd be good at it, especially with that scar.'

Herbert liked the villain. 'Thanks for the offer.'

He turned from the top of the stairs and grinned. 'And thank you for the coffee. And I don't mind you using that hundred watt bulb.'

Motoring lessons were advertised in a shop window on Walworth Road for a pound an hour, and he booked half a dozen, to practise driving around London. After the first session the instructor guided him over the river and into the thick of it. 'You've got the knack, pal.'

'All I want to know is how to pass the test,' Herbert said sharply, stuck behind a post office van in High Holborn.

'Oh, don't worry about that. You should get it first time.'

Thanks to Archie, but he wanted less talk and more knowledge. 'We'll see.'

'I know a nice car for sale, an Austin. Only a couple of hundred. You could practise all you liked, then.'

'Without a licence?'

'Get an international driving permit from the AA, then you can say you're on your way abroad if you get stopped by the law.'

'No thanks.'

Between motoring practice he walked up Villiers Street by Kipling's digs, across the Strand with a wave at friendly Nelson to his left, a white atoll of cloud in an otherwise blue sky. Adept at artfully dodging buses he jinked through Lamb Passage (careful of his head) on to Floral Street, and cut up into Long Acre. Idleness, the freedom to do as he pleased, which he had been wanting all his life, gave a spring to his step by the post office, a different walk than after absconding from school and sending the missive to his parents.

Coming out of the National Gallery, with its vacuous and self-satisfied faces of the famous dead, he dropped a well-deserved sixpence to the bony old man in a blue beret chalking portraits on the flagstones. Brilliant colours delineated Henry VIII and Queen Elizabeth, Nelson, Wellington, Disraeli and other great personages, each powdery base to be washed away in the next downpour.

In Lyons on St Martin's Lane he sat down to the fuel of pie and mash, glancing from behind his *News Chronicle* at elegant office girls out for lunch. Isaac had told him with a laugh that you had to be wary of saying good day to a pretty girl in London in case you were accused of being a white slaver about to needle her with drugs and bundle her off to South America. Herbert wouldn't approach them anyway, whether from reticence after so long in the Midlands or because he was still uncertain as to who or what he would finally turn out to be. He only knew that he liked looking.

'Don't you know me, then?' a woman called, when he was on the street and wondering which direction to go in next. The voice jerked his heart. He had heard it before, though this time the accent was different, the tone in no way vitriolic or accusing. She faced him. 'You should.'

She was gloved and hatted, carried a Harrods' shopping bag, and a smart umbrella. An Italian leather reticule hung from the other arm, and her smile showed delight at the chance meeting. A boy of six, and a girl a little older, stood close, each in the stiff new clothes of their prep school. 'It's a long time ago, I know, but I've often thought about you.'

'So have I.' Her corn-dolly beauty had faded in ten years, but the make-up and smell of perfume attracted him. There seemed more of a gap in their ages compared to then, but he recalled her naked, and in every conceivable sexual position – as if it were yesterday now that he looked into her blue eyes and met the same intimate smile – the pines of Cyprus outside the room. Pangs of love and regret came from so long back, as she vividly recalled the times they'd had. Such memories were a luxury, blossoming out of instantaneous recognition. She laughed excitedly, and touched his arm. 'I can't get over bumping into you like this. I knew you straightaway.'

He stroked his scar, as if to hide it, but she had already taken note. 'It's amazing,' was all he could say for the moment.

'Mummy,' the boy crowed, 'will we be going soon?'

'This is Samuel,' she pointed out. 'And that's Dorothy.'

Sam sneered, and Dorothy glowered when he touched their heads. 'Nice kids.'

'They're terrors.' Her remark made them smile. 'Are you happy these days?'

'Very.' Herbert thought it a strange question. 'How about you?'

'Oh, absolutely.' Her lips told him otherwise, as she had meant them to, but who could be as happy as in the old days? 'My husband has an accountancy firm,' she said, and asked what he was up to in Town. He told her most of what had happened since their affair. The girl put out her tongue from behind Alice's back, and Herbert glared, which delighted her.

'Marvellous. You spent all that time on research in a factory? How brave! It must be good. I'll look out for the reviews. But call me whenever you like. Here's my number. My husband's a great reader, when he has time, so I'll buy him your book. We must go now: we're for the National Gallery, then I'm taking these despicable sprogs to tea – just so's they can be sick, I suppose.'

'I'm not a sprog, I'm a schoolboy, aren't I, Dorothy?'

'No,' she shouted piercingly, 'you're a fat little sprog.'

'I'll kill you when we get home.'

'Oh no, not again,' she yawned, a pale but capable hand across her mouth.

Herbert smiled. 'They must be a handful.'

'Not really. I give them a good smack now and again.'

'Yes, and it hurts,' Samuel shouted.

If I have children will they be Gedling or Thurgarton-Strang? Probably neither, he thought, though I don't suppose I will have any. He turned to Alice. 'Buy a copy of my book for your husband if you like, but I'll send one for you alone.'

'You are a darling.' In a lower voice: 'I loved you, you know.'

'I adored you,' he said. 'I've always thought about you. None of it

248

was forgotten.' It wasn't true, but the situation required such remarks from a Thurgarton-Strang, and maybe also from Bert Gedling. He wouldn't call on her, but the picture of doing so, and resuming their passion, and eloping, and setting up house (maybe in Cyprus) unrolled itself like an obligatory film. The last words out of the pathetic group hurrying away came from the boy who wanted to know about that man's scar, and Herbert assumed a passing bus muffled the smack Alice gave him.

During two hours' practice on the day before the motoring test he was caught in traffic along Piccadilly and around Trafalgar Square, which made him confident that he could drive anywhere without fear or hindrance. 'I'll blind the bastards if I don't pass,' he said to his instructor, feeling as competent at the wheel as any of those brash pig-ignorant louts who had often tried to kill him on Belisha crossings in South London.

Ice-cold attention to the test course made him neither slow nor fast, as if the hypercritical eye of Archie overlooked him instead of the middle-aged jaundiced cloth-capped examiner with his little moustache and poised clipboard. A railway bridge, a blind corner, the slope for a hill start, an obstacle course of crossings and traffic lights along the main street, a circuit of the gasworks, and backing into a quiet avenue – all was normal and predictable. He could quote the Highway Code from start to finish and inside out.

The test man filled in a sheet of pink paper. 'I have to tell you that you've passed' – as if his liver was going through the mincer with chagrin. Herbert supposed he was expected to jabber with gratitude, but his lips stayed locked as he took the permit, and gave a thumbs-up to the motoring school man by the kerb so that he could be driven back to his digs.

Twenty

People on the stairs made room for him so that Humphries at the top could grasp his hand and crow for everyone to hear: 'Have you seen the reviews?'

'No, I ain't.' Bert felt rough and surly, out of the sunlight into the hugger-mugger, the party no more than a chance to meet good-looking tarts from the office. Copies of the book had been displayed in shops for at least a week before publication. Herbert had seen a stack in a window on Southampton Row. 'Is that by me? Did I write that?' 'You fucking bet you did,' Bert told him. He stood back on the pavement for a wider view, Bert's gloating stamped out by a sneer from Herbert, and confirmed by the horn of a taxi that nearly took his heels off.

'We've had three good ones so far, and I'm sure there'll be others.' He was disappointed by Bert's formal get-up, but Herbert knew that if he'd decked himself out in cap and muffler, and pulled a reluctant false pedigree whippet on a piece of old clothes line, people would begin to suspect, anyone in the know realizing that when a factory worker attended a party, or went out on a Saturday night, he wore the best in his wardrobe.

Humphries thought he looked like a slightly more eccentric Sir Richard Burton of Victorian exploring days – though without the beard – which was not surprising, since he had come from that largely unmapped expanse of territory beyond Potters Bar. Never mind, he'll seem the genuine article as soon as he opens his mouth. 'I'll be introducing you to Jacob Wright later.'

Herbert, playing the part of Bert, felt threatened, disgruntled, almost paranoid among such people. Time must pass before a modification of his uncouth accent would seem a natural development of living in the south. 'Who's 'e, then? Is 'e a window cleaner?'

'Oh, no.' He wondered what the devil that could mean. 'He's from *New Books Magazine*, a very influential rag. It should get you in all the libraries, including Boots, so talk to him. He wants to do a full page. They're even sending a photographer.'

'I'm only interested in the crumpet.' Bert turned to a woman with shapely breasts and a beehive hairdo, offering glasses of wine. 'What's yer name, duck?'

'Fiona,' she smiled, moving on.

'Maybe you'd rather have beer?' Humphries pointed to a gaggle of bottles on his desk. 'We got these in specially.'

Bert took out his Waterman to script his moniker in a copy of *Royal Ordnance* for the firm's archives. 'It's all right. This red vinegar's OK, but I'd like some chips wi' it the next time, and a bit o' salt.'

The book jacket showed a group of brutal-looking workmen standing by a machine – which could have been anything from a one-armed bandit to a coffee dispenser – undecided whether to dismantle the contraption and walk out with the bits under their coats, or pick up hammers and smash it to pieces as representing all that was ugly in their oppressed lives.

'Like it?'

He didn't know what to say. Humphries obviously thought it was the best thing since he'd been to Rome on ten pounds and seen the Sistine Chapel. Herbert wouldn't look at such a cover on a shop table. He'd run a mile. It was ghastly. Even a half-undressed woman on the front would be better. 'Love it.'

'We all do.' He named the famous artist. 'He did us a jacket for Walter Hawksworth's novel a few years ago. The book wasn't very good, though it sold well.'

Herbert was sure it did. Still, the cover wasn't the fault of his book, which he lifted high to examine as the one object that might join his disparate parts. The greater the distance between them the more he felt himself an author, whether Bert Gedling who everyone should be wary of (or feel superior to) or Herbert Thurgarton-Strang who carried a bag of iron filings in his soul. Either way, he sensed people's unease as he signed the book, and lifted another glass of wine as if such work was wearing to an extent that factory graft never could be, and he needed a reward for tackling the unfamiliar system with such panache. Despite its murkiness, the drink went down like a well-greased adder.

Dominic showed him into a small office. 'It'll be quiet in here.'

Herbert wondered whether sharp questions on his past weren't about to commence, but Daniel Sloper the photographer turned Dominic and a couple of others out so that the flashing could happen in peace. 'All the pictures I've ever 'ad took mek me look like the back end of a tram smash,' Bert grumbled.

'These won't.' Sloper was a tall and well-stocked man in his twenties. He threw his brown leather jacket over a chair in the best motorbiker's style, but kept his silk scarf tied on like a Battle of Britain fighter pilot, which garment seemed to Herbert the social equivalent of his own white muffler.

Bert offered a glass from a tray of drinks on the desk. 'Sup this, mate. It's good for a cough.'

'Chin-chin, old boy!' Sloper took a modest swig and, as if knowing what real wine was, poured the remains into an ashtray. He set up screens and tripods, holding a light meter here and there, Herbert noting the thoroughness of a man who knew his trade. Using few words but with amiable and persuasive gestures, he got Bert to stand by the window, and then the door and, lastly, against a solid background of books. A dozen scar-side shots made Bert, in his formal suit and tie, look both villainous and interesting.

Sloper folded up the photographic trappings, waved cheerio, and trundled downstairs in his riding boots.

Herbert felt knackered already, as if his soul had been sucked out and spat into the gutter. 'You'll have to get used to it.' Dominic tried for nonchalance in lighting a Black Russian cigarette, but the match broke in two, and fell flaring on to the carpet. Before he could get down and put it out, Bert stamped on it, glad to see Dominic's face red with futile exertion as he came up. 'Yer've got to be quick where I come from.'

'I suppose it will take you some time to become accustomed to life in London. We had thought you'd come to the party wearing overalls. Just to play the part, of course.' Being jocular, he was unaffected by Herbert's scowl, who was wondering how he could enquire about

Rachel he'd had such a crush on at school. 'Ah well, where I come from yer put yer best rags on for a party. My sister Rachel allus towd me I'd got to dress smart. She's good at that. 'Ave yo' got a sister, Dominic?'

'I did have.' The cold-blooded toad-faced bastard was barely interested. 'She married an oaf who works in the City. Hardly see her now. Got three nippers.'

'If you don't like her 'usband me and some mates can do yer a favour and kick the snot out of 'im. I'll get some o' the lads down from Nottingham, to mek a proper job of it. All *you* need to do is give 'em a bit of beer money and their train fares. It'll be a day's outing for them. They'll love it.'

Dominic shuddered in trying to stop him. 'No, I don't think so, certainly not. We don't do that sort of thing here.'

Herbert turned away. That was that, then. He knew Dominic's old style, of being too icy to say his sister was also called Rachel, and not chiming in about her for a bit. Can't let these low-born types get too familiar, was what no doubt swamped into his unfriendly prep school mind.

A girl with short brown hair leaned on the top rail of the stairs, glass in hand, talking to a man whose suit even Bert knew to be very expensive. 'In't she marvellous, that one there. Deborah, in't it?'

'Yes,' Humphries said. 'I think you saw her before. But come along, it's time to be interviewed.'

A short-arsed putty-faced bloke smoking a curved pipe lifted himself from the sofa to shake the toiler's hand. Touch it, rather. 'I've read your book, and liked it. It's unique, in its portrayal of the working class.'

'You don't say?'

'I'm not the only one who thinks so.' At least he had humour enough to laugh. 'But I'm sure you must have read a lot to produce a book like that. You can't deceive me. Impossible to fault it.'

'Neither could I. That's why I sent it 'ere. I suppose yer was just waiting for somebody to come up with that sort o' novel and barge his way in. Still, I would say summat like that, wouldn't I?'

Jacob looked as if thinking he might not turn out to be as naive as he appeared. 'How did you start writing? But let's sit down, and be comfortable.'

'I'm used to standing on my feet eight hours a day. Well, I don't know. I just got into it. When I was twenty-five I looked round and thought I might 'ave summat to say about the world. Are you doin' shorthand?'

'I am. But go on. It's interesting.'

'So I got a pen and a packet of paper, and wrote about what I knew. One o' my mates sold me a typewriter that fell off the back of a lorry, and I was on my way. Mind you, it took a few years to gerrit all clear.'

'So how many drafts did you take it through before sending it to Humphries?'

'You've got more questions than a copper who puts his hand on your shoulder after a bust-up in a pub. I lost count at fifteen.' Bert set the tone to be aggressive rather than complaining, wanting only to get back among the booze and women. What else was he here for? Such a party had nothing to do with *Royal Ordnance*, though it was obvious Jacob must be dealt with. 'It looks like you're writing your own book about me, putting everything down on that jotter.'

'It could happen one day. We haven't had a book like this before, from a real working-class novelist.'

'How is it different?' Bert asked naively.

'Well, you've written about men who don't even think to better themselves.'

'Better themselves? What would they want to do a thing like that for when they've got good jobs in a factory?'

Jacob's shorthand swirled along. 'I see what you mean. It does give authenticity.'

Bert thought a lecturing tone was called for. 'I'm not a working-class novelist, anyway. Where I come from, if you call somebody working class, they smash yer face in. But I suppose you want to pigeonhole me, like everybody else. I'm just a novelist, or I will be when I've done a few more,' which intention Herbert thought a fair ploy to confirm that he would go on to become a real writer, certainly a better occupation than standing at a lathe. 'In a few years the fact that I'm an author from what you fucking well call a working-class environment' – let him wonder where he got that word – 'won't get anybody on the hop, because everybody'll be doing it.'

Jacob wiped sweat from both sides of his face. 'I'll quote that statement, but tell me something about your family.'

'Family?' He gave a suitably grim laugh, and settled himself, as if the burden of revelation might become too great, and he'd collapse into a fit. 'The owd man was on the dole when I was a kid. Not that he couldn't get a job, though. He was just bone idle.' He recalled the unsolicited account of Archie's younger days, listened to one Saturday night in a pub when they hadn't been able to get a nobble on from any of the women, about his father and the means-test man and the starvo times in the thirties, before the war started that drummed everyone into work. Archie was too pissed and despondent to care what he was saying, and went on till Herbert felt he had lived through such miseries himself.

'The old man kicked me out to work at fourteen, to bring some beer money into the house. Then the family was killed in an air raid, except me, who was in bed with a married woman – or I would 'ave been if I hadn't bin a bit too young. She was a cousin at my auntie's, as a matter of fact.'

Jacob nodded, and tut-tutted, and scribbled, and nodded again, till even he thought Bert was trowelling it on a little heavily. 'Let's talk about politics.'

Bert scratched his left ear, which hadn't been bothering him, till the finger-chafing brought an itch out of its burrow and refused to be eliminated, so he stopped, and closed his right eye to gain more control, looking sceptically at Jacob with the other. 'Politics? Well, it's allus been Labour for me, like the rest of us up there, though you do find a few fuckpigs that vote Tory.'

'That's always been a problem,' Jacob said, showing his own colours as if to encourage him.

'My temperament,' Bert went on, 'is a bit bolshie. I happen to think Darwin was right,' Herbert interjected. 'It's the survival of the fittest in this chronic world, which suits me fine. I reckon the country's over-governed. I don't like the idea of conscription, and I think income tax should be scrapped.' Herbert, though in danger of spoiling matters, maundered angrily on against every ruling institution and useful organization in the country, and stopped just short of appearing a fool or, worse, betraying his real back-ground.

Jacob wondered what he would be able to make of all this. 'I don't understand how someone who left school at fourteen could write a book like *Royal Ordnance*. In a way I don't quite see it.'

Neither did Herbert, who hoped his test was close to the end, for he began to despise himself at such apparent success. 'Well, I read a lot, didn't I?'

'But what about the scholarship, and going to a grammar school?'

'A what ship?'

'A scholarship.'

'What sort o' ship is that?'

He told him, and after a few more fruitless skirmishes thought a touch of provocation would put him back on the ground. 'Before you came in this evening,' Jacob smiled, 'I heard someone say he thought your book was good, but he did wonder how long you would be able to keep it up. Do you have anything to say about that?'

Bert's face twitched, and set hard. He looked towards the window, as if able to see outside and turn dark into daylight – and back again. 'Is he still 'ere? I'll knock him down the stairs' – especially if Dominic had been the know-all loudmouth. 'They can blab what they like,' he said moodily.

'I forget who it was.' Jacob put book and pencil back into his pocket. 'It's been a pleasure talking to you,' and took out a handkerchief to get the steam off his glasses. Herbert stretched himself, and cracked his knuckles, as he and Archie had often done in a duet to amuse the women at the end of the day, to indicate that the interview was over for him as well. Humphries had been listening by the door.

'That was fine, Bert,' he said when Jacob had left. 'You're ideal for interviews.'

'I was only talking. Showin' off, I suppose.'

In the crush of the party, he excused himself between several backs, and lifted the last full glass from a tray before another hand could close on it. Deborah's hugger-mugger with Dominic enraged both Bert and Herbert. 'Fuck off, Jones,' they said, 'or I'll bash yer pretty face in.'

A ripple went up her body at the prospect of some mindless violence, ending in a giggle which spilled a few beads of wine. 'Look here,

Herbert,' Dominic said. And then he grinned. 'I hope you don't mind me calling you Herbert?'

Bert glared into his eyes. So the bastard had rumbled him. Or had he? If he was fishing he'd bury the hook in his finger. Dominic looked back, impertinence passing for courage, as in the old days. It was one to one again, though pride and upbringing might well stop Dominic letting on if he did know, at least before so many people. Herbert, at the same time, no longer wanted to keep up the illusion of being someone he definitely was not. But he had to, and wondered what resources of his actor's talent remained to help him if he started drowning in the morass of his lie – or if his so far solid chariot began breaking up.

'It don't bother me if you call me Herbert,' Bert said, 'as long as you don't mind being dead. Nobody's called me that since I went into hospital to have my heart out. I was about four at the time. Anyway, piss off, so's I can have a conversation with this lovely, intelligent, and smashin' bit o' stuff called Debbie.'

Dominic collected the blush of chagrin from one side of his smarmy clock with a cursory wipe and put it into his trouser pocket for a future emergency, but the other side of his face showed that he didn't seem in any way concerned at leaving them together, giving one aspect to Bert and another to Herbert, so that each could make his choice. Even so, Herbert was glad to note how he shouldered himself along a disgruntled track towards a flat-chested woman who looked like his sister Rachel and blushed as he came close.

Herbert's words to Deborah had jerked out after soaking up too much inferior booze, but he decided to stay with her, and to rein in Bert for the rest of the evening, come what may, and put on whatever charm he could of a Thurgarton-Strang. She would only think he was learning fast. 'I'm sorry about all that. It's just that I get drunk on plain English now and again, which I think's no bad thing in this place. Anyway, it 'elped to get rid o' that lounge lizard.'

'I'm glad you did.' She looked at him with the sort of open full-toothed smile he could never have got from Cecilia. 'If I'd tried it I'd have been given the push.'

Herbert sensed that she and Dominic were closer than just acquaintances at the office, and if so he was glad to break up their affair, which would serve Dominic right.

Twenty-One

A light of inspiration in Herbert's room shone from the picture by Briton Rivière. Phoebus Apollo drove his chariot of the sun over a flower-strewn plain, the sullen pack of lions in long shafts gnashing their teeth at the efforts of the lord and master to gibe them on. Powerless to strike back from the reins and drag him down, such rage could only be slaked by sensing a time when the inexperienced Phaeton would struggle to control them and become their victim.

The reproduction, one of an album from a secondhand furniture shop, *all houses cleared*, provided another stitch in the tapestry of his progress, as well as a warning. He was half in the picture but too much in the bad dream of his room: a boil on the ceiling was about to burst, and drown him with pus while the walls closed in.

The yen to work was dead, relief impossible, for the time unthinkable. He only felt secure when alone in his room, but even that no longer held back the sensation of being close to madness. The room had turned into a prison, in which his anchor found no rock to grip.

He had money to spend, and London was all around, but being his own gaoler stopped him breaking out, unless to buy a cleaver at a bucket shop and disembowel a stranger in a dark alley. Without a motive he would never be caught. Would God or anyone look askance if he threw a child in the moiling water from Hungerford Bridge? It was the worst of dreams.

There was no other self in the offing but the one that sought to overpower him, a stranger he would have to fight like Theseus and the Minotaur. The rite of passage, to he couldn't tell what or where, gave a mixture of lassitude and voracious impatience, out of which not even Bert from way back could show him an escape route, except to say that he ensconce himself in the nearest pub and talk to people, something he was totally unable to do.

To get on a train for the north and wallow in the life he had abandoned, or go to Norfolk and shoot a few rabbits, and falter under the questions of his ageing parents, would be annihilation. The bark of Simpson the games' master might get him running, or the old army shout of rise and shine, but that was no more than a laugh. Or he could call Deborah from the box along the street and, babbling out his confusions, show himself as a worm not fit to live. They'd been close to getting into bed a few nights ago, but she said they hadn't known each other long enough, and he steeled himself to be gallant and not push the opportunity into boorishness.

He sliced brown bread and opened a tin of sardines into a saucer: the survival of the fittest had to begin with yourself. A barb on the ragged edge of the tin drew copious blood, an encouraging sign. Maybe his despair had been brought on because nothing had gone into his stomach since a meagre breakfast of distant coffee and a slice of buttered bread. He had been too intent on opening letters from the mat downstairs to eat much. Those with typed addresses were seen to first, in case there were cheques inside. The second half of his advance came for the novel, and a few hundred for a paperback, as well as cash for an American edition, an unnerving cocked hat for one post. He unfolded and flattened them with his buttery knife: let the teller at the bank wonder what the stains were.

The top came easily off a bottle of White Horse and, filling a cup halfway, alcohol felt good at the lips, put pepper in his belly, to be mopped up by a sandwich. As if the blood was ink he pressed several folds of blotting paper over it till the skin was dry, and whisky could be rubbed into the cut.

Behind the window of a showroom in South Kensington he saw an Austin Healey Four Cylinder One Hundred Sports Car, on sale for five hundred pounds, a heartening object to spring into your sight on a Monday morning. He sloped back and forth along the low slung brutish panels, fingered the dark green wings as smooth as marble. 'I'm serious. It's a beauty.'

'Then sit in it, pal.' The salesman was a tall Germanic-looking man with rimless glasses and an amiable worldly squint. 'The boss isn't in yet. Cup of coffee while you wait?'

'That's very good of you. Yes, please.'

'No trouble.'

Herbert stroked the pristine wheel, and felt his prospects good enough to stick up two fingers at the notion of getting a job. Solvent for at least a year, it would seem like twenty at the rate time had gone in the last two decades. He called the man over. 'Don't care if I do go broke. I'll have it.'

The boss came in, overcoat, scarf and homburg, despite the warmish day, looking like a brother (or cousin) of Glenny the rackrent landlord, whose offer of a job Herbert had turned down. 'I'll have it, if I can drive it away.'

'How would you like to pay, sir?'

All problems solved, he drove on to the road. After the car had soaked its gallons out of a pump near Shepherds Bush, he took the paces slowly around quiet streets so that he could gauge the dimensions. Drops of rain splattered the windscreen, wipers leaving a clean Perspex after every heartfelt sweep. In the coffee bar his position by the window kept the car in view long enough for him to know it was his.

He rocketed from the starter's line at the Notting Hill Gate traffic lights, well in advance of any slow coach or happy saver, cruised along the Bayswater Road, and threaded a way through Mayfair and Soho, feeling like a kid who had been given a sparkling mechanical toy for his birthday.

Pulling up at a phone box he called Deborah. Could they meet after work? 'I'll take you to dinner.'

'Yes, please. Can't wait. I know a terrific place in Hampstead.' She wondered, putting the receiver down, if he hadn't been a hoaxer, not Bert Gedling at all, unless he was trying to bring his accent into line, which would be no bad thing.

At his solitary tea in the thirties splendour of the Hyde Park Hotel he imagined her thoughts, and smiled at their progress. She would analyse every nuance, and sooner or later get close to the right answer. Looking into the Bible he learned that Deborah was a prophetess, reason enough for falling in love.

The waitress brought extra butter and filled his pot with hot water whenever he called. She had a stout figure and dark straight hair, and Herbert, because of her accent, wanted to know where she came from. She told him she'd been a teacher in Australia, and was working her way around Europe. Feeling quixotic, he left a pound note for a tip.

Deborah, walking down the steps of the offices, heard him pip the horn from across the street, and paused at the kerb for traffic to pass. Herbert seemed to get his first real look at her face, her features usually too volatile to picture her properly when among other people.

As for what she was like inside – inside? Where the fuck was that? – whoever you looked at, and thought you had weighed up, and knew from the spleen outwards, could remain a mystery, and the weighing up had to begin all over again. No one realized that better than he, and you could but speculate: often wide of the truth, yet sometimes close to reality. People, like quicksilver, needed a lifetime to properly pin down, the only thing being that you couldn't afford to wait that long, and so used the imagination to fix them for better or worse at a particular moment and say that's how they were.

She was a little above middle height, and walked across the road in such a way as to show she had been carefully brought up but had enough independence to go her own way. Her nose pointed somewhat in the air, as if she considered everyone else as shit, which amused him, though he liked how her white and even teeth showed he deserved a smile. Either she was more beautiful than he had supposed, or it was marvellous what a sports car did for you.

He looked in no way, she thought, like the proletarian novelist he was said to be, when leaning over the wheel to unlatch the door, though on opening his mouth he couldn't help betraying himself. 'Come on in, duck, and I'll tek yer for a ride in this mechanical pram.'

His accent was bound to mellow after a while, unless he's playing it up because he hopes I find it sexy, which in a way I do. The interesting scar – a mark of Cain if ever there was one – hinted at a fair amount of

261

trouble in his life, never mind how he said he'd come by it, though without it he might look a bit more ordinary.

She thought him handsome, but unpredictable and hard to know, perhaps a man to beware of. Her father had warned her of people 'from further down the ladder', who tried to pass themselves off for what they hadn't a snowball's chance in hell of becoming. Otherwise the kindest and gentlest person, he said he couldn't bear social climbers. 'They're only out for themselves, so avoid them like the plague. You know what they say? "Put a beggar on horseback, and he'll ride roughshod over you."'

He was only trying to protect her, bless him, but she was quite good at looking after herself, thank you very much. Bert Gedling wasn't climbing anywhere, though he sometimes gave the impression of treading in hobnailed boots across the whole spectrum. Luckily he wasn't fat, or coarse, or bumptious, or anything like such a person might be as shown on television. Nor was he paranoid or set on murder. His nails were scrubbed, and hair smartly cut, shoes polished and cravat arranged into the neck of his shirt. He used deodorant, so didn't smell, and even if it was his only suit he knew how to use a clothes brush. Perhaps he came from a more respectable level of the working class than he let on or, going by his rough-beast streak, he was the black sheep who even so hadn't been able to throw off the cleanly habits of his family.

It didn't much matter that she would never be able to introduce him to her father, as he wove with aggressive skill through traffic up Charing Cross Road. She caught looks of curiosity and admiration from other motorists, and glares of vile envy from one or two pedestrians. Her father would probably have been among the latter, but she didn't care what he would think of Bert, and would do as she liked, which was what living in London was all about.

My lovely popsy girl, he laughed, shooting the amber towards Camden Town, is enjoying her spin with Champagne Bertie, and I'm wallowing in being with her. Like an air stewardess in the telly ad she lit a pair of cigarettes and put one between his lips. Life was on the mend, though he supposed Archie in his place would have preferred her to be married, peril being pornography to him. Herbert took a hand away to up the gear. 'You are the most beautiful girl I've ever met, seen, or even dreamed about, and I love you. I know you don't believe me, but I can't help that.'

He was lying, of course. The first words of any man who wanted to be intimate with you was to say he loved you. And the first move of a woman who wanted the man to make love to her was to light a cigarette and put it between his lips. Her laugh at his declaration carried them much of the way up Haverstock Hill.

She lived on the third floor of a large old house, which allowed him to park his precious motor off the road – and close the top to stop pigeons making a mess of the upholstery. There were trees along the drive, but the garden had degenerated into a jungle.

'That's my Mini over there,' she nodded. 'I don't drive it to work, though it's good to rattle around in at weekends, or go to see my parents in Woking now and again.'

A curvaceous bottle of old Cliquot was lifted from behind the seat of his Healey. 'Smart little buggy, the Mini. Do you have a room, or a flat?' Meaning that if she's sharing maybe I'll have a go at the other girl as well.

She drew him into the hall. 'A flat, and I don't have to share.' Rising damp, woodworm and deathwatch beetle, with a dash of Colorado thrown in, it stank like his old school, tingled at the nostrils as they went up creaking stairs. She leaned on the banister. 'Daddy bought me a ten-year lease.'

He wondered if the building would last that long. 'What does he do, your old man?'

'He was a barrister, but retired early.'

How a barrister's daughter levelled with the son of a brigadier-general he neither knew nor cared, all such stuff left behind decades ago, at least on his part. Maybe everyone would start to think the same, though he doubted that anything could fundamentally change in such a country. Even if her father was a docker he wouldn't have minded.

He followed her into a large sitting room, with bedroom, kitchen-diner, and bathroom attached. 'Quite a nice pied-à-terre, duck.'

'It used to belong to Dominic, till he got a place in Chelsea.'

'That fat worm.'

'He's a good editor. And it was kind of him to tell me the flat would be falling vacant. I'd always wanted to live in Hampstead, instead of the bedsit in Fulham. Oh, by the way' – she took a letter from her handbag – 'Dominic asked me to give you this. It came via the office.'

Postmarked Nottingham, he was glad to note, for it might help to establish his authenticity in Dominic's oyster eyes. He put it into his pocket, and looked around the room. She certainly did live here, everything neat and shipshape. 'A very cushy billet.' He took off his jacket only after she had shed her coat. 'Where are the napkins?'

'In the kitchen drawer. Glasses top left in the cupboard.' Like all the men she had been used to he was curt, but basically courteous, so why should she think him any better or worse? He came in with two glasses: the cork hit the ceiling. 'After we've polished this off we can go out to eat. I'm clambed to death.'

She would have preferred dry sherry, but maybe he had seen an old Charles Boyer film. 'I'm fairly hungry, as well.'

He stood by the bay window looking into the half-leaved branches, mouth down and brown eyes sharp but, she thought, seeing only himself, different now to the mad but gallant boyo who had driven her from the office. His saturnine aspect showed character, too broody perhaps at times, as if he was having a struggle coming to terms with himself – with his so-called success, probably – since whether he admitted it or not, it must be something of a shock, though so far she had to admit he was carrying it off with panache, unless he was a consummate actor.

Everything about him puzzled her, even so, because she had seen no supposed workman on the street with anything like the quality of his looks at certain moments. Perhaps experience in the matter was lacking, not having been further north than Whipsnade Zoo, and then only for a few hours, and gazing at faces not at all likely to help her speculations. It could be that there were many specimens like himself in the great unknown North, and that if she were to see him in overalls and cloth cap, with a spanner in one hand and a hammer in the other, and a cigarette between his lips as he puzzled out some difficult job or other, she would have no trouble in identifying him as a run-of-the-mill workman.

Another explanation – though this was really fanciful, as if out of a Victorian novel – was that he had been snatched from his cradle by some villainous woman who had, for the price of a bottle of beer, palmed him off to a family as low down in the social scale as his had been above it. Anyhow, what had changed him from one person to the other she couldn't know about, but she was more than half in love with the result, and felt like getting into bed with him this minute, whether or not it was because of the champagne, but didn't want him to think her cheap or easy to get in case he lost all respect for her, as her mother had said men would if she let them get that far, and in fact as one or two had already done.

He swung away, and set down his empty glass, deciding it wasn't the time to tell her who he was. It was necessary to avoid possible recrimination, or at best a long explanation as to why he'd got into the Bert guise at all, if he wasn't to forfeit his chance of seducing her. A confession had been urgent from the beginning, and though there would never be an ideal moment, it would certainly be stupid to make one now.

So after rehearsing the suitably crass lingo of his next announcement, he said: 'Come on, love, let's finish this bottle of bubbly, then we can go out and find one o' them posh troughs to scoff at. Maybe they'll light us a couple of orange candles, and somebody'll scrape out a tune on a fiddle when we spoon into each other's eyes.'

She broke away from his kisses and sat on the bed. 'Are you absolutely sure?'

What a question! – needing only a look for an answer.

Knowing there to be no option because of the way she felt, she began to undo her blouse, her eyes willing him to undress as well, though he wanted no telling.

Why and when she had decided to be intimate with him he couldn't say, but if it didn't happen now it never would, so he was more than ready.

She felt unsteady, after his topping up of her glass in the restaurant, and fumbled at her skirt, though it soon dropped. She nudged her shoes off.

He noted that her way of getting her underwear off was balletic, not only as if she had done it more than a few times before (he may be misjudging her, and yet who hadn't when you thought about it?) but that she believed, as a smart and experienced Home Counties girl would, in the no-nonsense utility of effort to get sooner to the point where pleasure could begin.

On the other hand you could say there was something puritanical in undressing so quickly, for he preferred to take his time, ploughing through fancy underwear, silk, cotton, or nylon, it didn't matter which, as long as, phase by phase, he reached what was inside and found it ready.

He kissed the closed lids of her eyes, and her delicious lips on which the taste of fruit and wine and coffee lingered, as if he wanted no more of her than that, stifling the crude language of Bert so as to spoil nothing and please both. The only way he could give his lust a patina of love and affection, and bring it to the level of romance which he assumed all women wanted – at least the women he had so far had – was to imagine her as a version of someone else. He worked his way backwards and forwards through every intimacy with other women, savouring the lechery, till he returned to the here and now of Deborah, the freshest of them all, whose love he was intent on winning till it matched his own.

The line of her naked back when she turned to pull down the bed-clothes made him fully stiff, as he held her breasts and embraced her gently from behind. Resisting the force of passion that threatened to overwhelm him, he proceeded subtly, even at the risk of her wondering how a man of his sort had acquired such tact.

Her lips voiced the usual request as to whether he had 'coped'. Nothing in the world would have been better than going in without, but the ultimate raw love of conception was only to happen after marriage. 'You know I love you, Bert. I can't hold myself back, but we have to take care.'

He stroked her hair and held her closer. 'I know, darling, and I love you too much not to.'

'When I can't resist,' she murmured, 'you'll know what it means, won't you?'

He saw it, at the moment, as a promise he could hardly wait to keep. It was better with her than with all the others put together, certainly better than it could ever have been with Cecilia. But then, the fucking you were doing at the moment was bound to be the best, and he was more than satisfied, after making her come for the first time.

The letter lay on the floor between trousers and vest. Frank said Mrs Denman was 'about to pass away, and is asking for you, Bert, and wondering how you're getting on. It's a crying shame she's having to go through so much. Ralph isn't any help at all, even though he is her son. He hardly shows his face, as if he's frightened of what's happening. He said he's got a lot of work on, would you believe it? And he's got to look after Mary, he says, because she's got varicose veins. After all his mam's done for him. That's what happens though when you pamper your kids.'

And so on. His unremembered dreams had not been of the sort to set him up for agreeable social intercourse but, even so, it was a matter of a shave, shower, coffee, and putting on a second-best suit so that she would neither think he had come down in the world, nor was making a show because she was about to die.

The drive through Watford was tedious. Maybe it was market day in St Albans. Luton and Bedford went fairly easily, and so did Kettering, but then came the final killpig of threading through Leicester, only useful for stopping to buy the best of flowers. He pulled in once for petrol and coffee, and twice to make notes on his impressions of the route.

Mrs Denman never left his mind, the cause of his tedious slog to the north, an obstacle race turning the hundred and thirty miles into a thousand. There was talk of a motorway opening soon, which would cut a chunk off the four hours – when it came – yet he thought it fitting that the expedition to see Ma should be anything but an easy option.

Nottingham looked livelier and brighter than six months ago, and on a midweek morning as well. Maybe coming in by road at the wheel of his own car, and knowing the place no longer meant hard labour, put him in a mood that overawed the reason for his visit. More traffic ran to and fro over Trent Bridge and, in spite of half a sky of cloud, sunlight found a way on to the tarmac as he passed the school where he'd enlisted, and turned off towards Wilford Road.

Frank opened the door. 'Thank God you've come. I knew it was you as soon as the car stopped.' His hand was dry and bony. 'You're a good lad, Bert, is all I can say.' Why was it that those who nursed the dying looked old and as if near death themselves? 'The doctor's just gone. He gave her enough painkillers to put a regiment down, but she's hanging on, bless her.'

Bert also felt himself ageing as he went up the stairs. 'Look who we've got here, my love,' Frank called. 'All the way from London. A real Prodigal!'

'I just happened to be passing.' So frail, it seemed as if she would sink through the bedclothes, a rag of her former self, soon to melt into the earth. But a hand came towards him, and he took it, turning back into the old Bert without effort. 'Hey up, Ma, what's all this, then?'

Her eyes opened. 'Hello, Bert.'

Tears were floating in his head, unable to find a way out, which was how it should be. As long as the stalactites were dripping somewhere inside. 'Thought I'd call and say hello. I'm on my way through.'

She smiled. 'Going to the moon, are yer?'

'And back,' he said.

'When I lit the fire last week . . .'

'I tried to stop her,' Frank said, 'the silly sausage!'

'Well,' she said, 'there was a bit o' burnt paper fluttering against the bars, like a moth it was, a black moth.' Her words came out one by one, as if torn by the teeth from a telegram. 'You know what that meant, Bert?'

'No,' he said.

'It meant a stranger was on his way to see me. And here you are. I thought it might be you.'

'That's right, Ma, and it was.' She was mistaken. A more important visitor was on his way.

Frank must have thought so too. 'I'll get a jug, and put these flowers in some water.' He hoped she'd noticed them. Her eyes closed, opened again. 'They're lovely. Thank you, Bert.'

'That's all right. I was walking past an allotment near Leicester, and went over the fence to nick 'em. I left a few bob on a stone, though, outside the hut door, so's the man could have a pint or two while he wondered what had happened to his blooms.'

She was away again, so he stayed silent, and hoped she would live, but knew she couldn't because the frayed piece of string she was hanging on to was about to give. Her voice came, weak but clear. 'Frank read me your book. You got it right.'

Wiping his face was the nearest to a waterfall of tears. He was in the house, so couldn't say it was the rain, hadn't been to work, so couldn't claim it was sweat, had A1 vision so couldn't laugh that his eyes had gone for a burton. 'Thanks, Ma.' His impulse of dedicating the book to her was the only good deed he could remember. 'I'm glad you liked it.'

'Write me another.'

He kissed her luminous forehead now so narrow, and then the cool damp lips. 'I am doin'. It'll be done soon. I'll write you lots.'

'I'll stay alive to read 'em. I'll get better now.'

'I know you will.'

She slept, crying in her sleep as if to get breath, or maybe down there was where she fought her pain, alone in the dark, sorting out memories and dreams. The usual sound of kids playing came from beyond the window, a little girl squealing every few seconds like a stuck pig. He'd done the right thing in coming to see her, but wanted to leave, go back to Deborah, who might wonder where he had gone. She wouldn't let go of his hand, though the grip grew more and more feeble. 'You can come down now for a cup o' tea, and summat to eat,' Frank whispered.

He didn't want to sleep in his old room, told Frank he would be staying with somebody in town. He put up at the George Hotel behind the Council House, then walked across Slab Square to call on Isaac. The front door was locked and bolted, windows boarded up. He went into a shop lower down the street to buy cigarettes, and asked about it.

'It's being redeveloped, duck, as far as I know.'

'An old man lived there. Do you happen to know anything about him?'

'Couldn't say. I expect they rehoused him. They don't chuck anybody on the streets, not now they don't.'

Which was a comforting thought. Yates's was crowded, and he positioned himself by the door in case Isaac shuffled in. It wasn't his night, and Herbert was irritated by the noise, so after his second pint he walked up the street to have dinner at the hotel.

The morning weather poured a deluge into the gloom, and he regretted having no workman's cap for his head. He took the two bags of groceries bought for Isaac to Mrs Denman's.

'You needn't have done this,' Frank said.

'Just a contribution to the household. How is she?'

Frank's face was wet with tears, a phenomenon in that Herbert hadn't noticed them begin. They were suddenly there. 'She's fighting, is all I can say. You know, Bert, I know I shouldn't say this, but it'll be a blessing when it's over.'

Herbert thought so, too. A faint untidiness made the house seem dead already. 'I shan't disturb her, then.'

'No, that's right. Come back this afternoon. She might be a bit better by then. Forget what I said just now. The only thing that's left of me is hope.' He sat in the armchair, almost fell into it, as if his legs had lost the strength to hold him up. 'It's funny, though. I told her to see a doctor last year, but she said it was only a cold that wouldn't go. Maybe every complaint that's going to carry you off starts with thinking you've got a cold. I shouldn't have believed her.'

'There wasn't much you could do,' Bert said.

After the funeral he avoided the main route out of the city by paying the fourpenny toll over Wilford Bridge to Clifton, practising the indirect approach for getting back to London. To his right were the dark trees of the Grove he had walked along with Cecilia, and he smiled at no longer regretting his lost love.

In the few days between death and burial he had called at various council offices, and put on his haughty Thurgarton-Strang voice to get Isaac's address out of a snotty-faced penpusher. The old folks' ground-floor flat was spacious and newly furnished, a living room flanked by kitchen, bathroom and bedroom. 'There's so little else I want', Isaac smiled, 'that I'm beginning to think my time's almost up. I've even got good neighbours.'

'You deserved this years ago.'

'No, I'm happy enough.'

Only the scattered books made it halfway familiar, and Herbert took a few off the settee so that he could sit down and unload his misery on to someone who had suffered more, and knew how to listen.

Working his way across country to intercept Watling Street, he thought maybe he should have stayed on a couple of days to console Frank. But Frank was strangely calm, icy almost, fully in control. The agony was over for Beryl so it was finished for him too, and he would grieve in his own way, for as long as it took, Herbert supposed, to get back to being only himself, when he'd maybe meet someone and marry again. His era of tears had ended, and Herbert was glad. In the past he'd been scornful of whoever shed them, cruel even – let the dead bury the dead – but the black dog of experience was firmly latched on to his shoulders, and the illumination of being a writer was always before his eyes – or mostly so – though in spite of his new tolerance he was inclined to scoff at such thoughts, unless impelled to pick up his pen and get them into a notebook.

By the aerials of Rugby and Daventry he was on the Roman road, and well on his way to London, beamed towards Deborah. She pulled him south, tarmac rolling under his car, distance lessened at every signpost. Wanting her nakedness to cling to, he cut his speed in case he never got there, despair vanishing now that Mrs Denman was dead and out of pain.

Twenty-Two

Awake, yet not awake, alert in the needle-grey dark but unable to open his eyes, the misty palisades closed in. Beryl haunted him through the deepest oceans of memory, till she had tracked him back to her lair. He must get out of bed on Monday morning, and reach for clean overalls, cram in his kitchen breakfast and, after as sociable a good morning as could be dredged up, bike his way through cold murk to the factory.

Such terror had its consolations when the limits of despair and indignation pulled away, and he felt the purest happiness to know that the factory had no more call on him, and that Deborah was in the kitchen pressing orange juice and brewing coffee.

To disperse the final wisps of nightmare he gloated, no less, on how the new year had brought more money from Humphries, and a thousand pounds advance for film rights which promised another fee on writing the script. There was much to be said for riches that fell so easily into your hands. 'It's as if I've inherited a coal mine.'

Deborah set the tray down, passed the Sunday papers, and put an arm around him. 'Darling, they nationalized them years ago. In any case, whatever you get, you've earned.'

He supposed he had, if it counted as back pay at so much a year. Such money didn't tempt him to waste time on the pleasures of London, a night or two each week at Deborah's taking care of that. Otherwise he stayed in his room to finish *The Wrong Side of the Tracks*, not as easy as writing *Royal Ordnance*, which had been put together as if time had no importance. On the other hand he couldn't afford to let *The Wrong Side of the Tracks* take nearly as long, not drawing a regular wage from the factory for his support. Since most of it had been done, or at least thought about before coming to London, he forced the pace through revision after revision till it was finished.

Time had to be found for interviews in certain newspapers: SENT OUT TO WORK AT FOURTEEN TO GET DAD SOME BEER MONEY. He hated their disgusting headlines, but couldn't deny that he was responsible. Keeping up the image of Bert Gedling was becoming more tedious and difficult, only manageable by exaggerating the role, which made the headlines worse. The deception was getting bad for his self-esteem, and he was terrified at being so much up to his neck in Gedling that he would never be able to come out of him, and have to stay fixed for life in the skin of a monster so mindlessly created.

The only way to go on was to separate himself into three compartments, one containing the all-seeing Herbert Thurgarton-Strang, another the calloused and resentful Bert Gedling, and the third a distillation of someone able to handle both in television interviews. Perhaps Deborah sensed his struggle when she gave a few hints on how to manage. He had worked out certain rules for himself, but nodded appreciatively, as Bert would, when her advice confirmed them. 'Don't you know', she said, 'that you never say a straight yes or no to any of their questions?'

'No, I didn't.'

'Now you do. That way they have less chance of making you say things you might regret. And it gives you time to think about what to say next. Also, never say anything that might lead them to think you're naive.'

He nodded. 'I'll try not to.' Having already decided to climb out of Bert Gedling's boots as soon as he unobtrusively could, he wondered, when Deborah went on, if she hadn't been put on to him by Humphries. 'You'd better do as I tell you,' he would say, 'and let him think you've fallen in love with him, or you won't have a job any more.' The only way to find the truth was by asking her to marry him, but she had to know who he was first. Even if she was Humphries' secret agent or, worse, that shitmouth Dominic's, her loving performances in bed were so genuine he had nothing to complain about.

At his first television interview she thought he'd scored about seventy per cent, which was good, she added, though it might have been better. The producer, Arthur Hornbeam, said everything was marvellous, but he would, wouldn't he? All the same, he seemed happy with it, and went on to wonder whether Mr Gedling would consider writing plays for the medium. 'Someone like you would be paid top rate. The time's just about right for that kind of stuff.'

He drained his paper cup of cheap whisky, and threw it into the bin. 'I'll think about it.'

'But can you go on churning out the same old thing?' Deborah asked, as they lay in bed.

'Standing on my head, I should think.'

He wasn't so sure, didn't care to deal only with the rough and tumble of low life for the rest of his days. After a few further books from the dustbin of his experience he would scribble about more worldly happenings, expand his imagination, alter the scenery, and become a real novelist, as everyone would expect him to do. Still, it wasn't yet time to disillusion Deborah about his ability to suck at the cow's teat forever, in case she let something drop to Humphries.

Waking in the morning, care had to be taken not to let his accent slide too far into the public school twang. 'I'll tell you another thing, luv, it's a lot better writin' books than it is sweatin' blood all week in a factory.'

'I'm sure it is, Herbert. You don't mind the Herbert bit, do you?'

'Call me what you like. Loves yer, don't I?'

'And I love you. More coffee?'

'Another thing is, I reckon it's time I did a bunk from my hole and corner billet near the Elephant. It's too far on the wrong side of the river.' People who assumed he was already a millionaire might wonder where he really came from if he stayed in such a squalid area.

She adjusted a fold of breast inside her brassiere, and reached for a pair of clean pants. 'Why not lease a flat for a few years in Belsize Park? That way you can commute between here and there.'

She used her London expertise, and looked at the Roy Brooks column in the Sunday papers. After a couple of weeks she found a place. 'They want three hundred and fifty a year, as well as five hundred for carpets and curtains. I went there this morning, and it's fine. Let's see it, before someone else makes an offer.'

A woeful Bert tone came up in Herbert's throat on hearing such sums spoken of so lightly. 'Eight 'undred and fifty quid's as much as I used to earn in a year,' but Herbert, who knew the price to be realistic if not reasonable, choked back more of the same on seeing the flat. 'I'll have it.'

Deborah led the helpless booby into Heals to buy the basic amount of utilitarian furniture that would fit with the newly painted walls. Selfridge's was for pots, pans, cutlery and provisions. Cheques fluttered away like leaves from an autumn tree, a day's shopping to suck out all energy. At lunch in the White Elephant neither could say much, though a surreptitious holding of hands and the warm touch of knees seemed to deepen their attachment, as if exhaustion was a more potent fuse than any talk about love.

The time was right to reveal himself as Thurgarton-Strang, yet he hesitated. The chariot was clicking along smoothly at the moment. 'You've got to tell her sooner or later,' Bert said. 'No use putting it off.'

'Tell her what?' – as if he didn't know.

'That ye're not me, and never was.'

'I'll do it in my own good time.'

'There's no such thing. And when you do she won't like it.'

'What do you mean?'

Bert laughed. 'Well, she likes me better than you. I know for a fact she won't want to see the back of me.'

'I doubt that's the case,' he said huffily.

'Oh, don't yer? You wait. It's me she fell for, not you. Yer can't deny it. You'll find out when you tell 'er.'

'It's got to be done, though,' Herbert sighed.

Bert changed his tone. 'Ye're not going to leave me, are yer?'

'Afraid I'll have to.'

'Well, I shan't cry about it. Good luck to yer, is all I can say.'

'You've been a good sport, Bert. I'll never forget you.'

'You wain't be half the man you was before.'

'Oh, I think I will. In any case I won't need to be.'

'You'd better do it now. I would if I was you.'

Deborah, from looking at two women waiting for a table, turned back to her coffee. 'I'd like to know what profound thoughts I've disturbed you from, darling.'

'Oh, I was only thinking how much I loved you.'

'What a simple uncomplicated mind you have.'

'That's how I am.'

'I know. And I love you, too.'

The Other Side of the Tracks had been in Humphries' office a week and Herbert went to see him. 'Well, what do you think?'

'We'll do it in the autumn.' He reached for a box: 'Cigar, Bert?'

'No thanks.'

'I read it on the train, going home the other night, after Dominic had finished with it.'

Herbert lit a cigarette. 'You must have read it as quickly as you can turn the pages.'

'Almost.' He cut his cigar. 'I think Dominic wants to suggest a few alterations.'

The stack of typescript lay on his desk, next to a new effort by Walter Hawksworth, and Herbert put a hand over his own. 'I'll buy a cross from an ex-service stores and crucify anybody who touches a word of this. You can come to the party if you like. There'll be champagne, not fucking red vinegar. I'll invite all the reviewers. Calvary won't be a patch on it, especially if I nail up two publishers as well.'

Humphries laughed. 'There's no need to go to such expense. The book's marvellous. It might even get a Book Society Recommendation, and do better than *Royal Ordnance*.' He didn't want the bloody fool taking his novel to another firm, after all they'd done for him.

'What about the advance, then?'

'Oh that? Well, we'll up it a bit this time.' He spun the fine gold chain till the watch hit his finger. 'We'll do you proud, in fact. What do you say to five hundred?'

Bert picked up the typescript. 'I'd better show it somewhere else – unless you make it a thousand.'

'A thousand?'

'Seems reasonable to me,' he said in a tone which suggested to

Humphries that he wasn't a bad mimic. 'And keep Dominic's hands off it, or I'll give him a good hiding.'

'Now look here, Bert, you just can't talk like that.'

He laid the typescript on a bookcase by the door, and flopped into an armchair, pushing out his legs. Deborah had Roneoed a letter which Humphries had written to Reginald Stone the paperback publisher, giving reasons for expecting a larger advance than the one offered.

'It's uncanny. He's writing about the workers in just the way we've always thought in our secret hearts they should be written about. We could barely have hoped for it, but now it's here. Of course, some strait-laced old vicars and JPs in certain places will complain about the obscene way it's done, and tell us that the "lower orders" shouldn't be written about at all, since it will give them ideas above their station, but Mr Gedling has given the working classes, whatever else one says, a genuine portrait of themselves, as well as a voice. All we have to do, as time goes on – if he doesn't do it himself, of course – is to steer him into our mouth instead of his mouth, a little more like Walter Hawksworth, if you see my drift. If we can do that we'll have real bestsellers on our hands, not retailing in tens of thousands but by the million. Meanwhile the joy of it is, he's absolutely one of them, and how he came to write novels I'll never know, because he's quite uneducated. But he certainly deserves what money he can get, and the wealthier he becomes, and the sooner he gets to depend on it, and is able to settle into a respectable life, the better it will be for everybody. So I think it's just as much in your interest as it is in mine that you see if you can't double your offer. You won't lose by it, I assure you.'

After several readings blind rage at the conspiratorial twist of Humphries' mind made him sweat more than he'd ever done in the factory. Veins on his temples jumped as he tried to stay nonchalant, barely able to resist saying he knew about the letter. Obtuse clod-hopper Bert had made him blind to such insulting views of his talent and intentions. He would go his own way whatever they thought or felt, even though he had as yet no clear notion as to what that way would be. It wasn't surprising that Dominic had itched to get his doctoring maulers on the typescript. Herbert would read the proofs word by word, to detect any clandestine tampering. 'I don't mind sitting here all day, till I hear your last word on what you're going to pay me for an advance.'

'Oh, all right,' Humphries' tone was no longer patronizing, 'we'll make it a thousand pounds. I only hope your royalties will run to it.'

'It's your problem if they don't. But I think I'd better find an agent.' Some good firms had written to offer their services. 'If I'd got one already they'd have screwed even more out of you.' He stood up and held out his hand. 'I'll 'ave that cigar now, if you don't mind.'

The flat was set up and finished, a home in which he relished being alone. He stood in the large study-sitting room, looking around as if in a dream, amazed at all that had happened in a short space of twelve months. The flat belonged to him for the forever of five years, by when he would have a bigger place to fall into a trance about, maybe even a house. Change was no problem, for didn't he get used to being a factory worker straight out of school? The staging post of a furnished room at the Elephant and Castle was easy to forget. He felt he was becoming a lover of comfort, and neither knew nor cared from what part of himself such maturity came. On the other hand he knew that not much was certain in life. Prosperity could any moment be snatched out of his hands by malignant fate. It was as well to be prepared, or at least not to be too surprised by the unwanted and unexpected. The picture of Phoebus Apollo, framed in thin black wood, hung on the wall above his writing table, and the hardworn copy of *Caged Birds* was available in the bedroom drawer.

Archie jumped from the carriage and strode along the platform. 'Hey up, fuck-face!'

'I'm glad you could make it,' Bert said, a handshake and then an embrace.

'I towd 'em I 'ad a bad back, and would be in bed for the day. The gaffer gen me a leery look, but since I've never 'ad a day off before in my life he couldn't very well say owt. Anyway, I'd a gen 'im a mouthful, if 'e 'ad.'

278

It was a tonic to hear the old accent from someone born and bred to it, yet disturbing to know how much of his own had already gone down the chute. 'The day's yourn, Archie, so what do you want to do with it?'

Archie gripped his arm by the ticket barrier. 'I wouldn't mind a black and tan at Dirty Dick's.'

'You still like the owd titty-bottle, eh? They wain't be open for a couple of hours, so we'll go to my place first.' A start had to be made on letting Archie see his altered style of living. Walking together into the Underground, Herbert wondered whether they could be taken for two workmen down for a day in the Smoke to see the sights. Though sartorially on a par in that Archie had donned his best suit, and Herbert wore his one for everyday, some difference between them must be obvious. He hoped so, but at the same time cared not to think about it. The connection had been false from the beginning, but he felt a brotherly responsibility for Archie, and nothing but gladness at having set the meeting up. 'How old is the baby now?'

'Three months, give or take an hour or two. He's a beauty, but the little boggerlugs screams his guts out from the colic, or if he don't get his own way. It teks all Josie's strength to pick 'im up. He'll soon be bigger than she is.'

'So when are you having another?'

'Give 'er a break, though I wouldn't mind. I don't want too many, or I'll run out of beer money.' The train rattled through Euston and Camden Town. 'I only know the middle of London from when I was in the army, but I don't think I'd like to live down 'ere.'

'I'm not sure I like it all that much, either,' Herbert said. 'I've got used to it, though.' Somewhere in the countryside might be more civilized, but he didn't feel ready for it yet.

'I suppose you 'ave. But you know, Bert, when you was in the factory and one of us, I allus knew you were up to summat and wouldn't stay forever. I couldn't be sure what it was, but you was different, and that was a fact. You used to try and hide it, but not from me you couldn't. I got the first clue when you wanted that typewriter.'

Herbert put a hand on his shoulder. 'And I knew you knew, but there was nothing I could tell you at the time.'

'I expect you thought it'd put you off your stroke. I'd 'ave called you a bleddy liar, anyway.'

Herbert laughed. 'Come on, we get out here.'

He looked on his bijou garden flat as the height of fine accommodation in crowded expensive London. Whatever family he came from, he had never expected such light and space for his own exclusive use. Archie's almost unnoticeable look around brought nothing like: what a marvellous place, you've really dropped into it you lucky dog, how much does it cost a day? He behaved, or so Herbert liked to think, in the same way as Bert would in a similar situation if Archie had won the pools.

Archie picked up *The Times Literary Supplement*. 'What the fuck's this newspaper?'

He had meant to stow it away. 'It's all about books. Let's have some coffee, shall we?'

'Yeh, I was up at six this morning. A lot of the blokes at work read your book,' he went on when Herbert came back from the kitchen.

Herbert stopped halfway in pouring the coffee. 'Did they like it?'

'Mostly. But one or two said you was giving them a bad name, about knocking on with other women. I towd the sanctimonious bastards to 'ave more sense. It worn't about them at all, I said. You'd made it all up. But they wouldn't believe me. They swore they kept recognizing themselves. I thought when I saw you I'd tell you, so's we could have a good laugh about it.'

Herbert wondered why he had never been able to match the fluency of Archie's lingo, whereas the screed at his desk came out with no trouble. Being on guard during speech could explain it, but not near as convincingly as that the language had never belonged to him. Reality couldn't finally exist independent of birthright. 'I suppose I'd better wear glasses and a false beard if I come up for a visit,' he said when they stopped laughing, 'or I'll get duffed up.'

'Nah! But don't yer mean when you come to hear more o' them lovely stories?'

'There is that, as well.'

'Yer did mek most of 'em up, though, didn't yer?' he winked. 'If ever you want any more, just let me know. They grow on trees where I come from.'

After a session at Dirty Dick's, and a meal upstairs, they traipsed back to Liverpool Street and got on the Underground for Tower Hill, quiet for the most part since neither by now had much else to say. Archie wanted to see the Crown Jewels and the Chamber of Horrors, and Herbert was glad to go, because he would never see such things otherwise. A boat to Charing Cross pier set them on a walk through Trafalgar Square to Piccadilly, which gave enough to talk about, Herbert telling Archie the story of his life.

They swing-doored into the Hyde Park Hotel, agreeing that enough had been done of London to last a long time. A thin young man at the piano tinkled out 'Somewhere over the Rainbow'. 'We can get a hearty tea here.'

'I'm ready for it.' Archie sat on a short sofa by one of the side tables, which gave a view of the 'talent' walking through to the rooms of the hotel. Niches to either side were filled with mirrors, in one a gigantic spray of orange and purple flowers. By the far wall square glass-topped tables were placed as if for writing at, each white sphere bulb making little impression because the salon was lit whiter from overhead than day outside.

Two dowager-looking women at the next table talked about their daughters who were soon to be married. Archie finished gazing. 'Do you have your tea here a lot?'

Herbert laughed. 'I've been a couple of times before, once with my girlfriend.'

'You dirty dog! When are you going to marry her?'

He signalled the waiter. 'Well, I'm thinking about asking her.'

'On'y thinkin'? Do it. Join the club. You'll never regret it.' He leaned across: 'Does she know all about what yer towd me just now?'

'I think she suspects. Some of it.' It was his problem, and nobody else's, certainly not Archie's. 'I like this place. Thought you'd like to see it, and get away from the crowds on the street.'

'As long as they mash a good pot of tea.'

'I think they do.'

'You'd better tell her, though. There shouldn't be any secrets between man and wife.'

'I know.'

Archie looked again at the mirrors and upholstery, at the orange globe lamps on expanding wooden tripods, and up at the flatly arched ceiling with yellow and orange panes of glass in the centre. 'Who pays the bloke at the jo-anna?'

Assailed by 'Tea For Two', Herbert speculated as to whether his parents had come here after seeing him off to boarding school. 'The hotel, I suppose.'

'He's good, not like some of the ivory bashers up in Nottingham. I like the old tunes, though. They mek me think of the days before the war,' he nudged, 'when we was clambed half to death.' A waiter in coat tails took their order for two full teas. 'Looks like he's got a ramrod up his arse.'

'Probably has.' Herbert laughed with him. I'm loosening up, he noted, enjoying himself again. The Australian girl must have gone on her travels. Archie would have fancied her.

'I prefer my job to his,' Archie said. 'I suppose he earns a lot more than I do, but fancy relyin' on tips.'

Herbert lifted the silver teapot with a folded napkin. 'Somebody has to do it.'

The hot handle didn't bother Archie. 'You've got soft.'

'I suppose I have.'

'No, I don't mean it. You're as hard as nails, Bert. Inside, anyway. But I'm glad you brought me here. I'm not bluffin'. I'm enjoyin' every minute of it.'

A longing in Archie's tone concealed a wish, Herbert thought, to see more and know more and feel more, a wish close to envy except that it had come from the heart. The fact that he could never grow into the life in no way lessened the sense of wanting to, and yet, if he won a million pounds, he would be a different man in a year, taking to a moneyed existence as if born to it. 'We'll do it again. Any time you can get down.' You're my friend for life. 'Bring Mary and the kids, if you like.'

Archie gave a familiar bang on the shoulder. 'She might fall for you and your posh life, and then where would I be? Anyway, yo' cum up to see us sometime, and it'll all be on me.'

'I will, you can bet on that.' But would he? Would he ever want to, or be able to? What would Deborah think of it up there? They'd go, nevertheless. He'd make sure to.

'I won't let the lads rip yer to bits,' Archie said.

They fell to laughing again, a few sour glances from the next table, one of the women reminding Herbert of his mother. 'Let's get this down us,' Archie said. 'Looks good. A thing I ain't told yer yet, Bert, is that I'm to be a shop steward at the firm. One o' the union blokes had a word with me the other night.'

'It took 'em long enough,' Bert said, as they settled down to the minuscule triangular sandwiches, and the scones, butter and jam, which called for more or less silence.

After a bath in the hottest water he donned a plaid dressing gown (a present from Deborah) and ate his cooked breakfast. Newspapers pushed through the door were read as quickly as he could flip the pages. The dream state had become normal life.

By ten he had put on a suit and Windsor-knotted his tie, polished his shoes, and sat at the desk to sort mail. Requests for talks and autographs were replied to, an onerous duty, and he cursed an upbringing which stipulated that every letter be answered. He paper-clipped a couple of fivers to a letter, and posted them to Isaac in his new council flat.

A magazine editor asked for a story, so he scanned one of the sketches slopped into his notebook over the years and worked it suitably up, putting it through the mill of his new Olivetti typewriter. He set it aside for posting to his agent, with an attached note saying that whatever sum was offered he should get double or else.

He dressed up because you never knew who might knock at the door and want to see an author at work. It could be someone who had admired his glistening green underslung road dog by the kerb, and clawked his initials on it. If any such caller found him slopping around unshaven, in a ragged old jersey and egg-stained trousers – after a lifetime's work in overalls – they would have little confidence in his future as a novelist.

A working-class writer dressed in anything other than a three-piece suit would give the impression of being a vile trickster. And since he was, that wouldn't do at all. Londoners weren't as daft as Bert had often wound himself up to assume, or as they often enough looked and were. Nor was Herbert Thurgarton-Strang so unknowing as to look down on anyone before they had revealed themselves as such. You had to treat people as if they knew everything, just as you wanted them to believe you knew everything. All in all, such thoughts were a wasteful way of passing the time, and he was glad to be interrupted by Dominic Jones, walking down the steps towards his garden flat. He decided to let Bert open the door. 'Hello, shag! Cum for a coffee?'

He sat comfortably in the armchair and opened *The Times*, irritating Herbert by making himself so free. Coming back from the kitchen he noticed how much weight he'd put on, cheeks puffier and skin more pallid. The white woollen fisherman's sweater under his jacket, and a pair of overall trousers called 'jeans', was a rig Herbert could only wear when it would no longer be suspect on someone like him. Anyway, who would tolerate overalls when you could afford something else? He passed his old friend a mug of coffee. 'What's up, tosh? Bad news from the firm?'

Herbert recalled their days at school, when Dominic had been a trusting pal, cherubic features turned up with an almost worshipping expression. My raddled phizog must bring back the same reflections in him. Dominic's eyes went positively piggy when he began to speak. 'I don't know how you got into all this proletarian writer business, Herbert, but I think it's time I let you know that I suspected you from the first.'

He was glad he had given him a spoonful of Distant instead of grinding the best coffee. 'You are a vile little rat, aren't you?'

He threw the *Times* down pettishly. 'Now you're sounding like your old self. It didn't take long, did it?'

'I'll tek just as long as I like,' Bert snarled.

'Well, you know,' he became more relaxed, a state which Herbert was dead set to alter, 'it isn't fair to deceive people.'

'What do you intend to do about it, you jumped-up publisher's pimp? I didn't think they paid you enough to suck their arses.' Stirring his coffee, Herbert went through the fantasy of murdering him and burying the corpse in the garden. A pleasant few minutes would be had, booting down the soil.

'What you have done', Dominic went on, 'is absolutely immoral, but at least I'd be interested to know how you did it. It wasn't a bad performance. The last time I saw you before you turned up at our office was when you absconded from school.' His face fizzled back into that of a frightened little boy. 'You never wrote to let me know how you'd got on. They were the most miserable months of my life.'

'I'm sorry about that. But I was too busy fitting into my new circumstances. I'll tell you how it was done, though.' He explained the metamorphosis, and at the end of his narrative didn't need to suggest he was more than halfway into another. 'Don't you think it was something of an achievement, living two different lives for so long?'

'I ought to, I suppose, but wouldn't it be even more of an achievement if you came clean, and told Humphries who you are?'

'He wouldn't believe me, and even if he did he wouldn't want to. I'm making him too much money, and making too much myself. To tell him so that he would be absolutely convinced might give him a heart attack. Not that I'd be bothered about that, but he does have faith in me as Bert Gedling, and that's flattering to my vanity.'

'You always had plenty of that.'

'So I did. I'm a writer, after all. Which also means I'm amoral.' As time passed, however, he'd relax his guard, and blend with the surrounding milieu, be tamed and controlled by the sort of people he would need to mix with. By becoming one of them, they would stop commenting on how he dressed, especially when he allowed them to see what a good job he was making of his integration into the accepted way of life. As his accent became indistinguishable from theirs, his Thurgarton-Strang stridence would be taken as just another of Bert Gedling's affectations.

On the other hand if Dominic decided to rip his disguise clear with something like proof he would be tempted to dissimulate to the end. Few would believe such an outlandish story, or care to. He would drive the chariot of Bert across the heavens till it broke up, or Herbert brought the whole caboodle into a controlled landing. No matter what change came about in his novels and filmscripts (or even essays: he was collecting notes for 'The Art and Metaphysics of Straight Narrative') he would never let them forget that plain Bert Gedling could come lumbering back into the ring any time he liked

– whether to their amusement or dismay was no concern of his. 'Why do you need to tell Humphries? I don't see what's in it for you.'

'Because I can't live within spitting distance of a lie, or allow you to do so. It's rather curious, but I still look on you as a friend.'

'You poor little worm who never grew up. You'd be an informer, would you? A nark. A sneak. You'd shop your own grandmother for that little *frisson* of school-prefect honour. Don't you know that that kind of thing is on the way out?'

Dominic winced. 'It's not. You're premature. I'll never believe it. The fact is, I'm leaving the firm.'

'Are you?'

'I'm going into the Foreign Office. I've always wanted to. Well, my parents never stopped hoping while I was at Cambridge. It'll be a far better job, so I must clear matters up before I go.'

'So that's your nasty little game? Want to go out with a bang, do you? Do you remember your last words to me when I lit off from school that night?' He looked at him with the most candid and intimate expression possible. 'I remember, if you don't.'

'What were they?'

'You said, "I'll never betray you."'

'Maybe I did. And if I did, that's why I want you to own up. Don't you see?'

'You'll do well at the Foreign Office. I will own up, though, in my own good time.'

'No, Herbert, it has to be in my time.' Dominic's expression was that of a satisfied cat with a half-dead mouse at its feet. 'I can't let you play false to yourself any longer.'

Herbert laughed at his language, and his sentiments from a dying age. He endured the silence, determined not to speak. If he'd had a cricket bat handy Bert would have broken it over the smarmy fuckpig's loaf.

'There's only one thing which will stop me blowing the gaff.' Dominic put on his sickliest face. 'Shall I tell you what it is?'

Herbert's ears were stopped as if by the noise of the factory, but through the roar of engines he choked out: 'Go on, then, Slime.'

'What I want to say is that I'll tell Humphries the truth, unless you stop seeing Deborah. I'm in love with her. Always have been. I want to marry her, if she'll have me.'

Herbert had never known there were words which could shock and oppress him to the extent that they would bring him close to fainting. He leaned against the desk. 'Have you asked her?'

'No, but I will.'

The poor honourable fool, not having the guile or gumption to lie and say she'd accepted him. He'd often wondered whether or not Dominic was his rival, and Deborah hadn't bothered to settle the matter, though he was hardly in a position to cavil about somebody keeping their past to themselves. 'Well, I have asked her, and she's said yes.'

'I don't believe you,' Dominic said with trembling lips.

Bert stood, thumbs wide-angled in the arm holes of his waistcoat, where they were safer than being free to punch Dominic's face in. 'Believe what you like, but it's true. You can do what you like, as well, but let me tell you this, you blackmailing runt: if you aren't out o' this flat in three seconds – no, two – I'll give yer the sort o' kicking' yer'll never forget. And if yer do blow the gaff I'll cum after yer wherever you are, even if ye're dyin' from malaria in the middle o' Borneo.' He freed his hands from the waistcoat, and smiled. 'Understand, old boy?'

He wouldn't bother, but let him worry. The door slammed, and he picked up the phone so that he could pop the question to Deborah. In love with her more than ever, the wonderful word yes came into his ear.

Twenty-Three

The telegram said: 'Father died of massive stroke in middle of night. Devastated. Mother.' Herbert thought him luckier than Mrs Denman, to go in such a way. The bullet zigzagging around the Arakan jungle nearly twenty years before had hopped on a plane and found its mark at last. So many people were dying it seemed as if God had got his hands on a machine gun.

He settled into the car, regretting he hadn't been there to see him go. Headlamps burning, he threaded the needle between trucks and the offside green verge, overtaking with a screeching hooter where no sane person would, but slowing down at the latter part of the journey because he didn't want either the shame or inconvenience of following his father so soon.

Maud stood by the window, gazing into the garden at the antics of the housemartins flying up and down to feed their young under the eaves. You won't see him stumbling around clipping the bushes any more, Herbert thought as he placed himself by her. 'I came as soon as I could, Mother. I'm very sorry about it. And sad, too.' Nothing else to say, though it was obviously the right thing.

'Darling, it's terrible. I can't believe it.' She could barely speak through her tears. 'I thought he'd live forever. He always joked he would. Longer than me, I hoped. I suppose everyone says that. The day I first saw him on the beach near Lowestoft seems only last week.'

He felt out of place, but told himself that nothing could be as affecting and important as the death of your father, especially to your mother. He tapped the black cat away when it pushed against his leg. 'Poor old Hugh!'

Maud looked askance at his use of his first name. 'He loved you more than you'll ever know, probably because you gave him more heartache than he ever deserved.'

It was as well Bert had no say in this, for he might swear at the notion that Herbert had made his father's life a misery simply by living as he'd wanted.

A plate of cold mutton and pickles was set before him at the kitchen table. 'You must be starving. There's a bottle of beer in the refrigerator if you want it.'

'I'll get it.' He couldn't deny that she looked handsome and forlorn in her black skirt and black jacket, black beads, and a black band across her hair, above a lined and pallid mask of loss. Such a hurried dressing into the part stopped her going to pieces. Fresh tears down her cheeks avoided the obstacles of those which had dried a few minutes ago. 'I think I'll go up to his study for a while.' Trying to find pity for this old woman, he hoped she would take his intention as a chilling sort of remorse, which he couldn't feel, though supposed it would seep into him during the next few months.

'Don't go in there yet.' She didn't want to be alone. No longer had to be. Impossible to say why he lifted her hand to kiss. She forced him to stand, and drew him between her arms, all bones, ardour and grief. 'Oh, Herbert, my life's finished. I can't tell you how it feels. My heart's breaking.'

It isn't, and won't. Grief doesn't last, he wanted to say. Everybody recovers. Live for me. I won't mind. I'll look after you as much as I'm able. We'll be closer from now on. He stood aside without speaking.

What madness, to talk about life being at an end. She wasn't much over seventy, and looked younger. Still, the old man had died, and they'd been nearly forty years together, ten more than he'd been alive. 'You'll be all right.' He held her, feeling pity, tears checked because a grown man didn't blubber. He forced the smile from his face: hadn't yet written about tragedy so close, could have felt worse if he had seen the old man die. On the other hand he might have been less disturbed. It would have been interesting.

'He was so honest. Such an upright person. I hope you find comparable love and devotion in your life, Herbert.'

In harness from the cradle to the grave, he'd had nothing to be dishonest about. Nothing important, certainly. 'I'll go into his study' – anything to get out of her way. 'I want to look at where he was happiest' – or to see if there'd be a clue as to what kind of a man he was now he's dead.

'No, Herbert, it'll take a while to get tidy.'

They'd lived such a neat life. If a single bibelot was out of alignment on shelf or table it had to be put back in case a hair's breadth of their life was going astray. Everything ordered and pre-ordained, a charmed but restricted existence he could never fall in with. Yet he envied them, and regretted that he couldn't live in the same way, though the barrack-room tidiness of his own flat suggested he might be on the way to getting there.

He couldn't care at all whether or not he saw the old man's study. It was a ploy to be alone, but his mother needed him every minute in her sight, and her overpowering sorrow was like warm mud too thick to swim from. 'Your father is in the living room. They'll be coming for his – him, at two o'clock.'

She was halfway to being dead herself, and wanted him, who couldn't recall when he'd been so much alive, to comfort her and coax her back. On the other hand he had never known her to be so vibrant. Before leaving London there'd been neither time nor thought of phoning Deborah. He wanted her with him now, to commiserate and hold him, to say she loved him, to lick his ears, anything to space out the millibars of such a bleak atmosphere. She would shield him from a sensation he shouldn't be exposed to, feelings only real if written about from the imagination. He didn't know what he wanted to be kept away from, since the experience must surely be good.

Deborah would know how to comfort his mother, or would try anyway. He saw them melting together, a very sexy scene, anger as he brushed the picture out. He would show her the house, walk her through the gardens, and take her to the orchard where he had once stood in the rain hoping to find out who he was, so long ago that he couldn't imagine the man he had been. Trying to find his true self – poor fool – he hadn't known that if he did nothing about it his self was sufficiently strong and centred to come out of the shadows and find *him*. He took his mother's hand. 'Let's look at him, then.'

'It'll be a big funeral. You can help send out the cards. Quite a few will go to his regiment.'

The idea pleased him. All the old buffers would come. A few young ones as well, maybe a platoon to fire a volley over the coffin. 'So they should.'

Hugh's moustache was greyer than grey, and the flesh it sprang from as white as if he had never been east of Suez. He looked satisfied more than at peace, about right for a soldier. His saluting arm seemed alive and set to come up for a final gesture of farewell. Maud kissed the cold lips, weeping as if to bring him back to life and walk with him arm in arm into the garden, talking about vegetables and what to have for dinner.

Real life's about to begin for her, as it is for me. 'We all have to die.' He regretted the callous remark, but its brutality calmed her: 'I know. It's the only consolation I have.'

'I would like to look into his study some time.'

'Not till after the funeral.'

Such peculiar fancies should be allowed to someone in a state of shock. 'Why ever not, though?'

'He must have known a stroke was coming on. I heard this weird noise, but thought he was just reorganizing his books. He did, from time to time. In fact you might say he did it endlessly. It calmed him. And he liked the room to be tidy. But when I found him I saw he'd made a bit of a mess. I'll never know why.'

She didn't bother to stop him when he walked towards the stairs. The tobacco smell from years of puffing was strong but stale, and the door wouldn't open its full arc, some obstacle preventing it. Her tone set off an alarm in him: 'I'm afraid you'll have to push.'

He slid through the gap, couldn't go right in for fear of increasing the wreckage. If his father hadn't found the maniacal energy maybe the stroke wouldn't have gripped him in such a vice. He might have halfway recovered and been in a wheelchair, the vilest horror to him. Or perhaps he sensed the inevitable, hoped it wasn't certain even so. He had tried to head it off by an animal rage against the injustice of death, or even against fear which had dragged out his utmost violence, giving him astounding strength.

Herbert found the curved pipe snapped in two behind the door, its bowl filled with slightly charred tobacco, as if Hugh's last wish had been to fill it and light up to face the end in familiar comfort. Finding the onset too quick, he had broken it before crushing half a dozen others underfoot and attacking everything else in the room.

Books and papers had been pulled from shelves, broken and torn. An orang-utan gone mad. Tables and chairs upturned, smashed, ripped, thrown, kicked, whirled about and trampled as if a fragmentation grenade had done its work. Not one piece belonged to any other.

He walked over paper and glass and set a chair on its legs, put the mahogany table back in place, awestruck at the damage yet light-headed with satisfaction that in old age his father had shown there to be more than one part to himself. At the same time as immersing himself in this wilful mayhem he had stacked maps and notebooks in a corner and left them – for me, Herbert knew.

He smiled, as if within the one seam that mattered he knew the old man almost as well as he knew himself, and in some quirky way even better. In his fight to the death Hugh had been influenced by a barbarous dignity at the iniquity of having to die, but within it had left a final message saying that he also had lived his life as two people. Unable to give in to it he had waited till the last moment to make the gesture.

Maud stood behind. 'Now you know. But it wasn't like his true self to do such a thing. He was never like that. Not in a million years. A week ago he told me about a pain at the top of his head. Only lasted a few minutes, while he was in the garden. He said it was like a small plate of steel pressing into his skull. Then it went away. I wanted him to get a check up, and he said he would if it came back.'

When everyone had gone from the funeral, a deadly calm set over the house. Lord of the manor – though his mother might dispute that – Herbert sat in the lounge. Two bottles of the best Languedoc had been finished at dinner, and he felt more than half drunk, while noting that his mother could soak it in like a trooper. 'He couldn't have had a better send-off,' she said ruefully.

Some of the mourners had looked curiously at him because he wasn't in the army, thinking what a pity he wasn't made of the same

292

stuff as his father. It was good that the old world stayed with us a bit to be written about. 'Yes, it was quite impressive.'

Such a verdict confused her, though maybe there was more of Hugh in him than she had supposed. 'That novel of yours, Herbert, it's very skilful, and I was amused by some of it, but I can't really feel people live like that, these days.'

An uncompromising retort was squashed. 'Father knew they did. They were his soldiers in both wars.'

She was happy at the mention of Hugh. 'I suppose they were. He was glad to know you had the decency not to use your real name. He appreciated that.'

The unceremonious attack needed no response. Maybe calling himself Bert Gedling had been nothing more than a long march towards finding a pseudonym – all that his deception and exile had been for. If so, what a waste. 'Did he like the book?'

'Yes, said it was first rate.'

'I'm sorry he didn't tell me.'

'He knew I would. Probably didn't think you needed to be told. On one level he was disappointed in you, but on another he was proud.'

You can't have everything, nor did he expect it. 'Are you going to stay on here, Mother?' He pulled another cork and filled both glasses, to dull his pain but most of all hers. 'Let's drink to Father. He'd like that.'

She laughed, whinnying and tearful. 'We've drunk to him already, but if we do it again I know he won't mind.'

'You could get a flat in Chelsea,' he said, lighting a cigar of his father's. 'We'd be able to meet nearly every day.'

'I belong here.' She looked around to confirm that the furnishings would support her. 'It's only a few miles from where I first set eyes on your father.'

'The house is rather large, though.' A bloody mausoleum that should go under the hammer.

The swig she took was enormous. 'I'm a soldier's widow. We know how to manage. But what are your plans for the future?'

A widow could meddle more openly. He didn't care about the future. Living a few days ahead had always been good enough, the only way possible. 'I'll go on as I am, and come and see you when I can. You're only a couple of hours or so from Town.'

'And if it were five or six?' she smiled. 'Don't feel obliged. I wouldn't put up with that.'

The cat used his stretched-out legs as a ramp to get on to his lap. Stroking its silky fur, he wanted to go on talking, as if his father's death made him more voluble. 'I see myself earning a living as a writer. But I can't be bothered to think about the future, which has a way of looking after itself.'

'It's a healthy attitude,' she said. 'That's how Hugh looked at life, and why he was so happy – or at least never unhappy.'

'I may get married, though. Deborah's her name.'

This interested her enough to pick up the glass again. 'Is that who you were on the phone to yesterday? You were talking in a rather strange voice.'

'I'm in love with her.' He wanted, as Archie would say, to go in raw. A new dimension was needed in his life, deepening attachments to give fresh limits to his nerve ends. 'She works at my publisher's.'

'Is she from a good family?'

'Good enough. You'll like her.'

'I'm sure I shall.'

'And she'll like you.'

'Do you know, darling, you really do remind me of your father.' She giggled, stood up, swayed and, just as he was beginning to think she'd got a bit too light-headed, sat down again: 'Got to surround Blue Force by morning!'

'What does that mean?'

'Oh, it's what your father said when I first met him, and he wasn't able to stay when my father asked him to tea.'

He poured more wine. 'I can just imagine him saying it.'

'You fill your glass too near to the brim, dear.'

'Sorry.' He was amazed at getting so drunk with his mother. 'I'll check it next time.' Back in Town he would disown Bert Gedling and become entirely his Herbert Thurgarton-Strang self, give out who he was, and see how they – whoever they were – liked it. They may not be so interested to know, though his next book would still be pseudonymed Bert Gedling, since there was no point in losing the advantage of that. Maybe he would walk into Humphries' office with a bottle of smelling salts and tell him straight out. Or he would get him to arrange a set-piece press conference and, performing a languorous recitation in the voice of his birthright, relate the real story of his life, so that, forced to believe, they would bray for his soul with howls of execration. Such a confrontation would be quite unnecessary, but he spun out the fantasy for his mother's enjoyment.

'I'd want to be there. Hugh would have, I'm sure of it. He would have been proud of you.'

'Never mind, Mother. Don't cry.'

'Why not, I should like to know?'

'Because we've got to surround Blue Force by morning!'

Life was good when they could laugh in the midst of death. He was crying at last, drunk, maudlin, the handkerchief from his lapel pocket in time to stop tears spoiling his waistcoat. He told himself not to be so damned weak. 'I'll stay on a few more days. Deborah will come up for the weekend.'

'I'd like to meet her. It'll give me time to get sober, sober enough to drive you both to the station anyway. She can have the room next to Hugh's study.'

'I thought you were a woman of the world, Mother.' He looked into her grey eyes, lines around them lost in the dimmed light. 'We don't bother about such things as separate rooms these days.'

'I want her to have her own room, and feel like a proper guest. What you would do in the night would be your own business.'

'Mine will be more than adequate for us both. As for driving to the station, we have our own transport now.'

'All right, darling, I won't say anything more. I know times have changed, since the war especially. And I don't want to lose you, Herbert.'

He envied her directness. 'You'll never do that, and you know it.'

'You're all I've got.'

True it was, and the circle had come around, stopped spinning and closed. He didn't really know how to feel about it.

*　　*　　*

Deborah's grey Mini nosed its way up the drive. He opened the door. 'Glad you found the place.'

Gentle auburn waves came out from her parting, telling him she'd been to the hairdresser's. White blouse and brown Liberty's scarf at the neck, beige skirt and laced brown shoes were right for meeting his mother. 'You look wonderful, darling. Let's go this way.'

'You sounded so mysterious on the phone. But what is all this about anyway?'

He led her on a slow circuit around the house. 'I want you to meet my mother, and stay with us for a few days.'

'Your mother? You said she was dead.' If not, maybe she works here, and he was ashamed of it. There was no sign of Bert in him today, though he could turn it on and off like a tap. 'Is she the housekeeper?'

He wondered how long it had been since a genuine loud laugh had ascended over the grounds. 'Good Lord, no! We own the place.'

She stopped, and looked at him. 'You said something on the phone about not being who you were supposed to be. Well, I'd gathered that much already. I'd been waiting for you to tell me for weeks,' though she hadn't felt it could be as important as what seemed on its way.

'It was difficult,' he said, passing the neglected old summerhouse. 'I really had to hang on until now. If I'd told you cold you might have thought it just another of my impersonations. Dominic knew, almost from the beginning. He never gave me away, though he threatened to. We went to school together.'

She was pale with loss, and chagrin, showing a new Deborah. 'I can't believe any of this.'

'I ran away from school when I was seventeen, went to Nottingham and worked in a factory. It was the best way to hide. After the army I drifted back there, and turned into a workman, you might say.'

'Well, I suppose someone like you might say anything.'

There was nothing but to go on remorselessly. 'I stayed at the factory. I don't know why, but the years rolled by. I wrote the novel to keep myself sane. And that's it. You know it now.'

The wind was warm, but she felt cold. He kissed her, and she pushed him away. 'It's just not feasible.'

'I hoped it wouldn't hurt you when I told you.'

'Hurt?' He was obviously telling the truth. 'I'm bloody blasted. And this is your family home?'

Not wanting to feel a worm, he became blasé. 'Yes. I thought you'd be pleased. Thurgarton-Strang is my real name.'

She'd heard the name but couldn't think where, picked a flower from the clematis, crushed it and let the petals drop. 'I didn't fall in love with a liar.'

'I never lied. I became someone else, but I wasn't so mean and despicable as that.' The chariot was weaving out of control, and he felt himself fighting for his life. 'I just did what I had to do, otherwise I'd probably have killed myself. I've been thinking about it. I had to become two people so as to be even one. As far as I know I've harmed no one, but I'm more than glad to give up all the Bert Gedling stuff. I only hoped it wouldn't make any difference to our relationship when I did. Maybe I put it off because I thought it might, out of funk. No, not that, either. I just waited, and let the right time come along.'

'*Your* time, not mine.'

'Well, there never was any right time.' How could there be? He saw a tear in her left eye, found it touching and gratifying, if not promising. She wiped it away angrily. He cleaned a white chair by the edge of the lawn with his handkerchief. 'Won't you sit down?'

A touch of Gedling there. Or was it? He forgot the 'duck'. 'Damn you,' she cried. 'I have to get used to you all over again.' She had noticed the obituary of Brigadier-General Thurgarton-Strang in the office *Times* last week, and now she knew who he was. Bert Gedling's father. It was almost laughable.

'Not entirely, I hope. There was a lot of me in Bert Gedling, as you'll probably find out. One person's very much like another, after all, when you rub the paint off.' Which he was sure she would be able to do, though he would take care always to be one move ahead.

She had speculated on whether his father had been a postman, or a shoemaker, or a plumber – he'd never given a straight answer – but to prophesy this had been beyond sensible reach. From a mixture of self-disgust and pique she thought it might not be difficult to stop feeling superior to him, which she had done in some ways. It was unjust that he'd been responsible for that. She supposed her father would be happy to meet the present version of whoever he

297

was, but could she trust Herbert when, as he said (and she felt it was true) there was so much of Bert Gedling in him whether he had played the role or not? Thoughts rushed through her mind. Anyone from his class who had acted the workman for so long was bound to be unpredictable for the rest of his life, and even if he hadn't been a workman he would still have been someone to be wary of.

'All I know', he was saying, and she couldn't disbelieve him, 'is that "love is not love which alters when it alteration finds". Or it shouldn't be.'

'You call that alteration?'

The chariot needed final and expert guidance at the reins, and couldn't be allowed to break up. He stroked her hair, ran a finger over her lips, and felt the wet grass through the knees of his trousers. 'It's the best I can do. I love you. That's all I'm trying to say. You're the love of my life, and we're made for each other. I knew it from the moment I saw you.'

Maybe getting to know the rest of him would be more interesting than putting up with the single phenomenon of Bert Gedling, and she wasn't the sort of girl to eschew an adventure. 'And I certainly love you,' she said, contemptuous of all caution.

He stood up. 'Ah! Here's my mother, coming from the garden. And she's carrying the vegetables.'

Deborah was also glad of a reason to stand. 'She looks as if she needs some help.'

Back in London, he would take down the picture of Phoebus Apollo and put it in the dustbin. 'Yes, she is rather like Ceres laden with abundance.'

The old folks had been assiduous in doing what they could to control the grounds and garden, which were ruinous and overgrown. A man from the village had helped, but he had died six months ago, and no one else was forthcoming.

'He was a thieving old devil,' Maud said. 'He took most of our tools, over the years. I expect his son's using them now. But you can see why we didn't say anything. It was too much work for Hugh. I do want to keep up the summerhouse, though. He loved to sit there and drink his whisky in the evening.'

Deborah said he ought to do something about it, so Herbert paced the large lawn, wondering where to start. A tree overhung the summerhouse, coating the reinforced glass roof with leaves and seeds. His mother was right: if it wasn't pruned the force of vegetation would crack the guttering, and the place would crumble.

He fetched a ladder from the garage, a handsaw and a pair of the strongest clippers, wondering where to start on the tangle of growth. Roll up your sleeves, to begin with, and put on an old cap of your father's. That done, he attacked the tree's outriders methodically, going round and round and slowly closing in, as if reducing the sinews of a besieged fortress. The trunk was too close to the wall of the summerhouse to get the ladder between, but he erected a platform of wooden boxes and sawed through overhanging branches.

Cut them from a tree on one side, and they would grow more forcefully out of the other. Enjoyment was part of the process, a renewal of his habit of labour. To reach the highest python-like limb he leaned with all the strength of his right arm against the roof and, with his left extended to the utmost, sawed through with a measured forward and backing of steel teeth, every second hoping that the boxes beneath his feet would keep their stability. The strength of his arm did not let him down, and he felt a certain pride at the force and endurance of his muscles.

A laugh from Deborah sounded from the open door of the kitchen, where they were cutting and scraping at vegetables. Maud said something he couldn't make out, and both laughters duetted into the air.

Every inch of gutter around the structure was clogged with seeds and leaves, embedded in black mud, and the only way to clear it was by trawling four fingers along the trough and throwing the stinking mess overboard whenever the ridge became too high. He rammed stiff wire through the pipes to make certain the rain would be carried away instead of streaming down the walls and rotting the wood. Rose bush tendrils between the drain and glass edge of the roof were clipped and pulled out. He unthreaded each growth and pushed them back in spite of their aggressive thorns.

In a few days he would drive to Woking with Deborah and meet her parents. She hoped he would behave, and he thought he might be able to. 'You'd better,' she said. There had been something more than usually stimulating, making love in his own house, and her cries were those of a shot fox when she came. He poured into her almost at the same time, on imagining her travails of giving birth.

His hand slipped, he grabbed a lower shoot but it was dead, came away with his weight. But it slowed his fall, and he landed without harm, persuading him to let only neutral matters go through his mind.

The branches were high above the hut, clear sky between, where they could do no damage. With a long-handled broom he swept the remaining seeds and leaves from the roof so that the sun would light through. Mindless though useful work was a tonic, and he was happy. The tree, cut back and rendered harmless, would only grow upwards. Its structure was neat and simplified, superfluous baggage gone, and a soft wind as of appreciation played among the remaining leaves. His mother would be happy too, though no doubt she'd blub a little at memories of Hugh when he brought her out to show what had been done.

Rounding off the job as a real workman should, he swept the inside tiles, and drew a bucket of water from the garden tap to mop them and enhance their black and whiteness. A table and two chairs streaked with green mould had to be wiped clean with a damp rag. The effort of his care and attention would impress because it was a mark of love, something to make up for not having been much of a son during most of his life.

He climbed the tree for a view of his work. The rectangular summerhouse, with its wide windows from waist to roof, stood in free space, renovated and accessible, a place complete. He got down to look across from the spot on which he had made his confession to Deborah. Instead of threatening, the tree stood guard, would grow tall and orderly, unencumbered by any rival encroacher.

Deborah called that coffee was ready. So was he. The work was finished. Out of something had come something more, a neutral structure for him, an edifice of memories for his mother. Next year the same would need to be done, and the year after that, for as many times as were thought necessary. He would live here with Deborah and the children when Maud was gone, so the maintenance would continue for as long as the summerhouse did not crumble, or for as long as he stayed alive.